SHADOW'S SON

JON SPRUNK
SHADOW'S SON

an imprint of **Prometheus Books**
Amherst, NY

Published 2010 by Pyr®, an imprint of Prometheus Books

Inquiries should be addressed to
Pyr
59 John Glenn Drive
Amherst, New York 14228–2119
VOICE: 716–691–0133
FAX: 716–691–0137
WWW.PYRSF.COM

14 13 12 11 10   5 4 3 2 1

Library of Congress Cataloging-in-Publication Data

Sprunk, Jon, 1970–
    Shadow's son / by Jon Sprunk.
        p. cm.
    ISBN 978–1–61614–201–8 (pbk.)
    1. Assassins—Fiction. I. Title.

PS3619.P78S53 2010
813'.6—dc22

2010006203

Printed in the United States of America

This novel is dedicated to my wife, Jenny,

Without whom none of this would have been possible,

And to our son, Logan,

Who is the twinkle in our eyes.

ACKNOWLEDGMENTS

The author wishes to thank the following for their support throughout this project:

To my father, who instilled in me a love for words.

To Lou, for turning the dream into reality.

To Eddie and Joshua, for their guidance and wisdom.

To Steve, Bruce, Dave, Adrian, Nicko, and Janick, for their inspiration through the years.

CHAPTER ONE

A killer stalked in the shadows.

Hidden within the gloom shrouding the hall's lofty ceiling, he crept across the rafters to the flicker of the torch fires below. As unseen as the wind, silent as Death itself.

Festive music rose from the chamber beneath him. The flower of northern Nimea, two hundred lords and ladies, filled the great hall of Ostergoth Keep. The sharp crack of a whip cut through the din. The centerpiece of the evening was an aged hillman, stripped to the waist and bound to a wooden frame. Livid welts oozing blood crisscrossed his shoulders and back. While Duke Reinard's guests gorged on fine victuals, his torturer performed for their entertainment.

The bullwhip cracked again and the old man shuddered. The duke laughed so hard he spilled wine down his ermine-lined robes and spoiled the yellow dress of the pale, shuddering girl on his lap. She quivered as he blotted at her bodice with a stained napkin and then squeaked at an indiscretion committed under the table. She tried to squirm away, but the duke held her fast and laughed all the harder.

Caim's gloved hands curled into fists. It was time to go to work.

He dropped down to an empty balcony outthrust from the stone wall. Crouched behind the railing, he unslung a satchel from his shoulder and took out its contents. With sure movements he assembled a powerful bow made from two curved shafts of laminated horn. He opened a lacquered case and took out three arrows. Each projectile ended in brilliant indigo fletching, the design favored by the hill tribes of eastern Ostergoth, as requested by the client.

Caim fit an arrow to the string and lifted the bow. He took a deep breath as he sighted along the shaft. An uneasy sensation rumbled in the pit of his stomach. *Nerves.*

He adjusted his aim to allow for distance and declination. The girl managed to escape the Duke's lewd embrace, at least for the moment.

Don't worry, honey. Caim pulled the bowstring to full tension. *He won't ever bother you again.*

Just as he was about to shoot, his target leaned over to chortle into the ear of a lovely noblewoman beside him. The duke's ringed fingers fondled the strands of pearls looped across the lady's plunging décolletage. Caim held his breath and counted by the slow, measured rhythm of his pulse.

Three . . . four . . .

Any moment now, the Duke would sit up and present the perfect target.

Seven . . . eight . . .

His aim was dead-on, his hands were steady.

Eleven . . . twelve . . .

A feathery tickle caressed his shoulders. Not taking his eyes off the Duke, Caim caught a glimpse of silver.

"Hello, lover," her voice whispered in his ear.

Ghostly fingers tickled Caim's waist, but his gaze never left the target. "Hello, Kit."

"Putting another notch in your belt, I see."

He winced at the volume of her voice as it carried over the revel. It didn't matter that no one else could hear her. She was throwing off his cadence.

"I'm busy. Go find a nest of bunnies to play with until I'm done here."

Kit pressed her face against his cheek to peer down the arrow shaft. Although he couldn't exactly feel her, tiny itches radiated everywhere she touched his skin. A strand of her silver hair fell across his left eye. Caim resisted the urge to blow it away, knowing it wouldn't do any good if he tried, and strained the bowstring another inch.

"Bunnies live in holes, not nests," she said. "And you're aiming too low."

"Leave me alone. I've got the shot."

"You're going to miss his neck by half a foot."

Caim ground his teeth as the duke turned away from the noblewoman to slap the back of Liram Kornfelsh of the Kornfelsh merchant syndicate.

The syndicate was backing Duke Reinard to the hilt, hoping to ride his rise to power all the way to the inner sanctums of the capital.

"I'm aiming for his heart. Now leave me alone for a minute."

Kit hopped up on the banister, as light as a butterfly in flight. Short for a human woman, she possessed a figure out of any man's fantasies. Tiny-waisted yet buxom, she had creamy skin with a faint olive sheen. The dress she wore, tight-clinging with an absurdly short skirt, barely left anything to the imagination. Caim supposed it made no difference, since no one could see her but him.

Balancing on her bare toes, she clucked her tongue. "What if he's wearing a coat of mail under that atrocious shirt?"

"The head is piled for penetration." Caim thrust his chin at the arrow's reinforced point. "Anyway, he doesn't wear armor. Detests the weight of it. That's why he surrounds himself with so many soldiers."

He rechecked his aim anyway. The duke was still manhandling his guests. Caim wished he would sit up straight. His fingers were getting numb.

Kit spun around and sat on the narrow railing. "For all the good they'll do him. Are you going to finish this anytime soon? It's loud in here. I can hardly hear myself think."

"Just a moment."

The duke leaned back in his chair, his shoulders framed by the wide oaken back. Caim released the bowstring. In that moment, the target glanced upward. Wine ran down Reinard's blubbery chins as their gazes met.

The arrow sped across the hall like a diving falcon. It was a perfect shot, a sure kill. But just before it struck, the torchlight flickered. Cups tipped over. Plates crashed to the floor. Caim's neck hairs tingled at the sight of Liram Kornfelsh, sprawled in front of the Duke. The arrow's blue feathers quivered above the emerald brooch nestled in the hollow of his throat.

Screams echoed off the hall's high walls as guests bolted from their seats, all except for Kornfelsh, who they left lying across the high table like an overstuffed ham. The duke grasped his hands together as his soldiers rushed to surround him.

Caim grabbed the other arrows and fired in rapid succession. The first caught a bodyguard through the left eye. The second penetrated the boss of a soldier's shield and through the forearm holding it, but the duke remained unscathed. Caim tossed the bow aside and raced down the balcony.

Kit skipped along the railing beside him. "I told you the shot was off. You have a contingency plan, right?"

He clenched his jaws tight together. The only thing worse than making a grand mess of a job was doing it in front of Kit. Now he had to get down and dirty. He reached behind his back and drew a pair of *suete* knives. Eighteen inches of singled-edged steel gleamed in the torchlight.

A sentry appeared at the end of the catwalk. Caim flowed past him, close enough to smell the wine on the man's breath, and the sentry stumbled against the wall, his life spilling through his fingers from a bloody gash across his throat.

On the floor below, the duke was ushered by his bodyguards through a door at the back of the hall. Caim vaulted over the railing, jumping right through Kit. For a moment as their bodies merged, he was covered from head to foot by tingling goose bumps. A thrown spear flashed just inches in front of his face as he landed on the central trestle. Flagons and dinnerware went flying as he dashed down the polished length of the table.

"He's getting away." Kit floated above his head.

Caim bit back a rude response. "Then how about you go follow him?"

She sped off with a huff.

Caim kicked open the door. The duke would be heading to his quarters on the top floor of the donjon where he could hole up until reinforcements arrived. If that happened, Caim was well and truly fucked. But he had never failed to complete an assignment before; he didn't plan to start now.

The corridor beyond was unlit. He started inside, but a nagging sense of caution made him pause. That hesitation saved his life as a sword blade swept through the empty space where his neck would have been. Caim ducked and jabbed with both knives. His left-hand *suete* cut through a colorful surcoat and got caught in links of mail underneath, but the right-hand blade found a gap in the armor. A gurgle issued from the shadows as the hidden guardsman slumped forward. Caim jerked his knives free and swept down the hallway.

A single staircase led to the higher levels. The steps spiraled clockwise around a thick stone newel post. Caim sprang up the stairs two at a time. As he came around the first landing, the twang of a crossbow string reached his ear a split second before a quarrel zipped past. Caim threw himself against the wall. From somewhere above echoed the staccato clack of a hand crank.

Caim pushed off from the wall and darted up the steps as fast as his legs would propel him. If there was a second archer lying in wait for him, he would be dead before he knew it. He rounded another turn. A lone crossbowman stood on the landing above, furiously turning the iron crank to reload his weapon. The soldier dropped the crossbow and grabbed for his sword, but Caim cut him down before he freed the weapon.

Caim crept up the last flight of stairs to the keep's highest level. The upper landing was empty. Candles dripping wax from brass sconces on the wall illuminated a juncture of two hallways. He put his back to the cool stone and peered around the corner into the corridor that led to the master suite. So far, the duke had shown an exceptional affinity for sacrificing his men to preserve his own hide. Two bodyguards were down. Two more to go. Decent odds. Caim sidled down the hallway. The door to Reinard's suite was reinforced with thick iron bands. It would be barred from the inside. Nothing short of an axe would get through the door, but he had another idea.

Caim was moving toward a shuttered window on the side of the hallway when Kit's head and one shapely shoulder poked through the door.

"You better hurry," she said. "He's packing up to run."

A cool breeze ruffled Caim's hood as he swung open the shutters. A sixty-foot drop yawned on the other side.

"He doesn't have anywhere to go."

"Not quite. There's a hidden passage that leads outside the grounds."

"Damn it! Why didn't you mention that earlier?"

"How was I supposed to know it was there? It's pretty well hidden, behind a wardrobe case."

Caim swung a leg over the sill. Time was running out. If the duke got outside the compound, he would be near impossible to catch.

"Keep watch on that secret tunnel, Kit. Follow Reinard if he makes it outside. I'll catch up."

"Will do."

She vanished back inside the chamber. Caim leaned out the window.

He still didn't know what had gone wrong in the great hall. The shot had been set up perfectly. Nothing he could do about it now except to correct his mistake and get out fast.

As he climbed out onto the sill, he spotted the outline of another window on the same level thirty paces away. Pale light flickered from within. Exit scenarios played through Caim's mind as he ran his fingers over the outer wall. Once the job was finished, he could drop down to the keep's courtyard to make his escape, or he could use the duke's secret tunnel. Either plan held its own set of risks. He'd hoped to be gone by now. Every passing minute reduced his chances for success.

The broad ashlar blocks of the keep's outer shell provided strong protection against siege weapons, but their wide seams made good purchase for climbing. He found a crevice in the wall and grabbed hold without stopping to consider the prudence of his actions. He hated rushing a job, but he was running out of options at this point. He focused on his holds.

A prickling itched down his spine as he reached a point halfway between the windows. He froze, clinging to the sheer stone face. Something drew his gaze toward the heavens. A thick blanket of clouds veiled the night sky. The light of torches from the courtyard below flickered upon the keep's crenellations. He saw nothing at first. Then, something moved among the battlements. Caim held his breath as a silhouette passed above him, a sinuous shape gliding through the dark. For one terrible moment he thought it had seen him, but then it was gone.

Caim waited several heartbeats before he dared to breathe again. What was going on? He didn't have time to waste. Trying to put the specter out of his mind, he lunged for his next hold.

Seconds later, he was at the window. The clear glass casement opened with a slight rattle, but no one inside noticed. The window led into the master bedchamber. Beyond it Caim could see entrances to other rooms and the stout door leading to the hallway he had vacated minutes before. Both bodyguards stood at the barred door, swords out, watching the portal as if expecting Caim to burst through at any moment.

The duke hunched over a heavy trunk. "Ulfan, leave off that damned door and help me!"

One of the bodyguards turned around as Caim crawled through the window. He opened his mouth to shout a warning, but never got the chance. Caim hurled a knife with a whip of his hand. The bodyguard jerked back, a runnel of blood streaming down his collar as he fell to his knees with the *suete*'s smooth handle protruding from his throat.

Reinard dropped a heavy sack that clinked as it hit the floor. "What—?"

Caim drew his other knife and crossed the room just as the second bodyguard turned. As the man raised his sword arm to strike, Caim lunged in close and drove his weapon full length into the joint under the man's armpit. The bodyguard gasped and slid off the knife.

"Caim!" Kit shouted from behind him.

He turned, knees bent with his knife at the ready. From this vantage he could see the wardrobe Kit had mentioned. It was pulled aside, and a black tunnel mouth yawned in the wall beyond. A young man in the duke's livery with fair hair and a short goatee emerged with a bared arming sword in his hand. Caim pivoted out of the path of the falling sword and thrust his knife into his opponent's side. The point struck a rib. Caim twisted the blade and punched it through the connective tissue between the bones.

The young man's last breath wheezed from the wound as he crumpled to the floor.

The duke cringed beside a massive, four-post bed. "Please." His jowls trembled as he held out his hands before him. An angry welt marred one of his palms. "I'll give you anything you want."

"Yes." Caim crossed the floor. "You will."

The duke died with considerably less effort than his bodyguards. Caim left the body stretched out on the bed with a bloody hole carved into the chest. He hadn't been able to take out Reinard in front of his dinner guests. His clients would have to be satisfied with butchery. The message was sent.

Caim retrieved his other knife and scanned the chamber. If he hurried he could be over the walls and outside the keep before the duke's men organized any meaningful pursuit. He didn't expect them to trail him for long. With their liege dead, they would be more concerned with finding and protecting Reinard's heir. By all accounts young Lord Robert was a decent boy, a far cry from his monstrous father. The duchy would be a better place.

Caim's gaze fell on the young man sprawled at the tunnel entrance.

He had never set eyes on Lord Robert, but he had a reliable description. Twenty-two years old, light brown hair with a wisp of a beard and blue eyes. The youth on the floor matched the description too closely to be a coincidence. Caim cursed under his breath. So much for leaving these lands in the care of a kinder, more tolerant liege.

Kit walked through the door to the hallway. "You're going to get some company very soon."

Caim considered the open window. "How many?"

"More than you can handle. Believe me."

"I do. What about outside?"

"All those pretty ladies and gentlemen have stirred up quite a commotion in the yard. Every exit is sealed and extra men have been put on the walls. Search parties are scouring the grounds."

"And the tunnel?"

Kit gave him a sassy grin. "Lots of stairs and the rest of the duke's bodyguards wait at the other end. They might not be happy to see you come out before their boss."

Caim wiped his knives clean on Lord Robert's tabard. Nothing was going his way tonight. He was going to have to use his last option. By the amused expression on her face, Kit knew it, too. He hated admitting she was right, but he'd probably hate dying even more.

He went around the room snuffing candles and lamp wicks to plunge the chamber into darkness except for a single lantern resting beside the tunnel mouth. He passed the Duke's traveling trunk and the sacks spilled on the floor without a glance. Just one of those purses would set him up for a year, but he was an assassin, not a thief.

Fists banged on the door.

"You'd better hurry," Kit said.

Caim tried to ignore her as he pressed his back against a wall in the darkest part of the room. There amid the shadows, he closed his eyes and shut out the outside world. He focused on the sliver of fear quivering at the center of his core. Fear was the key. It was always there, hidden beneath layers of denial and repression. Caim hated this. He had to tap into that feeling, allow it to possess him. At first, he didn't think he could. There were too many distractions. The pain was too far removed. But then a memory seized hold of him. It was an old memory, full of pain.

Raging flames painted the night sky in hues of orange and gold, and threw shadows across the yard of the villa where the tall bodies sprawled. There was blood everywhere, pooled in the gravel, splattered across the face of the man kneeling in the center of the yard, running down his chest in a great black river.

Father . . .

Caim opened his eyes as the dark came alive.

It gathered around him like a cloak. By the time the guards battered down the door, he was hidden within its inky folds. Just another shadow. The soldiers flitted about like bees from a jostled hive. Some dashed into the tunnel with lit firebrands. Others stood over the corpses of the duke and his son. None of them detected the shade that glided out the door and down the stairs.

Once outside, Caim scaled the keep's curtain wall and disappeared into the countryside. Dappled moonlight splashed over him like a gossamer rainstorm. A quarter mile away from the stronghold, he released the cloying darkness. He grabbed the trunk of a sapling to hold himself upright as a wave of disorientation overloaded his senses. The darkness swam before his eyes in a thousand shades of gray and black. Something lurked in the distance, just beyond the limit of his vision. He didn't know how he summoned the shadows. The power had resided within him for as long as he could remember, lurking within him, threatening to erupt whenever he was frightened or angry. He had learned to control those feelings over the years, but he never got used to it.

After a minute, the weakness passed and the normality of the night returned, and Caim resumed his trek through the fog-strewn moor. Kit danced ahead of him in the distance like a will-o'-the-wisp. The faint tune of a tavern song reached his ears. Same old Kit. Nothing fazed her. Yet he couldn't share in her frivolity. Not even the prospect of the sizable bounty he would soon collect lifted his spirits. Apprehension welled up inside him, rising up like the deep arm of the sea, dragging him into unknown depths. His steps slowed in the fog.

Overhead, a lone star pierced the cloud cover. Like a man grasping a lifeline, he stumbled toward it, following its shimmer through the gloom.

CHAPTER TWO

Josephine rushed from the carriage and into the house faster than the footman burdened with her purchases could follow. Her cheeks stung from the brisk autumn chill.

As she brushed past Fenrik, their family steward, she shed her jacket and the new hat she'd bought. He collected her garments with his usual aplomb.

"Welcome home, mistress. I trust your excursion was pleasant."

"Marvelous! Is Father upstairs? I must see him right away. I have amazing news! Anastasia is to be married this Yeartide Day and to such a dashing man. His name escapes me at the moment, but he's very tall and handsome. Did I mention he was an officer in the Sacred Brotherhood?"

"No, mistress. But—"

She flew past him without waiting for another word. Father would be ensconced in his study with his books and papers. Retired from his government post for four years, he still maintained his connections in political circles, a thing for which she was especially grateful. Someday those connections would net her a smart match like Anastasia had just made.

Josey paused on her way to the stairs. An unfamiliar overcoat hung from the brass rack on the wall.

"Fenrik, who visits with my father?"

"A man from the palace, milady."

"From the palace?" She raced up the wide marble steps.

"He does not wish to be disturbed."

Of course Father would want to see her straightaway. A visitor from the palace could only mean one thing. Her father was finally making a match for her hand, and to a man from an outstanding family. Her heart was ready to burst from her chest. Just to think, she and Anastasia could both be married by this time next year.

A curtseying maid passed on her way to the study. Josey paused for a moment at the door. She couldn't remember it ever being closed. She glanced down the hall. The chambermaid was gone. On an impulse, she pressed her ear against the wooden panels. The voices of two men murmured on the other side. A tendril of guilt knotted in her belly, but she didn't pull away. If this visitor was here to discuss her matrimonial options, it concerned *her* more than anyone. But she couldn't make out what was being said. She wished they would speak up.

The voices ceased and Josey jumped back as the door opened. She smoothed the front of her dress and did her best to look as if she had just arrived. The guest was a tall gentleman, younger than she imagined. A sigil of crossed keys was emblazoned on the breast of his gray mantle, which he wore over a suit of the same color. He had a sallow face with a nervous look about him, a look that amplified Josey's anxiety. Had their discussion not gone well? Had Father not offered an adequate dowry? She was bursting with questions. The man bent in a stiff bow before striding past her to the stairs.

Josey peeked inside. Her father sat at his perennially cluttered desk with a hand pressed to his forehead. The light from an open window illuminated his pate, bald save for a halo of sparse white hair around the crown. He would be sixty-two this winter. She remembered how strong and tall he had looked when she was a child. Now, he spent most of his time in this study, surrounded by the trappings of his former power. The room was stuffy and warm, but he kept a blanket wrapped around his legs.

He straightened when he saw her. "Josey. I didn't hear you return. How was your shopping? Did you find Anastasia well? I want to hear everything."

"Father." She entered and sat in the leather chair beside his desk. "Who was that man? Fenrik said he came from the palace."

He reached out to take her hand. His fingers were thin and cold.

"His father was a friend of mine. In younger days, the two of us were powerful men. Members of the Court vied for our attention and would give much for our patronage, but now he's dead and buried and I am an old man."

"You are still a great man. I just had this notion your visitor was calling about something . . . more auspicious."

"Ah." He placed a finger alongside his nose. "You thought he came with a betrothal offer."

She tried to blush, but it was a trick she'd never mastered. "It was silly of me. I'm only seventeen, I know."

"Seventeen and as lovely as a rose in bloom. I wish I had such an offer, Josey. Sadly, the news is not so gay. There are rumors of strange troubles in the north. Banditry and worse. Envoys have gone missing and things are deteriorating here in Othir. How would a voyage suit you?"

His question caught her off guard. "Suit me? Father, I can't leave Othir. Anastasia is to be married. That's what I've come to tell you. She's asked me to be her maiden of honor."

"I'm quite serious, Josephine. The political tide is shifting faster than I anticipated. I had hoped we could weather the storm, but I fear it's not safe anymore."

"Not safe? Why not?"

He eased back in his chair, suddenly looking old and feeble. "Affairs on the Capitoline are in disarray."

Father still used old-fashioned terms like the Capitoline, even though the Nimean Empire had died out ages ago and everyone else had taken to calling it Celestial Hill.

"There is unrest in the streets," he continued. "And the prelate's ability to contain it grows weaker. Just the other day, a man was killed not three blocks from our doorstep. Suffice it to say I wish you to adjourn to a safer location until these problems pass."

"I was out the whole afternoon and I didn't see anything amiss. The city is as calm as a summer day. Anyway, Anastasia is my best friend. I can't miss her wedding, Father. Not for anything."

"Josey, my dear. I promised your mother I would always see to your well-being. And I act from my own selfish desires. I couldn't bear to see you come to harm. You possess the key to my heart."

She placed a hand on her bosom. Under the lace fronting of her dress, the cool hardness of a pendant pressed against her skin. She knelt before him and folded her hands on his lap.

"Mother wasn't afraid of anything. She wouldn't want me to leave your side."

He brushed a rogue curl from her face. The corners of his eyes drooped amid folds of wrinkles. "She would want you to trust my judgment and obey my wishes. Please, Josey, pack your things. I have arranged for a ship."

"Father, please!"

"No, Josey. My mind is adamant on this. You will go to Navarre and remain there until I send for you. The new exarch is a good man and as trustworthy as we'll find in times such as these. He will see you safe—"

Josey jumped to her feet, her entire body trembling. "I won't go! You cannot make me."

"It is settled. Chide me no more on this subject, Daughter."

Cheeks wet with tears, she dashed from the study, brushing past Fenrik in the hallway loaded with wrapped bundles from the carriage. She slammed the door to her room and stood at the foot of the feather bed, hands clenched at her sides. How could he be so cruel? Why couldn't he see that she couldn't leave? They needed each other. She had no other family. Only him, and now he was sending her away. What would she tell Anastasia?

Josey took deep breaths and composed herself. Tears wouldn't get her anywhere. She sat down at her dressing table and began to brush her hair with short, hard strokes. She needed to think, to devise some argument to sway her father. She had to convince him to let her stay. She had to.

Raging flames painted the night sky in hues of orange and gold, and threw shadows across the yard of the villa where the tall bodies sprawled. Caim peered through the wooden slats of the fence.

"We have to go," a voice whispered behind him.

Caim wanted to turn away, but his limbs had turned to stone. The frigid wind flogged his small body. The cold slid through his veins like ice water. There was blood on his hands. He wiped them on his shirt, but they wouldn't come clean.

The world shimmered and he was standing in the yard. A large man slumped at his feet. Strings of red-black blood ran from the wound in his chest. A tremor ran through Caim as the corpse opened its eyes, black spheres without irises or whites. A whisper issued from blue-tinged lips.

"Justice . . . , my son."

Caim opened his eyes and was greeted by a razor-sharp moonbeam that pierced through the slats of the window shutters. A cool breeze flitted over his chest as the last vestiges of the dream—the images of fire and death—sifted through his mental grasp. He settled back into the fabric of the cot under him and stared at the ceiling, debating whether to get up or try to fall back asleep for another hour.

With a sigh he threw back the woolen blankets and dropped to his chest on the cold floorboards. His muscles stretched and contracted through a routine of exercises: push-ups, stomach tighteners, lunges, and handstands. Thirty minutes later he was sweating freely. After splashing his face with water from a chipped clay pitcher, he stood before his only extravagance, a full-length cheval glass in a bronze stand. Hard eyes stared back at him from the wavy depths of the mirror, chips of granite set in deep cavities beneath his thick, black brows. He ran his hands across his torso, examining the damage; a few scrapes and cuts, broken skin at his elbows and the backs of his hands, but all in all he was in better shape than he probably deserved. Fragments of the dream scudded through his mind. The words of his father's ghost haunted him. *Justice.* Had it been served in Ostergoth?

He pulled a clean chiton and breeches from his footlocker and went out into the kitchen. The rest of his apartment lacked for furniture: a plain table stood with a single chair, a coldbox and small brick oven in the kitchen, and a pantry. The living area was bare except for a wide mat and assorted pieces of exercise equipment, sand-filled bags suspended from the ceiling. A charcoal etching of a lighthouse drawn by a street artist hung on the wall in a plain wooden frame. In the picture, black frothing waves battered at the rocky base of the lighthouse as its beacon shone bravely in the face of the storm. Tiny lights flickered in the distance. They made him think of Kit.

He put on a pair of scuffed leather boots and wondered where she was. Kit came and went as she pleased. Sometimes he wouldn't see her for days, and other times he couldn't get rid of her. He didn't know what Kit was, not exactly. When he was a boy he had thought of her as an imaginary friend, but as he grew older and she did not leave, he began to suspect something else. No one else had invisible friends who tagged after them. But she was real. She knew things he didn't, things he couldn't know. Countless times she'd warned him of danger before it materialized.

His ability to meld with the shadows was another mystery. He had always been good at going about unnoticed, even as a boy, but where did the power come from? Had he been born with it or was he cursed? More trouble than anything, it was another quirk of a past he remembered only in murky fragments. Maybe he didn't want to.

Caim strapped on his knives and covered them with a fustian cloak as he went to the door, its olive green paint peeling away in strips to reveal the slab of old wormwood underneath. He peered down the hallway in both directions. As he secured the door's rusty latch, a small, pale face stared up at him from across the hall. He had seen the girl a few times before, playing alone in the hallway at odd hours. Her wheat-colored hair hung down across her thin shoulders in tangled skeins. She couldn't have been older than six, or maybe seven. Angry voices echoed from beyond the door beside her. Caim walked away.

He descended a flight of creaking stairs and passed through the dirty foyer. The tenement building might have been a stately manor house in its former days before the neighborhood took a turn for the worse. Still, he liked its location and found the current owner's policy of studied indifference toward his tenants convenient. As long as the rent was paid on time, the old geezer never asked questions.

As Caim reached the street, a stench assaulted him like a wet sock full of rotten eggs, a combination of sea air and human refuse that clogged his head and clung to the back of his palate. It was worse in the summer.

The ancient stone buildings of Low Town, once the heart of the city according to the local salts, were stained with centuries of weather, soot, and foul air. Over the years, the inner city had grown upward as well as outward. Buildings four and five stories tall hung precariously over the narrow streets. With the defeat of the pirates of the Stormcatcher Islands fifty or so years back and the subsequent expansion of trade on the Midland Sea, those with the means to capitalize on the sudden influx of new goods left the neighborhood to build bigger homes on the hills above the Processional. So High Town was born, eventually to become the glowing jewel of Othir. Things had only gotten worse for the Low Towners in recent years, such as increased taxes to pay for distant wars and expensive public works like the new cathedral under construction in the city center, and food shortages. The poorest families were put out on the street by landlords feeling the pinch. He saw them every day, begging on the main thoroughfares, selling their children in back alleys.

As he hopped over a fetid puddle on Prior's Cross, Caim caught a glimpse of the horned moon, perched over the roof of an abandoned dyer's factory like a silver sickle. Its otherworldly beauty, forever out of reach, always made him uneasy in a way he couldn't rightly describe. It was like being homesick, but for a home he had never known.

Othir had been his home for six years. He had originally begun plying his trade as a sellsword in the western territories. He'd done time in various mercenary crews during his teen years, earning his silver with one hand and spending it with the other. But after a bit of nasty business in Isenmere, his gang was run out by a posse bent on revenge. He drifted from town to town, always watching over his shoulder. When no lawmen showed up to arrest him, he passed into a new life.

A right turn onto Serpentine Way brought Caim to a tangle of back streets and alleyways known as the Gutters. Here the buildings were built of old, crumbling brick covered in dingy whitewash. Their sooty slate roofs tilted sharply, with tall steeples and shuttered gables. The Gutters were home to every sort of crook and deadbeat imaginable. It was a place to tread lightly, where anything could happen and often did.

Caim strode down the center of the street. Footpads slunk deeper into their hidey-holes as he passed by. Muggers found business elsewhere. He'd drenched these cobblestones in blood more than once. Still, he kept his cloak tight around his shoulders and one hand on a knife.

His first contract had been right here in Othir. Dalros was a luxuries trader whose business had suffered a turn of bad fortune. When he couldn't cover his debts to the local usurers, they decided to make an example of him. Caim was tapped for the job. It was a simple break-and-stab, nothing fancy, but Caim would never forget the shakes he'd suffered that spring night as he scaled the low wall surrounding Dalros's home. He was in and out in less than fifteen minutes. With the merchant's blood on his hands, he'd crept past a lounging sentry, slipped back over the wall, and gone on his way. He was paid twenty gold soldats for that job, a fortune to him in those days.

A shout from behind made Caim spin around. His knife slid out of its sheath as a squadron of soldiers on horseback rode down the street. On their bloodred breastplates gleamed a blazing sunburst in gold, the symbol of the Sacred Brotherhood, or the Knights of the Noose, as they were called behind their backs—a jest about the manner in which their patron saint had gone to meet his Maker. Some in Othir said they were the real power behind the prelacy, but Caim paid little heed to politics. It made no difference to him who ruled as long as he could count on them to sow discord and corruption; unrest made for good business in his line of work. And over the past few years, business had been extraordinarily good.

Caim slipped into the shadowed doorway of a cobbler's shop and sheathed his blade as they rode past. The soldiers' presence in the Gutters at this hour made the skin between his shoulder blades itch. The denizens of these squalid alleys were typically left to their own devices after sunset.

Once the soldiers passed from sight, he continued on his way. Another three blocks brought him to Chirron's Square. A marketplace by day, it brokered a different type of commerce after sundown. Pimps and drug peddlers lounged amid the marble pedestals of broken statuary. Ladies of the night trolled for interested buyers. In the center of the plaza rose a scaffold. Its weathered timbers supported a massive crossbeam from which dangled five bodies, adult, probably male, but it was impossible to tell for sure. They had been burned before they were hanged, their hands and feet lopped off, their eyes gouged out. No one paid the bodies any mind. Who had they been? Robbers? Rapists? Or just some poor souls foolish enough to criticize the ruling powers in public? Caim continued on his way, but the spectacle lingered in his thoughts.

He turned onto Cutter Lane. Windows were thrown wide open down the length of the street despite the chill in the air, spilling the rosy light of a dozen taverns and festhouses onto the grimy cobblestones. Pipers and lutists competed with the din of hard drinkers.

He ducked into the third house on the left. The cracked placard over the door depicted three buxom ladies in short frocks. Bright light filled the Three Maids. Wooden tankards clanked on the tabletops, and rough hands clapped in time with a zithern while a scrawny girl clad in only her snow-pale skin and long red locks danced under the glassy stares of tradesmen and stevedores. A shore party of sailors—Arnossi by their accent and swarthy features—sang sea ballads in a corner.

Caim threaded his way to the bar. Big Olaf was tending tonight. He grinned through a row of uneven teeth as Caim approached.

"Hey, boyo. You should've been here last night. I had to toss out a pair of uptown rakes with a mean-on. Swear they flew a dozen paces before they hit pavement. Each."

Caim slid a silver noble, double-penny weight, across the bar. "Is he in?"

The coin disappeared, and Olaf jerked a sausage-thick thumb at the back stairs. Caim headed around the bar. Mathias, the owner of the Three Maids, also handled several of the biggest fish in Othir's murder-for-hire game. He was their broker, their middleman, the one who ferreted out the contracts and matched them with the right talent for the job. He lived above the tavern, he claimed, to be closer to the people, and always acted hurt when anyone insinuated he was a miser. Caim didn't know why Mathias continued to live amid the dregs of the city. With the commissions he'd made in the last year alone, he could afford a comfortable house in High Town. Some folks couldn't bear to leave their roots, no matter how high they climbed. Caim had never had that problem.

The back stairs were unlit. As he started up, Caim heard the whisper of leather glide over wood a moment before a shape appeared above him. An image flashed through his mind: clinging to the walls of Duke Reinard's keep, gazing up at a mysterious black figure crawling along the battlements. A twinge quivered in his chest. Both *suete* knives were out in an instant, held low and pressed against his thighs to hide their shine. His knees flexed, ready to leap back or lunge ahead.

Two white circles appeared in the gloom above him, a pair of hands held open. "Peace," said a low voice. "Good evening, Caim."

"Ral." Caim slipped the knives back into their homes, but he left an inch of each blade free. "If you've got business with Mathias, I'll wait below."

Ral descended a step. The faint glow from the common room highlighted his features. Bright blue eyes peered from beneath coiffed spikes of stark blond hair. Dressed all in black leather, he melded with the shadows of the stairway. The intricate silver cross-guard of a cut-and-thrust sword jutted from his belt. Glints of steel at his wrists, waist, and boots hinted at other weapons; Ral was notorious for all the hardware he carried.

"No, we are concluded." His lazy way of talking reminded Caim of a dozing cat, always a moment from showing his claws. "I heard you did quite well up north. Reinard and his bodyguards slain in front of a hundred witnesses, but not a single person could identify the killer afterward. Not bad."

Caim chewed on his tongue. He didn't like discussing his business, especially where idle ears could overhear. He leaned against the wall of the stairwell, trying to appear casual.

"It's done. That's all that matters."

Ral came down another step. "Exactly, but you should be careful. There's been a citywide crackdown these past couple days."

"I saw the display in the square."

Ral chuckled. Despite his butter-smooth voice, it wasn't a pleasant sound. "A gang of roof-crawlers got pinched robbing a vicar's home. All involved were caught and hanged, but not before they tortured his entire family for the location of a cache of jewels. Word says they even cut off the youngest boy's fingers and toes."

A leader of the True Faith, supposedly sworn to vows of poverty and chastity, keeps a house in High Town with a wife and children, and no one cares to comment. But why should they? Large sins are easily forgotten. It's the little ones that gnaw at your soul in the lonely hours of the night.

"Of course," Ral said, "the fops up on Celestial Hill are terrified out of their wigs that it's another movement toward rebellion."

Caim nodded, uncomfortably reminded of young Lord Robert. "If you'll excuse me, I have business of my own with Mathias."

"I've no time for palaver myself. I'm heading out of town."

They passed each other on the stairs and Ral turned. "You know, Caim. It's not fair."

Caim paused with a foot on the top step. "What isn't?"

Ral opened his hand and a slender throwing blade appeared, too fast for the eye to follow. Caim tensed.

"Here we are," Ral said. "Two of the deadliest men in the city. We should be running things, lording it up in the palace. It's all wasted on those powdered fools whose only claim is their family name." His eyes lit up as he spoke.

Caim looked down at the other man without a shred of empathy. According to the rumors, Ral was a son of privilege who had enjoyed many a night rutting in Low Town until his inheritance ran out. Then, broke and desperate, he had weaseled his way into the assassination trade. He must have found the taste to his liking, because he came back again and again between benders on Silk Street. Knifings in the merchant district in broad daylight, pregnant mistresses found floating in the harbor—those were Ral's stock in trade.

What does that make you? A vigilante with bad dreams or a thug just smart enough to stay one step ahead of the law?

Searching for a way to end the conversation without giving insult, Caim decided on brevity. "It is what it is."

"I suppose so. Farewell, Caim. I'm off to a warmer clime to take care of some business. We'll talk another time."

Not if he had any choice in the matter, Caim thought as he climbed the last step. He was tired. He just wanted to get his money and go home. Maybe he would take some time off. He approached the only door on the upper floor, knocked twice, waited a heartbeat, and gave two more knocks. He opened it without waiting for an invitation.

If Mathias acted the skinflint with his patrons below, he spared no expense to make his living space look and feel like a mansion. Overlapping hand-woven carpets covered the floors. Silken arrays embroidered with eastern-style hunting scenes decorated the walls, hiding the bare panels underneath. Heavy furniture in glossy hardwoods cluttered the room, along with marble tables and expensive bronze artwork.

Mathias came through the archway on the far side of the parlor, dressed in a gaudy teal robe splashed with tiny golden cranes. He was a heavyset man past his middling years. He still had most of his hair and employed dyes to keep it black and lustrous except for a pair of silver wings brushed back over his ears. An admission of inevitability, he called them.

"Our good friend returns from the north!"

They shook hands, and Mathias offered him a choice of seats. Caim sat down on a high-backed chair with no armrests or cushion.

Mathias fetched a bottle and two glasses from a malachite sideboard. "By the gods above and below, I am glad to see you back."

"Blasphemy, Mat? At your age?"

"Aye. I'm too old to care anymore what the Church thinks. What has that prattle ever done for anybody? Nothing. But forget about that. Everything went well, yes?"

Caim accepted a glass of amber brandy and settled back into the hard seat. "Well enough, although trying to get anywhere in this country is becoming a right pain in the ass. The roads are a mess and tollhouses have sprung up over every hill."

Mathias flumped onto a banquette and sloshed liquor on his expensive robe. "The realm is coming apart like an overripe melon. Every warlord who can put together a dozen half-trained men-at-arms is trying to carve out a piece for himself. It's almost enough to make one long for the good old days of imperial law and order. Almost."

"Anyway, I stayed in Ostergoth long enough to hear the bells ring His Grace's departure from the world of the living before I left."

Mat lifted his glass. "To another job completed and another villain vanquished."

Caim took a sip before setting the glass down. "I've gathered there was some trouble in town while I was away."

"I had nothing to do with it." The rubies encrusting Mat's pinky ring gleamed as he placed a plump hand over his flabby breast. "You know I never touch that sort of smash-and-grab work. It's an unsavory business and a trifle pathetic. Now we all have to suffer through a few weeks of heightened security, but things will settle down. They can't stay on full alert forever, eh? More brandy?"

"I'll just have my fee and leave you in peace."

Mathias smiled. "That's the man I know. All business—and business is good!" He reached under his seat and tossed a bulging leather sack to Caim. "Five hundred soldats, just as the contract stated."

Caim caught the bag and slipped it into his shirt.

"Not going to count it?"

"No need to. I know where you live."

"Right enough. You're acquiring quite a reputation, Caim. That's why I know you're just the man for another job I'm sitting on."

Caim rose to his feet. "No thank you, Mat. I don't want to see anything you're sitting on. That cushion looks like it's had enough."

"It's not like you to pass up money, especially for a worthy cause."

"I'm sure. Another priest with a fetish for children, or a landlord who squeezes every last crumb from his destitute peasants. No thanks. I'm going to take some time off. Like you said, the city's heating up."

"That's why I'm turning to you, Caim. Believe me when I say this job is easy. So easy you could do it blind and one-handed."

"Not an image I want to ponder."

Mathias brushed the air with his pudgy fingers. "You know what I mean. But it has to be done fast."

He headed for the door. "Sorry, Mat."

"Caim, I'm desperate!"

Caim stopped with his hand on the knob. Mathias wasn't a stranger to theatrics, but he sounded genuinely worried, and Mathias Finneus never worried. The look of relief on his face was almost comical as Caim came back and stood by the high-backed chair.

"What's the job?"

"Please, sit, my friend," Mathias urged. "More brandy?"

"No more drinks. Tell me about the job."

"It's very simple. One target, living in High Town."

Caim's hand hovered over his glass, resting still on the table. "Inside the city?"

"Yes, you've done local work before."

"Who is he?"

"A retired general, a real hard case from what I've heard. He was responsible for some big massacre during the war. Up in Eregoth, I believe. You're from those parts, aren't you?"

Caim considered the carpet between his feet as a jumble of old feelings knocked around in his chest. "What makes you say that?"

"Nothing much. You just have a northernish look about you."

Caim looked Mathias in the eye. "I told you before. I'm from the western territories."

But he wasn't. As far as he could piece together from his shambled memories, his family had hailed from Eregoth, one of several border states that had once been part of the Nimean Empire. But it was a past he didn't want known, for no better reason than it was personal.

"Oh yes." Mathias winked. "I forgot."

"Go on."

"Well, what makes me nervous is the timing. This job has to be done in two days."

"Impossible. You know I don't do rush jobs. Go find some desperate sailor deep in his cups and slip him a few silvers."

"Caim, this client isn't someone to disappoint, if you get my meaning.

It must be done quickly, and with no mistakes. That's why I need you. You're the only one I can trust with a job like this on such short notice."

"I want to help you, Mathias, but there are too many things to consider. I spent weeks stalking Reinard before I took him down. I would need time to study the target, learn his habits and movements. After that I would have to do the same for his family and bodyguards."

Mathias bounced off the chaise and waddled to a rolltop desk against the wall. He held up a bundle of papers bound together with a red cord.

"I have all the particulars here: daily itinerary, personal security details, interior layouts, everything you'll need. He lives with a young daughter, but don't worry about her. The mother's dead. He doesn't keep any guards, just a broken-down manservant who sleeps like a log. It will be the easiest money you ever made."

Mathias held out the bundle, but Caim didn't take it.

"Who gathered all this?"

"A mutual friend. I vouch for its authenticity."

"It was Ral, wasn't it?"

"Why does it matter? Just take it."

"Damn it, Mat. He took the assignment and then dumped it back in your lap when a better job came up, didn't he? No wonder he was so chummy. No thanks. I'm passing."

Caim took two steps toward the door. Mathias reached out as if to grasp his sleeve, but drew his hand back before it made contact. Caim stopped as the bundle of papers was thrust in front of him.

"It's his loss!" Mathias said. "In and out, and a thousand soldats in your pocket."

"I don't clean up other people's messes."

Mathias cocked his head to the right. "My friend, that's precisely what you do. Please, don't make me beg. I'll throw in half of my end. That's another three hundred in gold. Then you can take a nice, long sabbatical."

Caim sighed as Mathias shook the papers at him. He couldn't do it, couldn't let down the man who had given him a chance as a young man on the run, a vagabond with no contacts or vouchers.

Caim took the papers. "All right. I'll do it. But hang on to your fee. You're getting old, Mathias. You should think about retiring soon."

Mathias gathered his robe around him as he returned to his chair. "I don't know what I'd do with myself if I ever retired."

"Buy a big villa somewhere nice. Live the life of a country gentleman."

Mathias laughed so hard he almost choked on his wine. "Can you see me as a country squire? I wouldn't last a month. Good fortune, my friend. I'll see you when the job is done."

Caim tucked the papers into his tunic. The bundle made a lump under his arm opposite the money pouch. He crossed to the door, but hesitated with his hand on the knob.

"By the way, what was the other job Ral took?"

"What?" Mathias twisted around to look at Caim over his shoulder. "Oh, something in Belastire. He'll be bow-legged and as dusty as a beggar by the time he returns."

"Belastire? It'll be cold on the Midland coast this time of year."

Mathias nodded. "Cold and bitter. The blackheart should feel right at home, eh?"

Caim thought back to the conversation on the stairs. Hadn't Ral mentioned a warmer clime? What game was he playing?

Caim checked his knives out of habit as he departed the Three Maids. Revelers accompanied by torchbearers filled the benighted streets, pushed out the door by exhausted tavernkeeps. The sun would be rising in another couple hours. He would have liked to go back home and crawl into bed for a couple sennights, but he had work to do. Two days wasn't enough time.

Tucking the pouch and the papers deeper into the confines of his shirt, Caim pulled his cloak tighter around his shoulders. The broadcloth wrapped around him in a warm cocoon as he delved back into the Gutters.

CHAPTER THREE

Josey had nearly worked herself into another bout of tears by the time her carriage stopped outside Anastasia's house on Torvelli Square. She couldn't get the conversation with Father out of her head. She'd never felt so helpless in her life. The only thing she could think of was to talk to her best friend about it. Between the two of them, she was certain they would find a solution.

An elderly footman ushered her inside. Handing her mink-lined cloak to one of the house girls, its silky hairs stiff from the chill, Josey filed away the changing seasons as another potential argument against her departure. Now was hardly the best time of year to undertake a sea journey. That wouldn't be enough on its own to sway her father, but when she talked to him again, she intended to have an arsenal of reasons why it would be best for her to stay in Othir, at least until after Yeartide.

"Josey!" Anastasia's cheery voice echoed through the atrium as she hurried down a winding staircase. They clasped hands and kissed each other's cheeks.

Anastasia stepped back to arm's length, concern written across her pretty features. With her honey gold hair, coiffed in wavy marcels, and her ocean blue eyes, Anastasia was a true beauty, doll-like in her perfection. Next to her, Josey had always felt homely, her complexion too pale, her hair too dark and stringy.

"What's the matter, Josey? Come in here."

Josey let herself be pulled into an adjourning parlor room and seated alone on a padded settee with tiny green leaves embroidered on the cushions.

Anastasia kissed her again. "Something's wrong, Josey. Tell me."

Josey told Anastasia about her father's decision to make her leave. By the time she finished, she was sobbing openly.

Anastasia lent Josey a handkerchief to wipe her face. "That's simply not fair. Othir is as safe as a nursery. Forgive me, Josey, but I fear your father may be feeling his dotage. You know how old men get. They see specters in every dark corner."

"I know. But no matter what I said, he refused to budge on the matter. I don't know what to do. That's why I came to see you. You have to help me, 'Stasia. I cannot miss your wedding. It will be the happiest day of my life!"

"You have to be there!" Anastasia looked on the verge of tears herself.

Before her friend started to cry, Josey rushed on. "I will be. I promise. But I need a plan. Father won't give in to emotional pleas."

"You could stay here with me. With the armsmen we keep, this house is virtually a fortress at night."

"I'm not sure Father would feel that's adequate. My safety has always been his chief concern. There were bodyguards everywhere when we lived in Navarre. Sometimes I could hardly breathe."

"But the westlands are abysmally lawless. This is Othir. It's entirely different."

"I know. I just don't know how to convince Father of that."

Anastasia squeezed her hand. "Don't worry, darling. We'll find a way." She reached up and touched the pendant hanging from Josey's neck. "I've always admired this piece, Josey. It's beautiful. So simple, but elegant."

Josey lifted the pendant, an antique-style key in gold. "Father gave it to me for my fourteenth birthday. It's my favorite piece of jewelry."

"It must be. You never wear anything else."

"Father says it's the key to his heart, that it would give me everything I ever wanted and more. Sometimes he's the sweetest, kindest man in the world. I wish he would see reason and let me stay here until your wedding day."

"It will work out, Josey. I know! We'll go to the basilica and say a prayer for it."

Josey dabbed her face with the silken cloth. "I don't think praying is going to solve anything, 'Stasia. This is serious." Then she saw the stricken look in her friend's eyes. "Forgive me. I'm just overwrought. Yes, let's go."

As they made to leave, a servant appeared at the entrance of the room. "Pardon, milady. A visitor has arrived for you."

"Let him in." Anastasia turned to Josey. "That must be Markus. He's been coming by every day since the engagement was announced. He's such a romantic. Do you like him, Josey? Tell me true."

Josey hugged her friend and laughed, glad to speak of something else. "He's a dream come to life. You two will be as happy together as a pair of larks."

Anastasia giggled. "Markus is nearly a knight, you know. Well, very nearly. Second prefect is a worthy rank, and soon he'll be promoted. I'm sure of it."

They turned to the clack of hard boot steps as a tall shape filled the doorway.

"Markus!" Anastasia ran to him and they embraced beside a bronze bust of one of her famous ancestors. Then, as if noticing Josey for the first time, the couple parted and came over to sit with her.

"I adore this uniform on you, Markus." Anastasia brushed her fingers over the circle emblazoned on his jacket. "It makes you look so handsome."

He smiled, revealing rows of large, white teeth. He was starting to grow a mustache and sideburns in the military style. Josey squinted, trying to imagine him with a full face of hair. Something in the way he looked at her made her uncomfortable.

"What do you think?" Markus asked. "Does it make me look dashing?"

Josey dropped her gaze to the floor. "Yes, quite dashing."

Anastasia patted Josey's knee. "Poor darling. Her father's sending her away, and we've been trying to concoct a scheme to keep her here."

"Sending you away?" The note of real concern in his voice touched Josey. Perhaps he was as genteel as a knight after all. "Whatever for?"

Josey folded the loaned handkerchief into a square on her lap. "He says it isn't safe here in the city anymore. He says people have been assaulted, even killed."

"How horrible!" Anastasia said. "Is it true, Markus?"

"Oh, it's not for you to worry about. The Low Towners are forever at each other's throats, like a pack of curs fighting over a bone. That's where most of the attacks have taken place."

"Most?" Josey asked. "But not all?"

He brushed at the breast of his uniform, dismissing the idea. "Sometimes a matter spills over across the Processional, but it's nothing to trouble you ladies. You're as safe as lambs in their pens."

Josey wasn't sure she liked his description, but she put on a smile for her friend. "I hope I can convince Father of that."

"I have a wonderful idea," Anastasia said. "Markus could escort you home and tell your father just what he said to us. I'm sure it will comfort him, coming from an officer of the Sacred Brotherhood."

"Would you?" Josey asked. She didn't like the idea of riding home with him, but she was willing to make sacrifices if it meant being allowed to stay in Othir.

Markus stood with a shake of his head. "I'm sorry, but I cannot. I have business to attend this afternoon. I just stopped by to remind Ana of our date for a late supper this evening."

Anastasia rose to embrace her betrothed. "I didn't forget. I'm having Maya make something special for us."

"Excellent." He bowed to Josey and gave Anastasia a peck on the cheek. "I shall see you later."

Josey remained behind as Anastasia walked Markus out. They whispered their good-byes out of eyesight. Several minutes passed before Anastasia returned to the sitting room. Her eyes danced with joy as she plopped down beside Josey.

"Isn't he magnificent? I'm so happy, Josey. I feel like a cloud floating high above the world."

Josey hugged her friend and murmured the words Anastasia wanted to hear, but she couldn't shake the suspicion that things might not remain so congenial between husband and wife after the wedding day. Markus was polite enough in mixed company, but his cavalier manner didn't suit her friend, who was the picture of a perfect lady, refined and unassuming. Yet Josey kept those fears to herself. Anastasia was clearly smitten, and there was no use spoiling her good feelings. And some part of Josey wondered if she wasn't just the tiniest bit jealous that her friend had found such love while she was still alone, chaste and waiting for the man of her dreams.

Josey listened with half an ear while Anastasia chattered about visits to the seamstress, finding the right orchestra, and all the other minutiae required to plan a wedding. She nodded at the appropriate places and made polite noises, but the greater part of her thoughts were on her own problems. Her ship departed in two days. The matter couldn't wait until she devised an airtight argument. She had to speak with Father tonight.

Ral watched them from the shadow of the Emperor Tronieger monument in the center of Torvelli Square, the strapping officer of the Guard and the young daughter of a respected statesman, as they shared a deep kiss on the front steps of the manse. The prefect's hands slid down to clutch his lady's slender bottom in broad daylight. Ral smiled to himself. The wagging tongues of High Town would wear themselves ragged.

Ral didn't understand the fascination with romance. Oh, he enjoyed the company of women aplenty, the sorts who were attracted to a man of means, and the girl was a pretty slip of a thing, but he didn't have time for anything that outlasted the night. Perhaps after his work was done he would take the time to find a companion, someone suitable for an upcoming man with a bright future.

Finally, Markus bid the girl farewell. Ral followed him, keeping his distance. The prefect, in his scarlet coat, was simplicity itself to shadow through the broad streets of Opuline Hill.

The sights and sounds of High Town did not distract Ral. Growing up, he had sampled every type of excess that wealth could buy. His life might have turned out differently if his father had lived to a ripe old age, but fate had intervened in the form of news off an Arnossi trader bound for Illmyn. Both of his father's ships had disappeared in a storm off the Hvekish coast, lost with all hands. In an instant, he went from a boy to a man of means. He sold his interest in the shipping company and bought a big house. He found new friends in the sons and daughters of the city's finest families, hosted lavish parties that went on for days, and lived the life he'd always wanted. Until the money ran out. Then the loan sharks started circling. He borrowed to keep up his sumptuous lifestyle, and then again when that ran out. By the time he realized the depths to which he had sunk, it was too late.

They found him dead drunk in the back room of a Low Town dive. Five big men with cold eyes propped him on a rickety chair and lashed his hands behind his back.

"Mr. Ayes isn't happy with you," the biggest of them rumbled. "You been spending his money like it's piss, and he ain't seen nothing back in more than a fortnight."

Another thug flashed a long-bladed dirk, so big it was almost a sword. "Not a smart thing to do, making Mr. Ayes angry. Now we come to collect."

They cut off his clothes and shook them out, but Ral laughed at them, too drunk to care whether or not they killed him.

The man with the big knife rested the point between Ral's legs and whispered in his ear. "If you can't pay, friend, then you have to make good some other way."

They gave him a simple choice: lose his skin or do one small favor for his debtor in exchange for wiping the books clean.

All he had to do was kill a man.

That job changed him forever—the apprehension as he stole into another man's home in the dead of night; the tingling of his skin as he found his quarry abed, oblivious to the doom looming over him; the euphoria that surged through his veins when he drove the knife into that soft belly. His victim's death moan had been a paean of rebirth, setting him free from all the constraints that had been ingrained into him by a society blind to his needs, apathetic to his desires. That night he had stepped into a world where the power over life and death rested in his hands. He had never looked back.

Ral followed Markus through the old Forum with its afternoon strollers out for their constitutional amid the rows of vendor stalls. The shouts of hawkers punctuated the susurrus of the crowd. Markus strode straight ahead like a charging bull, never glancing to his left or right. Complete obliviousness to the city's dangers, great or small—that was the prerogative of being an officer in the Sacred Brotherhood. Markus's stride didn't even slow to the sound of cracking whips.

Ral slipped behind a stack of cloth bundles as a band of men in bloodred robes burst from a merchant's tent. Their scourges split the air as they flung the object of their ire onto the dirty pavestones. The man was dressed in the tattered remains of a fine suit. His round cap rolled in the dust. The Flagellants surrounded him—Ral could now see he was the owner of the stall—and proceeded to beat him without mercy while a scrawny woman, possibly his wife, wrung her hands and sobbed in the tent's doorway. What had been the man's crime? Ral couldn't guess. It could be almost anything, from cheating his customers to failing to display a proper image of the prelate within his establishment. Like the Brotherhood, the Flagellants were a law unto themselves, answerable only to the Church.

Ral skirted the scene. He found his quarry on the other side of the forum and followed him into the Temple District. A few streets farther, Markus entered the Pantheon, a converted pagan temple. While the prefect entered the stolid building through the front via a set of immense bronze doors, Ral went around to a side entrance located in a constricted alley. Avoiding piles of garbage, he wedged the tip of a dagger into the keyhole and snapped the simple lock. The door accessed a crowded storage room. The deep tones of choral singing filtered through another door on the other side of the room. Ral took a moment to rummage through a varnished wardrobe, selected a white cassock, and pulled the garment over his head. A red stole stitched with circles in gold thread went around his shoulders. Smiling, he slipped through another door.

The Pantheon's circular walls bowed over the main worship chamber of the church. The building was an architectural masterpiece, dating back to imperial days when Nimea had enjoyed an era of magnificence unmatched by any nation in the world. The ceiling was open to the sky, another sign of its pagan origins. Prayer mats formed orderly rows on the floor's red-and-white checkerboard flagstones where priests and trains of dutiful acolytes walked among the faithful, swinging pots of smoking incense and murmuring prayers.

Ral pulled up the robe's hood and slipped behind a gaggle of old women in black shawls, their eyes downcast as they walked the stations around the perimeter of the great chamber. He slowed as they stopped before a hollow niche inhabited by the gray stone statue of some saint. So pious, they made him sick as they whispered fervent prayers over clenched fists. If any of them dared to raise their eyes high enough, they would see the marble base of the original statue that had adorned this shrine before the advent of the True Faith. Perhaps it had been the likeness of Torim, the Storm Lord, or Hisu, the patron goddess of love and nauseating poetry. Whichever god it had been, the name had been chiseled out of the pedestal as if it never existed. Ral smirked under the hood. It was a shame people couldn't be eliminated as easily as deities. His life would be a lot simpler.

As the old women shuffled off to the next station, Ral sank down beside Markus, who knelt in the last row, his large hands clasped together.

Markus barely looked over. "No, thank you, Father. I'm—" Then the prefect caught sight of his face. "Ral? God's breath! Isn't anything sacred to you?"

Ral glanced at the massive sculpture of the Prophet of the True Faith. Lord Phebus, the Light of the World, towered above the high fane at the end of the nave. The statue was clothed as a simple peasant, but glittering rays chased in real gold radiated from his bloodied brow.

"I'll worry about God when he starts worrying about me."

Markus looked around. "Someone could see you."

Ral had already checked during his approach. No other worshippers were in earshot.

"Not likely. These bleaters are too busy worrying about saving their souls. With all this praying, you'd think there was an army of Shadowmen banging at the gates, eh? Or old King Mithrax riding from the grave with his Hellion Host."

The scabbard of Markus's sword scraped on the floor as he shifted position. He moved easily for a big man. "What are you doing here?"

"Just making a last-minute visit. I take it you haven't heard the latest?"

"No, what?"

"Your grand master has been arrested."

"On what charges?"

Ral put his hands together as if to pray. "Treason. Sedition. It doesn't matter. Our benefactor will make sure he never sees the light of day again."

"I never thought—"

"That's your problem, Markus. You never think. But now that the head of your order is out of the way, the way is clear for new blood to rise to the top. Especially for those with allies on the Elector Council."

Markus sucked in a deep breath.

Ral let him ponder that idea for a moment. "Is everything in place?"

"Sure. The plan is simple. I'll get there a candlemark after sundown. The signal is—"

"How many men are you bringing?"

Markus glanced over, a flicker of annoyance passing across his pale blue eyes. "I got a few boys on board, just like you told me. A couple of them owe me money, and another guy is bucking for a promotion so he can move out of his mother's house. They'll do what I say without question."

"And afterward?"

"They'll keep their mouths shut."

"They'd better. Our patron doesn't forgive mistakes. If one of these men talks—"

"I know what I'm doing."

Ral leaned into Markus, hooking his right arm through the man's elbow. His left hand pressed into the prefect's side, the needle-sharp point of the stiletto held in his palm pricking through both surcoat and mail to touch the flesh beneath. Markus huffed and strained to remain still.

Ral pitched his voice to a low whisper. "Listen to me. You don't have to worry about the boss. If you mess this up, I'll peel your worthless hide from your back myself. Do you understand me?"

Markus nodded. With a hiss, Ral released him. The stiletto vanished into his sleeve. Markus clutched his side and stared at the floor with his lips compressed into a tight line. The prefect wasn't used to being man-handled, but he had to understand and fast. Both their lives hung in the balance if he messed up.

"Get more men," Ral said.

The prefect rolled his shoulders. "I'll need more money for that. God's soldiers don't come cheap."

Ral wanted to laugh, but he didn't let it touch his features. He reached under his cassock. Markus stiffened, one hand dropping to the hilt of his sword, but he relaxed as Ral passed him a heavy pouch.

Ral stood up and rested his hand on the prefect's beefy shoulder, the very picture of a pastor counseling one of his flock.

"Remember, Markus. No mistakes. No loose ends."

"Don't worry. We'll arrive just a moment too late to save them."

"And their killer?"

An evil grin dimmed the prefect's chiseled features. "Sadly, he'll be killed trying to elude capture."

"Perfect."

A moment later, Ral was out the side door and down the alley, heading toward home. He had his own preparations to finalize. A horse was waiting for him at the west gate, reserved by the offices of the Elector Council, with remounts at every roadhouse and garrison station between here and his target. Tomorrow night, the culmination of his dearest ambition would begin. He would rise higher than his departed father had ever dreamed. Soon people would call him the most feared man in the city, and in the process he would eliminate his only true rival to that title.

Tomorrow night Caim, Low Town's favorite son, would die.

CHAPTER FOUR

Kit showed up while Caim stalked down a narrow lane between two dark rows of houses. One moment he was strolling by himself, eyes darting back and forth in search of hidden threats, and the next she was walking beside him. Or rather, she levitated beside him; her dainty feet never touched the cobbles.

"Welcome back, Kit. Off gallivanting again?"

"I *don't* gallivant, darling. I might flit about sometimes, or stop to watch a caterpillar weave its cocoon. Did you know they could do that? It's amazing! But I never, ever gallivant. As it happens, I was looking after *your* interests."

Kit flipped over so she was hovering upside down in front of him. In defiance of gravity, her long silver hair stayed curled around her slim shoulders. Her violet eyes twinkled mischievously as she regarded him, and it was all he could do not to chuckle.

Those eyes were his first memory, peeking over the side of his cradle when he was a babe. She claimed to have been searching for a little brother and stopped when she found him, but with Kit the truth was often difficult to ascertain. Whether real or imaginary, she was without a doubt the most interesting person he'd ever met. She'd been everywhere, it seemed, and seen everything there was to see. She could fly so high into the sky he lost sight of her, or dive into the earth and return with tales of the secret lives of voles and worms. After he'd lost his parents, Kit had become his family. She was all he had left. If there were times, such as during his turbulent adolescence, when he tried to drive everyone else away, Kit always did as she chose. No one could sway her once her mind was made up. In that they were much alike, to his constant chagrin.

"Forgive me." He turned onto one of Low Town's many crooked, unnamed streets. "What interests are those, dear lady?"

A pair of drunken merchant marines passed him in the gathering dusk. If they thought him odd for talking to himself, they said nothing, but murmured behind his back once they were past. Caim chewed on the inside of his cheek and ignored the itch in his palms.

"Hubert's on his way to the Vine," Kit announced.

He touched the heavy lump of the purse inside his shirt. "Good. That's where I'm headed now."

"And he's not alone."

"Is that right?"

"He's got a whole gang of roughnecks with him. Most of them look like vagrants, but a couple might be able to handle themselves. One is the disinherited son of a former pimp."

Caim smiled to himself. Ever since he had taken up his current lifestyle, Kit had endeavored to be useful to him. He had to admit she was an exemplary judge of people's capabilities. She could look at someone and spy out what they hid from others. That ability had saved his ass too many times to count. The trouble was that Kit couldn't be relied upon to always be where he needed her. She had a disturbing penchant for leaving him for days at a time and, even more unnerving, showing up with knowledge of things she shouldn't know, things no one could know.

"Should I be worried?"

Kit shrugged, turning around to stand right side up again. "He seems in a good mood. I'd say he was scheming something, but not against you."

"Then I have nothing to worry about."

The faded sign of the Blue Vine appeared around the next corner. One of the oldest wineshops in Othir, it had been owned by innumerable men and women over the centuries, passed down through families and sold off dozens of times. The current owner was Mistress Clarice Henninger, but everyone called her Mother.

She spotted Caim as soon as he pushed through the rickety door. "Caim!"

He held open his arms as she waddled across the common room to wrap him in a fierce embrace. A thick-waisted woman on the hoary side of fifty, she was every bit as saucy as a wench half her size and a third her age. The money purse tucked in his shirt ground against her massive breasts.

"Happy to see me, sweetling?"

Kit giggled while Caim disentangled himself as politely as he could manage. The Vine's taproom was dim, its windows tightly shuttered. The only light came from small oil lamps suspended from the ceiling and two stone-lined hearths. Thick shadows clung to the brick-and-niter walls. It was crowded this night. Most of the Vine's patrons were teamsters and porters, large men who made their living by the sweat of their brows and the strength of their backs. A few nodded his way. He returned the gestures with a slight dip of his chin.

"Want your usual table?" she asked.

Mother led him to a dim corner, swaying her wide hips with every step. Caim took off his cloak and slid around the table to sit with his back to the walls. From here he could see the front entrance as well as the door to the back room where the wine casks were stored.

"A cup of Golden Swan?"

Caim started to nod, but stopped himself. "No, I'll have the Asper tonight. In a clean cup, please."

She laughed, grasping her breasts with both hands. "Of course, sweetling. All Mother's cups are clean!"

A pair of oldsters in shabby coats cackled over their stones game as she waddled back to the bar to fetch his order. Kit perched on the table and regarded Caim. Her large eyes glowed like purple jewels in the dim lighting.

"So you took another job?"

He flipped a penny to the wench who delivered his wine. She flashed him a welcoming smile, but he returned only a curt nod and leaned back into the shadows.

As the girl flounced off, he said, "You were eavesdropping?"

Kit twirled a wisp of silver hair in her fingers. "Mathias talks so loud I could hear him half the world away. I thought you were going to take a break."

Caim took a sip and sighed as the cool wine trickled down his throat. "I was, but sometimes people need killing. That's what I do."

"It didn't sound like you were too eager to take it."

"Well, I couldn't stand to see Mathias beg."

"You never say no to him."

"He's a friend."

Kit reclined on an elbow, staring up at him. "A friend wouldn't put you in danger for a few pieces of gilt."

Before he could think of an answer, the door opened and a young man entered. The newcomer's colorless eyes swept around the room as the door closed behind him. He was alone.

"Hubert's here," Caim said. "Why don't you go keep an eye on his roughnecks?"

Kit hopped off the table with a spin. "It doesn't sound like you need my help. Maybe I'll go watch fireflies instead."

"As you like."

As Kit vanished through a wall, Caim focused on the youth crossing the wineshop. Hubert Claudius Vassili looked every inch the foppish noble's son he was, from the floppy, wide-brimmed hat cocked roguishly on his head, complete with a ridiculous sky blue feather, to his fine cavalry boots, polished to a high shine. A slender rapier hung on his left hip, more of a showpiece than a real weapon.

Hubert stopped in front of Caim's table with a hand on his sharp, smooth-shaven chin as if considering where to sit, and said, "The blue falcon hunts at midnight."

Caim kicked out a chair. "Sit down before you draw more attention to us than you already have."

Hubert dropped his hat on the table and called for a cup of the house best before he settled into the seat. "Ah, Caim. It's good to see you again, but you don't have to worry. Every man in here is an ardent supporter of the Azure Hawks. They've pledged not to give up the fight until the theocrats are dragged down from their gilded thrones."

Caim glanced around the taproom. "Gathering quite the little army, aren't you? I thought I saw a few tinmen shaking in their armor tonight."

Hubert spread his hands as if delivering a benediction. "The people clamor for freedom, Caim. I am but a humble servant of the public welfare."

Caim tossed the purse onto the table. "And regular infusions of my money don't hurt either, do they?"

Hubert covered the purse with his hat and pulled it into his lap. "Not at all. The Hawks are very grateful for your generosity. It's donors such as yourself that fuel the engines of our progress."

Caim couldn't resist. "You've had progress?"

Hubert didn't notice the jibe. "Naturally. Our forces are marshalling. Plans are being laid. One day we will free the people from the Council's tyranny. One day very soon!"

He glanced around as if expecting a chorus to support his claim. A few tired drinkers nodded in his direction, but most simply stared into the depths of their cups.

"Well." Hubert turned back to Caim. "It will happen. And we'll have you to thank."

"So why did you feel the need to bring a gang of strong-arms to our meeting?"

"How—?" Hubert gave him a weak smile. "I should have known. They are merely waiting outside for my protection. The streets are dangerous these days. I would never dream of insulting a man of your talents."

"Good. I wouldn't want any misunderstandings, Hubert. I respect what you do, misguided though it may be at times. However, this will be my last donation for a time."

"But we need your support now more than ever. Things are heating up. We're staging demonstrations nearly every day."

"I understand, but I've got my own problems."

"But—"

"Look, Hubert. I'm taking some time away from the contract game."

"How long?"

"I'm not sure. A couple months, maybe more."

Hubert leaned across the table. "Then come join us. We could use a man like you."

Caim pushed his empty cup away. "No offense, but I'm not interested. Your little enterprise has been interesting, and anything that keeps the bigwigs off balance is good for business, but you don't need my help to burn down storefronts and break into warehouses. You've got plenty of supporters now, right?"

"Sure, I can assemble disgruntled clerks and teamsters by the hundredhead, but I need fighters, Caim. Sooner or later we're going to have to face the Reds head-on. We'll need you."

Caim sat back deeper in the shadows. He knew what Hubert wanted: another pawn to push around in his game of politics. But Caim wasn't interested. He had his own battles to fight. Giving to the Hawks had seemed like a good idea, a way of giving back some of the blood money he earned to help a worthy cause. Now he could see it had been a mistake.

"No, Hubert. I agree things in Othir are getting worse, but I'm not a revolutionary. I work alone."

Hubert put his hat back on as he stood up. "The offer's always open if you change your mind."

"I won't."

Hubert started to say something when Kit phased through his body. He didn't notice, of course, but the look on Caim's face must have been unexpected, because he stopped talking in midsyllable.

"Caim!" Kit blurted. "You've got comp—"

The front door crashed open. Conversations stopped as a crowd of City Watchmen filed into the common room. Without preamble they pulled patrons out of their chairs and pushed them against the walls. A stout man with an oily beard made a break for it. He got to the threshold of the front door before a soldier cracked open the back of his head with a baton. Everyone jumped to their feet. Even the old codgers stood up and shook their bony fists, but by then the watchmen were circulating through the room, seizing anyone who made a commotion.

"Your men couldn't bother to give us a warning?" Caim hissed.

"Some of them are new." Hubert inched away from the table. "And others may have outstanding warrants on their heads."

"Wonderful."

Caim surveyed the room, measuring distances in his head. "Go for the back room. There's a delivery entrance that leads into the alley."

"Good idea."

Hubert headed in that direction, but not fast enough. Most of the soldiers were patting down patrons, but a pair and their commander moved to intercept Hubert. Their mail armor rattled as the tinmen ran to catch the young noble.

Caim rose from his seat and reached behind his back. If he drew his knives, men would die. That would draw unneeded attention to himself and the Vine, but he didn't want to see Hubert apprehended either. True, he was a rabble-rouser and a hypocritical demagogue, but his heart was in the right place. Most of the time.

Caim let his hands fall to his sides and closed his eyes.

He only meant to release a tiny bit of his powers, just enough to conceal Hubert's escape behind a curtain of darkness, but the taproom's shadows swarmed around him like moths to a flame. The Vine was drenched in an impenetrable gloom so thick Caim couldn't see more than a few feet in front of him, which was fine by him, but there was more. As he slid along the wall, a cool sensation prickled at the nape of his neck.

The hairs on his arms stood on end and his mouth went bone dry as *something* entered the taproom. He couldn't see it. Whatever it was, it blended perfectly into the darkness. But he felt it moving through the room like a monstrous beast.

Shouts and curses filled the wineshop. Glassware shattered. Shutters banged open as someone scrambled out a window, or was tossed out. Throaty mews whimpered from the direction of the bar.

Caim sidled over to the back door and found it ajar. With one hand on the hilt of a knife, he ducked out, and left the taproom cloaked in darkness like a covered grave.

CHAPTER FIVE

Caim leaned into the Vine's dingy whitewashed siding as the sick-ness washed over him. Black lines wriggled before his vision. His stomach tried to squirm up into his throat, but he fought it back with firm determination.

Twilight's veil was drawing over the city. Angry shouts resounded from inside the wineshop. What had happened inside? His talent had never reacted like that before. It usually took every ounce of concentration he could muster to conjure a few flimsy shadows, but this time they had flocked to him like flies to a corpse, and whatever else had emerged from the dark . . .

He took a deep breath.

Stars filled the darkening sky. No light shone from the new moon, hidden as it crossed the heavens. A Shadow's moon, a night when the shades from the Other Side could cross over to walk in the mortal world. He shivered. The sweat under his shirt had turned cool. Gods-damned legends. Stories to spook little children. *Then why are you shaking?*

Caim pushed off from the wall and started walking. The alley was empty. Kit, as usual, was nowhere to be found. Neither was Hubert, which was a good thing. *Maybe he's learning.*

Kit appeared over his head. Her violet eyes shone in the twilight gloom. "Fun night, huh?"

"Sure. A little more fun like that and I could be enjoying the com-forts of a pinewood box."

Caim glanced over his shoulder. An uneasy sensation had settled in the pit of his stomach, the feeling he was being watched. He tried to pass it off as his imagination, but it refused to leave. There was something in the air tonight. The city, never a safe haven for fools, seethed with barely restrained frustrations. Like a boiling kettle, the steam needed to vent before it exploded.

"Oh, Caim. I'd never let that happen to you."

"I'm serious. Something happened in there."

"Yeah. You finally let loose. Felt good, didn't it?"

He shook his head. It had been terrifying to feel that much power flowing through him, out of his control. "That's never happened before, Kit. Why this time?"

Her dainty shoulders lifted in a shrug. "How should I know?"

"You're supposed to know about this kind of stuff, but you never tell me anything useful."

"Well then, since I'm not useful . . ." With a mighty huff, she disappeared in a shower of silver and green sparkles.

Caim sighed and continued on his trek.

Three streets later, he turned a corner and stopped before a monolithic structure. The dark mass of the city workhouse eclipsed the skyline like a colossal black glacier. The building had been closed years ago, but the specter of its presence hung over Low Town like a bad dream. Among the Church's first creations in the chaotic years following its rise to power, the workhouse had been heralded as an opportunity for the unlawful to repay their crimes against society. Thousands of convicts had entered its iron doors. Most of them died before their sentences were complete, killed by either sadistic guards or the miserable conditions. A mournful wail rose from behind the weather-stripped walls. It was the wind, no doubt, blowing through a broken window, but it was unnerving nonetheless.

Caim picked up his pace to put the unpleasant edifice behind him. He wished now he'd been smart enough to turn down Mathias's offer. With the city in such a state of turmoil, the last thing he wanted was to risk his neck doing Ral's secondhand work. This job had better be the easiest he'd ever done or someone was going to regret it. Hell, he regretted it already.

A pair of painted slatterns called out to Caim with promises of earthly delight from the mouth of a cramped alley and flicked their chins at him as he walked past. The street branched ahead of him, both lanes crowded with street-level shops and sprawling tenement houses above. Murmurs of life filtered through their faded, whitewashed walls, sounds of laughter and tears, talking voices and wordless moans. The city was a living creature, hungry and untamed beneath its thin veneer of civilization.

In the kaleidoscopic days and weeks after the attack on his family's home, he and Kit had trekked across the countryside like hunted animals, moving at night, holing up during the daylight hours under whatever cover they could find. He ate whatever came his way—wild berries and nuts, the few animals he was able to catch or knock down with well-aimed stones, stolen goods from the occasional farmstead. Chicken coops were his favorite. He became adept at pilfering eggs without disturbing the sleeping hens.

The towering gray walls of Liovard, the first real city they encountered on their flight south, amazed him. They stretched up to the sky several times the height of a grown man. Beyond those mighty stone ramparts protruded the peaks and turrets of more buildings than he had ever seen in one place. His father's estate, including the fields and bordering woods, would have been lost inside the walls, and Liovard, as he would learn later, was petite compared to the great cities of the south: Mecantia, Navarre, and Othir were all larger and more diverse. Yet, walking through the iron-shod gates was like passing into another world, a realm of noise and commotion where everyone hustled on vital business. *Business* was a new word he'd learned in Liovard. Just the sound of it quickened his pulse. That's what he wanted to be reckoned: a man of business.

It didn't take him long to learn about the messy underside of city life. For a young boy with no family and no prospects, the city was a frightening place. He slept in alleyways and inside piles of garbage. A stack of discarded shipping crates provided shelter for almost a month until the street cleaners took them away. He moved from place to place, always hungry, always searching for his next meal. If he thought he was safe from harm amid the bustle of the city, he learned better the first time he encountered a street gang. He'd been rooting through a barrel of half-rotten apples when cutting laughter erupted behind him. A dozen older boys surrounded him. As a lesson for trespassing on their territory, they beat him bloody. After that, he learned to avoid them. He snuck like a rat through the slums with Kit, his only companion.

But if the street toughs were dangerous, the tinmen were worse. The bully boys only wanted your food and whatever you had hidden in your pocket, and maybe to rough you up a bit. Yet when he was dragged into a backstreet by two looming guardsmen after stealing a pomegranate from a vendor's stall, he knew with sinking certainty they wanted more than to thrash him. While Kit swatted ineffectually at their heads, one held him fast while the other ripped open the laces of his breeches. He struggled, but they cuffed him hard across the face, knocking him to the ground. A white-hot ember of rage burned in the pit of Caim's chest as he remembered that day, but also a thread of euphoria, for no sooner had the guards begun pawing at him with their big, clumsy hands than something erupted inside him. At first, he thought he was going to be sick as the feeling bubbled in his belly. Then, the colors of the waning day faded before his eyes. As he was turned onto his stomach, a new spectrum of shades emerged from the bleak drabness of the alley, blacks and grays of marvelous, vivid tones. While his tears mingled with the dust beneath his face, something extraordinary happened.

A shadow moved.

He had seen shadows move before, when a cloud passed in front of the sun or the object casting the shadow shifted, but this shadow stretched out from under a heap of broken boards like a black tentacle of tar. Strangely, he wasn't afraid as it oozed toward him, and the guardsmen were too distracted to notice. One held him down by the shoulders while the other tugged down his pants. Caim didn't recoil; he wanted to know what it was, this crawling, amorphous darkness. When it touched his hand, he yelped as a sensation of burning cold slid over his skin, like dipping his hand into a bucket of ice water. More shadows crawled into the light, swarming over the alleyway until Caim couldn't see the ground under his nose. The guardsman holding him down shouted and let up enough for Caim to wriggle. He kicked and scratched. When a hand seized his face, he bit down hard until warm, salty blood filled his mouth. A strangled scream pierced the gloom, and then he was free.

He didn't hesitate, but hitched his breeches around his waist and ran. Fear thundered in his ears with every stride.

Caim let the memory fade away as he turned his footsteps toward High Town. Two things were clear to him. First, he couldn't risk using his powers until he figured out what had happened at the Vine. He couldn't risk losing control. And second, he would avoid contact with the

Azure Hawks for the time being. Those decisions made him feel a little better. Then he remembered that he'd left his cloak back in the taproom.

Caim hunched his shoulders against the night's chill and hurried through the umbrageous byways of the city. Yet the haunting images of his past followed him down every street.

CHAPTER SIX

Caim awoke to the faint glow of dawn. Long shadows crept across the floor of his bedroom. Two plum pits and a crust of rye bread lay on the nightstand.

Remnants of a dream lingered in his head. The same old dream. The burning house. The corpse-strewn yard. The same questions without answers.

Caim blew out a long sigh and got up. After his ablutions, he went to the cabinet and pulled out his work clothes.

Kit appeared behind him as he climbed into his breeches. "I like the view. Ready yet?"

"Almost."

Caim tucked a black hood and a pair of soot-blackened gloves into his belt. He didn't anticipate any difficulties tonight. He had studied the workup supplied by Mathias. An old man with no guards; a simple enter-and-kill and he'd be gone before the clock on Septon Chapel struck midnight. He strapped on his knives and settled a medium-length cloak, the color of old dishwater, over his shoulders. He'd let his whiskers grow; the stubble would make his face more difficult to distinguish in the dark.

He turned around to see Kit, levitating above his bed. She wore a short emerald dress. Sparkles danced across her chest.

"I confess," she said. "I still don't understand why you're going along with this. Even after throwing most of your money away, you've got enough to last for weeks, maybe months the way you live." Her eyebrows rose in wry disapproval as she looked around the apartment.

He didn't feel like a debate. His mind was already working the job, combing through the details for anything he might have missed, checking every angle for flaws.

"Mathias was in a bad spot. I took the job as a favor. What else is there to say?"

"And when has that overstuffed bladder ever done you any favors? He treats you like a half-trained wolfhound. He snaps his fingers and you jump to do his bidding."

Caim grabbed the rest of his gear and headed for the door. "You know better than that."

Kit flipped her hair as she followed after him. "All right, I don't want you to go out tonight. There's a strange vibe in the city."

Caim paused at the door. He had felt something when he first woke up—a raw, indeterminate feeling of dread. He hadn't dwelt on it, chalking it up to anxiety about tonight's work, but now it returned, stoked by Kit's words.

"What kind of vibe?"

"I don't know. It's just a bad feeling, okay? It doesn't matter. Let's just go. I'm tired of watching you fidget."

"I wasn't—" He took a deep breath. "Fine, I'm ready."

"Good. See you outside." She sank through the floor.

Sometimes I wish she was real. Caim undid the locks securing his door. *So I could wring her pretty little neck.*

He peered out. The hallway was empty. He pulled the hood of the cloak over his head as he slipped down the corridor.

Kit joined him on the city's mist-shrouded streets. She whistled an eerie tune while she skipped beside him. It sounded like a funeral march. He considered asking her to shut up, but knew it would only encourage her to whistle louder. At least it was a good night for working. A blanket of clouds occluded the stars. The moon peeked out every few minutes, only to be hidden again behind the shroud of dark.

He took a roundabout way to the target as a matter of habit. There were few pedestrians about. As winter approached and the days grew shorter, people tended to make their way home earlier, but Caim enjoyed the brisk weather. People closed their minds to the outdoors when the temperature dropped; sentries spent more time seeking warmth than manning their posts.

He paused at the Processional. The broad avenue continued downtown to the Forum. The minarets of prayer towers jutted above the stately roofs of government buildings, all silent at this hour. Beyond them and taller still rose the unfinished towers of the new cathedral. Fires burned at the zenith of every overlook, proclaiming the supremacy of the True Church for all to see.

Caim crouched behind the weathered statue of a dead civic hero festooned with pigeon droppings as a patrol of night watchmen marched along the thoroughfare. Their spear butts struck the ancient cobbles like the hooves of a forty-legged beast. When they passed from sight, he darted across, just another gray shadow in the twilight. A six-foot wall ran along the other side of the street, intended to keep out the riffraff, but it was broken by so many gates and posterns, most of them unguarded, as to make for no barrier at all. Once on the other side, he was inside High Town.

Caim kept to the smaller avenues and avoided the wider boulevards that crisscrossed the burg like the warp and weft of a weaver's loom. Glass lamps lit the tree-lined streets. Mansions of stone and timber stood silent behind tall gates. Caim passed a party of nobles attended by linkmen and bodyguards at an intersection, but they paid him no mind. With his stooped shoulders and quick steps, he was just another servant attending to his master's business.

"Where are we going, anyways?" Kit stopped to tickle the whiskers of a stray tomcat. The animal followed her, which meant it trailed behind Caim like a lost child. He resisted the urge to boot it over a fence.

"Esquiline Hill." He indulged her, hoping some conversation might make her forget about the stupid cat.

Instead, she blew in its tufted ears, which made the animal yowl like a wounded groundhog.

"You're coming up in the world, Caim. I hope you were smart enough to demand a bushel of money. Hey! Maybe we could stay in the house for a couple days after the job. It would be nice to hang out someplace livable instead of that shack you call a home."

"I'm not sticking around afterward," he replied.

"Spoken like a true man, gone as soon as the deed is done. Why not stay? I doubt the owner will protest after you cut his throat. If you're squeamish, we could just avoid the room with the body. We'd have plenty of space—"

"You're a nut. You know that?"

"It was just a suggestion."

As they started up the long incline of Esquiline Hill, the homes became larger, each more opulent than the one before. Their walls glistened in ivory and salmon marble, unstained by the city's ordure. Smooth pavestones replaced the street's cruddy brick.

Caim went over the job in his head. Two days wasn't much time, but he had put it to good use. He had located the target's home, a three-story Graccian-style manse at the apex of Founders Circle, and spent most of the first night casing the site. The house had a gloomy look. Tall windows gaped in the dark stone façade like empty eye sockets. A high wall encircled the property. The gate was a gaudy monstrosity of wrought iron.

"This is nice." Kit floated up to peek over the wall. "A lot nicer than that old barn you live in."

"Just get inside and take a look around, will you?"

With a smirk in his direction, she walked through the stone. Caim ducked into a spacious alley between the wall and the next property, a similarly impressive mansion. Around back he found a servants' entrance, a simple wooden gate secured from the inside. In less than a heartbeat, Caim was over it and crouched on the other side. He listened for signs of alarm, but the yard was silent. True to the report, there were no sentries and no dogs, for which he was grateful. Even though his information explicitly stated the target owned no animals, Caim had brought a pouch of pepper-laced meat just in case. No lights showed in any of the windows.

Caim darted across the yard. The outer face of the house was stone brick. His information suggested forcing the rear door and stealing up the inside of the house. Detailed plans of the building were included in the packet, with the stairs and entry points clearly marked. The target's chambers were situated in the northeast corner of the top floor. The only servant, a middle-aged butler, bunked on the second floor. While it was a sound plan, Caim had discarded it at once. Forcing doors was a noisy affair, which meant an added chance of attracting attention. Plus, he didn't like anyone telling him his business.

As he crouched in the lee of the house, he reached into his satchel for a bundle of thin rope. He portioned out a loop and tied a slider knot. A grappling hook wouldn't bite on the slate shingles and would make an awful clatter, but like most large homes the roof of this manse sported several chimneys. Caim hurled the lariat up and over the lip of the roof. On the third throw it caught on something. Caim tugged several times and the line held. He had a solid anchor. After one last glance about the yard, he went up the line hand over hand.

He found Kit at the top, lounging on the canted tiles.

"Are you going to take all night?" she asked.

Caim gathered up the rope behind him. He left it coiled around the chimney stack it had snagged on. "I thought you wanted to stay a bit."

She sat up. "Can we? It's really beautiful inside! You have to see this crys—"

"Any guards?"

Kit huffed and laid back on the rooftop. Her hair spread out beneath her head like a silver pool. "No."

"Is the servant asleep?"

"I suppose."

"You didn't check?"

"Of course I did. All the lights are out and no one is moving."

"Good."

Caim ignored Kit's glare and crossed the tiles. At the northeast corner, he lowered himself onto his belly and leaned over the edge. The window he wanted was directly below his perch. He swung his legs over the side, lined it up as best he could, and let go.

He landed on the pitched gable protecting the window with barely a sound. From there it was an easy shimmy down to the casement. Caim stepped out onto the narrow stone shelf projecting from the windowsill with care. With some old houses, the masonry was weak and prone to collapse. But it held.

The shutters were closed and secured from the inside. Caim took a thin steel bar from his belt and slid the hooked end between the wooden doors. After a moment of searching, he snagged the latch and lifted it out of the catch. The hinges swung open without protest. The window was closed, but not locked. Caim pushed the misted panes open far enough to slip inside.

He paused as his soles touched down on the floor of a hallway, one hand under his cloak to grip the hilt of a knife. This was the most precarious moment. Had his entrance been heard? He listened for sounds of movement, for the sharp intake before a cry was given. Even an old man could raise a hue, and in this neighborhood the tinmen would come running. Fortune favored him tonight. All was quiet.

The hallway ran the width of the top floor and joined with a staircase winding down to the levels below. The target's room was the third door on the right. Caim crept across the hardwood floor and paused at the first door to listen. According to the packet, the target's daughter was a child of five. She should be sound asleep at this hour, but children could be unpredictable. The crack under the door was dark and no sounds issued through the wooden panels, but Caim stood at the door for several moments. He didn't like the idea of harming innocents, especially children. Yet by his actions tonight he would be making an orphan of this girl.

I'm serving the greater good. The target was a vicious man who had earned death a hundred times over. The daughter would be better off without him. *Sure. That worked out well for Duke Reinard's son, right?* Caim put the thoughts out of his head as he continued to the third door, the master suite.

He drew his right-hand knife, turned the knob, and eased the door open. By the orange glow that emanated from the stone hearth, he could make out the details of the long room, which was larger than his entire apartment. A four-poster bed against the far wall dominated the floor space, but there was room enough for a large desk and chair, a sideboard, and rosewood cabinets. The bed was empty, its blankets flat against the tall mattress.

Caim turned his head very slowly until he located his target, slouched in a chair beside an antique desk. Wisps of white hair rose above the seat back.

Caim glided across the bedchamber floor and yanked the head upright by the hairs with his free hand. The *suete* knife came up. Its point hovered as Caim stared down at his victim.

He could not believe his eyes.

"Can we go now? Please?"

Kit sat on the desk and regarded the old man's body. She'd appeared moments after Caim's discovery. Upon hearing that it hadn't been him who put the victim's lights out for good, she had lost her zest for sticking around, but he wasn't ready to go, not until he made sense of this.

Was another contractor working the same job? This was a good score and there were plenty of knives looking for work. Throat-slitting had been a time-honored tradition in Othir since the days of the emperors, long before Caim had set foot within the city limits. The viciousness of Nimean politics was legendary throughout the world, and it hadn't lost any of its ferocity with the rise of the Church. But Mathias usually made sure he had exclusive rights before farming out an assignment. In fact, he was obsessive about such things. It was just good business.

Caim leaned against the victim's desk. Curled sheets of parchment were stacked on the cherry surface, held down by brass equestrian paperweights. The inside of a glass tumbler was smeared with a glazy film. He smelled it. Ground fennel root, a tonic for headaches. A ceramic frame rested on the shelf above the desktop with the portrait of a young girl with striking green eyes. She sat in an elegant pose, black tresses curled around her heart-shaped face, gloved hands folded upon her lap.

Caim looked back at the old man. He didn't look much like a fabled general. He more resembled a scholar with his long, somber features and aquiline nose. The loose folds of his nightgown showed where his chest had been hacked open. Hacked was the operative word. The cuts looked like they had been made with a meat cleaver.

He bent down closer. Some blood was pooled in the old man's lap, but not nearly enough for such a traumatic injury. And the carpet beneath the seat was dry except for a few coin-sized dots of blood. The victim's eyes were open wide, the muscles in his face tensed. Both hands hung straight down at his sides. No signs of rope burns, but rings glittered on both hands, one gold band set with a large beryl. Caim frowned. A Gutter-bred thug wouldn't have missed those pieces, which would bring a good price at any fence in the city. There were no other signs of distress, so either the old man had been taken unawares, or he had let his killer do the bloody work without a struggle.

Or he had been dead before he was cut open.

Caim searched for other means of death. A quick inspection ruled out strangulation, poison, and blunt force. He knew of a few poisons that left their victims paralyzed, but they were expensive and difficult to procure. In any case, why use poison when you intended to carve up your victim afterward? The only reason was to send a message. But to whom?

"Caim?" Kit said.

He walked around to peer over the victim's shoulder. The angle was poor. The killer must have worked from the front, or he had an accomplice. Possible scenarios played through Caim's head as he came back around to the front. He squatted beside the corpse and reached out with a gloved finger. The flesh around the wound was discolored, turned almost tar black, and the hole was deeper than he first thought. The victim's breastbone had been shattered by the impact. Forget about a meat cleaver. The killer must have used something heavier. Like what? An axe? It seemed to Caim as if he had seen something like this before, but he couldn't remember where. He slid his fingers deeper into the wound, ignoring Kit's *ewww* of disgust, and made another discovery.

The old man's heart was gone.

Kit twirled a piece of silver hair in her fingers. "Okay. The job is done. Let's just get out of here before someone finds us with this old relic."

"No one's going to—"

The door opened. Caim had a knife out before he was fully turned. He checked his movement as a girl entered. No child, but a lady in the first bloom of womanhood. Her delicate frame was wrapped in a high-necked nightgown; its diaphanous panels glowed bright in the wan light of the bedchamber. Wavy midnight hair curled about her ivory shoulders to frame aristocratic features. Her eyes, twin gimlets of emerald, pierced the darkness like jewels of green fire.

"Father, I want you to reconsider—" She froze as she saw Caim.

Then, her gaze fell to the old man in the chair. She lifted a hand to her abdomen as she swallowed a sob and opened her lips.

Caim leapt.

CHAPTER SEVEN

Josey stared up at the sheer white canopy draped over her bed and tried to get comfortable on the feather-down mattress, but sleep was the farthest thing from her mind. Her stomach twisted in knots. Despite cudgeling her brain for the past two days, she hadn't found the solution to her dilemma. At supper Father had told her that her ship was set to depart tomorrow morning with the rising tide. Tomorrow!

After Father had retired, she had called for the carriage and went to vespers—not to the basilica that, despite its gold-plated finery, she found cold and forbidding, but to her childhood parish off the Forum. Though small and unassuming with plain plaster walls and a simple altarpiece, the priory at St. Azari's exuded a comforting atmosphere, like having Father's arms around her as a child. Safe. Protected. However, not even the familiar hymns and solemn liturgy had been able to quell the angst raging inside her. Unable to find solace in prayer, she'd returned home as despondent as before.

Before bed she had written a letter to Anastasia, an earnest apology splashed with genuine tears. In it she explained how sorry she was to miss her dearest friend's wedding. With every word her heart moved farther away from her father's love, and by the end she could almost say she hated him. Despite her agony, Josey realized he was doing what he thought was right. As a dutiful daughter she ought to respect that. Instead, it made her want to fight him all the harder. She was not a child any longer. She could decide things for herself.

Finally, she could take the tumult inside her head no longer and got out of bed. She didn't pause to light a taper for fear she would lose her ire in the delay, but marched straight from her room in the dark. She hesitated for a moment in the hallway as she considered what to say. He had defeated all of her logical arguments for staying. How else could she sway him? For a moment the specter of apprehension almost overcame her. She could wait until morning, appeal to him when he was rested and most inclined to indulge her. *No, I must do this now.*

She tiptoed to his bedchamber. The door was partway open, and a faint light shined from within. He was awake, likely reading as was his habit at night. With a deep breath, Josey grasped the knob and pushed open the door. She began her argument right away, before her willpower could falter.

"Father, I want you to reconsider—"

The words died on her lips as the ghastly scene unraveled before her. The dull glow of the fireplace showed Father sitting at his worktable, his head thrown back. A deep, red wound gaped in his breast like an obscene second mouth. Over Father hovered a man clad in muted gray and black from head to toe. A gush of hot bile filled Josey's throat. She put a hand to her middle as her stomach threatened to void the remains of her supper. Terrified, she began to scream.

The man in black leapt.

She had never seen anyone move so swiftly. His movements were sure and quick, almost graceful. Before Josey could get the scream out of her chest, he had seized her with one arm and clapped a gloved hand over her mouth, bruising her lips.

Josey stood rigid with terror, the taste of leather in her mouth. The killer's hands were strong, too strong for her to break their hold, but when he dragged her toward the bed, a will to resist bubbled up inside her. She shook and flailed, kicked with her feet. The man in black lifted her like she was a child and thrust her down on the firm mattress. He let go for an instant and she clawed to get away, but a heavy weight pushed her flat onto her stomach. The sound of ripping cloth presaged her hands being yanked behind her back and bound in strips of torn blanket, and the same for her ankles. A wad of cloth was forced between her teeth and tied behind her head. She lay on the bed, chest heaving, straining to hear a sign, a clue of what the killer intended next. Suddenly, the weight was gone from her back. She waited for something dire to happen.

"Now we can go," the killer said.

Josey twisted her head around. Was he talking to her? She wasn't about to go anywhere with him! Yet the room was empty except for the two of them and her poor, departed father. The horrified expression on Father's face bludgeoned her from across the room. Every time she tried to comprehend what he had suffered, she shivered with fury.

A loud crash from downstairs shook Josey from her misery. Heavy boots pounded on the stairs. Someone was coming! Fenrik must have awakened and called for help. Elation surged through her. *Now you'll face justice!*

The assassin didn't wait to be caught. He darted to the window and climbed out. Josey struggled against her bonds. If she could get free, she could tell her rescuers which way the killer had gone. However, the bindings refused to cooperate. Every wriggle she made only seemed to twist them tighter.

The bedchamber door slammed open and four men in the uniforms of the Sacred Brotherhood burst into the room. They fanned out with naked blades in their hands and lanterns raised high to pierce the shadows. Josey shouted as best she could through the gag, but the soldiers paid her no mind as they searched the chamber. She tried to nod toward the window and could have sighed with relief as one guardsman went to the aperture, but he was satisfied after a cursory look and turned back to face the murder scene. She kicked and screamed.

One man came over to peer down at her. He held his light up to her face. "What's she doing here?"

A young guardsman with a chubby face said, "Maybe she heard a noise and came to check it out."

"She ain't supposed to be breathing anymore," the first said. "This is all screwed up."

"What's screwed up?" a voice asked from the doorway.

Josey was perplexed by this bizarre behavior, but calmed as Markus entered the room. He looked so gallant in his prefect's uniform that for an instant she felt the tiniest bit jealous he was betrothed to Anastasia, but the feeling passed as she focused on the here and now. She grunted through the gag and shook her bound hands.

The first man pointed at her with the point of his sword. "He didn't kill her. He just left her trussed up."

"So I see." Markus came over to the bed. "Where's the assassin?"

"He wasn't here," the guardsman with the lantern replied.

Markus smacked his hands together. "Damn! Epps and Lauk, go search the yard. Whistle if you see anything."

As the two soldiers dashed out, the lantern-holder said to Markus, "We could make this one look the same as the other."

Markus nodded to the first man. "Take care of it, but make it fast."

Josey tried to wriggle free once more, but the soldier straddled her hips and yanked back hard on her hair. She screamed as a blade's edge pressed against her exposed neck.

"No!"

Josey shook with relief as the blade stopped. A large tear ran down the length of her nose.

"Not here," Markus said. "Take her back to her own room."

What were they doing? Josey tried to shout, but the air whooshed from her lungs as the guardsman hefted her onto his shoulder. The room spun; the tableau of her dead father flashed before her eyes. She sobbed as her captor headed toward the door.

Then, the room exploded into violence.

From Josey's vantage point it appeared that the shadows along the wall came alive and attacked the man standing by the window. He fell to his knees, his face as pale as a bedsheet. A ribbon of blood spilled from his open mouth. Markus drew his sword. A silvery blur flashed. Markus fell to the carpet, bleeding from a gaping cut across his throat. Josey's bearer dropped her without warning. She landed hard on her hip. A moment later, the man gasped before joining her on the floor with a ghastly wound where his nose had been.

Josey curled into a tight ball and squeezed her eyes shut. *This can't be happening!* But it was. She rocked and prayed for the nightmare to end.

It was over as quickly as it began. Silence fell over the chamber, except for the crackle of the hearth embers. Josey yelped as powerful hands lifted her into the air. She imagined a knife blade sinking toward her bosom, its red tip eager to end her life. The room spun between the cracked slits of her eyelids, and a cool breeze rustled the hem of her nightgown.

The window! The beast was abducting her. She squirmed to get away. She clawed with both hands. One of her kicks landed squarely and the killer paused. Fingers grasped her hair. Then, a terrible pain shot through her skull and her sight dimmed.

A cold wind caressed Josey's face as she floated through a gray-black world of shadows lit by a smiling, silver moon.

CHAPTER EIGHT

Caim's insides trembled as he stole across the midnight lawn. It was all he could do to keep his hands from shaking. Five members of the Sacred-fucking-Brotherhood lay in a High Town mansion, dead by his hand, and a plethora of questions raced through his head. Most of them concerned the limp, sweet-smelling form slung over his shoulder.

He regretted dashing the girl's head against the wall, but she had been wriggling so hard he thought she might pitch them both out the window. Anyway, it gave him some much-needed silence to think. He climbed over the gate and dropped into the alley behind the house with a grunt. The girl stirred, but did not waken. He couldn't help noticing her long legs under the flimsy nightgown and the soft breasts pressed against his shoulder. With a sigh, Caim shifted her weight and started hiking.

As he crept down the dark alley, he considered the carnage he'd left behind. He had run into his share of crooked lawmen in his time, but he had never seen any operate as boldly as the soldiers inside. They had been downright cocky. How had they gotten there so quickly? Had they been tipped off? That was a possibility. Even the men of the Brotherhood weren't above the graft and corruption that flowed through Othir like a foul air. The old man's death hadn't concerned them in the least, but finding the girl still alive had caught them off guard. Why? What was her place in this mystery? He needed answers, and he'd wager tonight's earnings she knew something.

At least one thing had gone right tonight. He had resisted the urge to call upon his powers, but it hadn't been easy. He'd wanted that edge, felt it calling him. Just a sliver; that's all he would need. But the memory of what had happened at the Blue Vine and the monstrous presence that had answered his summons were enough to deter him. Caim shook his head in the dark. What was happening to him?

Kit hovered over him. "How did the tinmen get here so fast?"

"Good question." He kept his voice low. Sounds carried a long way on these quiet streets. "I wish I knew."

Kit floated closer to the girl. "Why did you take her? Not having enough fun as a cutthroat, you've sunk to kidnapping now?"

The question was bothering Caim as well. Why had he gone back? The job was a bust. He could have left the girl and fled the house, content that his part in the events would remain unknown. But overhearing the soldiers' conversation, it became apparent that they meant to eliminate her, and something in him couldn't let that happen. So he had risked everything he had built—his livelihood, his freedom—to save her. What the hell was he thinking? The girl's bosom expanded and contracted against Caim's cheek. She smelled faintly of lavender.

"You'd be better off just killing her and dumping the body," Kit said. "She'll scream for help as soon as she comes to."

"Kit, go scout—"

"Maybe you should hit her on the head again, just to make sure."

"Kit!" He clenched his jaws shut as his voice echoed off the stone façades on either side.

She put her hands on her tiny hips. "I looked already, all right? There's no one around, which is weird. I mean, High Town is always crawling with the law. But tonight it's like they all have something better to do. There's no one out except for a couple youngsters over on Duchess Street."

"Then check them out. I don't want to be caught by surprise again tonight."

"They're harmless. Just a couple kids out for a ride on their daddies' ponies. Not like this one." She swatted at the girl's drooping head, her hand passing through the wavy locks. "She's going to be nothing but trouble. Mark my words."

Caim ground his teeth together until he thought he might shatter a tooth. Nothing about tonight made sense, especially his reaction to this strange girl. He didn't like snags in his routine. With Kit staring at him, he felt something give.

"I couldn't leave her there. All right? I can't explain it. I just felt, I don't know, like it was wrong. The whole thing stinks. Anyway, she might know something about what happened up there."

"And I'm sure she'll be eager to tell you everything, what with you looking all guilty standing over her father's corpse."

"He was already dead when I got there."

She wiped an imaginary tear from her eye. "I'm sure she'll believe that. So what really happened up there?"

Caim glanced back at the manor falling into the background of the cityscape. The sensation of being watched itched between his shoulder blades. More imagination. No one could track him in the dark. "I don't know, but I intend to find out. Now go scout a path home, the long way around. I don't want any tails."

"So you're really taking her home with us?" She exhaled a loud huff. "Sometimes, love, you're dumber than you look."

Caim batted a hand at her ethereal backside. "Scoot."

"I hear and obey."

She darted away on the wind, leaving Caim alone with his thoughts and the girl. He studied her while he walked. She was young, maybe eighteen or nineteen, with a proud aquiline nose. Her mouth had fallen open, which made her appear even more innocent and fragile. Caim shook his head. What was he doing? He didn't pretend to know. But it was too late for subtlety. He increased his pace to a quick jog and wished he could leave this night behind.

The moon hid behind a curtain of clouds. That, and the lateness of the hour, allowed him to leave High Town unseen. Once across the Processional and back on the streets of Low Town, he felt better. He paused at the corner of Clesia and Julian streets, caught at the intersection of two thoughts. He could still dump the girl somewhere and forget this entire night. There was an abandoned house on Clesia used by drunks to sleep off their rotgut dreams. Certainly, that would make Kit happy. But something gnawed at Caim's insides. Someone had tried to set him up. The Brotherhood's arrival had been too well timed. Had they taken him, no magistrate in the city would believe he found the man already dead, nor care. His story would have ended with a speedy trial and a brisk walk to the gallows. It all stank like last week's garbage.

Caim turned onto Julian Street. An hour later found him at the door to his apartment. Once inside, he laid the girl on the cot in his bedroom. After checking to make sure the window shutter was latched, he went out to the kitchen. He grabbed a half-filled jar of wine from the cupboard and drowned his thirst with a long swallow.

Kit perched on the edge of the table, her pretty legs crossed. Her dress had changed to a fierce shade of indigo. The color accentuated her pale skin and brought out the purple in her eyes.

"You know what I'm going to say," she said.

He set down the wine jar. "You've said it half a dozen times already. Let it go, Kit. It's too late to change what happened."

"Then let's leave town. Tonight. That High Town bitch is only going to bring you more headaches. Steal a horse and ride. We could be in Michaia in a fortnight."

"There's a price on my head in Michaia."

She jumped up and wrapped her arms around his neck. Her touch tickled his chest. "Go east, then, to Arnos. We could see the City of Jewels or hide in some tiny village by the coast, lounge by the ocean in luxury."

"I'm not leaving. I won't be chased away."

"Why not? We could make a fresh start. Othir is a stinking sewer. You could be a powerful man somewhere else, with servants and a big house."

"That old man had a big house and servants. What did it gain him? He's dead this morning, just the same as any drunk knifed in the Gutters."

"Exactly. Life is short, so enjoy it while you can."

Caim walked over to a wooden shelf beside the coldbox and took down a small stone vial sealed in brown wax. He peeled it open and measured a spoonful of mealy yellow powder into an earthenware cup, then poured some wine into the cup and swirled it around.

"I'm just saying you could do better," Kit said as she followed him to the bedroom.

The girl was still sleeping soundly, but buffets to the head were difficult to judge. She could awake any minute, or not for hours. He dribbled the cup's contents into her mouth and got most of it to go down. He stood over her for a minute, watching the slow rise and fall of her chest. Her full lips glistened from the wine. He untied her bonds and arranged her limbs more comfortably.

He left the room, closing the bedroom door behind him as he went back out to the kitchen.

Kit trailed behind him. "Caim, your mother wouldn't—"

He held up the cup, one finger pointed at her nose. "Don't, Kit. Just let it go."

"You know she wouldn't want to see you like this."

"Give it a rest! This is my life. Either help me or leave me be."

She puffed out her cheeks and bit her bottom lip, but she didn't go. "Fine. What do you want me to do?"

He grabbed his cloak. "Watch over the girl. She should sleep till daybreak, but just in case. She might be important."

"I'm not a nursemaid! Where are you going?"

He opened the door and peered down the hallway. "To get some answers."

"What if she wakes up?"

"You'll think of something."

He closed the door and padded down the hall, leaving two of his problems behind. It was past midnight and he had a host of questions with no answers. But he had an idea where to start looking.

The Luccian Palace perched atop Celestial Hill like a harpy poised to swoop down on the city. Built during the old empire, and added to extensively in the decades since, the palace was as much a symbol of Othir's prominence as the True Church itself. Though the prelate abided at Castle DiVecci, most of the Church's administrative and bureaucratic activities were performed here.

The wing where Ral was met by a young manservant was decorated in an antique style oozing with old money and power. Gold leaf dripped from every conceivable surface. Huge silk tapestries covered the high walls. The atrium's ceiling was painted with scenes from scripture displaying the majesty of the Church Fathers. There was hardly any evidence of their fabled mercy. One painting showed the current prelate, Benevolence II, with a golden orb in one hand and a bloody sword in the other, an impressive pile of dead sinners at his feet.

Ral reached down to clutch the hilt of his sword while he paced across the black marble tiles, but his hand came away empty; the guards had confiscated his weapons, the ones they could find. He hadn't volunteered the few they missed.

Waning rays of moonlight streamed through the tall windows lining the hallway. Oil-soaked flambeaux crackled in wrought-iron cressets on the walls. Two bodyguards in white surcoats over black mail stood at attention, poleaxes held rigid in their hands, on either side of an oaken door.

Ral wanted to laugh. *They believe their guards and these stone walls make them invincible.* But violence could reach anyone, at any time. That was a lesson he had taught to more than one aristocrat.

He ignored the costly objects d'art surrounding him, the jeweled diadems in their crystal display cases, even the rack of ancient weapons that might have interested him another time. He was not looking forward to this meeting. He had considered not coming at all. He was tired from his journey, which, although it had been successful, had taxed him more harshly than he anticipated. He would have much preferred a hot bath and a fine meal followed promptly by several hours of undisturbed sleep, but he wasn't likely to see any of that anytime soon.

The summons had been waiting for him at home when he arrived, the archpriest's soldiers insisting in excruciatingly frank terms that he accompany them at once, regardless of the hour. So instead of procuring that hot bath and sweet slumber, he had ridden through the early morning streets of Othir and answered the call he could not afford to ignore. Not yet.

He knew why he was here. News had reached him on the road: the Esquiline Hill job had been botched. The archpriest must have his own informants close to the scene. Ral didn't like that. He had told Vassili he would handle it personally and to hell with the fallout, but the archpriest had insisted on doing things his way. Now matters were even more mucked up than before. Of course, Ral would be expected to make everything all right. And he would do it, with a smile if that's what was required. The rewards made it all worthwhile.

The manservant returned and ushered Ral into the archpriest's office. Lustrous parquet replaced the marble floor tiles. Comfortable furniture was arranged about the room at precise angles. An immense stone hearth stretched along most of the west wall; a company of silver figurines crowded the mantelpiece in strict formation. As he entered the chamber, Ral got the fleeting impression someone had just left. Yet the parlor's frosted-glass windows were closed tight against the night air and there was nowhere else for a person to hide. A faint odor hung in the air. It reminded Ral of a spice, pepper perhaps, or cloves gone stale.

Archpriest Vassili sat behind a heavy chalcedony desk. Draped in a wine-colored robe trimmed with mink, he was at least sixty, and in the stark candlelight he looked every year of it. A silk tonsure, the color of blood from a lung wound, capped his close-cropped white hair; matching rubies sparkled on stick-thin fingers. Around the loose folds of his neck, inscribed with sacerdotal icons, hung a bulky golden medallion on a thick chain of the same noble metal.

Vassili was reading from a scroll when Ral entered. His desk was littered with long sheets of parchment. A platter of *piscis* galantine on a bed of black caviar sat at his elbow, hardly touched. The papers were architectural plans for the new cathedral under construction in the heart of the city. Ral had seen the building often in his comings and goings, and noted its stark white marble walls, the legions of frozen angels and saints frowning down at passersby in stern disapproval.

The archpriest continued reading for an uncomfortably long interval before he acknowledged his visitor. When he did, his glare was cold and penetrating. "How could this happen?"

Ral started toward a cushioned chair, but stopped as his patron raised a snowy eyebrow. He settled for tossing his cloak over the back.

"How could what happen?" A moment later, he added, "Your Radiance. My mission was a complete success. The grand curate of Belastire has suffered an unfortunate mishap, as did his mistress, their three children, and a maidservant. Even better, one of his own underlings was fingered as the culprit. Seems the poor man has a drinking problem, woke up in the victim's cellar with a nasty hangover and covered in blood. They were preparing to hang him as I departed."

"Not that, idiot. How could an entire squad of the Sacred Brotherhood, handpicked by you, manage to get themselves killed doing a job you told me would be routine?"

Ral held his tongue as the servant reappeared with a silver tea service.

He took a steaming cup out of courtesy, but didn't taste the contents. What he wanted was a tall draught of good wine.

"I did as you demanded," he said. "You wanted men who could be trusted to keep their mouths shut. Ambitious men, you said, who could be manipulated with ease. I found the best available. If they failed, it is no fault of mine. I wanted to handle the matter myself, but you commanded otherwise."

Vassili glowered over the rim of his cup. "Mind your tone."

Ral bowed his head, as much as it grated. "Apologies, Your Radiance. I only mean to point out that matters would have gone smoother with my hand on the knife."

"You know well that my plan could not allow for that. The timing of the Belastire job had to take place exactly as it did, far from Othir and with no suspicion thrown in my direction. That you did well, but still it was a mistake to involve the other assassin."

A spider crawled from under the desk and scurried across the hardwood floor. Ral extended his foot to crush it.

"Caim is lowborn scum who needed to be put in his place." He examined the sole of his boot. "Anyway, it makes little difference. With Donovus out of the picture, another obstacle on the Elector Council has been eliminated."

Vassili slammed down his cup, splashing tea on the desk. "Earl Frenig was the crux of this scheme! His daughter escaped from your men and ran off to God-knows-where. And what's worse, your dupe is free as well. With them loose, all my plans are in jeopardy. Do you know how long I have labored, how many assets have been expended, all to see this day? I will not waste this opportunity."

Ral tugged at his chin. Was it possible Caim had taken her? But why? What did he think to gain from it? He couldn't possibly know her value.

"I don't see the problem." Ral held up a hand to forestall any protest. "Please, Radiance, hear me out. All Caim knows is that he killed an old nobleman and a few soldiers."

"He knows more than that. Earl Frenig was dead before your man ever entered the house."

"Dead? I don't understand. The plan—"

"I modified the plan. I did not trust your men to time their entrance with precision. A moment too soon and they would be party to murder, leaving more loose ends to clean up. Too late and we'd have what we have now, an unaccounted asset free in the city with knowledge that could destroy everything. Two assets, if the girl saw anything, and she likely did. So I sent another agent."

Ral chewed on that for a moment. What other machinations had the archpriest devised without consulting him?

"You never told me why we're making all this effort over an old man, not even an elector at that, and his brat of a daughter."

"Never mind the reasons. Your job is to carry out your orders to my satisfaction, and I am very unsatisfied tonight."

"Be that as it may, it hardly makes a difference. Caim is alone now, a fugitive with an entire city searching for him. He cannot go to the authorities. If he's hindered with a girl, he'll soon be caught, and then we'll have them both."

"You mean the prelate will have them. Don't you think this thug, this Caim, will spill everything he knows for a chance to save his life?"

"He doesn't know anything of import. Besides, he'll never make it to the dungeons. I will make sure of that."

Vassili shook his head. "I'm not willing to gamble with happenstance. I want them both eliminated immediately. My forces are in place. Before the next new moon, Benevolence will suffer an untimely mishap. The Council will convene to elect a new prelate, and I will offer myself as a candidate for the high office, a motion which will meet with quick approval."

"And as your faithful servant, I expect my promised reward. Our agreement called for a lordship, lands, and title."

The archpriest picked up another scroll. "You will receive your due compensation when this matter is completed. Mind the task I have laid before you. I want the girl and this man dead. You may go now."

Ral grabbed his cloak and left. The manservant preceded him through the doorway. Just as Ral crossed the threshold, Vassili called out, "Don't fail me again. My patience is almost at its end."

Ral turned and made a bow. "As you command, Radiance."

The soles of Ral's leather boots slapped on the tiles as he stalked through the atrium, past the bodyguards who didn't look as if they had so much as blinked since he entered. Ignoring the manservant who held open the door, he strode out into the brisk night air. This business was getting out of hand. Once he had thought Vassili would be the herald to all his dreams, but more and more of late he was beginning to doubt the archpriest's true intentions. If Vassili managed to gain the prelacy, he might decide that his old allies were too dangerous to keep alive. Ral had no intention of being discarded after his work was done. Perhaps it was time to form a contingency plan. One couldn't be too cautious in matters such as these. A man had to look out for his own interests.

Another thought nagged at Ral as he vanished into the shadowed streets of the city. If it wasn't Caim, who killed the old man?

Vassili frowned at the water-stained parchment in his hand.

> *Your Radiant Grace,*
>
> *Conditions in the state of Eregoth continue to deteriorate. An influx of Uthenorian mercenaries—brigands in all but name—into the usurper's armies has foiled our latest efforts to undermine the local viceroy. Rumors of strange happenings in the highlands continue to persist. Most of the peasants have fled or been taken to parts unknown.*
> *We beg Your Radiance to send additional men and monies, as both are in perilously short supply.*
>
> *Your Servant, with all humility,*
> *Jacob Mourning, Aspirant*

With a curse, Vassili tossed the letter on the desk amid a pile of papers, all bearing similar reports from his agents in the north. Some had not bothered to report at all. He was tired of their complaints, the endless wheedling for additional funds and soldiers. He was more concerned with events here at home. Banditry and lawlessness plagued the countryside. Arnos encroached from the east, and the prelate's "holy war" against the god-kings of Akeshia in the distant east had left Nimea with inadequate forces to guard her own borders.

Vassili broke the elaborate seal on the next missive and unfolded its stiff parchment. This one he found more to his liking.

Brother in Faith,

We most happily accept your gracious gift to the impoverished unfortunates of Parvia. As the Holy Texts profess, surely your heartfelt generosity shall be remembered forever.

Furthermore, we hereby agree to an alliance of purpose on all matters that come before the Council.

Archpriest Gaspar, Viscount of Parvia

After reading the message, Vassili folded it with care and placed it in the hidden compartment under the bottom drawer of his desk. A dozen archpriests presided over the twelve holy districts of Nimea. Together, they formed the Elector Council, a body ordained to advise the prelate and, when necessary, elect his successor. With Donovus gone and Gaspar's support, he held half of the Council securely in his pocket. Now, if only Ral could be counted upon to perform his task with alacrity, all would be set.

A shiver went through Vassili as the temperature dropped and shadows stirred in the corners of the room. A figure emerged from the darkness. Tall and lean, almost to the point of gauntness, he wore a simple monk's robe, black as the night, cinched at the waist by a plain length of cord. His pale face hovered in the candlelight. Its stern lines came together to form a powerful jaw, a twisted nose. White scars creased hollow cheeks, old wounds poorly healed. Shadows smudged the sockets of his deep-set eyes. Black pupils like cold, bottomless pits swallowed the light.

"Levictus." Vassili made a show of looking over the latest plans for the cathedral's baptistery. "You overheard?"

The figure moved to the spot where Ral had stood only moments before. His voice, though only a whisper, carried through the chamber.

"Nothing remains hidden from the Dark."

The archpriest reached up to touch the medallion on his chest and forced himself to look upon the man's ruined features. Levictus winced as candlelight reflected off the symbols etched on the golden surface, and

Vassili allowed himself a satisfied smile. Sometimes a pet, no matter how faithful, needed to be brought to heel.

He jerked his chin toward the doorway through which Ral had departed. "That one grows bolder every day."

Levictus opened his left hand slightly, and then made a flicking gesture as if to say, *The man is insignificant, an insect*, but there was something ominous in his gaze.

"In any case," Vassili continued, "there is a more dire matter at hand. Namely, your failure in Ostergoth. You assured me that your necromancy could protect Reinard. I made guarantees based upon that assurance, guarantees which are now returning to haunt me. The duke's brother sits on the Council. He will no doubt demand concessions as a result of this debacle, concessions that will cost me dearly. Well? What say you?"

Still, Levictus said nothing.

Vassili exhaled a long breath. He was tempted to reach for his medallion again. The sunburst sigil of the True Faith was perhaps the only thing his servant feared in the entire world, having been tortured and scarred under its standard. Yet he kept his hands on the arms of his chair. He would show restraint.

"For the love of the Light, man. What is it? Speak."

"Have I not done all that you asked of me?" Levictus stood perfectly still as he spoke, but the scars on his cheeks rippled with every word. "I have spied on your enemies. It was I who discovered the old one's intentions, and I who silenced him. I have done all that you asked, to the letter of your expectations. Would you agree this is true?"

"Yes, Levictus. And forget not that it was I who saved you from the Inquest's torture cells."

Vassili would never forget that day. Twenty years ago, the Church hierarchs saw the filth and immorality lurking throughout the realm and, having secured the emperor's sanction, launched a pogrom to rid the nation of its heretical pagan roots. The fanes of the old gods were rooted out and destroyed, their priests imprisoned or slain on the spot along with any others who refused to convert to the True Faith. Levictus's family was among those swept up by deputized officers of the Holy Order of Inquest. Vassili had been merely an ambitious praetor at the time. On a tour inside the Inquest's dungeons, he'd noticed a particular young man. According to the jailers, his parents and brother had expired under questioning, but this young man refused to repent, though he had been tortured for weeks and was slated for execution on the next day. Vassili sensed something special in this youth, as if their paths had been destined to cross. He used his authority to have the prisoner released and took the waif into his own household. Not long after, his new protégé began to display certain unusual traits. With time and study, Vassili realized the amazing treasure he had unearthed.

"Have I failed in any task you set before me, master?" Levictus stepped toward the desk. "Or given less respect than was due?"

The archpriest folded his hands within his sleeves. "No, Levictus. You have served me faithfully. I do not debate it."

"Then when, master? When shall I have my revenge?"

There it was. Vassili chided himself for not seeing it sooner. He never expected the man to forget the torments of his past, but sometimes it slipped his mind. When he'd saved Levictus from the stake, he had promised the youth his vengeance against the Holy Inquest for what they had done to his family. Over the years, he had sustained Levictus on tidbits of revenge, the odd Inquestor or misogynous cleric, fools caught sodomizing their acolytes or plundering the Church coffers. But he understood what Levictus truly wanted.

Vassili composed himself. "Soon, Levictus, if you follow my instructions. It is no easy thing we aspire to achieve. Our realm seethes with corruption. Merchants scheme and bribe their way to high position. Harlots peddle their wares on every street corner in Low Town. Debauchery reigns in the houses of God. Civilization itself teeters on a precipice."

"When, master?"

"Degeneracy is festering in every corner of the realm. Heresy breeds in the streets of our very city. And yet Benevolence does nothing to halt the corruption, but squats in his fortress like a bloated leech and dreams of past glories."

Levictus stared at him.

"Find the girl! By the Noose, Levictus, find her and we can move on to the final phase. Then, you will receive everything you desire."

Levictus maintained his gloomy stare a few seconds more, and then dropped his gaze to the floor. "Yes, master."

"Good. Now go and do not return until you have good news for me."

He made a show of comparing blueprints as Levictus retreated into the shadowy corner from which he had emerged. Moments later, the chill faded from the room.

Vassili leaned back and released a long sigh. Levictus was becoming increasingly difficult to manage, and the thought of the sorcerer running free, no longer under his control, was enough to send him reaching for the bellpull. He needed a drink—something stronger than tea.

While he waited for his servant to appear, Vassili played with the idea of pitting Ral against Levictus. With luck, they would eliminate each other and rid him of both problems. It was an interesting line of thought, one he filed away for the future. He didn't dare upset the delicate balance so close to the fruition of his dream. At this moment, the prelate slept soundly within the walls of Castle DiVecci, never suspecting that his doom approached on silent steps. Vassili almost wished he could see the look on the old fool's face when the end came.

Smiling to himself, he took the scroll from his desk drawer and read its contents again.

CHAPTER NINE

The feeling of being watched followed Caim through Low Town as dawn's first rays painted the city in shades of purple and orange. He glanced over his shoulder from time to time, mixed up his pace, and took wrong turns on purpose, but never caught sight of a tail. Meanwhile, the events of the previous night played over and again in his head. Questions piled up, but they lent no answers.

He emerged between two brownstones and hooked a right onto Fulcrum Close. It was a bit of backtracking to get to his destination, but the habits that had kept him alive all these years were ingrained into his bones. When the hairs on the back of his neck tingled, he knew better than to ignore it.

He turned down a street and skipped to a halt as the iron gray walls of the city workhouse emerged from the morning mist. Strands of pearlescent fog snaked through the hollow window sockets of its squat towers and clung to shadowed doorways where the sunlight could not penetrate.

Caim huddled within his cloak as he continued on his way. He made several more turns before he reached the Three Maids. A soft knock at the back door summoned a plump scullion girl who gave him entrance with a smile. The cooks paid him no mind as he slipped through the kitchen. The common hall was empty except for the dregs of last night's carousing, sleeping off their hangovers on the floor. The morning bartender, a lanky six-footer with a floppy crop of orange hair, nodded to him.

Caim placed a silver coin on the bar. "I need to speak to Mathias."

"He hasn't come down yet. He had company last night. Might not be a good idea to disturb them."

This whole night's been a bad idea. "I'll risk it."

The bartender made no move to stop him as he headed for the back stairs. Caim thought back to his last visit, when he met Ral on the stairs. How would Ral have handled last night? Probably would have slit the girl's throat and been gone before the law arrived. *That's what I should have done.* But he couldn't muster any real enthusiasm for the idea. Killing innocents never appealed to him. Then again, it seemed like the whole world was going to hell these days. Maybe innocence didn't exist anymore.

The upstairs hall was dark. Caim paused at the door. Mathias was a friend, as much a friend as he had in the world, besides Kit. He might not take kindly to someone barging into his abode at this hour. Then Caim remembered the imbroglio on Esquiline Hill and his anger returned. He was a marked man. With the city already cracking down on illegal activities, it was the worst time for such a catastrophe. Maybe Kit was right. Maybe he should leave Othir and start a new life someplace else.

No. He'd been running all his life. It had to stop somewhere.

Caim turned the knob, pushed open the door, and froze with one foot over the threshold as an icy finger of caution slipped down his backbone. Everything appeared ordinary at first glance; the furniture was laid out just as it had been on his last visit. The scent of the exotic incense Mathias favored lingered in the air. Heavy window shades shut out the morning light, but there was nothing sinister about that; Mat was a notoriously late riser. Still, something wasn't right.

Caim drew one of his knives. "Mathias?"

He crossed the room on quiet steps. The suite consisted of several interconnected chambers. Caim parted a curtain of blue silk dividing the front room from the living areas. A short corridor gave entrance to three archways. The doorway at the end was blocked by another curtain.

Caim went down the corridor on the balls of his feet, knees bent. The floorboards flexed under his weight, but did not squeak. He peeked into the side archways as he passed. The left led to a spacious kitchen. Everything appeared in order, from the pristine marble countertops to the copper pans and utensils lined up over a big iron stove. The right arch opened into a private salon. There was a small desk shoved into a corner, its surface piled with loose papers, pens, ink jars, and ledger books.

Caim moved to the last doorway and pushed aside the curtain. He paused a moment for his eyes to adjust. This room was the darkest of all, the windows not only shaded but covered by heavy curtains. A massive canopy bed, large enough for three adults, rested on the far side of the room. Two shapes nestled under the diaphanous awning.

"Mat." He let his voice rise from a whisper. "It's Caim. I need to talk to you."

The shapes on the bed did not stir. Caim eased the other *suete* from its sheath and circled around to the side of the bed. He watched the dark corners of the room for movement. His ears strained, but there was only the whisper of his own footsteps as he stepped across the carpet.

He stopped at the bedside. Two bodies stared up at the ceiling with dull, blank eyes. Lyell had been one of Mat's favorite pretties. He looked like a doll, pale, with long blond hair fanned around his head like waves of beaten gold. Someone had opened a second smile across his throat with a narrow blade, very sharp. Dark lines of blood were encrusted on his chest. Caim doubted the youth had wakened until the last throes of death were upon him.

Mathias lay beside his paramour. Even in death his bulk was impressive. His slick hair was mussed in disarray. His throat was uncut. Instead, a bloody hole gaped between his breasts. The edges of the wound were tinged with black discolorations. Caim didn't need to check to know Mat's heart had been removed. It was just like the Esquiline Hill job.

Caim stood motionless. Death was an old companion to him, but his hands shook as he looked down on the man he had known and worked with for six years. He gripped the hilts of his knives until his palms hurt. *Stay in control.* He took a deep breath as he catalogued every detail of the scene. The boy had likely been killed first, and quietly. Mathias hadn't awakened until he was already dead. That gave the killer as much time as he needed to do his grisly work. The sheets were drenched in blood, but there wasn't a drop on the carpet.

Caim went to a window and peered through the curtains. A grille of stout iron bars secured the entry. There were no signs of forcing. The killer must have entered from the front. He was good, a professional. That shortened the list of suspects considerably. Most hired killers were elevated street thugs with more muscles than brains. Only a handful achieved the level of skill it took to enter a locked room and kill without rousing the neighbors. There were a few who could have done this, and most of them worked for Mathias. Sadly, this sort of thing had probably been overdue. Men who murdered for a living came in two categories. One type killed for the money; it was a job for them, the same as hauling crates on the docks or sweeping out stables. The other type was a completely different animal. They took pleasure in their work, deriving some sort of twisted satisfaction that Caim had never been able to fathom; but he had ridden with men in his early days out west who would take their time with a kill, making it last while they watched with sick smiles.

In Mat's line of work, he dealt with both types of killers. *Had* dealt with them. It had only been a matter of time before one of them came after him, because of a perceived slight or a disagreement over money, but Caim didn't believe this was a coincidence. It wasn't a random murder. It was meant for someone to see, and Caim had a suspicion that someone was him.

A footstep from the hall shook Caim from his thoughts. He cocked his arm for an underhand throw even before he finished turning. He held the action as the outline of a tall, mop-haired man filled the doorway. The bartender stood stock-still with a wooden platter in his hand. The smells of fried eggs and bacon cut through the stale air.

"Mr. Finneus?"

"Dead." Caim lowered his knife. "Sometime in the night. Did anyone come up here last night except Mathias and the boy?"

The bartender shrugged. The tray rose and fell with his shoulders. "I don't know. Olaf was working last night. He went home."

"Go back downstairs and send someone to fetch the law. Don't mention I was here. Understand?"

After a long look at the bed, the bartender turned and shuffled back down the hallway. Caim waited until the apartment door closed. He looked down at his dead friend. *You were a good man, Mat, and a good friend. You never did me wrong.*

Not the most elegant of eulogies, but those were the best words Caim could come up with. Hell, they were the best words he could say about anyone.

He left via the back stairs and ducked out the kitchen. The streets were filling up as the denizens of Low Town left their homes to begin another day, none of them realizing that one of their own had been lost during the night. Most wouldn't care if they knew. That was the sad truth of it. Like him, Mathias had been a product of society's underbelly, a creature both loathed and feared even though he served a necessary function. Caim had come to terms with that realization a long time ago. He hoped Mathias had as well.

Despite the rising warmth of the day, he pulled his cloak tighter around his body. The hood hid his face from view. A mix of emotions roiled inside him over Mat's murder: sadness, regret, perhaps a touch of guilt, but anger burned hotter than all else. Anger at whoever had killed his friend, at himself, at Mathias for leaving him when he needed answers. The game continued, and he was falling farther behind. Worse, he was running out of sources of information. The girl was the key. He only hoped she knew something worthwhile.

Otherwise, he might have to take Kit's advice.

From the rooftop across the alleyway from the Three Maids, Levictus worked his knife as he watched his target depart. White-gray wings fluttered in his hands.

With the fat man's blood still wet on his blade, he had waited here while the city awoke to the new day. He had taken no joy in extinguishing the death merchant's life, nor that of the elder on Esquiline Hill. They were simply tasks consigned to him by his master. Ordinary tasks, as mundane as cleaning a pair of boots or beating a mattress. Over the past decade and a half he had given up on the idea of finding a challenge worthy of his talents.

Until now.

He tightened his grip, and tiny talons scrabbled inside his fist as he considered the man below. This one might prove entertaining. Vassili was growing more arrogant and demanding by the day; treachery dripped from his every word. If not for the power he wielded through the Elector Council, Levictus would have left him long ago. But his family's souls cried out for vengeance. Through the long years, he had utilized his sorcery to track down those who had tortured and murdered them. He had dragged Inquestor agents by the dozens out to the forgotten sanctuaries beyond the city walls and given them over to the dark powers of the nether realms. Yet his thirst for vengeance would not be slaked while the initiator of the pogroms, the man who had devised the doctrine of bigotry that had resulted in the death of thousands of innocents and then ridden the tide of bloodshed and torture to the very pinnacle of his order, yet lived. The prelate of the True Church. Until Benevolence himself lay dead at his feet, Levictus would not stop. All that he had done, it meant nothing if he did not accomplish that.

He flicked the blade of his knife and wished he could eliminate the prelate now and be done with it, but Vassili preached patience and Levictus waited. Yet he would not wait much longer. The archpriest's plan had brought certain opportunities to light. The assassin with the lazy smile and eyes like blue crystal was an interesting prospect. Headstrong and ambitious, that one would be easier to manipulate. Perhaps it was time to make a change, or he could do as Vassili wanted and kill the man in the street below.

Or he could do both.

The target reached an intersection and vanished around a corner.

Levictus put his knife away and reached into his robe. From a pocket in the lining he took out a small object and placed it on the rooftop. The bead gleamed black and glossy in the morning light like a pebble of polished obsidian. Warmth pulsed within its ebon depths. He knelt beside the egg and whispered in soft, lilting tones. Tendrils of smoke rose from the bead as its surface dulled. With a pop, it cracked down the center and an inky stain emerged, a tiny serpent as long as his forefinger. Speaking softly, he gave the creature its instructions. It listened, and then disappeared into a chink between two roof shingles.

Levictus straightened and stepped into the lee of an arched gable. As he entered the shadow's embrace, plans formed in his head. Death would reign over this city before he was done, a scourging storm to wash away all the wickedness and iniquity. For a brief moment, he considered his loyalty to Vassili, but then reminded himself that he was a dead man. He had died on the day he was dragged into hell by the foot soldiers of the True Church. And dead men held no allegiances.

A whisper on the wind left the rooftop vacant save for smears of blood and the headless carcasses of a dozen pigeons.

CHAPTER TEN

Josey giggled as her nanny crept past the pantry closet. She put her eye to the crack between the door and the jamb and ignored the demands that she present herself immediately. Hide-and-seek was one of her favorite games, and this big new house was the perfect place to play. It had even more nooks and shadowy corners than the hedge maze of their last home. She could hide for *days* if she wanted.

She was six years old, but Father still left her in the nanny's custody while he attended to business. She didn't know what business was, but it took up a great deal of his time these days, something she was decidedly not happy about. She was used to being the center of his world, his little princess, and anything that took Father away from Josey made her obscenely jealous.

While the nanny went calling into the next room, she snuck out from her hiding spot. She wanted to find a better one, someplace no one could ever find her. In her stocking feet she ran through the cavernous kitchen with its high tables and racks of cast-iron pots, down a wide hall, and around the corner. After several more turnings she found herself in a part of the house she had not yet encountered. Overjoyed at the prospect of exploring new territory, she forgot her game and wandered the long, windowless corridor. Tall wooden doors, their bronze latches dark with age, refused her entry, so she kept going. At the turning of another corner, she looked back. A line of footprints trailed behind her, a clear path she could follow back whenever she wanted.

The hall ended in a shallow niche, its blank walls encased in wooden paneling. A rusty hook for hanging a picture jutted above her reach. Josey crouched in the niche. It was too exposed for a good hiding spot. Dejected, she started to get up when a twinkle of light caught her eye.

She bent down and found a crack near the floor. She would have missed it if not for the yellow glow filling the narrow gap. She wriggled her fingers into the crack and grinned when a section of the wall swung out like a narrow door. Deep steps of bare rock descended into the tunnel beyond, from which issued smells of earth and smoke. Below, more light flickered and strange sounds whispered in her ears like distant singing.

She stole down the steps like the daring thief Jangar Bey, her favorite storybook hero. Her fingers followed the curve of the stone wall as the cool steps wended beneath her feet. The lower she descended, the louder grew the sounds. The light got stronger, too. At the bottom of the steps a wide chamber opened before her, cut from the foundation beneath the house. Flaming torches lit the cavernous room and threw deep shadows across its painted walls. People in funny costumes stood in a circle and swayed in rhythm with the rising chant. Deep-blue hoods covered their faces except for dark eyeholes. Fanciful designs were sewn onto their clothes, shaggy birds with rearing claws depicted in golden thread.

There was so much to see, Josey didn't notice the song had ended until the rustle of clothing caught her attention. The hoods came off and faces emerged into the torchlight, men and women smiling and nodding as they finished their play, or whatever it was. A head turned and Josey's breath caught in her throat as familiar eyes cast their gaze across the chamber. With a startled gasp, she ran back up the steps, not sure why she fled, but only knowing she had seen something she wasn't meant to witness. When she reached the niche, she slammed shut the paneled door and darted down the hallway, but the eyes followed her like a bad dream.

The cool eyes of her father.

The hallway stretched into darkness before her. Her breathing thundered in her ears. A haunting dread pursued her through the gloom. She grasped for something to hold on to, but there was nothing there as she tumbled down a well of endless night.

With infinite slowness the darkness resolved itself into shapes. At first indistinct, they loomed large and frightening over Josey's head, until their edges came together into long shadows across the ceiling. Her body didn't seem to want to work. She tried to turn her neck and waited for what seemed like hours before anything came into view. She remembered her dream and shivered. She had forgotten about that day in the old wing of the house and the secret door in the wall. She had gone back to the niche days later only to find a bare wall and tight panels that refused to budge no matter how hard she pried at them. She left the wing convinced it had all been a bad dream.

The musty smell of the secret cavern lingered in her head.

She sat up. She was lying on a crude bed, little more than a length of coarse fabric stretched over a wooden frame. The room was unfamiliar, with walls and ceiling of cracked plaster, devoid of color or décor.

Her head felt strange, like it was wrapped in wet towels. She lifted a hand to her forehead and groaned as a sliver of agony slid across her temple. The skin wasn't broken, but she could feel a bruise rising beneath the skin. What had happened? Fighting back a wave of nausea, she moved to get up. She was still wearing her nightdress. All of a sudden, the events in her father's room marched through her mind. She saw Father sitting in his favorite chair, his chest ripped open in a bloody gash, and the hulking specter in black standing over him. She remembered the rough hands that had bound her tight. The authorities had arrived to save her, but the man in black had killed them all. Was that right? Her thoughts were all jumbled. But one thing she remembered with crystal clarity: her poor father was dead.

And now she was a captive, likely held for ransom. But who would pay for her release? She had no other family. The terror of her situation crept over her like an army of biting ants. She shivered on the cot, unable to move. Heavy tears slid down her face as the image of her dead father played over in her head. Poor, poor Father and poor her. She was truly alone in the world.

The sound of talking silenced her sobs. She wiped her face with a silken sleeve and tried to stand up. The pain wasn't so bad now. She listened. A man's voice filtered through the room's only door.

"—must've been killed right before I arrived," the speaker said. A moment later, he added. "No, this was a real slick job. No broken windows. No blood trail."

Josey couldn't make out any other speakers. As quietly as she could, she stole up to the door and pressed her ear to the peeling wooden panels. She heard a little better, but still only the one voice.

"I can't yet, Kit," he said. "Mat was a friend."

Who was Mat? Or Kit? Josey tried to follow the conversation.

"I don't know," the voice continued. "She's part of this somehow, or the old man was. Either way, she knows something and I intend to find out what."

Josey stepped away from the door with her heart pounding in her throat. It had to be the man in black. He was crazy, talking to himself. From the sound of his ramblings, he meant to interrogate her. Imaginings of torture popped into her head. She wrapped her arms around her body, shivering. *I have to get away!*

She took another look around the room. At the foot of the cot sat a heavy locker bound in bands of old bronze. A full-length mirror, actually a very nice piece she wouldn't have minded owning herself, stood beside a wooden cabinet opposite a narrow window. She hurried to the window and threw back the shade. There was no glass in the casement, just two heavy shutters secured with a slide-lock. She pulled the lock's handle, but it refused to open. The darkness seemed to deepen around her. There was something in the room.

She yanked harder, biting her bottom lip as the shutters rattled. Her fingers encountered something wrapped around the lock, a piece of wire tied around the slide to keep it from opening. A shadow moved in her peripheral vision. She clawed at the wire with her fingernails as a tide of fear swelled inside her. She had to get out.

She screamed as a brutal grip seized her from behind.

The sun had begun to set as Caim turned onto the street of his apartment building. All day he had scoured Othir's backstreets and alleyways for information about Mat's murder. Nothing happened in the Gutters without someone hearing about it. For the right price, or faced with the proper motivation, the denizens of Low Town could be very forthcoming. Caim had plied both coin and intimidation with every street hood and gossipmonger he could find, but no one knew anything. He hadn't believed it, not until he'd bared his knives and seen the truth in the stark eyes staring back at him.

About the only thing he'd learned were vague whispers about a new player in town, but nothing solid. It was all just rumors and gossip. People had turned up missing, not an unusual thing in the Gutters, but some were people who knew how to survive, like Molag Flat-Nose, an ex-mercenary and one of the prime suspects on Caim's list. Now that list was shorter and he was out of leads.

As he entered the front door, Caim considered his situation. He could always cut and run. Kit would be thrilled. But it didn't sit right with him. This had gone far beyond a botched hit. Somewhere along the line it had become personal for him. He'd never had many friends, not besides Kit. Mathias had treated him well, better than he'd expected when they first met at a dingy tavern on the west side. The tavern was gone, replaced by a newer establishment that catered to a better clientele, and now Mathias was gone, too.

Caim took a taper from the pot in the foyer, lit it from a tiny lamp set aside for late-night arrivals, and climbed the stairs to the second floor. A small shape huddled in the unlit hall. Caim started for a knife with his free hand until he recognized the shape and let it fall back by his side.

The child sat on her haunches against the wall across from his door. Her large eyes watched him while her spindle-thin fingers traced the wall's discolored plaster. He paused at his door for a moment. A woman's soft crying issued from across the hall, punctuated by loud, angry shouts. Suddenly uncomfortable, he fumbled with his locks and ducked inside, closing the door to the sounds and the little girl's eyes.

He lit a lamp and went over to the coldbox, trying to push the child's gaze out of his thoughts. Everyone had problems. Whether or not she learned to cope with life wasn't his concern. He grabbed a wine jar and drained it in several deep swallows. He looked at the last dregs of wine gathered at the bottom of the jar. Something tugged at the back of his mind. An unquantifiable urge to action tickled his nerves, like some nameless doom poised over his head, waiting to strike. *I'm just tired*, he told himself, but he almost jumped when Kit appeared behind him and threw her arms around his neck.

"I missed you," she said. "What did you find out?"

Caim put the jar down. He wanted to drink more, to get completely wrecked and forget these past couple days, but he needed all his wits about him.

"Mathias is dead."

Kit rushed around to face him. Her fingers brushed across his hands like faint cobwebs. "What happened?"

"Someone cut his heart out while he slept."

"Oh, Caim!"

He poured out the whole story. Once he started talking, it all gushed out of him, like pus from an infected wound. Afterward, he felt a little better. The wine helped too.

"So are you going to listen to me now?" Kit sat cross-legged on the kitchen table. "Will you leave Othir? Tonight?"

Caim let out a long sigh. He didn't feel like fighting, but he couldn't walk away from this problem. It was too big, cut too close to the bone.

"I can't yet, Kit. Mat was a friend."

"What's the girl got to do with this?"

He tried to explain it to her, but he could tell by her rigid expression that he might as well be talking to the table. Why, why, why, she asked, until finally he collapsed in a chair, exhausted.

"I give up, Kit. Maybe you're right. Maybe I'm just chasing my tail, but for as long as I can remember I've been running from something. I'm tired of looking over my shoulder."

Kit set her hands on her tiny hips. "That's what I'm saying. A new start, someplace where nobody knows—"

Before she could finish, a scream came from the bedroom, followed by muffled pounding. Caim leapt across the room and swung open the door. The old man's daughter was pulling frantically on the bindings that secured the window. The feeling of dread returned as Caim stepped into the room, so intense that he ducked his head between his shoulders. He crossed the narrow room and pulled the girl away from the window. Her screams sliced away the last remnants of his euphoria.

He dragged her out into the kitchen and wrestled her into the chair. She started to rise again until he stood over her. Sucking in deep breaths, she stared up at him with a sullen expression. Her eyes were red and swollen, and her hands were clenched into tight fists. For a moment, he thought she might try to attack him. The image in his head made him smile. The girl glared with a hard set to her mouth. At least she had stopped screaming.

Caim turned away and filled a kettle with tepid water from a jug. He had thought the girl was pretty before, but unconscious she had been only a distant presence, like the moon on a frigid winter night. Now, awake and animate, she was even more breathtaking. He squeezed his right hand into a fist until the fingernails cut into his palm. He had to keep his head on straight. He was a hunted man. He had to play this smart.

With one eye on the girl, he lit the stove and put the kettle on to boil. He had a feeling he was in for a long night. Maybe Kit was right. Maybe he should have dumped this problem in an alley and left for greener pastures. He shook his head. No, he was too stubborn, or too stupid, to give up that easily. One thing he knew for sure. He wasn't letting this girl out of his sight until he found out what was going on. He owed Mathias that much.

His hands tightened around the lid of the tea tin.

CHAPTER ELEVEN

Josey concentrated on her hands, clutched together in her lap. She had always liked her hands. They were small-boned, with long, tapering fingers. Her nails needed painting; the pink lacquer was flaking off at the tips, but besides that, they were very nice hands.

The killer's hands, however, the hands that had murdered her father, were wrapped in hard sinew. Tiny scars dotted his knuckles. One long cicatrix started on the back of his left hand and ran up into the cuff of his shirtsleeve. She stared at it as he held out a cup to her.

"Take it," he said.

She grasped the round porcelain cup with both hands. It was deliciously warm. A pleasant green tea smell rose from the rim, but her stomach quailed at the idea of ingesting anything given to her by this beast. She let the cup rest in her lap.

He glanced at her temple. "Does that hurt?"

She shook her head to prove it didn't. His voice sounded different than she expected, more normal. *He's not normal. He's a cold-blooded murderer.*

Her teeth clenched together so hard her jaws ached, but she knew if she didn't keep them clenched she would start screaming again. Everything about him repulsed her. His shoulders were too broad for his frame; his wrists were thick and ropy with muscle. His face wasn't uncomely, but it had a stoniness that made her think of the statues that decorated the walls of the new cathedral. Although she considered herself a good, pious woman, the sight of the immense edifice disturbed her, especially the stern faces of the statuary, which didn't resemble the kindly saints of her imagination. The killer had the same hard look about him. His chin was too sharp to be handsome. It made him look sinister, like a fox out to pilfer unattended chicks. And his eyes. They were chips of granite, cold and impervious. She looked away and tried not to think of his gaze upon her.

The apartment was modest, barely larger than her bathing chamber. A shoddy table and the single chair in which she sat comprised the only furniture. The boards were bare wood, but clean-swept. A thick mat sat in the far corner. Leather bags hung on long cords from hooks set into the ceiling. Were they some sort of crude torture device? Metal bars of various lengths leaned against the wall. The kitchen area was likewise spare, with its antique coldbox and simple oven, some cupboards. Something unexpected rested on the countertop, a book. She couldn't make out the subject, but its illuminated pages were held open by the blade of a dagger.

A thought struck her from out of the blue. *He lives alone.* Strangely, she wondered if he was lonely. Then, he turned to fetch a cup for himself and she saw the huge knives strapped to his back. One of them had stolen her father's life. In her imagination, she ripped the knives from their harness and plunged them into his neck.

"What's your name, girl?" he asked, startling her with his brusqueness.

"Who were you talking to before you grabbed me?" Josey congratulated herself on how steady her voice sounded. She started to lift the cup to her lips, but then set it back in her lap.

"I was talking to no one."

"I heard you through the door. You were talking, but I didn't hear anyone else."

"You and I are the only ones here."

She nodded to herself. *So he's either lying to me, or he's a madman who talks to himself and kills defenseless old men.* Her fear was receding. In its place rose a gush of burning anger from the pit of her belly.

"What do you want with me? If you're after a ransom, you ruined your chances when you killed my father."

He watched her with his stony eyes. "The only people I killed were the men intent on doing away with you."

"I saw you standing over him!" She couldn't stop shaking. The cup trembled in her hands. "I saw the blood and . . . his chest. I saw everything!"

"Yes." He was remarkably calm in the face of her rage. "There was blood and the old man was dead, but I didn't kill him. He was already dead—"

100

"Liar!"

She threw the cup at him. He dodged faster than she had ever seen anyone move. The cup shattered against a cabinet door, spattering hot tea and pottery shards across the wall. She steeled herself for his rebuke, but he stood there and sipped his tea.

"I had the contract on his life," he said. "And I would have killed him. It was under false pretenses, but I suppose that matters little to you. Still, I'm telling you the truth. Someone else had been there before me."

"Am I supposed to believe you?" The scorn in her voice made her feel invincible. He could hurt her, even kill her, but he couldn't stop her from speaking her mind. "Was there a whole legion of assassins waiting to kill my father? He was a harmless old man, well loved and respected by everyone."

"Not by the person who killed him, nor the client who hired me. That's two fairly serious enemies. A bit much for a man loved by everyone."

The dryness in his voice made her want to claw his eyes out. She crossed her arms across her breasts. She didn't have to listen to this. Her father was a good man. A great man! He had connections to the palace and all the best families. Now he was gone. Moistness crept into her eyes when she thought of how she wouldn't be able to attend his funeral. *Who will attend mine?*

"You killed Markus, too," she blurted.

"Your servant? I never touched him. He's still alive for all I know."

"*Second Prefect* Markus, one of the Sacred Brothers you murdered when you were abducting me. He was the betrothed of my dearest friend."

"Those tinmen were after you, not me. I saved your life by stopping them."

"Markus would never hurt me. He was my friend, and you killed him like he was nothing."

He regarded her for a long moment. Her stomach quavered. Was this it? Was he going to kill her now?

Instead, he asked, "What's your name?"

"What does that matter?"

"I'd like to know."

She straightened her posture. "I am Josephine Frenig, daughter of

Artur Frenig, seventeenth earl of Highavon. Now, what of you? What are you called?"

"It makes no difference."

"What's fair for one is fair for both. Since you surely mean to murder me, it should be of no consequence to you."

"Caim."

"Caim." She had to choose her words carefully. "If you have any shred of decency, you will release me immediately, or at least allow me to write a letter to my father's friends."

"And if I intend to murder you?"

Josey's tongue dried up in her mouth, but she forced her lips to work. "Then be done with it, craven."

He shook his head. "I didn't take you just to kill you here."

"Then why? Why did you do it?"

He glanced at the wall over her head. He hesitated before saying, "It all comes back to your father. I didn't kill him, but someone wanted him dead. You must know someone who wished him ill, someone jealous of his success."

"No."

"A business partner? Some lady's husband?"

"No!" she shouted, and then sat still, frightened by her own anger. "He had no enemies. No lovers. Just me. He was a good and decent man."

"Decent men have plenty of enemies. I know." He started to pace back and forth past the table. "What was your father's position?"

"He was the exarch of Navarre when I was a girl. Afterward, he received the Golden Sword for his service and retired to a life of ease here in Othir. He was a great man. Infinitely better than a lowborn killer."

If the comment stung, he gave no indication. "Yes. That could be. It almost makes sense."

"What does?"

"Never mind. Was your father involved in any overseas ventures? Did he belong to a social club?"

Josey remembered the nightmare of the people in funny robes meeting in the basement of their house, but shunted the memory aside.

"I don't know. I don't think so. He spent most of his time in the study, writing letters to old friends. Nothing to do with me."

Caim didn't seem to be listening, so she stopped talking and studied him. Now that she had a better look at him, he didn't appear like she imagined a killer would. He was strong, but not overly big or brutish. In fact, his features were rather refined. He might have even been fetching if put into proper clothes. When he turned to look at her, she quickly glanced away, a shudder racing through her insides. He had a gaze like a corpse.

"No," he said to the air over her head.

"What?"

"Nothing."

The man was clearly deranged. What would he do next? One thing was sure. If she remained here much longer, she would never leave this dingy apartment alive. There was a window behind her, but it was shuttered and locked like the one in the bedroom. Josey glanced at the door across the room. It had to be the way out. There was a slide-lock holding it shut, but if she could distract him long enough to work the bolt . . .

"Do you want more tea?" he asked.

"Yes. Have you anything to eat? I'm famished."

He nodded with his back to her. "I might have some victuals about if you're not too particular."

While he rummaged through a pinewood pantry painted with faded flowers, Josey slid off her slippers. They were soft lamb's wool, but she would move faster and more quietly in bare feet. As she watched his back, something stirred in the shadows above his head. She froze as a long, sinuous shape emerged from the corner of the ceiling. Without a sound, it glided down the wall. A violent shiver ran through Josey. It was the most revolting thing she had ever seen, a serpent of pure blackness, and it was headed straight for Caim. She almost called out a warning, but clamped her lips shut.

No, I won't help him.

Watching the awful creature slither toward her father's killer, Josey rose from the chair. She tiptoed across the room. A single sound would betray her. She reached the door without alerting her captor. The bolt was a thick affair of iron. She grasped it with both hands and pulled. The slide shot back with a loud click. Without looking back, she yanked open the door and dashed out into the dark hallway beyond.

Her naked feet slapped on the floorboards. Fear lent speed to her steps. She reached a narrow stairwell at the end of the hall and raced down the steps, and gasped with relief as she spied a large doorway at the bottom. With a grunt, she shoved open the door and ran out into the night.

Caim suppressed a sigh as he peered into the pantry. This conversation was going nowhere. The girl, Josephine, obviously didn't trust him enough to give him straight answers. And why should she? In any case, he was beginning to doubt she knew anything pertinent. She was just a pampered socialite without any cares beyond the lacy confines of her perfect world. Kit was right again. Bringing the girl here had been a mistake.

He was pushing aside a sack of old flour to see what might be lurking behind it when the weird sensation returned, stronger than before. Fear was a thing he had learned to live with. It was part of his life and his livelihood. Every time he faced a drawn weapon or crept into a strange location for a job, it perched on his shoulder. He had learned to control it, to harness its energy to do what had to be done. This feeling was different. It refused to be repressed or ignored, but roiled in the pit of his stomach like a bad meat pie.

"Caim!" Kit yelled. Her shout made him jerk upright, almost banging his head on the roof of the cupboard.

He extricated himself and turned in time to see his captive dart out the doorway into the hall. With a curse, he took two steps after her and halted in his tracks as a bitter chill descended over him like an avalanche of snow. Kit stared up at the ceiling. Caim dove to the ground and rolled. A sharp pain pierced his right ankle, cutting through his boot. He kicked and spun around.

A great serpent reared above him. Its inky scales gleamed in the lamplight like diamonds of polished jet. The tail end disappeared into the shadows of the ceiling. The wedge-shaped head hovered before him, jaws wide enough to swallow a dog splayed open to display rows of glistening fangs.

Caim slid one of his knives free of its sheath. The serpent watched his movements with cold, cerulean eyes. Its head swayed from side to side.

"Are you all right?" Kit's gaze remained on the black creature as it floated nearer.

"What in the hell is that thing?"

"Something very dangerous," she whispered, and dropped her voice even further when the serpent's head swung toward her. "I could distract it while you run."

"It can see you?" He gathered his feet under him and bit his bottom lip as a bolt of agony shot up his right leg. But it supported his weight. "No, go after the girl."

"But—"

"Go! We can't afford to lose her."

With a last glance at the serpent, Kit vanished into the floor. Caim crouched and backed away as more of the creature's body emerged from the ceiling. All the while it moved closer, its great eyes stalking him. Caim studied its movement. Like him, the serpent was a predator. It would keep maneuvering closer until it pushed him into a corner. Then, in a sudden rush, it would lunge.

He retreated step by step. His ankle was throbbing. He drew his other *suete* and waved the knives back and forth to draw the serpent's attention, but its gaze never left his face. Caim got the uncomfortable feeling the creature wasn't a dumb brute, but possessed some semblance of intelligence. He remembered the invisible beast that had torn apart the Blue Vine. Was this it? Had this thing somehow come from him?

As he backpedaled onto the cushion of the woven-reed exercise mat, a pulling sensation stirred behind his breastbone. A familiar tingle of energy ran down his spine. He didn't need to seek out his fear; it ran through him in terse, nauseating waves. The shadows wanted to come out and play, but he pushed them away, back down into the dark recesses of his mind from whence they came. He couldn't afford the risk. If he had inadvertently summoned this creature, calling upon his powers again might make matters worse. What if more appeared?

The room shortened as the inky serpent backed him toward a corner. Caim ran through his options. The only window was shuttered and locked, but the front door hung open. He could make a break for it. The beast was large. He might be able to outrun it. As if sensing his thoughts, the serpent looped around to block his path. Caim's shoulder brushed against a target bag suspended from the ceiling. He didn't have much time left. A few more steps would bring him to the wall and nowhere else to go. He eyed the scaly hide and wondered if cold steel could even harm it. There was only one way to find out.

He lashed out with his left hand and set the target bag to swinging. The serpent kept coming for him, lowering its head to stay out of the arc of the swaying bag. Caim took a quick step to his right and punched another bag. As it swung toward the creature, he crept sideways toward the window. When the serpent reversed course to cut off his escape, he attacked. He lunged with his right-hand knife extended, the point aimed at the serpent's blunt snout. As the creature reared back, Caim threw himself forward onto his knees. He slid underneath its bulk and thrust upward with his left-hand knife. Its point skittered along the monster's belly, unable to pierce the tough scales.

Caim gasped as the pressure in his chest returned, twice as strong as before. Unprepared for the sudden onslaught, he almost lost control. Every muscle in his body tensed as he fought his powers. They clawed against the walls of his mind like a pack of sewer rats trying to escape the rising tide. Above him, the serpent reared.

Caim leapt away, evading its curved fangs by inches, but the creature looped around and pulled him close. So quick, it flowed like a rushing stream. Pain blossomed around his rib cage as the rippling, muscular body wrapped around his middle. His legs strained under the enormous weight. The knife fell from his left hand and he stabbed at the beast over and over with the right, but it had no effect. Every breath was a struggle. Black spots appeared before his eyes. His muscles slackened. And still, his powers fought for release. Caim clamped down on them with every scrap of resolve he could muster. This battle had become more than a struggle for release. Either he would control his abilities, or they would control him. His lips stretched back in a grimace as he strained.

Then, as suddenly as it appeared, the pressure vanished.

Its abrupt departure left a hole in Caim's chest, a void that bothered him almost as much as the pressure had, but he had more urgent concerns. The serpent had looped another layer of coils around his midsection. Its crushing embrace threatened to squeeze him in two. He reached up with his free hand. The giant wedge of the creature's head swayed above him, just out of reach. His fingers found purchase at the back of the neck. Smiling through the pain, he struck.

The serpent shuddered as the knife pierced its eye. Caim tried to hang on, but the writhing coils flung him about like an infant. A mighty convulsion threw him across the room. Battered, he lay prone on the floorboards. His lungs burned as fresh air hit them. The serpent thrashed in the center of the floor, his knife still stuck in its eye socket until its violent throes hurtled the weapon free.

Caim crawled to his knees, but the creature had given up the fight. Black ichor dripped from its ruined eyeball as it undulated into the far corner of the room. Draped in shadows, it vanished like the remnants of a dream, and the eerie sensation with it.

Caim climbed to his feet. He ached from neck to toe, but he had survived. He tore his gaze away from the corner and hobbled to the door, down the hallway. The girl had a good lead on him, too damned good by half and him with an injured foot, but how well did she know Low Town? Not at all, most likely. He glanced through a grimy skylight as he passed under it. Night had settled over the city. That worked to his advantage. The darkness would make her flight more difficult. She might wander the Gutters for hours before finding her way to a landmark she could recognize. If Kit was doing her job, he would find Josephine in plenty of time, unless someone else found her first. An image of the girl, cornered in an alley by a Low Town street gang, blasted through his mind as he reached the stairwell. He leapt down the steps three at a time, heedless of the burning pain in his ankle. Down the stairs and across the foyer. He shoved open the heavy door.

Knives bared and ready for anything, he limped out into the night.

CHAPTER TWELVE

Fog swirled around Josey's ankles as she dashed across the slick cobblestones. The night's cold went right through her nightgown. She had to find help. But who would aid her? She didn't even know where she was. Shabby buildings leaned over the street like drunken titans. Where were the streetlights? Impenetrable darkness swathed everything.

She went to the nearest door and found it locked tight. The windows were dark. She pounded on the thick timbers, but didn't wait for an answer. The killer would be right behind her. She dared not glance over her shoulder. If she saw him, chasing behind her like the shadow of Death incarnate, the fear would paralyze her.

A faint clink of metal echoed in the fog somewhere ahead. Josey couldn't identify the sound in the dark, but she was past caring. Anything was better than falling back into the clutches of her father's murderer.

She ran toward the noise. Her breath came in short gasps. A nimbus of spectral light illuminated an intersection of three streets. At their nexus stood a man holding a lantern, the point of a pike glittering above his head.

"Who's that?" he called out.

Tears sprang to Josey's eyes as she made out the black coat of the night watchman's uniform.

"Help me, please!" she cried.

The watchman raised a hand to his lips. A whistle's shrill call cut through the gloom and fog. More watchmen appeared behind him. Josey staggered toward them. Leather-clad arms caught her as she swooned. Piercing eyes stabbed at her from behind steely faceplates.

"She ain't no Gutters wench," said one. "Think she's the one we was told about?"

"What's your name, girl?" asked another, rolling his *r*'s with a thick western accent.

Josey drew in a deep breath. Her heart bounced hard against the inside of her ribs. "I am Josephine . . . of the House Frenig. Please, help me."

The westerner nodded. The stripes sewn onto his sleeve marked him as a higher rank than the others. "We've been looking for you, m'lady. Your disappearance has caused quite a stir."

Josey allowed herself to nestle in his arms. She wanted to cry. It was over. She was safe. Then she remembered what the killer had done to the men in her father's bedchamber.

"There's a man after me!" she said. "He's dangerous. He killed my father."

"You're safe now, m'lady. Can you walk?"

"Yes, I think so."

She leaned on the watchman's strong arm and let him escort her down the street. The lantern-holder led the way. She glanced over her shoulder, but there were only fleeing shadows. She let out a cleansing breath. *He's gone. He can't get me now. But I'll see him hanged, for Father's sake.*

Caim. That was his name, the name of a dead man. She tried to convince herself it was over as the watchmen fell in around her, but the memories of her trials buzzed inside her head like a swarm of cicadas.

There was no sign of the girl at the intersection of Winder and Silverpike Row.

A night fog had rolled in from the bay to blanket the cobblestones. Two shapes slouched in the alley across the way. He couldn't tell if they were drunk or dead, but both were decidedly male and not his girl. He'd heard footsteps running in this direction, but the fog caused weird echoes, making noises difficult to pinpoint. He wished Kit would return with some good news. He was a blind man searching for a hare in a field of willowtails.

His foot burned where he'd been bitten. His toes squished with every step as his boot filled with blood. Was it envenomed? Probably not. A snake that big would pump out enough poison to kill a herd of warhorses. He tried not to think about it.

A glowing shape appeared from a nearby alley.

"Did you find her?" he asked.

Kit shook out her silver hair. "She's not in Buckwald Den or Dyer's Lane. I doubt she could have gotten farther than that before me."

Caim shifted his weight to his good leg. The pain was moving up his calf.

"Is it bad?" Kit glanced down.

"Not bad enough to stop me. We have to get her back. We can't have her wandering into the wrong hands."

Kit rested her fists on her slim hips. "She's probably already facedown in some alleyway. The ragpickers will find her body tomorrow. You need to forget about her and get back inside so I can take a look at that foot."

Caim squinted down each street and tried to pierce the darkness for any clue that might lead him in the right direction. The events of the past twenty-four hours had ripped him from his comfortable life and sent him veering into unknown territory. He didn't like the feelings of unease and doubt knocking around in his gut.

"Kit, what was that thing back at the apartment? Did it come from me? My gift . . . powers . . . whatever they are, they've been acting strange lately."

Kit floated a few inches off the ground, her outline blurring with the fog. Her eyes turned dark and unfathomable, the way they did when she didn't want to pursue a subject. She could be downright obstinate when she chose to be. He stared back until she finally relented.

"It's called a *queticoux*," she said. "And no, it didn't come from you. At least, I don't think so. They're rare. I'd never actually seen one up close before. They live Beyond."

"Beyond?"

"Beyond the barrier separating this world from the Shadowlands."

Caim gripped his knives tighter. She was talking faerie realm nonsense again—ghouls and goblins, bogeymen who abducted children and left changelings in their place. Ridiculous. *But you've seen the shadows yourself, haven't you?* He ground his teeth together. His thoughts were scattered in a hundred different directions tonight. Shadows. Mathias. Spoiled rich girls out alone in the dark. He had to focus.

"Okay. So how could such a thing cross over?"

"It couldn't." She twirled a finger through her hair. "Not on its own. It would need help to cross the Veil."

He pretended to know what she was talking about. "You mean like sorcery?"

"I suppose."

"How could a High Town lord's daughter do that? She didn't strike me as a witch. Hell, if she knew magic, why didn't she use it to escape?"

Kit shrugged. At the same instant, a keening whistle cut through the night like a siren's wail. It sounded like it came from Three Corners. Caim started running. Kit didn't need to be told; she skittered ahead of him like a shiny pebble across a smooth, black pond. A filament of concern threaded its way into Caim's chest, winding tighter around his insides with every painful stride as the whistle led him farther away from the Processional and High Town.

Josey shivered.

Her feet felt like blocks of ice on the freezing cobblestones. The four watchmen stood tall around her. Their hobnailed boots rang loud upon the street, a comforting sound in the late hours of the night. She was protected. Safe. Her father's killer couldn't touch her now. By morning she would back at home, wrapped in familiar surroundings. A new sense of courage settled over her. She had survived kidnapping at the hands of a vicious lunatic, navigated the treacherous streets of Low Town, and found succor. After she settled her father's affairs, she was determined to put her life back in order. Perhaps she would obey his dying wish and leave Othir, go to Navarre or Highavon. Maybe even find a suitable husband. After this night's events, the idea of remaining in this city had lost its allure.

Ensconced in her thoughts, Josey didn't realize the direction they were taking until a muted roar caught her ears. It sounded like a forest of leaves rustling in a windstorm. The streets had become even more fog-clogged, the cobbles shrouded under a wispy mantle, but she could tell they were heading away from High Town, away from her home.

She spoke up. "Where are we going? I live on the Esquiline."

The lead watchman removed his helmet. Tall and sturdy, he cut a fine figure in his uniform. He possessed a rugged face, but kind in its own way. His bright hazel eyes gleamed in the lantern light, and Josey found herself wishing he was noble born. With regret, she pushed her thoughts away from that direction. Any man she married would come from a proper family to suit her station.

"Orders, m'lady. We're required to report to our station commander."

He said this with natural aplomb, but tossed a wink to one of his comrades. Josey's throat tightened painfully. Could it have been a twitch or a trick of the light? No, she had seen it. Something whispered in the back of her mind. Caim had said the soldiers at the manor had been after her, but she hadn't believed him. How could she? Who would believe the words of an admitted killer over the honor of the Church's duly appointed officers? Her father had been a great champion of the law. Yet as she walked among her guardians, she took notice of their silence. Shouldn't they be trying to reassure her? Why hadn't they asked for the identity of her kidnapper? They hadn't even made a cursory search for Caim. Her stomach flipped in sickening loops.

Shouts rose and fell in the distance as they passed down an avenue of boarded-up storefronts. Noisome odors mingled with the fog. A stream of brown water trickled across their path, dammed at the center by a large lump. Josey put a hand to her mouth and swallowed as she made out the body of a dead dog, its fur matted and crawling with maggots. Pottery crashed on the street behind them. Throaty laughter cackled in the dark. The watchmen brandished their weapons as they hurried her along.

She clutched the leader's arm. "I am not feeling well. Might we head to High Town at once?"

None of them answered. They turned onto a new street, and a gust of fresh salt air met Josey's nose. She drew in a deep breath to clear the miasma of the streets from her lungs as cobblestones gave way to coarse wooden slats. A boardwalk wended between a row of long whitewashed buildings to her right and the black void of the open sea. The briny air sang with the slap of waves against worn pilings and stone quays. Tall masts of ships secured in their moorings swayed to the roll of the breakers, empty as beggars' bowls.

Josey slowed as the watchmen started down the boardwalk. Their leader tightened his grip on her arm.

"Sir, unhand me!" she shouted aloud in the hope that some sympathetic ear might overhear.

The watchmen laughed, all chivalry dropped from their demeanors. Josey bit down on her tongue as the leader leered at her. How could she have imagined kindness in his brutish eyes? He dragged her along with alarming ease.

At first glance, the harbor was empty of people. Then, a point of yellow light appeared over the spit of an ancient wharf. As she was drawn closer, Josey made out a gang of men gathered under the light. Their coarse laughter echoed through the night air. Josey's legs shook as she spied the symbol emblazoned on their tunic. She would have fallen if she wasn't held up.

Every man wore the golden sunburst of the Sacred Brotherhood.

The lead watchman thrust Josey into the circle of light. Tears ran freely down her face as cruel gazes raked her body. Why was this happening to her? Wasn't it enough that she had lost her father? Must she also be molested by these brigands? She knew what these men lusted after, and knew she was powerless to fight so many of them. She looked around, hoping to spot some passerby, someone who would hear her screams, but they were alone. Her stomach twisted into knots as she realized she should have listened to her father's killer.

A tall man shouldered his way through the crowd. Josey sobbed as a familiar face appeared.

"Markus!"

She tried to go to him, but rough hands threw her down on the pier's hard boards. Josey stared up at Markus, her lips parted in a silent appeal. Spots of blood showed on the bandage wrapped around his neck. One look into his eyes told her that she would find no succor with him. Suddenly, she was terrified for Anastasia.

Markus ignored her. "Where did you find her?" His voice was low and coarse, like grinding millstones.

"Three Corners." The westerner grinned at Josey in a way that made her insides tremble. "She ran right into our arms."

"Anyone follow you?"

"Nah. The streets were empty. What'll we do with her?"

Markus pulled a sloshing green bottle from inside his coat and thrust it at the watchman. "Go take a walk and forget you saw her."

"Wait!" Josey wailed, but the watchmen marched off without giving her a second glance.

Once they were gone from sight, Markus signaled to the others. "Get rid of her. No mistakes."

Josey bit her lip. A scream fluttered in her throat, but her mouth refused to work. Her fingernails scrabbled across the wooden spars.

A broad-chested Brother with a shaggy red beard stepped forward. "Hell, we can't waste a cunny like that! I'll have a crack at that before we finish her off."

A raucous chorus of chuckles greeted the pronouncement. Josey backed away as Red Beard reached for the ties to his baggy breeches. A wall of sturdy legs halted her retreat. She shut her eyes and prayed harder than she'd ever prayed before, for deliverance from this horrible night, for the sweet embrace of unconsciousness, even for death before she must succumb to this nightmare.

Markus produced a coil of rope and tossed it on the ground. "No messing around. Just kill her and get it done with. She'll wash out with the tide."

The men grumbled, especially Red Beard, but they grabbed Josey and set to binding her arms and legs. A rusty iron weight was produced and secured to her ankle. The men carried her down the short dock. One of her bearers took the opportunity to knead her buttocks. Josey's sobs had grown to near convulsions, but the waves crashing against the pilings drowned out her mews. She tried to kick and only succeeded in making them laugh.

"Be quick about it," Markus rasped. "And slit her throat before you dump her off the end."

"Let me do it," a skinny Brother said. His ropy lips turned up in a grin as he pulled a long dirk from his belt.

They put her down on the weather-worn boards, and someone yanked back her head. Josey lifted her eyes. Stars sparkled overhead, blurred by her tears. She panted in terror. *This can't be happening!* But it was. She was going to die.

Josey braced herself for the touch of the steel. The waiting seemed to last for ages. Then, something warm spattered the side of her face. The hands holding her let go. Boots pounded on the pier. She lifted her bound hands to wipe away the wetness. Three Sacred Brothers sprawled on the slats, bleeding out their wretched lives. The rest watched the night with their swords out.

Caim!

She knew right away it was him. Her suspicion was proved correct when Red Beard fell at her feet with his throat sliced open. A sliver of bloody steel flashed in the dark and was gone, only to reappear on the other side of the melee to drink again.

Josey struggled with her bonds. If she could get free while they fought, she might be able to slip away in the confusion. Her gaze fell on the slim dagger sheathed on Red Beard's belt. She scooted over to his corpse. Suppressing her revulsion, she caught hold of the leather-wrapped hilt and tugged the knife free, then began sawing at the thick rope that bound her wrists. Strand by strand the rope parted. Though the blade was sharp, her range of movement was limited and she had to hold the knife at an awkward angle. Josey sobbed with relief when the last piece gave way; she went to work on the loops binding her ankles.

The fighting continued around her and more men died. Caim was out there, killing to save her. For the second time, if he'd told the truth. Josey's head spun. She ought to be terrified out of her mind as the man who had killed her father, or *would* have killed him, battled her present captors. And yet, she was calm. Something had changed within her. The darkness didn't frighten her as before. She brushed the thoughts away. Caim was an admitted killer. Why would he care to keep her alive? He must know she would go straight to the authorities, the proper authorities, as soon as she was free. He had to have an ulterior motive, some secret he was keeping from her.

She almost cut her leg as the dagger slipped and sliced her nightgown. She concentrated on severing the rope's last fibers. Once free, she scrambled to her feet. Her escape from the pier was blocked by the melee. From what she could see, only Markus and a handful of his men remained, but it would only take one to notice her and finish the job.

As Josey took tentative steps toward the edge of the combat, a shadow emerged from the dark. It swept past the swarm of men, evaded their attacks, and raced down the wharf on whisper-quiet steps. Hard gray eyes peered from the depths of a deep hood. Josey was relieved in a way she'd never thought she would be. Caim grabbed her around the waist as he ran by and snatched her off her feet.

"Wha—!"

He leapt.

For one marvelous moment they were airborne. The bay breeze swept up her hair in its cool fingers as she floated in the night sky. She clutched Caim about the shoulders, and let her fingers roam over the play of powerful muscles beneath his black shirt.

The steely twang of a bowstring broke the spell. Josey felt the impact as Caim jerked like a giant fist had punched him in the back. The force of the blow knocked their trajectory askew. Instead of a graceful landing, they hit the dark waters like two falling stones.

The impact knocked the breath from Josey's lungs. She gasped, and icy seawater flooded her lungs as their combined weight pulled them under the surface. She struggled against Caim's grip, but his arm remained locked around her waist.

Her limbs grew heavy; her thrashing slowed. She screamed out her last precious bubbles of air as the choking abyss closed around her.

CHAPTER THIRTEEN

Caim collapsed at the water's edge, unable to crawl another foot. Every movement sent spasms of red-hot agony racing through him. The frigid bay waters had leeched away the last of his strength and left him a shivering mass of exhaustion.

Echoes of lapping water reverberated off stone walls, barely discernable in the darkness. After hitting the water, he had managed to find one of the submerged sewer pipes that carried effluvia into the bay. An iron grate had once barred the entry, but it'd rusted away long ago—a convenient access into the city he'd discovered a few years back while prepping for a job.

He took a deep breath and regretted it as a tremor of pain wracked his body. He hadn't heard the crossbow fire, but the bolt's impact had almost been enough to kill him outright. He managed to hold on to consciousness long enough to swim down deep into the inky waters, away from their enemies. No one had followed them. No surprise there. Whoever shot him must have thought it was a killing blow. Unfortunately, time might bear out that assumption. He'd lost a lot of blood. He could tell by the way his hands shook when he tried to pull himself out of the water that he wouldn't survive long without a chirurgeon, but he wasn't likely to find one down here. Even if he could walk, it wouldn't be safe. He knew a couple of cut-men who would treat an injury like this with no questions asked, but they might be compromised. Whoever was behind this fiasco had proven to be both intelligent and savvy.

A weak groan murmured behind him. Caim pulled himself over to the girl. She lay half in the water, facedown. He rolled her over despite the agony it caused him. Her nightgown was a tattered mess, stained with blood, mud, and worse. The wet silk clung to her body like a second skin.

Yet she had the heart of a lion. She hadn't screamed while he fought her captors or cowered at the sight of blood. Instead, she'd gotten hold of a knife and cut herself free.

The girl's teeth chattered between blue lips. The pipe was freezing, but Caim didn't have anything to make a fire. *This is where I'll die.* He had been dealing in death for so long it held little mystery for him. He would close his eyes and drift away to the sound of the water. It was probably a better end than he deserved. With one hand on the girl's stomach, he listened to her breathe. She would live, at least. For some reason that made him feel better.

A voice intruded on his solace. He smiled as Kit descended through the ceiling. The violet glow of her tight smock illuminated the tunnel, showing ancient walls caked with mud and lichen. The grime of the sewer didn't touch her. Caim had often wished he could fly like her, just take off and leave the world behind. He could never understand why she hung around with him when she could be soaring among the clouds. Kit said it was because he needed her, that without her he would get into all sorts of trouble. It seemed she was right yet again.

"Caim, what have you done to yourself?" Kit asked in a choked voice as she alighted beside him. Strangely, she seemed more concerned about his foot, which throbbed on the periphery of his awareness.

Before he attacked the Sacred Brothers holding the girl, he had told Kit to keep an eye out for trouble, but she had flown off in a huff. That was Kit, always marching to the rhythm of her own song. She hadn't changed a dram in all the time he'd known her. His whole life. Now she would watch him die. The thought made him laugh, which turned into an excruciating grunt.

"I had a little help." His throat was dry and cracked. That struck him as funny with all the water lying around him, but he refrained from laughing. He put on a brave face for her. "It's not that bad."

"Yes, it is. We need to get you to a barber."

He ran the fingers of his left hand through his hair. "You think I need a trim?"

"Don't play games, Caim. This is serious."

"It'll all be over soon. We had a good run, Kit. No one can say we didn't."

She *tsk*ed at him. "It's not over yet."

"You going to carry me out of here, Kit? That would be something to see."

She turned to the girl. "She's stirring."

This time Caim couldn't hold back his laugh, but it came out in a hissing cough as coppery bile bubbled in the back of his throat. "You think she's going to help me, Kit? She couldn't weigh more than seven stone soaking wet. Even if she could, why would she? I'm the bad guy. Just let me be."

With a sigh, Kit rested her head against his chest. Soft sounds echoed in his ears—either sobs or chuckles, he couldn't tell which. It was getting hard to keep his eyes open. He closed them knowing they would never open again. The sweet escape of oblivion beckoned.

"So long, darling," he murmured as he drifted away.

Josey dreamed she was lounging up to her chin in a giant, warm raspberry pie floating in the midst of a gorgeous, starry sky. Surrounded by gelatinous filling, she watched the twinkling stars streak by. A feeling of utter tranquility filled her. All was well.

Opening her eyes was like a slap in the face. She lay on a slanted plane of cold, coarse stone. Her legs floated not in warm sugary goodness, but in foul, frigid water that lapped at her thighs like a gaggle of icy tongues. Wherever she was, it stank worse than anything she'd ever smelled before, a combination of garbage and night soil and blood. Every breath made her want to throw up.

With shaking hands, Josey pulled herself out of the water. Her whole body felt like one massive bruise. The last thing she remembered was being knocked off the pier and the black water swirling over her head. She must have washed up here, wherever this was. No sky stretched over her head. There was a breeze of sorts, but it was fetid and moist. Perhaps she had floated into an old cistern. *No, not a cistern.* By the smell, she was in some section of the sewers. The urge to retch came over her again.

Josey clamped her lips tight against the nausea and tried to crawl farther, but froze as a groan echoed beside her. Wild fancies of trolls and hobgobs flashed through her mind. Was she still dreaming? Water dripped in the distance, making her want to use the privy. She almost laughed. She was in a gigantic water closet. A little more urine wouldn't hurt the smell, but a lady didn't answer the call of nature out in the open.

She crawled until she was out of the water entirely. The groan rose again before drifting away. It was nearby. Josey sat up on her knees, trying not to think of the damage to her nightgown. She had a dozen of them at home. She would burn this one as soon as she escaped from this horrid place. Whatever was making the noise, it didn't sound dangerous. It reminded her of a wounded animal, like a squirrel, but bigger. *A big rat.* She started to shy away until a raspy cough echoed around her.

It's him.

Josey had almost forgotten the reason she was still alive and breathing. Her father's killer was here with her, and by the sounds he'd suffered for his efforts to save her. He sounded sick.

"Hello?" she whispered.

Her only answer was another wet cough. Inhaling through her mouth, Josey crawled in the direction of the sound. She found him slumped against a damp wall. He, too, was drenched in foul water and chilled to the touch. She thought he was dead until he coughed again and his chest moved beneath her hands. She searched him with timid hands and found a patch of warm wetness on his right side, a gaping hole plugged with a wooden shaft as thick as her thumb, right beneath his ribs. He mumbled something, but she couldn't make it out. She leaned closer.

"Go."

Josey sat back on her heels. Her first impulse was to follow his advice and leave, but to where? She couldn't go to the authorities. That much was clear. And now that her father was gone, she had no family. Friends? She had only one true friend in Othir, Anastasia, but as much as she loved the girl, Josey didn't believe 'Stasia could help her. For one thing, her father was elderly and infirm, and he hadn't been active in politics for a long time. Also, Josey didn't want to drag her friend into this nightmare.

She considered the man lying before her. She could leave him here to die. It was no better than he deserved. He had probably murdered a lot of people—people with families and friends who cared about them. He was the most despicable sort of man, one who killed for money. He had no honor, no couth, a sore on the flesh of humanity. Yet he had saved her life. Twice. And he claimed he hadn't killed her father, though he would have if someone else hadn't done it first. If that was true, then whoever really killed her father had escaped free and clear, and this assassin dying at her feet might be the only one who could find out who did it and why.

Josey made up her mind. She had to save him, tend to him until he was strong enough to protect her again. But how? She was a good swimmer, but she didn't think she could pull him through the water back to the pier. What if those men were waiting? No, she couldn't go back. That left only one direction. She stared into the darkness of the tunnel. Far in the distance a tiny light flashed, like the brief burst of a firefly, but it was enough to show her the way. What was it? Some fearsome creature of the deeps or an angel sent from Heaven? Either way, she was out of choices.

Josey stood up and hooked her arms under the assassin's armpits. She tugged as gently as she could until he rested flat on the ground. Then, she pulled. Her feet slipped on the slimy floor of the pipe and her muscles complained of the unaccustomed exertion, but she kept pulling toward the distant light.

before the empire reasserted itself on the world stage, emerging from its own ashes like the legendary phoenix. Now, centuries later, those ruins festered beneath the city, only seen from above whenever somebody's cellar caved in. This chamber may have once been part of a villa, or a food merchant's shop. Somehow the girl had carried him here, or dragged him more likely. Still, it was no small feat for such a tiny waif. The lantern looked like an antique, probably leftover from the days of the empire, but it still had some oil in the reservoir. Another miracle. It would be nice to die with some light.

As he looked around, Caim almost missed Kit sitting in the far corner, arms around her knees. She watched him with sad, tearful eyes. He offered what he hoped was a cheery smile, but the pain transformed it into a grimace. The frown she tossed back at him didn't hold much hope. Good old Kit. She never pulled any punches.

"Thank you," he mouthed.

Josephine frowned as she glanced into the corner where Kit sat, and then turned back to regard him with a pensive expression. "What are you looking at?"

"Why did you help me?"

She shrugged, a simple raising and lowering of her shoulders, but he could see the pain behind her eyes. It raged like a beast within her, a feeling he knew all too well.

"What else could I do? You're hurt."

"You could have left me."

"Maybe I wanted to look into your eyes as you died."

He took a deeper breath and let it out. "You don't seem the type, Miss Frenig. But I'll do my best to make it quick."

"Caim!" Kit chided through a veil of tears.

"Call me Josey."

"All right, Josey. You'll get your wish soon enough. Just keep that lamp burning a little while longer."

"You can't die. I need you alive."

Caim couldn't stop the racking laugh that erupted from his belly. When he had recovered from the agony that almost sent him reeling back into the darkness, he ventured to speak again.

"I'd sooner believe the first answer," he said. "You're harder than you look, Josey. So, now you get your revenge. After I'm gone, go find somewhere safe. Get out of Othir if you can."

"Where can I go? I can't go to the authorities. I don't know who will try to kill me next. Whom should I trust?"

"Trust no one."

"What about you?"

"Especially not me. I don't know what to tell you. Go back to your lord father's estate until things settle down. Or find a nice farm boy and start a family."

"I don't want to run." She glanced down at her hands resting in her lap. "I want to find out who killed my father. For that, I need your help."

Caim tested his strength by pulling himself up into a sitting position. The wound didn't pain him much when he moved slow and took small breaths.

"I'm no use to anyone anymore, girl."

She gazed back at him. Wetness gathered in the corners of her eyes. He hadn't realized how green they were, like glittering jewels. Even bedraggled and mud-stained, she was beautiful.

"Those men meant to kill me, and Markus is part of it," she said, softly as if she couldn't believe the words coming from her own mouth. "But you risked your life to save me. You're all I have."

Caim closed his eyes. Deep inside his chest, the old anger smoldered. He wasn't ready to relinquish this life. He had things to do yet, debts that needed settling. The dream loitered in the back of his mind, and the vow he'd made on that night with his father's blood on his hands. Somehow, other things had gotten in the way of fulfilling that oath, but he saw it clearly now. His life up to this point had been a path toward that goal, if he lived to see the end.

"You'll have to get the bolt out."

"What?" She shook her head, sending her straggly ebon locks flying in all directions. "No. We'll find a physician. There's got to be a way out of these sewers."

"I'll never make it. I'm losing too much blood."

"But I don't know how to do that. I've never—"

He reached under his back and drew a knife. He held the blade up to the light. "This is a good time to learn."

She recoiled from the weapon. "No, I can't. We need help."

Caim hissed. The pain was spreading up his arm and through his chest. He flipped the knife and offered it to her, handle first.

"I'm running out of time. You can't make it any worse than it already is. Don't worry. I'll talk you through it."

She took the *suete* with both hands. "You've done this before?"

He peeled off his tunic, careful not to jar the shaft of the bolt, and rolled onto his left side to give her better access to the wound.

"Not exactly." As the apprehension returned to her eyes, he added, "But I've cut open enough people to know where the important parts are."

She looked at the knife in her hands, and for a moment he thought she would balk, but her brow came together in a determined frown.

"All right," she said. "I'll try."

Caim let out a long breath. "First thing, get that lantern down here. You'll need to be able to see what you're doing."

She did as he instructed and set the lantern on the floor beside him.

"Now open the shutter and hold the edge of the blade over the flame for a few seconds." When she looked askance at him, he said, "It cleanses the blade. The wound is probably going to get infected in any case, but no use in stacking the odds."

"Should we wash your side first?"

"Not with any water you'd find down here. And we'll need something to pack the wound afterward."

Josey set down the knife and reached under her skirt. Caim watched with amusement as she rocked and shimmied. A petticoat of delicate lace appeared, only slightly damp and shielded from the worst of the effluent by her nightgown.

"That will have to do," he said. "Now, it's time to start cutting."

"It's so deep." She peered into the hole in his side. A dewy sheen of perspiration beaded on her cheeks and upper lip.

"Don't think of it as flesh you're cutting. Think of it as a piece of meat."

She put a hand to her mouth. "I'm going to be sick."

He grabbed her wrist hard. The bones under her skin were thin and sharp. He forced his voice to remain calm.

"You can do this. Just start cutting until you can see the steel head."

She nodded and he released her. He clenched his jaws together. The first cut, when it came, didn't hurt as bad as he feared. The wound was already throbbing so terribly he hardly noticed. He tried to distract his mind while she worked. He thought about where they might be in the undercity, how they could find their way out, and where they should go if they did.

As he was considering how to get them both out of Othir, a wave of coolness fluttered over his injured foot. He glanced down to see Kit kneeling beside him, her brow furrowed as she ran her hands over his foot. He opened his mouth to ask what she was doing when a sharp pain stabbed his side. His hands curled into fists as he struggled to hold himself still. Josey gnawed her bottom lip as she worked with the knife point. Rivulets of blood ran down his stomach and formed tiny pools on the floor beneath him.

"I see it!" she said. "I see the head."

Caim let out a slow breath. "Do you see any barbs curving back to you?"

"No."

"That's good. All right. You'll need to make small cuts on either side, just enough to pull it free. Now grip the shaft near the head and . . ."

Caim's vision dimmed as Josey tugged on the bolt. He pressed his forehead against the floor and focused on staying conscious, but his exhaustion and the blood loss conspired against him. He was fading. As he tried to describe how to dress the wound, the rising darkness swept over his head and carried him away on its inexorable tide.

Ral turned away from the window's roseate glass panes. The morning light, usually so soothing, gave him a headache.

"Tell me again." He pressed a hand to his temple. "How did they escape from you and a dozen of your best men?"

Occupying the entire upper floor of the Golden Wheel, Ral's suite was decorated in a style more fitting to a fine manor house than a gambling hall. He had chosen the furnishings himself, everything from the brass fixtures and window treatments to the expensive carpets. The walls of the main living area were painted in terra-cotta murals. His favorite faced him across the room, a vivid rendition of the hero Dantos descending into the underworld to rescue his dead bride. It was an image Ral found inspiring. Sometimes he thought of himself as a tragic figure like Dantos, doomed to fight impossible forces to get what he justly deserved.

Markus stood at attention before him. A white bandage peeked over the collar of his uniform. Ral was beginning to wish Caim's blade had cut a little deeper. The prefect was incompetent. Worse than that, Ral still needed the man for his connections in the Sacred Brotherhood. But that need would evaporate as soon as Caim and the earl's daughter were found. Then, Second Prefect Arriston would meet with an unfortunate accident. Ral smiled at the prospect.

"He came out of the night like a demon from hell," Markus said in a raspy voice. One of his hands stole up to touch the bandage and dropped back to his side. "I swear the man is a wizard. Half my men were down before we even knew he was there."

"So much for the prowess of our city's vaunted defenders." But the words lacked fire. Ral knew he had been sending lambs to the slaughter when he instructed Markus to organize a citywide manhunt. Still, Ral had expected better than this debacle.

"Find your backbone, Markus. Caim is just one man. Don't tell me the Brotherhood can't deal with a single lowborn thug. What will I tell the archpriest?"

"One of the Brothers got off a shot as they went into the water," Markus said. "I think it hit him."

"You *think*?"

"It was damned dark out there."

Ral clasped his hands together to help resist the urge to bury a stiletto in the prefect's eye socket.

"And what are you doing now to find the fugitives?"

Markus shrugged and grimaced as the gesture jostled his throat wound. "I've got men dredging the bay, but its slow work. I need more manpower."

"Then get more men!"

"I'll need more money for that."

"I've already paid you more than your life is worth. Find the girl, Markus, or your men will be dredging the bay for you next."

Markus left the suite. Ral listened to the click of his boots descend the stairs to the hall below. If Markus didn't find Caim soon, he would have to take steps to improve the situation. He didn't like his options. Vassili wasn't a forgiving man, and Ral had burned too many bridges over these past few months to remain in Othir if their scheme failed. As much as it galled him, he might have to leave the city. Ral hummed a mournful ballad as he contemplated the mural of Dantos.

The tickle of a cool breeze on the back of his neck was his only warning. He stood perfectly still, every nerve quivering. The window had been shut a minute ago. He flexed the muscles of his right forearm to loosen the throwing blade strapped under his sleeve. He shifted his weight to his right foot in preparation for a quick spin-and-throw, but stood very still as a sharp point pressed against his spine, right between his kidneys.

"Sit," a voice whispered in his ear.

Ral took two slow steps and lowered himself into an antique, slat-back chair. His unexpected visitor stepped to the center of the living area in plain view. The hood of a night-black robe concealed his features. For a moment Ral thought Caim had come for him, and an icy caress slid down his back. But the stranger was too tall and rather thin, though broad through the shoulders. His hands were tucked into the sleeves of the robe, lending him the semblance of a cloistered monk.

Ral palmed the throwing blade. It would be an easy toss from this close, and his sword leaned against the armoire if he missed. He started the motion when his gaze rose to the shadowed depths of the stranger's cowl. A weird sensation rolled over him as he tried to penetrate the darkness inside the hood, like looking up at the night sky, into a darkness that went on forever and forever. The icy feeling returned. He lowered the weapon. He had seen this man before, in the shadowed chambers of the palace. Vassili's pet sorcerer. A cold dread washed over him.

"You work for the archpriest."

"I am Levictus."

Ral shifted in the chair and forced his lips to form a small smile. Many men had trembled to see that smile just moments before their deaths.

"Tell your master I am doing everything I can. We'll find Caim and the girl. Don't wor—"

"I come on my own behalf. With an offer."

What was this? Ral sat up.

"For many years," the sorcerer continued, "I have worked tirelessly in the archpriest's service, but in recent days I have come to discover that his aims no longer reflect my own."

That was interesting. Yes, very interesting indeed. "You mentioned an offer."

"I seek a new partner, one whose goals are more closely aligned with my own."

"So what brings you to me?"

The cowl dipped slightly. "You are ambitious. You chafe under the yoke of servitude, just as I do. Separate we are formidable, but together . . . there would be nothing to stop us."

"There's Vassili and the Church. And the Sacred Brotherhood. Even without a grand master, they aren't going to sit idle and let us take over."

Levictus drew up straighter and the room suddenly felt too small for the both of them. Ral squeezed himself farther into the chair.

"The Church is not as unified as it appears," the sorcerer said. "The prelate's gaze is turned across the sea. The electors are divided by their lusts. As for the Brotherhood, you already possess the leverage you need."

"Markus."

Ral worked his tongue around his mouth to drum up some moisture. He didn't like feeling small. He hated it, in fact, worse than anything else he could think of. Yet there was something to this figure standing before him, an awful power he could not deny, and one he dared not ignore. "And His Sublime Radiance?"

"All men die, the small and the great alike."

Ral tapped his fingers on the arm of the chair. Despite the theatrics, this man meant business. The deadly serious sort. The kind of business he enjoyed best.

"Sounds like you have it all figured out. What do you need me for?"

The sorcerer loomed closer. "The archpriest's plan was too timid. We will eliminate the Elector Council, down to the last priest. Then, as the only powers left in the city, we collect all the spoils."

"Is that all? Do you want me to knife the Holy Father himself while I'm at it?"

The intruder said nothing.

"God's balls, you're serious! Listen. I didn't mind working for Vassili. He made me certain assurances, but what's my end of this grand scheme?"

The other leaned forward. Despite his best efforts, Ral pressed back against the chair to keep the distance between them as a sibilant whisper issued from the dark cowl.

"I will deal with the prelate, but it is time for Nimea to regain her soul. For that, the realm needs a strong hand on the reins. You were content to accept the scraps from Vassili's table. Would you pass up the chance to hold this entire city in the palm of your hands? Unfettered. Answerable to no man. For once, your own master."

Ral sucked in a deep breath. "How—?"

Levictus extended a scroll sealed with a dollop of black wax. Ral reached for it as though it were a serpent. The parchment was stiff and strangely textured as he unrolled it, like cowhide but much smoother. With a start he realized it must be human skin. He held it aside so he could watch the man while he read.

"These are your new targets. Complete this task and all that you desire will come to pass."

Ral read through the list and appreciated the straightforwardness of the plan. Yes, it could work. With these individuals out of the way, there would be no one left to defy them. If this man could be trusted to do his part. Ral wished he could see the sorcerer's eyes. This was a risky gambit, but the rewards were beyond anything he had previously dreamed. Governorship of the greatest city in the world. He would have everything he had ever wanted: respectability, money, prestige.

"What about funding? An operation such as this—"

The sorcerer opened his other pale hand, and a stream of coins spewed forth like a fountain. "Do we have an accord, Lord Governor Pendarich?"

Ral gaped at the fortune in gold and silver rolling across his carpet, and up to the sleeve from which it had come. The hairs on the back of his neck tingled. *Lord Governor Pendarich. I can live with that.*

"I accept."

Heat flared in Ral's hand and he dropped the scroll, which had erupted into sizzling flame. He coughed and waved his hands. When the smoke cleared, the scroll and Levictus were gone.

Ral stood up. Long shadows filled the corners of the room despite the bright sunlight that shone through the windows. Thirteen square boxes rested on the table beside his armoire. Identical in appearance, each was constructed of a creamy wood, beach or maybe white pine, bound with brass fittings.

Ral went over to investigate. Fearing some trap, he abstained from touching them at first, but then his impatience got the better of him and he lifted one of the lids to peek inside.

He swallowed as he shut the box. An unsightly business, but necessary. He looked at his hand. A black smudge marred the smooth patch of skin between ridged calluses. He rubbed it on his shirt, but the mark remained. With a frown, he held it up to the light.

In the center of his palm gleamed a silhouette of an ominous black tower.

CHAPTER FIFTEEN

Caim awoke on his side with one hand tucked under a pillow. Thoughts drifted through his mind like clouds through a murky gray sky, memories of his wild days riding with Jame's band of marauders. The brawls, the comrades, the sultry nights in Brevenna where every woman was a beauty and the wine never stopped flowing. Sometimes he missed those days. They were a more innocent time in his life, a time when he'd never had to watch over his shoulder unless it was for an angry husband or a suspicious lawman, and either could be dealt with by coin or blade. He wondered what had happened to the fiery-tempered rogue he had once been.

He rolled onto his back and stretched, fully believing he was home in his cot until the shifting of the soft mattress beneath his frame made him sit up in alarm. The piercing agony that ripped through his side drove away the last vestiges of sleep. He groaned and settled back on the mattress. His stomach did a little flip when he opened his eyes. The pink walls, the frilly lace canopy, tin ornaments on the shelves polished to resemble silver. The smells of rose petals and talcum. There was only one place he could be.

Madam Sanya's Pleasure House on Paradise Lane.

It was a bolt hole he had used a few times in the past to recover from arduous jobs or just to clear his head. By the slant of the sunbeams filtering through the window slats, it was early morning. Sounds drifted in from the street—people talking, bartering, and arguing over the hum of the city. A familiar scent floated in the air. Another look around confirmed it. He was in Kira's room, and he wasn't alone.

Josey sat in a chair beside the bed. Part of him was amazed to see her. He would have wagered she'd come to her senses before now and taken off. Another part of him was irked. He was losing his edge if he could sleep soundly with someone else in the room.

She had changed outfits, replacing the tattered nightgown with a maroon off-the-shoulder kirtle. It was a decent fit, if a little tight across the bosom. High, buttoned boots peeked from beneath the hem of the flaring skirt. He marveled at the spoiled aristocrat's daughter, who probably spent more on shoes in a sennight than most people scraped together in a year, sitting in a whore's bedchamber in a borrowed dress and looking absolutely gorgeous. Though he wasn't partial to red, the color brought out the glow in her cheeks. He couldn't look away, and didn't say a word for fear he might lose this moment. He felt her beauty tightening around his soul like a web of steel. Then, he thrust it away before the spell could settle over him for good. It was harder than he expected.

His good feelings faded under her fierce glare.

"You brought me to a . . . a *bordello*!"

Kit dropped from the ceiling and plopped on his bed without disturbing the covers. "Hey, look who's finally awake! You gave me a good scare, Caim. Don't do it again."

He cleared his throat and started to sit up, but stopped himself. He was naked. Worse, he couldn't remember how he'd gotten that way. Kit couldn't touch him and Josey . . . He banished the thought. Surely, she hadn't . . .

"You look, um, very nice," he said, and meant it for both of them.

"Don't say a word about the dress."

Kit snickered.

"I was just—"

"Not a word!"

"Fine."

"Good!"

He was glad to hear the fire in her voice. The things she had seen in the past couple days would have broken many people, especially a young woman from the fair streets of High Town. But Josey had responded with good instincts and poise. Unfortunately, those fine attributes wouldn't count for much if they were found. Twice now the Sacred Brotherhood had come for Josey, and had risked a great deal to see her dead. Twice he had saved her. Laid up with a hole in his gut, he didn't want to find out if three was his unlucky number.

"Actually," he said, "you brought me here. I was in no condition—"

"You gave me the directions!"

A knock at the door broke off whatever he was going to say next. A cold wave of dread washed over him as he tried to sit up again, and he clenched his jaws as a ripple of pain tore through his side. Where were his knives? He spied a familiar strap hanging from the bedpost by his head and grabbed for it just as the door opened. A familiar face peeked in. Caim suppressed the urge to groan again. Instead, he pulled the bedsheets up to his chest. Of course, it had to be Kira. He should have known.

Kira beamed at him as she swept into the room with a wooden tray and set it on the nightstand beside the bed. Caim returned a small smile, not wanting to appear impolite. After all, he and Kira had spent more than one night together in this very room on the few occasions he had felt the need for companionship.

Kira ignored Josey as she stood over him. "How are you feeling, Caim?"

Josey's mouth tightened in a way that made Caim glad to have his knives close at hand. Kit grinned like a cat with cream on her whiskers as she reclined beside him and watched the exchange.

The door opened again to admit the lady of the house. The panels of her lavender gown were wide to accommodate Madam Sanya's exceedingly ample bosom, which threatened to spill out of the low-plunged collar at any moment. It was widely whispered that she had been a great beauty in her youth, the most sought-after courtesan in Othir. Caim could almost believe it. A striking woman still lurked in the depths of her apple-shaped face, but she had been concealed under too many layers of makeup.

"All right, Kira." Madam Sanya made with a shooing motion. "Out now. Leave them to their rest."

The girl departed, after shooting another heated glance at Caim that earned him further mouth-tightening from Josey.

"I'm sorry about that," Madam Sanya said. "That girl can be a proper pain in the backside, but she's popular with the men."

"No." Josey came to her feet. "She's been very generous, as have you all."

Madam Sanya gave a lovely chuckle that could have come from a much younger and slighter lady. "It's no problem, darling. Caim is a good friend of the house. We're glad to help."

Josey leveled a bemused gaze at him. "Oh? Is he a regular at your establishment?"

Caim cleared his throat, ready to defend his reputation, but Madam Sanya didn't give him the chance. "Not quite a regular, but he's helped us out of some unpleasant situations. Not every man is a gentleman like Caim. Some have to be convinced to behave themselves, but it's just me and my girls here. I've never kept a bruiser at the door, and I never will if I have my way."

Arms crossed over her chest, Josey studied him with a mysterious expression like she was weighing him on some invisible scale. He didn't like the look one bit, but naked and abed there wasn't much he could do about it.

"Once," Madam Sanya continued, "we had a real hard case in the house, a Hvekish sellsword with more muscles than brains. Well, he hadn't been upstairs with Abilene for more than ten minutes when I hear an awful commotion. He was beating the vinegar out of the girl. Some men are just like that, mean to the core. Anyways, I sent Suri to fetch help, and she came back with Caim just as quick as you please. Without a word, he goes upstairs. We heard a mighty ruckus, but I was too scared to go up and look myself, not till afterward. There was Abilene, all busted up and bleeding like a lamb at market, but alive. The sellsword was stretched out with enough holes in his gullet to sink a man-o'-war. We threw the body out back with the garbage. Since then, everyone knows to keep civil in my house."

Caim changed the subject. "What's the latest, Sanya? Anyone looking for us?"

"Well, most tongues are flapping about the murders up in High Town."

"My father," Josey said.

Caim saw the pain written on her face and felt a stab of remorse. He hadn't killed her father, but he would have, and the knowledge of that made him feel just as guilty as if he had been the one holding the knife. Not for the first time, he reconsidered the direction his life had taken. Was it too late to give it all up? Would anyone ever see him as anything but a killer? Would he?

"You said *murders*, Sanya. There's been more than one?"

"Three all told," the madam replied. "Two was members of the

Elector Council, killed in their own homes and no one's seen nothing. The whole city is buzzing about it. Personally, I think it's one of them southern death-cults at work. Did you hear about how that high priest got his head cut off down in Belastire? And by one of his own servants, mores the worse."

Belastire? That rang a bell in Caim's head. Someone had mentioned that city to him lately. Then he remembered who—Ral. *Rotten bastard, what are you up to?*

"I tell you," Madam Sanya said. "People are crazy these days, worshipping snakes and cats. Anyway, there's more tinmen on the street than I've seen in twenty years on the Lane. Someone will be hanging in Chirron's Square come sunset, mark my words."

"You didn't answer my question, Sanya," Caim said. "Is anyone looking for us?"

The mistress of the house gazed down into her generous chest. "Some say it's you behind all those killings, Caim. They say you've gone mad. But I don't believe it. You've been nothing but a gentleman to my girls and me."

"Thank you," Caim said. "For everything."

This time it was the big woman's turn to blush. She did it with grace and left, closing the door behind her.

"What does it mean?" Josey asked.

"It means someone is making their move."

"What kind of move?"

Thoughts tumbled around in Caim's head like pieces of a giant puzzle, each obscure on its own, but all of them hinting at a bigger picture. Othir had always been a hotbed of backroom dealings and political intrigue. Unrest had been the watchword since the day the Church deposed the last legitimate emperor and installed itself as the new regime. It was one of the reasons Caim had chosen here for his base of operations. Turmoil was lucrative in his line of business. Now it worked against him. With the rumors flying about, he couldn't go anyplace he was known. Madam Sanya had taken a big chance letting them stay here.

His gaze moved to Josey, seated once more in the ladder-back chair. Her proud features were out of place in the cheap room. He was missing something, some bit of vital information sitting right in front of him.

"Your father. You said he was a governor."

"The *exarch* of Navarre, but he retired when I was little and we moved to Othir."

"My contact told me he was a general responsible for ruthless massacres in Eregoth."

A look of horror crossed her features. "My father never harmed anyone."

"Sure," Kit murmured. "I bet her old man was a pussycat. Probably ate like a king while his people starved in the streets."

Caim shook his head. Kit pouted, but he didn't care. This wasn't the time for a debate on social injustice. He was onto something. He could feel it, like a fish wriggling on the end of a line.

"So he wasn't a military officer?"

"No, he was never in the army. He had a lame foot since childhood."

Caim considered that. Mathias wasn't one to make careless mistakes. He was purposely misled, and by someone he trusted.

"You think my father's death is connected to these other murders?"

"I don't believe in coincidence. The same person who set me up at your father's house is somehow involved."

"How does that help us? We can't go to the authorities. The Sacred Brotherhood is trying to kill me, and you're wanted for about a thousand crimes."

"When was the last time you saw your father alive?"

He instantly regretted his boorishness as bright spots of moisture formed in the corners of her eyes. To her credit, she didn't break down.

"Earlier that day in his study," she answered. "We had an argument."

"About what?"

"He wanted me to leave the city. He said it wasn't safe for me here. He wanted me to take a trip abroad. He said he would send for me when things got better."

Caim sat up and received a sharp reminder of his condition. He ignored it. He didn't have time to be hurt. "Did he say who he thought was such a threat?"

"No." A hint of gold sparkled under Josey's neckline as she ran a hand over her forehead. "I told you. My father was a well-loved man. We never had trouble like this before."

Caim wrapped the blanket around his waist and swung his legs over the side of the bed. He thought better on his feet. He exhaled slowly as tiny slivers of agony crawled under his skin. Josey started to get up, but he waved her away. Using the bedpost for support, he managed to stand up on his own. The first step was uncomfortable, but it got easier after that. Kit hovered at his side. Whatever she had done to his ankle, it felt a world better.

As Caim shuffled across the small room, he tried to think of other avenues of information he could pursue. When he reached the wall, he turned back. "Did your father have a mistress?"

"Of course not!"

He grimaced as another jolt of pain rippled through his side. "Forgive me. I'm trying to find loose ends."

"What?"

"People who may have been involved with your father. Associates, business partners, lovers. People who had a vested interest in his survival, or his death. Most assassinations are arranged by close relatives."

"That's atrocious!"

"That's human nature."

"Well, it's disgusting. I—" Josey looked at the floor.

Caim halted and watched the play of thoughts across her face. "What is it?"

"The day my father died he was talking with a man, someone I'd never seen before. I didn't think much about it at the time. My father had many well-wishers. But there was something odd about the conversation."

"What?"

Her shoulders fell as she leaned back in the chair. "I don't know. I just got the feeling they didn't want anyone to overhear what they were saying. My father was never a secretive man. He told me everything."

"Except that."

"Yes. It bothered me at the time, but I forgot about it in the heat of our argument. When I found you in his bedchamber that night, I was coming to convince him not to send me away."

He felt the urge to touch her, perhaps brush the strands of hair from her face, but he suppressed it. "Was there anything odd about this man? A feature you'd recognize again. The way that he spoke—"

"Keys." She looked up. "He had a pair of keys stitched on his breast, crossed like a pair of swords."

"Does that symbol mean anything to you?"

"No." She slumped back in the chair.

He scratched his bristly chin. "Me neither."

"This is pointless," Kit complained. "She doesn't know anything, Caim."

He shushed her and got an odd look from Josey. Then, a sudden inspiration made him smile. He headed toward the pile of his clothes on the dresser. "But I think I know someone who can help us."

"Wait a minute!" Kit jumped up to bar his way. When he passed right through her, she spun around and floated past his head. "Enough is enough, Caim. You've done your civic duty. You rescued the wench and gotten yourself shot in the process. Now let's do the smart thing and get out of this place. East, west, across the sea—I don't care which direction as long as it's away from here!"

"I can't," he replied.

"What?" Josey asked.

"Nothing. Listen, I'm going to go meet this person. I want you to stay here. And don't leave this room."

"You're crazy!" Kit said.

"I'm not staying here," Josey replied.

"Be quiet!" he shouted. To Josey, he said, "It isn't safe on the streets. You'll be better off here."

Kit crossed her arms across her chest. "Since when did you start caring about other people, Caim?"

He almost choked when Josey adopted an identical posture. "It's my life," she said. "You're not my father. You have no right to tell me what to do."

Caim sighed. This wasn't fair. No man should have to put up with this much harassment.

"Fine," he said. "But you can't go out like that."

Josey lifted the skirt of her borrowed dress. "What's wrong with this?"

"Oh, the dress is fine." He winked at Kit as he put on his pants and the figments of a plan coalesced in his head. "But the look's not complete yet."

Savoring the confusion on their faces, he hobbled over to the door and called for the lady of the house.

CHAPTER SIXTEEN

Step, clack, slide.

Caim kept his head down as he shuffled through the door to the Blue Vine. A grimy, rust-colored robe covered his leathers, compliments of Madam Sanya, who had closets full of clothes left behind by old clients. The robe's deep hood concealed his face. A cane, gnarled and fire-blackened, completed the ensemble.

Step, clack, slide.

He winced as he stepped into the wineshop's cool interior. His side pained him, but by leaning on the cane and dragging his right foot he could get around reasonably well, and the limp made his mendicant act all the more convincing. He just hoped he wouldn't have to leave in a hurry like last time.

The disguise had been his idea, but in truth he'd had little choice in the matter. Kit and Josey both agreed he shouldn't leave the brothel room without one. They argued that he wasn't up for fighting if it came to that, and he didn't disagree. Of course, his knives rested against his back under the heavy robe just in case.

His disguise, while serving admirably in the streets, was severely out of place in the Vine. As soon as Mistress Henninger noticed him, she rushed over with a look of alarm.

"Out you! There'll be no begging in here. Come round back later on and Cook will see if we have any scraps for you."

Caim winked from under the hood. "Relax, Mother. It's me."

She sucked in a deep breath, which threatened to burst her bodice. Thankfully, she kept her voice down. "Caim? You in trouble, sweetling?"

"Nothing I can't handle. Got a table for an old friend?"

"An old friend, eh? Of course."

Caim looked around as he followed the wine mistress. Nothing had changed in the Vine. He had half expected to see the place in shambles after his last visit, but whatever he released from the shadows hadn't caused as much damage as he feared. Except for some new holes in the grimy wattle, the place looked the same as ever.

Then he noticed the empty tables. It was past midday, a time when the Vine would normally be filling up. Yet there were only a handful of patrons scattered through the common room. Caim hid a grimace of discomfort as he slid into a hard wooden chair.

"Some wine?" Mother asked. "I got a good Calamian in stock this week."

"Just a small beer. And Mother?"

"Yes?"

"Don't hassle the chit in the red dress."

"What?"

Caim nodded in the direction of the front door, where Josey stood. With shutters over the windows and smoky hanging lamps, the Vine was kept dim. Everyone who entered paused for a moment on the stoop to let their eyes adjust. It was an effective way to size up newcomers, which was one of the reasons Caim liked the place. That, and Mother never watered down the drinks.

As he'd said at Madam Sanya's, the dress hadn't been enough of a disguise, but now even her own father, had he been alive, wouldn't recognize her. Her jet black locks had been dyed with henna and chamomile. The resulting hue was a peculiar shade of reddish gold that was actually rather fetching. The whole coiffure had been pulled up into a gravity-defying design that drew eyes away from her face, the only change to which was a sassy beauty mark nestled in her left dimple.

"As you say, sweetling," Mother said as she eyed Josey. "I'll just go fetch your beer."

While Mistress Henninger waddled off to the bar, Caim watched Josey survey the room. Kira and Madam Sanya had tried to give her some pointers on how to act like a lady of the streets, which Caim observed with much amusement until they booted him from the room. When Josey emerged an hour later, all dolled up like a courtesan, he was genuinely surprised. She strutted ahead of him on the way to the wineshop and looked every bit the part.

Of course, Kit had been furious. She argued every step of the way, rattling off the many reasons Caim should cut his losses now while his head was still attached to his neck and flee the city for greener pastures.

"Don't let that pretty face fool you," Kit said. "And don't think I haven't noticed the way you've been watching her! She's just using you. She'll leave you high and dry the first good chance she gets."

He listened to her tirade all the way to the Merchant Quarter before he lost his temper and muttered some very pointed things about meddling spirits and the ugly head of jealousy.

"Fine!" she said. "I guess you've made up your mind."

With that, she left in a puff of sparkling silver dust and he hadn't seen her since. Now he regretted his words. He didn't have enough friends that he could afford to lose one, but Kit would be back once her temper cooled. Sooner, he hoped, rather than later.

As he watched Josey saunter around the room, lingering at the occupied tables, Caim began to think she was enjoying the charade. That is, until she turned in his direction and transfixed him with a venomous glare. Thankfully, Mother arrived in time to save him. While he handed her twice the price of the drink, plus a sizable tip for the inconvenience, Caim caught Josey's gaze and jerked his head to a nearby table.

She stalked across the taproom and alighted gracefully into a chair. She started to sit up like a proper lady until she saw his expression and slouched, hips thrust forward and legs dangling askew, the perfect picture of a bored streetwalker taking her ease. Mother avoided looking in her direction, but every other eye in the place was plastered to her every move. That was exactly what he wanted. If they salivated over the lusty whore, they wouldn't notice the noblewoman behind the act.

The sound of the door swinging drew Caim's gaze back to the entrance. He breathed a little easier at the sight of Hubert. After the way they had been forced to flee the last time they'd met, Caim had feared the young man wouldn't show. He signaled.

Hubert came over. He grinned as he took in the disguise. "Going back to your roots, Caim?" He helped himself to a seat at the table. "Or shouldn't I be using your real name?"

Caim set down his half-empty cup. "It's safe enough here, but I'm trying to cover my tracks."

"I was a little surprised to get your message. I thought you were done with us. To what do I owe the pleasure?"

"Mathias is dead."

Hubert's smile vanished. "What happened?"

"Someone dealt me a poisoned job, and then went back to make sure I couldn't get more details from Mat. Now they're after me. And my friend."

"Friend?"

Caim gave a slight nod in Josey's direction. Her seat was close enough to overhear their conversation without appearing obvious. She looked Hubert up and down before turning away with a bored yawn.

"Hubert," Caim said, "meet Josephine."

"She's lovely." Hubert's eyebrows rose. "A friend or a *friend*?"

Josey's smile curled up into a feral smirk as she pretended to examine her nails.

"Careful," Caim said. "She bites."

Hubert tipped his hat in a way that included Josey, or perhaps he saluted the entire room. "Charmed, milady. Hubert Vassili."

Josey frowned. Out of the side of her mouth, she whispered, "Vassili?"

Hubert nodded. "No doubt you've heard of my father, the archpriest."

Josey inhaled sharply. Caim glanced around the taproom. Few in Othir dared to talk openly of the Elector Council these days. People had been known to disappear for voicing opposition to their edicts.

"Do not be alarmed, milady." Hubert touched the blue feather in his hat. "Despite my father's office, I am a sworn enemy of the theocracy that holds our fair city in bondage."

He called for a drink as he turned back to Caim. "Say, are you behind those funerals up in High Town?"

Caim gave the young man his best deadpan face. "No."

"Ah, just as well. So I gather you've got a problem that you need my help to solve. Let me guess. The lady has a jealous husband?"

"Not exactly."

"A jealous pimp?"

Josey's smile became a strained grimace as a patron approached her with a lecherous smile and a cocky swagger. Caim slipped a hand behind his back, but Josey rejected the fellow with a dismissive flick of her fingers. Not precisely in character, but it worked. The man turned around and went back to his table with a glum frown. Mother shot Caim a frown of her own as she hustled over to soothe the jilted lover with a fresh flagon of ale. Message received. She didn't want any more trouble in her place. He needed to hurry this up.

"I'm trying to find someone. A city official, maybe high up." Caim gave a brief description of the man Josey had seen in her father's study, complete with the sigil stitched into his clothing.

"Crossed keys?" Hubert asked as a decanter of wine arrived with a semiclean glass. "That would mean a minister of the Church treasury. From what you've told me, I'd guess you're talking about Ozmond Parmian. He's the assistant to the keeper of the Holy Coffers."

Caim digested that for a moment. "Any idea why he would be meeting with a retired exarch just hours before that respected man should be killed?"

Hubert tasted his wine and made an unpleasant face. "You're talking about Earl Frenig."

Caim's nod was so slight as to be almost imperceptible.

"Oh ho! Caim, you've gotten yourself into a real wasps' nest, haven't you? Old Frenig had his hand in all sorts of interesting business."

Josey spun around on her chair. "If you're insinuating he had anything to do with underhanded dealings, you're severely mistaken, sir! He was a—"

Caim held up a hand. "Josey, I'll handle this. You're drawing attention."

Hubert looked between them. "Josey . . . Josephine." His eyes widened. "As in Lady Josephine of House Frenig?"

"One and the same," Caim said. "Now you see my problem."

Hubert sat back in his chair and scratched his forehead. "Maybe better than you do. You're frogged seven ways to Sun Day, my friend."

"Tell me something I don't know. Like this Parmian guy. Was the earl dealing with the prelacy?"

Josey stiffened in her seat, but Caim ignored her. He didn't have time for niceties. They could be found out at any moment. He had no illusions about what would happen if they were caught. He'd never make it to Castle DiVecci's infamous dungeons. A convenient accident would silence his involvement in this matter for good, and Josey might not survive much longer.

"That's the thing," Hubert said. "Frenig was well known to be an active opponent to the Church, one of the last loyalists to the old imperium. That's why he was recalled back to Othir."

"He retired!" Josey hissed under her breath, loud enough to make Mother jump as she passed by with a tray of drinks.

Hubert shook his head. "I beg your pardon, milady, but that's not how I heard it. The Reds didn't like some of the things he was saying and so they cancelled his commission. His choices were return to Othir where they could keep an eye on him or be branded an enemy of the people."

"It doesn't make any sense. Parmian is a bright star in the prelate's administration, but he wouldn't treat with someone like Frenig. It would be a death sentence if he was ever found out."

Caim's gaze wandered around the room. The place was filling up as people got off from their day's labors and sought solace in a wine cup. "We have to get hold of this guy. He knows something about the earl's death."

"I can help with that," Hubert said. "Let me contact a few friends and we'll set up a meeting."

"Is Mr. Parmian going to know about this meeting?"

Hubert tipped back the last of his wine and stood up with a flourish of his silk-lined cloak. "Not until it's too late."

"Good. You can send word to me at Madam Sanya's."

Caim nodded to Josey as he got up and shuffled toward the door. She followed him outside, where a crowd had gathered. People holding lit candles and sticks of burning incense marched down the street. Then, he saw the coffins: six boxes of raw pinewood.

Caim pulled down the hood of his shabby outfit and led Josey down a side street, away from the procession. His side ached something fierce. It put him in a foul mood. His palms itched for the handles of his knives. He almost wished to see a squadron of red uniforms converging on him.

The sky was clear, its cerulean perfection marred only by the smoke of the city's chimneys, but he could feel a storm coming. He searched every passing face and glanced down every alley in expectation of an ambush. Only the soft patter of Josey's boots at his back kept him from melting away into the dim recesses of the city. He continued his tottering, stumbling gait while the anxiety grew inside him.

By the time he sighted the gauzy festoons of the pleasure house, his nerves were scoured raw. And he had to admit, even though she annoyed him to distraction, he missed Kit. Wherever she was, he hoped she was all right.

He went around to the brothel's back entrance. As he made his way around puddles of mud and offal, Caim tugged his hood down a bit farther. The sun was dipping in the west. Suddenly the night didn't feel so friendly.

Step, clack, slide.

CHAPTER SEVENTEEN

Caim rubbed his hands together in the dark alleyway and tried to ignore the cold. A frigid southerly had blown in from the bay, sending the inhabitants of the city's better neighborhoods home early for the evening. The windows of High Town's homes glowed cherry red around the edges of their lowered shades as families gathered indoors. Caim cursed them one and all for their comfort and wished he'd thought to bring a flask of something warm.

"It's freezing out here." Josey huddled next to him in a long wool coat, another loan from Madam Sanya. Underneath, her pretty dress had been replaced with a boy's tunic and breeches that didn't quite fit. A linen scarf hid her nose and mouth. Caim fought the urge to grin at her, the very image of a dainty little bandit.

Hubert breathed into his folded hands and nodded. He wore a mask, blue of course, smelling of whiskey.

"Nice and brisk. A good night for some fun."

Caim grunted. This wasn't his idea of fun. It was business, down and dirty. He meant to have some answers tonight, even if it meant exposing Josey to the rougher side of his trade. He didn't have time for civility. One way or the other, Ozmond Parmian would give him what he needed.

As Caim peeked out from the mouth of the alley, he wished for the hundredth time that he'd been more diplomatic with Kit. She would return, of course, in a day or a month, whenever she got bored of wandering the byways of the world. She always came back. Once he had remarked that she was too much in love with him to stay away for long. Now, he wasn't so sure. Recent events had put a strain on their relationship, and Josey's presence didn't help. Caim didn't understand why it should matter. It was like she was jealous, but Kit was immaterial, a ghost without the cares and troubles of the physical world. Yet sometimes she confused him every bit as much as a flesh-and-blood woman.

The streets below Sabine Hill were quiet, with only occasional revelers out to enjoy the evening air, but he couldn't shake the uneasy feeling that had settled between his shoulder blades. Like he was being watched.

Hubert had brought along a few of his "friends." One skulked in a doorway on the other side of the boulevard. From time to time a ruddy glow illuminated the man's hiding spot, probably from a tinderbox brought to warm his hands. Caim exhaled a jet of white steam into the night air.

Amateurs.

"How dependable are these men?"

Hubert's answering shrug raised and lowered the stiff collar of his twill jacket. "They're all good men, handy with a cudgel or a knife in a scrap, but they won't stand up to armed soldiers."

"I don't think it will come to that."

"I thought you said we were just going to talk to this man," Josey said.

A sharp whistle saved Caim from the need to respond.

"That's the signal," Hubert said. "He's coming."

Caim reached under his cloak and eased his knives in their sheaths. He hoped Josey was right. He wanted answers, not more bodies, but anyone who didn't prepare for the worst was as good as dead in this city. She'd have to learn that sooner or later.

A gate stood at the end of the street, a remnant from Othir's younger days when the city was much smaller. Rough umber bricks composed a wide archway inset with bronze doors. A flicker of light emerged from the gate, followed by footsteps. As the glow came nearer, Caim made out two figures. A linkboy in a white tunic held a lantern on a pole for a narrow man wrapped in a long gray jacket. Their footsteps clacked on the cobblestones as they approached the intersection where Caim and Hubert had positioned their ambush.

Hubert started to move, but Caim grabbed him by the sleeve. "Not yet."

"Sorry," the young aristocrat replied. "I always get a bit jumpy before some action."

Caim glanced to Josey. "Is that him?"

She studied the figure coming toward them for a moment, and then nodded. "Yes. He's the one."

Caim waited until the target was directly between the alleys. He motioned for Hubert and Josey to stay behind him as he glided out from his hiding spot. The Church man never saw him coming. The linkboy looked up, but not until Caim was within arm's reach, too late to do more than give a tiny squeak before Caim threw his left arm around the target's throat. The point of his knife touched the man under his ear, firmly enough to get his attention, but not to draw blood. The linkboy stood like a statue, his eyes stretched wide open. They fluttered as a fist bashed into his cheek and sent him to the ground. The lantern smashed on the stones as Hubert, rapier drawn, loomed over the boy and delivered sharp kicks.

Josey flew out of the darkness. She shoved Hubert aside and knelt beside the fallen servant. "He's just a boy. Help me get him up."

With a sheepish look to Caim, Hubert hooked an elbow under the boy's arm and helped Josey walk him to the alley.

Caim got there first. He pressed his captive against a wall with a knife point against his neck. "Are you Ozmond Parmian, assistant to the treasury keeper?"

To his credit, the man held himself erect. He stood a couple inches taller than Caim, but his slight build and sloping shoulders made him seem smaller. The symbol of crossed keys was displayed prominently on the breast of his jacket. Caim noted a silver chain under his collar and two rings of plain gold. He wore no weapons on his person, not even a knife.

"I am not in the custom of answering street ruffians," he answered. "Unhand me."

Hubert dropped the linkboy against the wall. Josey knelt at the boy's side and dabbed at his bleeding lip with her coat sleeve.

"Yep." Hubert's breath puffed through the fabric of his mask. "That's Ozmond in the flesh."

"Do I know you, sir?"

Caim nudged Hubert back a pace and shifted to put himself between them. The young man meant well, but his presence could be a hindrance.

"Why did you visit Earl Frenig's home two days before his death?"

"You have no right to interrogate me," Parmian replied. "I promise you, the night watch—"

Caim pressed the knife tip deeper. "The watch is too far away to help you at the moment, and a moment is all you have left if you don't answer me. Why did you go to see Frenig? Was the earl involved in a government plot?"

"Who are you working for? Whoever it is, I'll see that you receive more if you will just release me."

Caim scratched the man. A bead of blood trickled down into Parmian's collar.

"Frenig despised the theocracy!" Parmian said, almost shouting.

"Quietly," Caim admonished.

Parmian drew in a long breath, but shallow so as not to impale himself on Caim's knife. "If you had known the late earl, then you would know what I say is true."

"I knew him." Josey came over to stand beside Caim. "Very well, in fact. And you're right. He despised the Church and what it had become, although he didn't air his grievances in public. How did you know him?"

Parmian took in Josey with a long glance. "The late earl was a family friend. He'd known my father many years ago. He helped me achieve my position in the treasury. I visited him on a social call."

"From what I've been told"—Caim leaned closer and dropped his voice to a whisper—"it didn't sound very social. It sounded like an argument."

When Parmian didn't reply, he moved the knife point to the groove of the man's neck, where the big artery throbbed. "I'm losing patience, Master Parmian."

Something changed in the man's eyes. A bulwark of resistance crumbled and he collapsed against the wall. Caim pulled the knife point back to avoid killing him by accident.

"I went to warn him."

"About what?"

Parmian's eyes shined as he lifted his head. "The Elector Council was moving against him."

"That makes no sense," Josey said. "He was retired, a hero of the realm. Why would they want to kill him?"

Parmian hesitated a moment, until Caim caught his attention with a pinprick. "They'd found out about his activities."

"What activities?"

Parmian drew in another deep breath. "Earl Frenig was the head of a secret society sworn to restore the empire."

The words hit Josey like a runaway coach.

She reached for the alley wall, forgetting for a moment about the crud and grime coating the bricks. "You're wrong," she said. "My—the earl withdrew from politics after he resigned his post."

If Parmian caught her slip, he gave no indication. "I'm sorry, but it's true. My father was a member of the same society before he passed."

No, no, no! The denial echoed in her mind, but deep inside she knew it was the truth. After all, she had seen it herself.

Hubert whistled. "No wonder the Council did him in. They've got enough trouble on the streets without the nobility trying to bring back the old regime."

"Shut up!" Josey shouted, much too loudly, but she didn't care.

She spun away as Caim looked at her. She couldn't face him like this. Cold splatters fell on her face like the pieces of her world falling apart. The hidden chamber beneath her family home appeared in her mind, just the same as it had looked all those years ago. The hooded participants of the bizarre ritual stood in a circle in the dim light. Their chanting echoed across the gulfs of time.

Her hand crept up to the cool talisman dangling between her breasts. Her father had said it was the key to his heart, a sentimental gesture she had thought little of over the intervening years, but it had been more than that. She knew now what the key truly was, what it would unlock.

Caim's voice intruded on her thoughts. "So you were their spy."

"No," Parmian answered. "I never wanted any part of their schemes. I'm little more than a glorified accounting clerk, but I see everything that crosses the keeper's desk, and everything that happens in the city eventually makes its way through the treasury. We control the funding. When I saw the indications of a coup, I went to warn the earl. For my father's sake, I felt I owed him that much."

"I don't buy it," Caim said. "Why try to resurrect an extinct regime?

What's the point? The emperor and his family were killed when the Church came to power."

"I was just a kid," Hubert said, "but I remember. They called it an execution, but it was murder, true and simple. Anyone related to the imperial family was either eliminated or forced to show their support for the prelate."

Parmian's voice regained some of its initial confidence. "When I spoke with him, the earl said he possessed a secret, something so powerful that if it was revealed, it would bring down the Church."

"What secret?" Josey blurted before she realized what she was doing, but she had to know.

Parmian shook his head. "He never told me. He said it would be safest if kept to himself until the time came to unveil it. Those were his exact words."

"What else?"

He lifted his empty hands, but dropped them as Caim applied more pressure with his knife. "That's all. I urged the earl to leave Othir as soon as possible."

"What do think, Caim?" Hubert asked.

Parmian perked up. "You're Caim? The one they're searching for?" He looked at Josey. "Then you're . . ."

A bevy of whistles split the night. A cry went up from a nearby roof as hard footsteps pounded on the cobblestones. Josey wrapped her arms around her body, but her shivers had nothing to do with the cold. She couldn't catch her breath. She felt like she was running, so fast her lungs might burst, but her feet never moved.

"We're done here," Caim told Hubert. "Take your men and disappear."

"Sure. I'll go rally the rest of the boys. Once word of this reaches the streets, every hand will rise against the Reds."

As Hubert disappeared into the night, Caim turned back to Parmian. The man stood up straight, his shoulders squared as if expecting the worst.

"What do you intend to do with me? My family will—"

Caim stepped back. "You can go."

The man didn't move. "Just like that? I know who you are. I could have every able-bodied soldier in the city searching for you."

Caim sheathed his knife. The whistles were getting closer. "Can't you hear? They already are. Go home, Ozmond, and think about taking your own advice. Things are heating up. Othir's going to be a very dangerous place, no matter which side you support."

Caim turned away, but Parmian stopped him. Josey watched a host of emotions play across the treasury man's face. He grimaced, shook his head slightly, and then settled into a look of resignation.

"Wait. There's something else."

He looked at her. "The order to have the earl killed came from the highest level."

Icy fingers constricted around Josey's windpipe. She couldn't breathe. *What did he mean, the highest level? The Church hierarchs? The prelate himself? They killed Father, and now they want to kill me.*

She gasped and shook. Then, Caim put an arm around her and the air rushed once more into her lungs.

"Come on," he said, pulling her away. "We have to get out of here."

Josey leaned into him and felt his warm breath against her cheek. She needed the contact, to feel the touch of another living person. She felt like she was surrounded by ghosts. She looked back over her shoulder, but the alley and Parmian were gone, hidden in the night. For the first time, she realized it was raining.

"I know," she said. They hurried through the slick, black streets. "I know where we have to go to find the next piece to the puzzle."

Caim regarded her with an amused expression. Something flickered across his eyes, too quick to follow. A blossom of heat spread through her chest as she realized she trusted him.

She turned her head as the warmth spread into her face. She gazed into the sky, into the rain and gloom, to the heights of Esquiline Hill.

"I have to go home."

CHAPTER EIGHTEEN

Ashadow crouched by the riverbank where a gentle breeze pushed through the riparian jungle of rushes and cattails. Dark masses of silver-black clouds scudded across the starless sky. Somewhere an owl hooted, and the shrill howl of a coyote carried on the wind.

Amid the Memnir's sleepy currents, where the river slid past the fortified walls of Othir, Castle DiVecci perched on a spur of bare rock. The castle's white parapets loomed over the water like cliffs of alabaster in the waning moonlight. Banners hung slack from the sturdy towers.

A stone span joined the isle to the mainland, guarded at both ends by a gatehouse manned by soldiers of the Prelate's Guard. Othirians called it the Bridge of Tears for all those who had crossed and disappeared into the dungeons beneath the castle, never to return.

The shadow had no need of bridges. One moment it stood on the riverbank. The next, it appeared inside the castle's mighty donjon, in a hallway on the top floor.

The shadow listened as its sandals touched down. The rhythm of the castle was slow and steady, like the heartbeat of huge slumbering beast, broken only by the discordant groans of the damned far below in the catacombs.

Content, the shadow began to hunt. It crept past rows of closed doors and paused as it came around a corner. Firelight spilled from a doorway at the end of the hall. Two bodyguards in white-and-gold livery stood outside, leaning on the polished shafts of their immaculate halberds.

One of the guards looked up as the shadow approached, but too late to give warning as a swarm of inky globules dropped from the ceiling. The men jerked and tried to shout as the shadows wrapped them in tight cocoons, but nothing emerged from their straining mouths. The little darknesses devoured them in silence.

The shadow stepped over the dying men, through the doorway. Shelves of books lined the chamber walls from floor to ceiling. Logs crackled behind an iron grate in the broad hearth. A water clock on the mantelpiece dripped out time's passage. Above the fireplace was mounted a graphic bronze sculpture portraying the Prophet of the True Faith. The half-starved demigod hung by a noose on a twisted rope with an expression of supreme sorrow etched on his long, pained face.

The crackle of paper drew the shadow's attention as a thin hand, spotted with age, appeared over the arm of a massive cushioned chair beside the fireplace. It turned the page of a large tome before sinking once again out of view.

Levictus pulled back his cowl. There was no one else in the room. The darknesses, finished with their meal, pooled around his feet. He shivered as they scaled the hem of his long black robe and vanished within the garment. A long knife appeared in his hand. For many long years he had waited for this moment. He wanted to make it last, to savor this thing that had consumed his thoughts since the day, long ago, when armed soldiers came to his family's home and took them away, depositing them into cells under this very castle. His parents, both elderly and in failing health, had died under torture on the first night. His brother expired a few days later. Only he had survived.

A voice rose from the chair. Perhaps once strong with authority, time had left it weakened and wavering. "Gunter? There's a chill in the air. Could you bring us another warm brandy?"

Levictus crossed the intervening distance as a bald pate leaned around the side of the chair, followed by rheumy eyes and a wide nose. He made no attempt to hide, but strode purposefully toward his prey. The old man's rubbery lips formed a hollow O as the knife rose. The blade's dark surface drank in the light of the fire.

"Mercy!" the prelate cried. "Mercy in the name of Almighty God."

But Levictus had none. The knife sliced through the man's wrinkled flesh. Thick streams of blood poured down the breast of his snowy robes. It splashed on the book that fell from his hands. The firelight caught the spine and illuminated the golden words printed there. *By Fire and Blood: Bringing the True Faith to the North.*

As his victim tumbled to the floor, Levictus opened the folds of his robe and brought out a wooden box. He set it on the floor as he knelt beside the prelate's corpse. Blood pooled beneath the body while he worked.

When the deed was done, as Levictus stood and put away his prize, he studied the man at his feet. No archangels had rushed in to defend His Sublime Holiness; no thunderbolts had fallen from the heavens. For all his majesty, the prelate had died like any other man, less well, in fact, than most. So much for the vaunted power of the True Church.

A strangeness passed over Levictus while he stood over his victim. Something buzzed in his ear like a flying insect. He made a pass with his hands, whispered a sibilant phrase, and the sensation fled on soundless wings.

Levictus went to a cabinet on the wall and rifled through its contents. Leaves of parchment fell to the floor. Then, he held up a sheet to the flickering light. His eyes followed the neat handwriting down to the surprise at the bottom, stamped in a blob of old wax. He stuffed the paper into a pocket. Then, he stepped into the dark space between two massive bookcases and vanished.

He reappeared inside the city, speeding through the slumbering avenues, just another shadow under the sequestering cover of the night.

Caim pulled his cloak tighter around his shoulders as he hunched on the rooftop. Below him, a blanket of silver fog shrouded the street in front of the Frenig mansion. Moisture dripped from the iron spikes atop the walls.

At least the rain had stopped.

Josey sat beside him, her arms propped on upraised knees, her chin resting on her forearm. He watched her in silence, studying her profile, not wanting to break the spell of her beauty. After Parmian's interrogation, Josey had been convinced that the answers to their problems lay within her father's house. Caim had given all the reasons they couldn't return to the scene of the crime—it wasn't a smart move, the place would likely be guarded, it was precisely where he would expect them to go if he were behind this whole charade—but his arguments had withered under her intense stare. Somehow she convinced him.

He almost suspected witchcraft.

Since then, she hadn't said much. Sitting beside him in the dark, she could have been a thousand leagues away.

Caim tried to put himself in her place. To find out that her late father had been the ringleader of a rebellious cult couldn't be an easy thing to swallow. It was simple for him. You lived and you died. What you did in the time between was your own business. And yet, how much of what he believed had been shaped by the uncaring world into which he had been thrust, a world that ground the weak and helpless into grist beneath its colossal wheels? Would he be so nonchalant about existence if his own past weren't so mired in brutality?

Caim sighed and concentrated on the silent house across the way. By his reckoning, they had been hunched up here for almost two hours. Dawn would come soon. If Josey was serious, they had to go now or never.

He whispered her name. When she didn't respond, he nudged her shoulder. She blinked as if coming out of a deep sleep.

"You sure you want to do this tonight?" he asked. "We could come back tomorrow."

"No." Her gaze returned to the spaces below. "Is this where you watched our house before coming to kill my father?"

Caim swallowed. He would have rather not answered, but figured he owed it to her. "Here and a couple other places." He indicated a flat-roofed brownstone down the street, and a pair of alleys with good vantage points of the mansion.

"Have you killed many people?"

"I suppose."

"Tell me how you do it. How do you kill people day after day, without regard, without feeling?"

He took in the meager offering of stars strewn through the overcast sky and the gulfs of darkness between them. "You think I like what I do? I didn't ask for this life."

"Then why—?"

"Because killing is the only thing I've ever been good at." The answer rung hollow in his ears, but damn her. He didn't owe her anything, didn't care a whit for what she thought of him.

"How old were you when you first . . . did it?"

A cloud passed across the moon, hiding Josey's expression, but he felt her gaze in the dark. "I'm not sure. Fifteen, maybe sixteen."

"What happened?"

"I was passing through some little thorp in Michaia. I forget the name."

He wasn't sure why he lied about that. The town had been called Freehold. It looked and smelled just like any of another score of settlements scattered across the dusty plains of Michaia, just a place to wash the road from your gullet and maybe find a woman before moving on.

"Anyway, some men started a fight in an ale hall. Things got out of hand. By the time it was over, I'd killed two of them."

"So you were defending yourself."

"I guess. I had to run after that, but I learned a lesson. There's always someone looking for trouble. You try to avoid it when you can, but—"

"But sometimes it finds you anyway," she finished for him.

"Yeah, well. Now it's just another trade to me, the same as a butcher or a carpenter."

Josey's face lifted out of the shadow. Her skin gleamed like polished ivory in the moonlight.

"But pigs and wooden beams don't have feelings," she said. "People do. Everyone you've killed had a family who cared about them, who grieved for them after they were gone."

He shifted a foot that had fallen asleep under him. "That makes no difference to me. I do a job and I get paid."

"Don't you ever want more from your life? Something bigger?"

"Like Hubert? You've seen his band in action. A bunch of shopkeeps and pot-boys spoiling for a fight they can't win. That's not me."

"Why not join the army? You're good with your hands. You could lead men."

He didn't try to hide his disdain. "Why is it that if a lord or a king sends you to kill a man, it's somehow noble? But if you do this for yourself, it's murder. Explain that to me."

Josey's eyes glistened. Was it the onset of tears, or just the way the light touched her emerald irises?

"If you asked me, I'd say you were afraid."

He recoiled as if she had stabbed him. The soles of his boots scrabbled on the hard shingles as he got his feet under him.

She kept going before he could muster a reply. "You're afraid to let people get close to you. So you keep them at a distance, pretend that they don't matter to you. But it's just a ruse."

He peered over the side of the roof. "You don't understand the least thing about me or what I do."

"Fine."

She pulled away and sank into herself like a flower folding its petals after the sun went down. For a moment, she sounded just like Kit and he realized how much he missed his friend. Where was she?

"Look," he said. "I'm—"

She reached up and pulled a something out of her collar. It shined in the muted starlight, a golden medallion in the shape of a key.

"Keep it," he said. "I don't want payment."

"It's not payment. It's the answer to the mystery."

"How's that?"

Josey told him the story of her childhood, how she had stumbled into a secret meeting in the cellar beneath her father's house, and how her father had given her the talisman years later.

"I didn't realize its significance," she said. "Not until tonight."

"So it's true. Your father was the head of a cult."

"Not a cult. A secret society aimed at restoring the empire."

"You believe Parmian now?"

She tucked the necklace away. "I knew it for truth as soon as he said it."

"And now we're here to traipse through your daddy's secrets in the basement?"

"Do you have a better idea? Someone killed my father for what he knew. He must have left some clue in that chamber. My father was a careful man. He would have foreseen the event of his death."

"All right. If we're going to do this, let's get started. I can get you inside. That shouldn't be a problem."

"So now you believe, too?"

"I believe we need to find out what's going on. After that, well, we'll just have to wait and see."

He led Josey to the corner of the roof and showed her where to put her hands and feet. She was a fast learner. Minutes later, they crept around the side of the earl's manor house, their footsteps muffled by the swirling fog. The neighborhood was quiet, almost unnaturally still. Caim wished Kit were here and damned her for her obstinacy. But neither wishing nor damning made her appear. He had to do this on his own. For some reason, the thought was more disturbing than he had anticipated.

The mansion looked the same as on the night Caim had first broken in. Its tall gables frowned in the darkness as if forbidding them entrance. The back gate was closed and secured by a new chain.

Caim jumped and caught the top of the wall, lifted himself up, and, after making sure no nasty surprises awaited them inside, reached down to hoist Josey. Caim dropped to the other side first, and then helped her descend.

Caim pulled her down into a crouch as he surveyed the yard. Everything looked clear; all the windows were dark. In all likelihood the City Watch had locked up the house and left it alone. The estate would be auctioned off eventually unless a legitimate heir turned up, and Josey's enemies were determined not to let that happen. If the Elector Council was behind the murder of Josey's father, then he was setting himself up against a host of powerful adversaries. And his list of allies was pitifully short. Without Kit or Mathias, he had Josey. And possibly Hubert. A meager force against the most influential men in the realm, and their armies. Yet despite the odds, he found himself thrilled by the prospect.

He motioned for Josey to follow, and together they crossed the grounds, which had grown over during the past few days. Weeds and tall grass brushed against their shins as they made their way to the rear wall of the mansion. He bypassed the door. He hadn't brought his line and grapnel, but he thought he could climb to the second floor easily enough. If he could find something to lower, he should be able to pull Josey up. He was studying the wall for good handholds when a faint click reached his ears. He whirled about to catch Josey opening the door.

"Wait!" he whispered too late, and jumped in front of her as the door swung open with a shuddering creak.

"What's—?" she started to ask.

He held up a finger to silence her. The door entered into an empty anteroom. An archway in the opposite wall led deeper into the interior. He drew his knives.

"What's the matter?" Josey whispered over his shoulder. "Did you expect the Third Legion to be waiting in the parlor for us to swing by?"

"Not exactly." All was quiet, but that didn't banish the invisible fingers plucking at his nerves. "But you didn't expect your friend's fiancé to give the order to have you drowned either, did you?"

Chastened, Josey hung back while Caim encroached farther into the house. A quick survey of the rooms on the ground floor confirmed his hunch. The front door was locked, but except for a few muddy boot prints on the carpets there was no sign anyone had been inside in recent days.

"Where's the cellar door?"

But Josey had gone to the stairs leading up to the higher floors. She stared up into the gloom. "I want to go upstairs."

"Wait a moment. We can't—"

"I need to see his room."

Caim hissed between his teeth, but didn't argue. He took the lead up the winding staircase. His feet found the soft spots in the boards out of habit; he winced with every creak she caused. To his ears they rang as clear as alarm bells. If anyone was waiting for them, they had ample warning to ready a welcome.

On the top floor, Josey passed by the first two doors without a glance. One was a maid's room. The second led into a cozy bedchamber with feminine décor. By the large bed with its frilly lace canopy and pastel colors, Caim guessed it had been her room.

Josey stopped at the entrance to her father's bedchamber. Caim remembered standing in this very spot, prepared to take the old man's life. The memory bothered him. Despite his hard words earlier, he couldn't deny some reservations over the direction his life had taken. In reexamining his choices, one fact was unmistakable. Yes, he had been a victim of violence, but every decision he'd made since that dire day had been his own. He had chosen this life for himself. No amount of rationalization could change that.

Josey lifted the latch and pushed open the door. Caim stood beside her as she surveyed the room. The bodies were gone, but otherwise it looked exactly as it had three nights ago. Dark stains marred the carpet. Caim replayed the battle in his mind, matching each blemish to its maker, until his gaze came to the table and the small dots under the padded chair. Josey took a step in that direction and stopped. Burning shame rose in the back of Caim's throat. There, but for some strange chance, was the spot where he would have killed her father. He would have done the deed and left without a care for how it might affect this woman standing beside him.

He took her arm with a gentle touch. "We have to get going."

She lifted her fingertips to her lips and blew a kiss at the empty chair. With a firm nod, she turned with him to leave.

Caim's eyes darted back and forth as they descended the stairs, but his adrenaline was fading in the absence of a credible threat. On the ground floor, he let Josey lead him through a series of rooms into a side wing of the house. From the dusty smell, this part of the mansion saw little use. Paintings decorated the walls of a long hallway, portraits mostly, of old men and women dressed in the fashions of previous generations.

Josey stopped at the end of the hall, at the opening of a narrow niche. It was empty, its paneled walls bare, although pale rectangles showed where pictures had hung in the past.

"This is it," she said. "The door was hidden in one of these walls. I could never find it again afterward."

Caim moved past her and searched the small space. He knocked on each wall. They were insulated, probably with cork. The floor felt solid enough. He was bending down to check the bottom panels when cracks in the strip of rosewood wainscoting caught his eye. He tapped the odd section with a finger. Nothing happened. Then he twisted it, and a piece of the molding pivoted away to reveal a small hole in the bare wood underneath.

A keyhole.

He smiled at Josey and moved aside. She approached with the golden talisman in hand. The key's smooth shaft slid into the hole without difficulty. Turning it produced a faint click, and a portion of the wall sprang open. He eased it open with the point of a knife. Stone steps wended down into the darkness beyond, flanked by walls of heavy blocks. Odors of earth and mold rose from the depths.

"Wait here," he said, and jogged back down the hallway to a sitting room.

He fetched a table lamp and returned to Josey. She stood at the top of the steps with her arms wrapped around her body, staring down into the dark.

He came up beside her. "Ready?"

"I guess so. Caim?"

"Yeah?"

"Thank you."

He inclined his head. "Let's go."

Caim went first, with the lamp in his left hand, a knife in the right. The steps were steep and irregular in their spacing, almost as if they had formed naturally. Trails of niter ran down the walls like melted wax. Josey stayed close to his back. He wanted to whisper for her to give him more space, but held his tongue. This place held a lot of memories for her, most of them scary and confusing. Anyhow, he didn't expect any trouble. The hidden door didn't look as if it had been used in years.

The steps entered into a large, round chamber. The ceiling was double-vaulted and formed with rows of square stones. Down from the center hung a cast-iron chandelier. A vivid fresco illuminated the smooth walls. In the painting, twelve figures in hooded blue robes stood under a starry night sky. Each clutched a yellow dagger in the left hand and held forth the right, dripping blood from the palm, as they gazed upon a dead man sprawled under a burning tree. It was all very strange, and probably symbolic, but he couldn't make hide nor hair of it.

"All the years you lived in this house." His words reverberated back to him from the walls. "You never suspected this place was down here?"

"No, I told you. There was only the dream."

Shelves and casements stood against the walls. They held books and racks of scrolls, strange ornaments and miscellanea. It was like walking through an old person's memories, everything placed in no particular order.

"Looks real enough to me."

While Josey wandered around the chamber, Caim went to the center, where a design had been painted on the stone flagstones. It was a yellow lion with an eagle's head and wings on a field of navy blue. A griffon, symbol of the old imperium. So it was true. Caim wondered what else Parmian could have told them about the meetings if he'd applied more pressure. Perhaps nothing. The man had sounded sincere in his desire to leave his father's schemes behind. Whatever secrets the earl had possessed in life had likely died with him.

"Caim!"

He hurried over to Josey's side. She stood before a display stand. A row of ceramic plaques lined the top shelf. Josey's gaze was fixed on the center picture, which was a rather good likeness of her late father, Earl Frenig.

"Are you okay?"

"Fine." Her voice sounded odd, as if she were speaking to him from far away.

He studied the plaques closer. Twelve sober faces stared back, two of them women. "So these are the members of your father's society. Not a lot of people to challenge the might of the True Church."

"Twelve members." Josey ran her fingertips over the face of the shelf. "Same as the number of theocrats on the Elector Council. Father liked balance. He was a little odd that way. Making everything tidy, he called it."

"I wonder what came of them. Are they still alive? Or has the Church . . . ?" He remembered her father's fate too late.

"Silenced them?" she finished for him.

"I didn't mean to—"

She placed a hand on his forearm. "It's okay. I'm fine."

A large tome rested on a beveled table beneath the portraits. Its heavy cover was bound in smooth leather, possibly sheepskin, dyed a deep sapphire blue. Tarnished silver studs shined in the lamplight. Caim opened the book. The yellowed pages were covered in a concise scrawl of black ink. The characters were Nimean, but he couldn't understand a word of it.

"This looks like a code."

Josey broke her gaze away from the picture. "You don't read Old Nimean?"

"No. What does it say?"

"It's a journal. It looks like my father's hand. The title says 'Revolution Day.'" She ran a finger across the page. "'In the eleven hundred and twenty-sixth year of the empire, a coalition of ministers and nobles from the outlying provinces gathered in secret. Dissatisfied with the influence held by the imperial court, and further motivated by liens against their properties and titles, these individuals plotted to depose the emperor. Key legionary commanders were involved by a variety of means, including bribery, blackmail, and at least one known murder of a state official. This inaugural meeting was held at the Basilica of St. Andros in the free city of Mecantia.'"

She glanced at him. "The presiding minister was Praetor Terentius Vassili, count of Leimond."

"*Archpriest* Vassili?"

"Before his ascension to the Elector Council, it seems, and before Mecantia was annexed by primal decree. It goes on to say that the coup succeeded. The coalition armies defeated the imperial garrison and seized control of Othir."

Caim set the lantern on the table. "I thought it was the Church that led the uprising against the emperor."

"That's what we were taught," Josey said. "Since then, the prelate has held temporal power over Nimea in addition to his spiritual authority."

"For the good of the people, no doubt."

She frowned as she bent over the text. "Listen to this. After the usurpation, elements of the Sacred Brotherhood took the palace. The coalition leaders were tried by an ecclesiastic court and executed. Thereafter, select churchmen were put in important positions in a government imposed by the Council and supported by the Brotherhood. Any who voiced dissent were imprisoned, or killed outright, and their lands forfeited. There's a list of nobles who switched allegiance to the new regime and were allowed to retain their titles."

She read off the roll of names. The muscles in Caim's jaws bulged at the mention of a familiar name: Reinard, duke of Ostergoth.

He cursed behind clenched teeth. Mathias had vetted every detail of the Ostergoth mission because of the high-profile nature of the target. He had convinced Caim everything was in the clear, but it was too convenient to be coincidence. They had been played like fools.

Mat, what did we get ourselves into?

A thought struck him. "What was the date of this Revolution Day?"

She flipped back to the beginning. "The fifteen of Maises, 1126."

Seventeen years ago. That would be the spring before his father's estate was attacked. Another coincidence, or were the two events related? As the Church consolidated its power, chaos would have run rampant through the rest of the empire, alliances between neighbors forgotten in the rush to address old grudges, small estates swallowed by more powerful landowners pushing to extend their borders without fear of imperial intervention. Caim bit down on his tongue as a chilling touch tickled the base of his spine. He was more invested in this struggle than he'd known. His rage bubbled to the surface.

"Vassili set them up," he said. "He convinced those nobles to rebel, and then sold them out when the deed was done. After they were gone, the Church was poised to take over."

Josey straightened, her features pallid in the lamplight. "It's ghastly. I remember hearing stories about those days. The emperor and empress were convicted of heresy and burned for their crimes, along with their children. There's a horrible painting of it in the Lyceum."

"Is there anything else?"

"It says the extermination of the imperial line was not as complete as the Church wanted everyone to believe. One child, the youngest, escaped with the help of a loyalist faction. The emperor's daughter . . ."

"What?"

Josey's lips trembled. Wetness gathered in her eyes and threatened to spill over.

"What is it?" he asked.

She shook her head as the first tear ran down her cheek, to be followed by a choked sob. Caim clenched his jaws. He wanted to shake her. Instead, he placed a hand on her arm.

"It's all right. Just tell me what's wrong."

With a halting voice, she read, "'The emperor's daughter, Josephine, was removed from the city by Artur Frenig, earl of Highavon, who thereafter raised the child as his own daughter, to be kept until the date of her majority.'"

Caim looked at her. He had felt there was something special about her, something beyond her beauty and wit. Now it made sense. He marveled at the boldness of the man who had raised her as his own.

"Parmian was right," he said. "If this gets out, it will shake the Church to its foundation."

"No," Josey said. Tears cracked her halting voice. "He's my father. He is."

Caim reached out, but dropped his hand before he touched her. Why would she want his comfort? She shocked him by rushing into his arms.

He patted her on the back, unsure of what to do but keenly aware of the firm body pressing against him.

"It makes sense," he said. "Frenig claimed you as his daughter to protect your identity. He remained loyal to the old empire, but when the politics became too hot he retired from public life and returned to Othir to start this secret society. He was waiting."

"For what?" The question was squeezed between choking sobs.

"For you to become old enough to claim your birthright."

Josey looked up. Her eyes were red, but warm and glowing beneath the pain. The smell of lavender soap swirled in his head. He bent down over her until their faces were inches apart. Then, as if realizing where she was, Josey extricated herself from his embrace and stepped back.

"So," she said, "you're saying you believe all this?"

"It all fits, Josey. Or should I call you 'Your Highness' or 'Your Majesty?' I always forget."

"Stop that!" Her face turned vermilion.

He glanced around the chamber and took in the stacks of documents, the pictures, the pike with a golden griffon headpiece leaning next to a faded banner.

"There's no denying it. This is what Frenig died to protect. You are the lost heir of the imperial family."

"That is interesting."

A raspy voice echoed through the chamber. Caim spun around as heavy footsteps descended the stairs. His knives came up in a defensive posture.

"Yes. Very interesting indeed."

CHAPTER NINETEEN

Caim pushed Josey behind him as a squad of men came down the steps. Swords and axes gleamed in their hands. Mail armor rustled beneath surcoats of the Sacred Brotherhood.

A familiar face appeared behind the soldiers. Markus had shed his uniform for a coat of boiled leather armor. He strutted into the chamber, holding his sword aloft like he was leading a holyday parade, but his men meant business. They fanned out in a half-moon formation.

Caim sunk into an open stance. Six-to-one were long odds even for him, especially when hampered by Josey and the wound in his side. He took a step to put himself more firmly between her and the Brothers, but she moved with him.

"We've been waiting for you to show up," Markus said. "I have to tell you, Caim. It is Caim, isn't it? I'm not impressed. I mean, for such a dangerous killer, you're not terribly imaginative."

"Is that so? How's your throat feeling?"

The prefect's face darkened. He pointed his sword at Caim's chest. "You'll be begging me for a quick end before this is through."

"Markus," Josey said. "This is madness. Did you have something to do with my father's death?"

Markus chuckled from behind the wall of his men. "Something? I was the one who engineered it, my dear Josephine. My only regret is that I didn't cut his throat myself. I'll have to be satisfied with killing your paramour here."

Caim reached out with his arm to hold Josey back, fearful she might rush into the waiting blades in her rage, but she stood her ground and glared at Markus with tears running down her face.

"You're nothing but a coward," she said. "You're not worthy of Anastasia, or any woman. You should be whipped through the streets and cast out into the wilderness."

Markus's chuckle filled the chamber as his men edged farther into the room. Caim balanced on the balls of his feet while he studied his adversaries. A sheen of sweat glistened on the brow of the Brother on his far left. That was his first target. After that, the tall one with the bruised eye. Caim shifted his weight by a fraction. They would rush him at any moment. He'd only have a split second to react.

Josey pressed against Caim's back. "Let us go, Markus. You're not an evil man."

"No, not like the man beside you," Markus replied. "But I've chosen my side. You both have to die. Those are my orders."

"The electors are nothing but a band of traitors!"

The prefect laughed. "Oh, this is rich! You think I'm here under the Council's orders? Josey, nothing could be further from the truth. I answer to a higher calling now."

"Money, you mean."

"That's right, bitch. Not that you'd know anything about that, what with your ball gowns and pretty baubles."

"Don't"—Caim turned his injured side away from the soldiers—"call her that."

Markus smiled behind the point of his sword. "You seem a bit stiff, friend. Not as nimble as you were on the pier, or upstairs for that matter. So the bolt found its mark. It stings, eh?"

"Come a little closer and find out."

Markus clicked his tongue. Caim beat their rush by a fraction of a heartbeat. He jumped just before the Brothers advanced. Pain ripped through his side, but he shoved it to the back of his mind as he rolled on his left shoulder and came up inside the guard of his first target. The clammy soldier fell to the floor, bleeding from a gouge in his belly and a slash across the face.

There was nothing fancy in Caim's technique. He shifted and lunged, ducked and riposted. His left-hand knife cut a jagged furrow along the tall Brother's arm while the right-hand blade beat aside a sword thrust and drove its author back. The tall soldier whipped his sword up into a guard position, but Caim sunk underneath and drove both points into the man's upper thigh where the artery pulsed. The Brother shouted and dropped to the floor.

As Caim moved to engage the others, a vicious spasm pulsed in his chest like his heart was trying to burst out of his rib cage. Steel flashed all around him in the lamplight. He retreated under a slashing sword stroke and slid away from a swipe at his head, but hampered by his wound he couldn't move fast enough. A boot stomped on his knee and almost spilled him to the floor. A sword gashed the sleeve of his shirt. In desperation, he launched a whirlwind of stop-thrusts to keep the Sacred Brothers at bay.

A bulky missile soared over his shoulder, accompanied by a dainty grunt. The oil lamp shattered on the floor behind the Brothers, and a wall of burning oil erupted at their backs. By a stroke of good fortune, Markus was stranded on the far side of the inferno.

Caim saw his chance. He darted in close, switching to the offensive. The *suete* knives cut through gabardine and flesh. Blood spattered the flagstones. A Sacred Brother screamed as his sword fell to the floor, his hand still attached to the hilt.

Caim was pressing the last two Brothers when another blade flashed at him from the darkness. He pivoted as Markus, his boots wreathed in flame, launched a barrage of furious attacks. Caim evaded the wild swings, but the action forced him back a step. He made two swipes with his knives to gain more maneuvering room, but the prefect's arrival had tipped the scales. Caim couldn't defend both himself and Josey. He retreated with a sinking feeling in his gut. He had lost the advantage. In a moment they would regroup and overwhelm him.

He risked a glance over his shoulder at Josey, backed against the wall with the ceremonial pike clutched across her chest. They were both going to die in this stinking cellar. The flash of her warm green eyes inflamed him. A tingle in his chest was the only warning before the chamber plunged into absolute night.

Icy sweat broke out all over Caim's body as he fell back against the stone wall. Even knowing what was happening didn't prevent the tendrils of fear from sliding through his veins. The shadows had come.

But he hadn't called them.

There was no mistaking the screams that echoed through the

chamber. He caught a glimpse of something out of the corner of his eye, just for an instant, but it was enough to melt his insides. Sleek and powerful, it prowled the darkness, and the fall of its massive paws made no sound on the chamber floor. Caim's breath caught in his throat. He couldn't move; his muscles had turned to jelly.

Josey's cry shook him from the stupor. He felt along the wall until he found her, huddled against a bookcase. She shuddered at his touch and tried to slap him away.

"It's me!" he hissed in her ear. "We have to get out of here."

She buried her face against his shoulder. Careful of his aching side, he cradled her as tenderly as he could. His eyes were adjusting to the gloom. The oil fire was burning down. Flashes of metal near the center of the room showed him where the surviving Brothers were making their stand. There was no sign of the shadow beast, but Caim could feel its presence like a great, black wave rolling through a midnight sea. He only hoped the creature would focus on the soldiers, leave him and Josey alone.

With an arm around her shoulders, Caim steered Josey along the periphery of the chamber. He kept the knife in his free hand ready, but the soldiers were focused on the greater threat. A gurgling squeal rose beyond the range of human vocals.

Josey gasped as they approached the burning pool. The heat of the fire was intense enough to warm him through tunic and cloak.

"Trust me." He picked her up. Her arms encircled his neck.

Caim carried her along a narrow path between the fire and the wall. The heat climbed up his boots. They were almost through when a shape appeared before them in the gloom to cut off their escape. For a moment, Caim feared the shadow beast had turned on them. Then, Markus's face emerged from the shadows. His sword rose into the smoky air.

Caim lowered his shoulder and charged ahead. He slammed into Markus. The momentum of the blow sent Markus hurtling into the greedy flames. Spurred by the prefect's screams, Caim raced up the stairs as if the lords of hell were on his heels. But halfway up the uneven steps, the pain in his side forced him to put Josey down. They crawled through the secret door, and Caim slammed it shut behind them. The Brothers' screams died away to ominous silence below.

As he staggered out of the niche, Josey pulled him close in a fierce embrace. Her soft lips mashed against his so hard he feared she might bruise herself. In the midst of this passionate display, he collapsed in her arms.

Somehow she half carried him down the dusty hallway. The rest of the mansion was empty, which was good, as he was in no condition to fight. The sickness was worse than ever before. He ached over every inch of his body. While he waited for the effects to leach out of his system, disturbing thoughts caromed through his head. The truth about Josey's identity hadn't struck him yet, not fully, but he could already feel his attitude changing toward her. He stood a little straighter beside her, then scowled when he noticed this and deliberately slouched.

They left the mansion by the back door and crossed the yard. Every step jarred Caim's side. Scaling the wall was a brutal experience, but he survived it. As they stole away, a jarring crash from the mouth of an alleyway caused him to raise his knives, until a small, furry shape darted away. He squeezed his fingers around the hilts. He was getting jumpy. It was Josey's fault. He had been a successful, self-possessed professional before he met her. Now, he was a mess.

Perhaps guessing his mood, Josey asked, "What do we do now?"

The foggy street stretched before them into the gloom. "Back to Low Town."

"The brothel again?"

The note of indignation in her voice made him smile despite the fierce throbbing in his side. *Already acting the part of a princess.*

"Not yet. I want to stop by my place first and pick up some things, a change of clothes."

"Wait." She stopped, which forced him to halt as well or leave her behind, something he wasn't willing to do.

"I need your help." She straightened her shoulders and faced him. "I want you to help me track down those responsible for the death of my father . . . and my real family. I need you to help me punish them."

Determination burned in her gaze. So much like his own, it gave him pause.

"You mean kill them."

"I mean do whatever it takes. Whoever is behind this has taken everything from me. My father. My home. My whole life. I want them dead. Help me, and all I have is yours."

He forced a laugh, although it came out as more of a croak. "You're wearing borrowed clothes under a borrowed jacket. Any wealth your father possessed has probably been seized by the city. You're poorer than me."

"What do you want?"

He stepped closer. A look of uncertainty crept into her highborn features, but she held her ground. His mouth remembered the taste of her kiss. "How about a full pardon?"

Her smile returned. "We can negotiate that."

"It's negotiable?"

She took his arm as he steered her toward Low Town. "Everything's negotiable, Caim. But you know what this means, right?"

"What?" he asked, suddenly wary.

"It means you're fighting for a cause."

Caim didn't reply, but let those words drift inside his skull for a while. Neither of them spoke on the long walk out of High Town. He figured they both had enough to occupy their minds. Gods knew he did. The thing in the cellar prowled through his mind like a bad dream. What the hell was it, and why did it keep appearing to him? More important, how could he get rid of it? The questions dogged him all the way back across the Processional.

Caim smelled trouble before they reached the Gutters. It smelled like smoke, and blood. A commotion stirred in the streets ahead. He pushed ahead of Josey as a throng of men poured out of a side street. Brandishing lanterns and makeshift weapons, they vanished down another lane. Their shouts echoed off the house fronts and rose into the night.

"Death to the prelate!"

"Swords rise for freedom!"

The crowd took up the chant as they marched off into the night. Caim started forward, but Josey dragged him to a stop. "What if we went to the palace instead?"

"Are you crazy?"

"If I announce myself, who I am, the people may rally behind my claim. A lot of bloodshed could be avoided."

"Or you might be seized and bundled away before anyone hears your claim. It's suicide. Look, you said it yourself. The ones in power don't play by any rules but their own. We've got to be smart about this. I don't know much about politics, but even if the prelate and the Elector Council vanish overnight, someone else will seize the reins. And they aren't likely to hand them over to anyone without a fight."

She tapped her chin with a chipped fingernail, but didn't argue. For that, he was infinitely thankful. He didn't have the energy for any more fighting tonight. He just wanted to get home and crash in his own bed for a few hours. Everything would look different in the morning.

They turned off Hooper Street and halted in their tracks. The end of the block was engulfed in an inferno. Towering flames licked at the night sky and cast off swarms of burning cinders. Maybe they had come down the wrong street. He searched for landmarks. No, this was it.

"Is that . . . ?" Josey asked.

"Yes."

His apartment building was burning down.

A crowd of people milled about in front and watched the conflagration. Some sobbed; others stood enraptured as the towering flames licked at the underbelly of the night sky. A firefighting brigade was on the scene, but their efforts, though valiant, were useless. Unable to stop the blaze, they concentrated on keeping the fire contained.

Caim's fists quivered. This wasn't an accident. Even though the rickety building had been a disaster waiting to happen, the timing was too convenient. This was a message aimed at him. *We know where you live, and we can reach you any time we want.*

He wanted to stab someone, to fight something tangible. Instead, he stood with the rest and watched the immolation of the place he had called home for the past three years. He glanced at the faces reflected in the firelight. It had been a mistake to come here. Just like the mansion. Their enemies were a step ahead of them, looming at the end of every path they took. He had to do something unexpected, change his patterns. Otherwise, sooner or later, he was going to get them both killed.

Then he saw her.

The little girl sat at the edge of the crowd, her thin legs drawn up under her tattered smock of a dress. Tears carved pale lines down the mask of soot and grime plastering her delicate features. By her feet, a heap of charred corpses were stacked under a grubby tarp like so much cordwood.

A man stumbled out of the crowd. Unshaven, bloated, bleary-eyed, he staggered over to the girl. With a snarl, he grabbed her by the arm and yanked her upright. Her father, her uncle, her mother's pimp—it didn't matter. Something unhinged inside Caim. He crossed the distance in three strides. An open-handed blow to the wrist broke the man's grip on the child; a clout above the ear with a knife pommel put him down. Some people in the crowd turned to watch, but Caim didn't care. Ignoring the pain in his side, he bent over the fallen man and put the point of the blade to his throat.

The hand holding the knife quivered, just a little, but to Caim it was like the tremor of an earthquake. His emotions were raging out of control. He wanted to kill so badly he could do it without thinking, without caring.

A pair of small arms tugged at his leg. Caim looked down into a pair of wide brown eyes, and he remembered the night, long ago, when he had watched his father die.

Go ahead, hero. Destroy her world, too.

He put away his knives and picked her up. She squirmed for a moment, but then buried her face into his shoulder with a shudder.

"Shhhh," he whispered. "It's over."

Josey waited for him at the end of the lot. She didn't say anything as he carried the child away from the burning building. Together they walked the narrow streets of Low Town, three ghosts alone in the night.

CHAPTER TWENTY

Caim drew the *suete* blade across the smooth river stone. Steel whispered along the grains of the stone, turned over, and came back in the opposite direction. When the edge shimmered like foxfire over the moors on a cool summer evening, he put it away and started on the other knife.

The girl's name was Angela. She sat at a table in Madam Sanya's kitchen, fast asleep beside a half-empty bowl of apple slices and clotted cream. Cleaned up and wearing a fresh smock, she looked a damned sight better than the waif they had found outside his ruined apartment building.

Madam Sanya crossed the kitchen in her nightgown to hand him a cup of warm tea. "Sure, she's welcome to stay here, Caim. It's no bother. I've had a gaggle of little ones running through this house before, and our business being what it is, I gather I'll see more before they put me in the ground. That is, if I can stay in business."

Caim accept the cup with a nod. "Getting bad?"

"As bad as I've ever seen. Parnipos came by today with news. Seems some citizens tried to stop a band of Flagellants from burning down a tavern on Rye Street. Just everyday folk, but they had the Beaters hemmed in tight until the Brotherhood arrived. Fourteen dead, all told. The bells on Septon's Chapel have been ringing all afternoon, and now there's talk that the holy prelate has died, God rest his soul." She drew a circle over her breast. "We've gotten more people at the door looking for a safe place to hide than actual customers these past few days, but things will look up."

Caim reached into his tunic and took out a leather purse. It was the last of his money. The rest had been hidden in the floors and walls of his apartment.

"This is for taking in the girl. See that she gets some learning. And I don't want her working a room here, Sanya. Not ever. I'll have your word on that or I'll take her somewhere else."

Madam Sanya made the purse disappear inside the folds of her gown. "I promise. She can fetch and cook until she's old enough for schooling. I know just the right teacher. He's retired from the university, a real scholar and a gentleman. No, she'll be fine as a spring rain, but what about you two? Need to borrow Kira's room for a while longer?"

Caim looked over at Josey, sitting across from Angela with her head nestled in her arms. She looked almost like a child herself, despite the blood and soot marring her borrowed clothes.

"No," he said. "It isn't safe here, for us or you. We'll be moving on."

Madam Sanya observed him over the rim of her cup. "By the way you speak, doesn't sound like you intend to be back."

"You never can tell, can you?"

Caim went over to Josey and woke her with a gentle nudge. She looked up with squinty eyes. "Hmm?"

"It's time to go."

Madam Sanya gave them each a hearty embrace before they shuffled out the back door. Outside, the deep purple of night's final hour lightened into the faint glow of dawn. Umber streaks etched the sky, forecasting poor weather ahead.

Caim led Josey out the fence door and down the narrow alley behind the brothel. Their situation was bleak, to say the least. They couldn't trust anyone now, couldn't go anyplace he normally frequented. Not even his secret bolt holes in dives across the city were safe. He was known throughout the underworld, and his passage would go noticed. Disguises wouldn't hide them forever, not as long as they stayed in the city. The only thing left was to leave.

It wasn't an easy decision. Josey opposed it, of course. Caim put himself in her position and understood why. This was her home, all she had known since she was a little girl. But he had to rely on his instincts, and they screamed that as long as Josey remained in Othir, she was sitting in the jaws of a bear trap, just one ill-fated moment away from being snapped up. So he was taking her to the only place in the world he thought she'd be safe.

Josey started to shake off her drowsiness as they paused outside a chandlery on Fafstall Lane. "Are you sure about this?" she asked.

Caim peered down the street. Folks would be rising soon. He didn't want anyone remarking on two people seen hurrying through the predawn streets.

"No," he said. "But it's what your fathers would have wanted. Both of them."

"We'll return as soon as it's safe, right?"

"Sure." He let it go at that. Would it ever be safe in this city again? "Come on."

They stole across the street and down another alley. As they came around the next corner, they almost walked into a desperate melee. The ancient walls and cul-de-sacs of Low Town sometimes played tricks with noises. Caim didn't hear the fighting until they were upon it. In the middle of a crowded street, a score of militiamen, rural conscripts by their mismatched brown coats and crude wooden pikes, struggled to hold off a mob. Angry cries on both sides were punctuated by the clash of arms. Blue scarves dotted the crowd, but Caim didn't see anyone he knew. He drew Josey away.

Four blocks eastward, she grasped his wrist as the cemetery's dingy walls appeared from the night fog. The stonework was cracked and pitted like old cheese, caked with clumps of moss and climbing vines. Fallen chunks of masonry were scattered about. Wrought-iron spikes, now rusted and bent, lined the top. Once, there had been a contingent of watchmen assigned to protect the final resting spot of Othir's citizenry, but it had been deemed a waste of resources.

"What are we doing here?" she asked.

He nodded to the gate, slouched in its crumbling hinges. "This is our way out. Trust me?"

She pulled herself up straight and nodded. Caim opened the corroded lock with a quick twist of a knife point, and grimaced as he heard a snap. The hinges squeaked as he shoved it open. He ushered Josey inside, then shut the gate behind them. There was nothing for the lock; it was busted well and good. How long before someone noticed that? *Maybe we're the only ones out here tonight. Sure.*

Josey shivered beside him. Caim put an arm around her shoulders, partly to comfort her and partly to keep her from stumbling. The atmosphere of the boneyard was pungent with a miasma of noxious vapors. Swirling fingers of fog wafted across the sparse, gray grass through storm grates in the River Wall.

They didn't dare risk a light, but Caim knew the way. He navigated a winding path through the rows of gravestones. Some were so old their dates couldn't be read. A dozen centuries of corpses lay in repose beneath their feet. A sobering thought and not something he pondered often, but these past few days had illustrated his mortality in ways he'd never thought about before. He doubted whether either of them would survive this fiasco. *Where will I be put to rest when my time comes? Dumped in an alley for the street sweepers to take out with the morning trash? Or thrown in the Memnir with stones tied around my neck?*

Caim stopped Josey at an old mausoleum near the east end of the cemetery. The words carved into the stone lintel above the heavy bronze door were faded and eroded by time, but still legible.

Pieter Ereptos
The Last Honest Man of Othir,
From His Grateful Brothers.

Caim smiled at the private joke as he heaved on the door. Flecks of verdigris came away in his hand from the handle, but the door opened without a sound. Its hinges were kept well oiled by the deceased's large family of "brothers."

Caim drew Josey inside. Her hand was cool and slick in his grip. He squeezed to reassure her as the door shut behind them. The inside was as dark as the proverbial tomb, but Caim was able to make out a stone ledge with several objects. He found a wedge of flint and struck it against the iron plate resting beside it to produce a spark. After a couple attempts, the old storm lantern flickered to life.

Josey pressed against him as he turned. The interior of the crypt was cramped by a massive sarcophagus in the center of the floor. Great attention to detail had gone into the bier. Upon the lid was carved the likeness of a man in white marble. He was of middling years, dressed in plain but well-cut clothes.

186

Caim gestured with the lantern. "Josey, meet brother Pieter."

To her credit, she didn't shy away from the crypt. "I take it he wasn't really your brother."

"In a manner of speaking."

There had never been a man named Pieter Ereptos living in Othir, or anywhere else to Caim's knowledge. About fifty years ago, some elements of the city's underworld sought a reliable and secret means to enter the city. Gate sentries could be bribed, of course, but human agents were vulnerable to sudden attacks of conscience. So the various thieves, con artists, sellswords, and other scum pooled their resources to have a fictional "brother" interred in the cemetery. Workers were smuggled inside the crypt night after night for many long months to work on the clandestine project.

Caim reached out with his free hand to toy with the decorative shapes carved into the side of the sarcophagus. He found the one and pushed. Josey yelped as the lid of the stone coffin slid away. Caim caught her hand and drew her closer to the sepulcher. Instead of holding the moldy remains of a corpse, the interior was hollow. Steps disappeared down into the darkness of a long tunnel. A cloying smell rose from the aperture, not fetid and charnel, but the smell of clean, moist earth.

"Come," he said.

He held the lantern before them as they went down into the darkness.

Vassili swept the mass of architectural plans from his desk with a blasphemous oath. Outside the door, footsteps that had been approaching the door wisely turned away.

Robbed of the chance to vent his anger, he dropped into his throne-like chair behind the desk. Scents of sandalwood and ambergris wafting from the hearth did nothing to soothe his ire. He had been at the site of the new cathedral, basking in the realization of his genius wrought in marble, when the news of Benevolence's death reached him. His first thought had been to curse the heavens for their poor timing. Later, he shook with rage as he read the first reports out of DiVecci. The prelate had been murdered. The deed had Levictus's name written all over it.

Vassili mashed his hands together while he paced. Did the man think he was a fool? What with the rogue assassin on the loose killing electors, men he had counted upon in his bid for the prelacy, it was too soon to precipitate the final phase of their plan. This could ruin everything!

He paused with his hand over an Illmynish porcelain figurine. Perhaps things were not as bad as they appeared. The deaths on the Council were a setback, but no one else had enough votes to swing the election. That meant he was still in a position of strength. If he moved swiftly and with purpose, his plan could still succeed. But first he needed to rein in that bastard Levictus. The second thing he'd done upon returning to the palace had been to summon the sorcerer. It was time to remind the man which of them was the servant and which the master.

The lamp over his desk fluttered as if in a stiff breeze. The windows were closed.

Vassili turned, and stepped back reflexively as the slim figure appeared behind him.

"God's blood, man. What are you doing here?"

While he took a moment to catch his breath, the assassin took a seat by the fireplace. The archpriest's fingers curled into fists, but he forced a calm tone into his voice. Ral still had his sword with the ostentatious silver handle belted at his waist. The security lapse only increased his ire.

"Have you found them yet?" Vassili asked. "I need that girl, and the man—what's his name?"

Ral produced a knife and twirled it between his fingers. "Oh, we're still searching for them. No good having such hazardous tools lying about where anyone could snatch them up."

Vassili frowned. This was a different Ral than the one he was accustomed to dealing with. He went behind his desk and sat down. He considered calling for his guards, but held off.

"What are you getting at?"

"You've been colluding with dangerous people, Your Luminance. All those rumors about war in the north must be driving you mad."

"I don't—"

"Don't waste your breath." Ral reached into his jacket and dropped a scroll on the desk.

Vassili stiffened as he saw the wax seal on the parchment. How could this be? All his most secret documents were kept under lock and key. Then, he knew.

Levictus.

Vassili brushed a hand down the front of his robe as he composed himself. "Yes, I have had dealings with certain entities in Eregoth. What of it? We are surrounded by foreign powers that work toward our annihilation, from the pagans of Arnos to the godless heathens of the western realms. The prelate understood the use of clandestine means to further the Church's mission. The use of assassination as a political lever, for example."

Ral didn't take the bait. "Dealing with the Shadow is sacrilege, and treason to boot."

"Don't prattle to me about sacrilege and treason! I have spent my life in service to the Church. After Immaculate passed, I should have been elected to the high office. Me. Not that dotard, Benevolence. Your failure may have altered the timing of my plans, but nonetheless I will be the next prelate."

Ral frowned as if perplexed as he examined the palms of his hands. "I'm afraid there's been a change of plans. You see, it's not Caim who's been killing your peers on the Council."

Vassili grasped the desk. "I'll have you whipped through the streets for your inso—"

His words dribbled to a halt as he gazed down at the knife's shiny handle protruding from his chest. It was a curious sensation, more pressure than pain, radiating out from his breastbone. A thin line of warmth trickled under his robe, down his belly and into his smallclothes.

Another figure appeared before his desk. Levictus in his black robe. Nothingness reflected in the opaque depths of the sorcerer's eyes.

Vassili wanted to reach for his sacred medallion, to cow the man in his tracks, but his hands refused to obey. His body was too heavy; he couldn't move. He looked to Ral, who had risen to stand beside Levictus.

"You don't know," he whispered, barely able to summon enough breath to speak. The wound began to throb. "You think you've won, but you don't . . ."

The room spun, and then he was lying on the floor staring up at the ceiling. Little shadows crawled across the coffered surface, so many of them, like a hive of formless black termites burrowing through the palace. Something tugged at his sleeve. Papers rustled in the dark. Ral was going through his desk. Clever boy, he found the secret compartment under the lowest drawer that held the secrets he had killed to protect. Now they were laid bare like his body would soon be, dressed in a white funeral shroud and placed in his stone tomb. He hoped his son would honor his wishes and give him a mahogany coffin. He'd always loved the luster of that dark wood.

The sorcerer leaned over him. An object came down beside Vassili's head—a pale wooden box. It resembled an offering box. When he was a boy his father had allowed him to place their family's alms into the box. The young parish priest had had such fervent, penetrating eyes, always watching him. The pain was fading. It wasn't so bad, dying. He would close his eyes and drift into a deep, endless slumber.

Strong hands rocked him. Metal clattered in the distance. Vassili frowned at this disturbance of his peace. He was a distinguished principal of the Church. He should be accorded all due dignity and respect, not pawed over like a fish at market.

Levictus bent lower. Words fell into his ear, soft as goose down. "Benevolence spilled his last secret as he died, old man. I know who ordered the arrest of my family."

A crumpled piece of parchment was placed on his chest. The indentation of the Vassili family seal stared at him from the bottom of the document like an evil eye. The archpriest strained to speak, but only a dry wheeze issued from his lips. A final surge of indignation constricted his chest, and then evaporated, leaving him empty and weak.

Footsteps drifted away across the cold tiles. Ral departing. Levictus crooned softly as he reached out to the archpriest. Was this a last caress, an act of compassion for a dying man? No, something approached from beyond the misty edges of his sight. A knife, its blade as black as the new moon, colder than the depths of the midnight sea, descended toward him.

Closer . . . closer . . . closer . . .

Vassili's final kiss came not from the lips of his mistress but from the bitter bite of Shadow-tainted steel. He screamed, but there was no one to hear.

CHAPTER
TWENTY-ONE

Caim swayed to the rocking pace of his stolen horse. They were on the road, if the term could be applied to the rutted pathway wending between hedges of wild golden-brown wheat through the wilderness of rural Nimea. A colossal stone aqueduct ran parallel to the road, its arches clogged with ivy vines and detritus. A century ago it had carried water to Othir from the purple hills staggering away in the distance. Now, it was a monument to a tribe of humble origins that had gone on to conquer most of the world. But even empires died eventually.

Josey rode beside him on a piebald nag; the animal's mild temperament matched its rider. Since they'd left Othir, Josey had lapsed into a quiet reticence. Caim was content to leave her to her solitude. After their escape through the underground tunnel leading from Pieter's tomb, they'd emerged in the foulburg of ramshackle homes along the western banks of the Memnir River. Caim liberated a pair of steeds and gear from a tavern stable, and they set off into the night. There was only one place in the world where Josey would be safe until he settled their problems, only one person he trusted to protect her.

They rode west past sleepy villages and isolated homesteads. As the miles wore on, the farms and vineyards fell behind and they entered into a vast tract of wilderness. Still, Caim kept one eye over his shoulder. Even though they hadn't seen a living soul in hours, he couldn't shake the feeling they were being pursued. Invisible phantoms prickled his imagination, and not all of them originated from the events in Othir; with each passing mile he slipped deeper and deeper into his past.

A yawn broke the morning silence as Josey stirred and stretched. Caim watched her without embarrassment. The last few days had taken their toll; she was thinner than when they'd met; her face had lost some of its color. Still, there was a core of iron in her that could not be denied.

She caught him staring. "What are you looking at?"

"Maybe we should talk about it."

"Talk about what?" But a blot of color crept into her cheeks.

"About what happened in your father's house when you kissed—"

"I was overwrought," she blurted, "and you had one foot in the grave. It was just a moment of weakness."

"Weakness, huh?"

She fixed her gaze on the road. "It won't happen again."

"That's good to know."

He shifted in the saddle. He wasn't used to riding anymore. His thighs would be sore tonight. Up ahead, trees limned in shades of bronze and gold emerged from the flatness of the plains. Far in the distance, rounded hills pushed back the horizon, and beyond them towered the shoulders of lofty gray peaks.

They passed an old marker beside the road. Half hidden by weeds, there was no telling what it said, but Caim didn't need to read it. A cardinal perched atop the stone marker watched them as they passed. Caim tried to remember the last time he'd seen a bird besides the filthy pigeons that infested Othir.

"So where are we?" Josey asked.

"Dunmarrow."

Josey stood up in her stirrups for a better look around. "I've never been so far outside the city walls. Do people actually live out here?"

"Few. At least, not many you'd want to meet. We're getting into bandit territory."

"Caim, are you sure about this? We could turn back. There might be people who would help us in Othir."

He snapped the reins. His gelding trotted for a few steps before falling back to a lazy walk. Josey caught up a moment later, handling her mount with practiced ease.

"This person you're taking us to," she said. "He can help us? Who is he? Your teacher?"

"Not exactly. But I trust him, and I don't trust many people. Neither should you."

"All right. So where does he live? On the other side of this wood?"

The path entered a stand of red maples. Cool shadows played across the ground. These woods were no mystery to Caim. He had explored their length and breadth extensively as a boy. They had been his refuge, his castle, his haven from a host of memories that refused to fade, but he had never considered returning until now.

Half a mile after they passed under the leaf canopy, a humble dwelling appeared beside the road. Caim pulled his mount to a halt. Not much had changed since the last time he'd seen the place. A tendril of wood smoke rose from the clay-brick chimney. Roughed logs formed the walls, insulated with thick layers of wattle. The roof was bundled thatch.

"Is this it?" Josey asked. "How long since you've been here?"

"A long time."

Their horses whickered as a heavyset man came around the corner of the cottage. He had a wood axe with a black iron blade in one ham-fisted hand and a load of firewood tucked under the other arm. He looked to be somewhere in his fifties. His broad frame was clad in a homespun tunic tied with a rope over buckskin breeches. His face was uneven from an old war wound that had smashed in the left side of his jaw, giving him a menacing appearance, like a mangled wolf that'd been in too many fights. Watery blue eyes watched their arrival without expression.

Caim leaned forward in the saddle. The old man had changed. His beard, as scraggly as always, had grown down to his chest, and he'd lost some hair on top. Extra weight now clung to his middle, but his shoulders were still massive, rolling on either side of his head like tumbling boulders. Caim supposed he had changed somewhat himself. He'd been little more than a half-grown boy when he left. Would the old man even recognize him?

Those fears evaporated with a nod. "Caim."

Caim returned the nod. "Kas."

The axe man scratched his leg with the blade. "Looks like your taste in company has improved. You two jumped a broom yet?"

Caim's tongue clove to the roof of his mouth. "Uh, no. Kas, this is Josey. Just a girl I know."

The old man started toward the door. "Well, come inside. I've got a pot of *cha* on the fire. It should be about ready."

Caim climbed down and moved to help Josey from her horse, but she beat him to the ground.

"So I'm not good enough for you?" she asked, wearing the same feral smile Kit gave him whenever she wanted to pull his tail feathers.

With a grunt, Caim headed toward the cabin, hobbling with every step from the long ride.

Caim ran his hand across the surface of the table in the larger of the cabin's two rooms. The whorls and knots brought back memories. He and Kas had spent a lot of time at this table, conversing over meals of home-ground sausage garnished with whatever they could coax from the garden. Well, Kas had mostly talked while he listened. He remembered less pleasant things, too: angry words and all-out battles, the bitter winter when everything in the cabin except themselves had frozen solid. Caim could still imagine the chill in the tips of his fingers after all these years.

The interior was just the way he remembered it, except smaller. A layer of dust covered everything. Cobwebs hung from the rafters and the old spear over the fireplace, and the window shades looked like they hadn't been cleaned since the cabin was built. A pile of threadbare blankets was stacked in the corner where he used to sleep. The smells of wood smoke and Kas's joint liniment hung in the air.

The old man hadn't said much since they arrived, just dropped his firewood by the hearth and puttered around the squat iron stove. Josey sat back in the homemade chair and studied the two of them like animals in a menagerie.

Caim shifted to alleviate the stitch in his side. *Maybe this wasn't the best idea.* He was trying to come up with an excuse to leave when Kas came over with a steaming kettle, a rag wrapped around the handle. He poured a cup for each of them and lowered himself onto a stool made from a tree stump. Josey offered to give up her chair for the third time since they arrived, and for the third time Kas refused.

"No, I'm fine. I made those chairs, you know. Hope you don't get a splinter." He made a smile at that like it was a private joke.

Caim took a sip from his cup and winced. The *cha* was just like in the old days, horrible, but it was hot.

"So," Josey said, "are you and Caim related?"

Kas glanced across the table with raised eyebrows. Caim shrugged. They were past the point where his secrets could do him much more harm.

"Not exactly," Kas replied. "I served his father for a time after my soldiering days. After his father and mother were killed—"

"She wasn't killed." Caim squeezed the cup tight. The old resentment bubbled to the surface as quick as marsh gas. "She was taken."

Kas nodded. "All right."

Josey looked Caim. "Your father was killed, and someone took your mother? How old were you?"

Caim took another sip. "Eight."

Josey reached out as if to touch his arm, but stopped before her fingers made contact. "I'm so sorry, Caim."

"Ancient history."

"Who did it?"

"We never found out," Kas said. "Caim ran off during the attack. I searched for weeks before I found him scrounging around the streets of Liovard, skinny as an alley cat and almost as feral. I brought him out here and we built this cottage."

Caim could feel Josey's stare. He could guess the thoughts running through her head, trying to piece together the shambles of his life, to trace the journey from that small forlorn boy to what he'd become. He could have told her not to bother, that he had chosen his path with his eyes open wide, but it didn't matter what she thought. Nothing could change the past, so the past didn't matter.

"We had some good times here," Kas continued. "That is, until he up and ran out on me. You were what, Caim? Fifteen?"

"Thirteen." He remembered the day like it was yesterday. They had argued over something; he couldn't remember what, but it had seemed like the most important thing in the world at the time.

"We had a fight," Kas said with a shrug, as if that explained everything. "I can't even recall what it was about. Anyways, Caim turned in early that night. The next morning, he was gone. You know, I went back to Liovard searching for you."

"No one asked you to."

"Dammit, boy. I thought you were long dead by now."

"Well, I'm not." Caim got up. The room was cramped and stifling, the air thick with regrets.

"I know I made mistakes," Kas said. "I couldn't replace your family. The gods know I tried."

"Save it."

Caim left the cabin. He went around back to the wide meadow lined by a bulwark of ancient boles. This had been his playground, the place he went to escape with his thoughts. Years had passed, but the sights and smells of the cabin brought it all back like he was still just a boy, wrestling with the same problems, asking the same questions. And still finding no answers. What had really happened all those years ago on that cool spring night? Was he truly alone in the world?

Footsteps crunched on the carpet of dry leaves behind him. "I come out here a lot," Kas said. "In the evening with my pipe. It's relaxing."

"Where do you find tobacco this far out?"

"A trader comes by every few months. I got a new adze last spring."

Caim's gaze wandered to a boulder at the edge of the woods. Almost as high as his waist, half sunk into the earth and covered in gray lichen, it had to weigh as much as a prize steer, if not more. He remembered watching Kas lift the boulder and toss something underneath before dropping the stone back into place. It had happened so long ago, and yet the memory was as sharp as a knife.

"You're thinking about your parents," Kas said.

Caim nodded.

"You think you're strong enough to lift that stone yet?"

Caim considered the boulder, and the mountain of history heaped upon its craggy face. "I don't know if I'll ever be strong enough."

"I think about your father a lot," Kas said. "Your mother, too. I wonder if I should have searched longer for the ones who did it. Maybe I didn't try hard enough."

Caim scuffed the toe of his boot in the dirt and kicked up a pebble. It landed beside his foot, flat and smooth like a river stone. A band of red twisted through the white surface. What could he say? Nothing. He had his own reservations about the past.

"But you know, Caim, I'm glad I didn't go back, because then I'd never have found you. Your father was a great man, the best I ever knew.

He would have wanted me to take care of you until you were old enough to look after yourself."

"What about what I wanted? What if I'd been willing to trade a few years on the streets in exchange for the knowledge that what happened to my parents had been made right?"

"You still want revenge? Boy, listen to me. I've seen war and more than enough killing for a lifetime, and I can tell you from experience, that's an endless hole. You can pour everything you got into it, but every morning it's still going to be empty. It doesn't matter how many men you send to their graves, what's past is never going to change. It's time you learned that and moved on."

Caim ground his teeth together until sharp tingles of pain ran along his jaw. "I still see him in my dreams, Kas. He dies again and again right in front of me, and he keeps asking for justice, but I can't give it to him. What am I supposed to do? Just let it go and forget they ever existed?"

Kas sighed. "Caim, you've been walking a line between light and dark your whole life. Maybe it's time to choose a side and stick with it."

Caim stepped away. A sick feeling uncoiled in his belly. Suddenly, he didn't trust himself. Was he doing the right thing? How could he know?

"There are no sides, Kas. Just everyone looking out for themselves. That's the truth my father couldn't face."

"You don't see it, boy. You're in trouble."

"It's nothing I can't handle." He turned to face the man who had raised him. "But I need a safe place for Josey to stay. It'll just be for a couple days."

"Of course, she's welcome. What about you?"

Caim headed back to the cabin. "I've got things to take care of."

Josey stood in the tiny kitchen area. She looked over as he entered. "I'm not staying without you," she said as if reading his thoughts.

"It's for the best."

She crossed her arms across her chest. "You don't get to decide where I go and how I live."

He waited for the anger of her outburst to subside. The blush of her cheeks faded, but her fingers were knotted now, into a hard, white ball. She looked like she was searching for something to throw at him until Kas stepped through the door.

"We'll have a grand time, lady. We can talk about Caim while he's gone. I'll tell you all his childhood secrets."

Her eyes bore into Caim. "What if you don't come back?"

"I will."

"But what if——?"

He came around the table and wrapped his hands around hers. "I will return. Believe that."

She bobbed her head before collapsing against him. "You better," she murmured into his chest.

Kas cleared his throat. Caim gently pushed Josey away. He gave her his most sincere smile and a wink, and then he headed for the door. Kas stood in his way. Caim tensed, but the old man simply stepped aside.

"Hope you find what you're looking for, boy."

Caim kept his head down as he stepped over the threshold.

"Caim!"

He turned in time to catch Josey. She clutched him hard for a moment, and then pushed a small object into his hand. It was cool against his palm.

"Take this," she said, and stepped back.

He looked down into his hand. A golden key nestled there amid a jumble of leather string. Her necklace. With a nod, he wrapped the cord around his wrist as he went out to his horse.

Back in the saddle, he took a deep breath, filling his lungs with the scents of pine and maple, good earth and sweet smoke. Then he rode away and left behind the two people he cared about the most.

CHAPTER
TWENTY-TWO

Othir's gates were barred when Caim returned, their wardens replaced by soldiers in the hunter green livery of the Nimean army. So he entered by the underground tunnel. After snuffing the lantern inside Pieter's mausoleum, he stood for a moment with his hand on the crypt's bronze door. If he failed, it was only a matter of time before they got to Josey. The girl was lovely, smart, charming, but she was also haughty and headstrong. She wouldn't be content to wait with Kas for long. And where had Kit gotten off to?

Taking her own sweet time getting over being mad at me just when I need her the most.

Caim shook his head as he slipped through the cemetery gate, and wondered how he had acquired so many responsibilities.

A wild wind whipped through his hair as he navigated the cemetery. With Mathias dead, there was only one person who knew he'd be at the earl's mansion that night.

The streets bordering the boneyard were quiet, but only a block away the clamor of fighting resounded. Though muted by the fog from the river, it sounded like a full-scale war. He turned onto Acacia Avenue and found the way blocked by a pair of overturned wagons. Beyond the barrier, soldiers clashed with angry citizens. Bodies clogged the street. The ululation of rage long denied, now suddenly unleashed, filled the humid air.

An explosion lit up the night as a firebomb landed amid a cluster of soldiers. Orange flames engulfed them. Their screams made an inchoate chorus to the cheers of their attackers. The citizens pressed harder, eager to get at the men who had previously protected their homes and property. Sparks swirled in the air and were caught by the wind until the bombers were forced to scramble to avoid getting singed by their own handiwork.

Caim stayed in the shadows and bypassed the brawl. After several minutes of skulking, he arrived in the merchants' district. The fighting hadn't reached this part of the city yet, but it was only a matter of time; the fires of Low Town would spread quickly.

On Silk Street, the Golden Wheel stood between a *chirash* den and a brothel to form a triumvirate of earthly pleasures. The confirmation linking Ral to the plot behind the earl's assassination stared Caim in the face: a squad of Sacred Brothers slouched on the stoop of the front entrance like they were paying rent on the place.

Caim avoided the street's tall lampposts as he slipped around to the back. A narrow wooden gate gave entrance to an alley behind the gaming house. Dim light reflected in the windows overhead. Three located on the top floor were secured with stout shutters. Those would be Ral's rooms.

Caim started his ascent with slow movements, conscious of the wound in his side as he pulled himself up. The amulet dangling from his wrist was an unfamiliar hindrance, but he didn't remove it. He focused on the task one hold at a time until he reached the center window. There, he clung onto the narrow ledge and listened. No sounds issued from inside. He boosted himself higher to peek over the sill. The room on the other side of the rose-colored pane was spacious and well appointed. Light shined from a tiny lamp above the bed. A large four-poster bed of varnished oak rested in the near corner to his right, a tall wardrobe against the opposite wall, one of its doors partway open. Upon a sideboard next to the wardrobe sat a row of wooden boxes. Boots, capes, shirts, and other articles of clothing were strewn across the floor and draped over furniture.

Caim counted thirty heartbeats, until his hands and toes began to cramp. Nothing moved inside.

He yanked open the shutter and pulled. A jolt of pain seared his side as he heaved himself over the ledge. He fell forward, onto a thick piled carpet. In the scramble to sit upright, his elbow collided with a wooden stand. The hollow scrape of sliding metal triggered his reflexes. He caught a heavy object wrapped in silk before it hit the floor. As he let out a long breath, he regarded the item in his hands, a brass icon of St. Jules, patron of the chaste and good-hearted, wrapped in a lady's undergarment.

Caim set the statuette back on the stand and stood up. There were two exits: an archway to another room to his left and a narrow door on the other side of the bed, which was probably a closet. Except for the wooden boxes lined up on the sideboard, there was nothing unusual. He was about to check the boxes when footsteps approached from the archway. Caim flattened against the wall and drew his *suete* knives.

Ral stepped into the room. Steel glittered between the fingers of his left hand. The arm was whipping back to throw when Caim stepped into the light.

Ral lowered his arm. "Caim. I wondered when you might turn up."

Caim adopted a relaxed pose, but his muscles were as tight as iron cables under his clothes. He held his knives by his sides to keep his hands from trembling. He needed answers, not more deaths.

"Why is that, Ral? Didn't you expect your pet tinmen to finish the job?"

Ral walked over to the sideboard and set down the stiletto to pour himself a drink from a tall decanter. "Not really. Brandy? It's imported."

Caim didn't reply, but he watched every move.

Ral shrugged and lifted the crystal tumbler to his lips. "It wasn't personal. You didn't need to get involved. You should have left the girl to my men."

"You're the one who got me involved. You set me up with that job from the start. Thought you'd bag a nobleman and pin it on me."

"No harm in a little gamesmanship between friends, eh? I thought you'd make your escape and leave town, hopefully for good. Either way, I get what I want and you're out of the picture."

"Who's behind the murder of Josey's father? Who are you working for?"

Ral put a hand on the sideboard. "Josey is it, eh? I'm disappointed, Caim. I always figured you for a smart guy. I'm done with serving others. I've taken matters into my own hands."

"And you killed Mathias because he knew too much."

"Actually, that wasn't me, although I'll admit I didn't shed any tears. But it makes no difference. There's no one to stop me now."

"There's me."

"Don't be an imbecile, Caim. Think of this as an opportunity. Yes, I wanted you out of the way, but now I see a better way. We can work together. We can both be free to live how we want with no one to tell us otherwise."

Caim had trouble keeping his knives from leaping into Ral's chest as anger flared in his belly. "You think you can buy me off?"

"Think of the team we would make."

"I'd rather think of you lying in your own blood."

Ral set down his glass and faced Caim. "That's not going to happen. Even if you could kill me, you're still a wanted man sought by the entire nation. You've been implicated in the murders of several government officials, including a retired exarch and half the Elector Council."

"All lies—"

Ral flashed a humorless smile. "Articles of a personal nature were found at the scenes, all of them leading back to you."

Caim suspected the fire that burned down his apartment building had been no accident, and now he knew. "You stole those things from my place before you torched it."

"You're out of control, Caim. A blood thirsty animal. The Sacred Brotherhood has orders to kill you on sight."

"Then maybe I'll just kill you. One more murder attached to my name wouldn't make any more difference."

"I just want the girl."

"You'll never set eyes on her. I'll make sure of that."

Ral laughed. It was an ugly sound. "Caim, did you really think she'd be safe in that little cabin in the woods?"

Josey laughed as Kas filled her cup with another round of his homemade wine. Crickets chirped outside the window while they ate and drank and talked. Kas kept a modest home, but he was an enthusiastic host. They dined on wild pig with squash and tomatoes from his garden.

"Enough!" she said as the cup threatened to overflow.

Kas chuckled. He had a friendly laugh, warm and deep. It made her think of her father. Poor father. She brushed melancholy aside before it could spoil her mood. She focused on Kas's hands. Large and strong despite the passage of years, they were covered with thick ropy veins. A tracery of white scars climbed the thick, hairy planks of his arms. When he smiled, his jaw slid sideways as if it were about to fall off his face. Their eyes met and Josey glanced down at the tabletop.

"I'm sorry. I wasn't trying to stare."

He ran a hand down his cheek, under his bushy chin, and up the other side. "No offense taken. It's been a long time since this ugly mug felt the eyes of a pretty lady."

Josey looked around for something to change the subject, and her gaze wandered to the fireplace. "Why do you have a stick hanging on your wall?"

Kas turned to look at the weapon mounted over the hearth. Dust covered its shaft and metal head. "Ah. That, darling, is an old friend of mine."

"A friend?"

"Aye. I was first spear of the emperor's Fourth Legion. That old pike and I tramped across more earth than I care to remember. She got me through the Border Wars and back from the Long March."

"My father—" Josey's voice caught in her throat for a moment. She pressed onward. "He told me about the crusade into the Northern Wastes. He said hardly anyone came back."

Kas carved another slice of ham for himself. "That's so. Only one company in ten returned to Nimea. That was my last campaign. After watching so many friends die, I just wanted a little plot of land for myself and as much peace as any man deserves. Even an old warhorse like me."

Josey lifted the cup to her lips. "So tell me about Caim."

"I was under the impression you knew him better than I, young miss."

"I—?" She understood the connotation and managed to blush. "No, sir. Caim and I are only companions by happenstance. We're just friends."

"Well, what would you like to know?"

She leaned her elbows on the table. "Was he always . . . the way he is now?"

"You mean the dark clothes and hard eyes?"

"Exactly!"

"No, not always. He was a pleasant lad when he was smaller, before his father was killed right in front of him and his mother taken away to parts unknown."

His words sobered Josey faster than a shot of his bitter *cha* and reminded her that she wasn't the only one who had lost her parents. She couldn't imagine what it had been like for a small boy, alone, suddenly thrust into the world.

"It must have been hard for him."

Kas nodded over his plate. "Aye. It broke his little heart, and perhaps his mind, too. He didn't hardly speak at all after I took him out of the city and brought him down here. I thought I could raise him up proper, take care of him, but there was always something different about Caim after the attack."

"Different how?"

"Well, it wasn't so much what he said, or didn't, as how he acted. He spent most of his time alone. He had no interest in playing children's games anymore. In fact, he wanted nothing to do with me at all unless it had to do with weapon play. I tried to put him off, but I could see early on that he wouldn't be long for this little cottage. So I figured I'd best make sure he knew how to take care of himself."

"So you're the one who taught him how to fight."

Kas shook his head. "I can't take much credit for that. Oh, I taught him how to handle a blade without sticking himself, but not much more than the basics. You see, soldiering is all I know, but Caim wasn't satisfied with the simple drills I could teach him. He always pushed himself harder. No, he learned more in those woods, stalking the forest creatures and whatnot, than from me. I'll never forget the day he came home with a fine young buck slung over his shoulder. The thing weighed damned near as much as he did. He didn't have no bow or arrows neither. Not even a spear."

"How did he kill it, then?"

Kas chewed on a piece of ham for a moment. "When I asked him that, he took out the hunting knife I'd given him and laid it on the table just as bold as brass. I nearly cuffed him for lying, but I could see it in his eyes."

"He wasn't lying."

"Nope. Near as I can tell, he ain't never lied to me."

Josey let that tumble around in her head as she thought about how to phrase her next question. She couldn't let go of the things she had seen in the cellar of her father's house. Caim had done something, or become something. She wasn't sure which, but it wasn't natural.

"Kas, did Caim ever do anything . . . strange?"

The big man put another hunk of piglet in his mouth and nodded. "All the time. You've seen it. He's a strange bird, but loyal to the bone.

Was always like that. He'd wrangle like a snake to get out of a chore he didn't like, but if he gave you his word, he was as true as steel."

"No, I mean did you ever see him do anything odd? Something you couldn't explain."

Kas met her gaze, his sea blue eyes twinkling in the candlelight. "You mean his powers."

Josey understood what he meant by the way he said it. She nodded.

Kas sat back in his chair and reached for his cup. After a long drink, he sighed. "Aye, I've seen it. It started not long after his father was killed. Caim went from a bright, happy lad to moody as the Sea of Torments in winter. But that wasn't all. He started doing things—things I couldn't explain. He always had light feet, but I swear he could pop out on you in an empty room. And trying to find him when he didn't want to be found? Forget it. He was like a ghost."

"Yes, what is it?" She hesitated, but then plunged headlong into her next thought. "Is he a . . . I don't know what you'd call it. A magician? A warlock?"

Kas shook his shaggy head. "Nay, lady. I've known that boy all his life. I watched him grow up from a tiny babe, and I tell you on my life he didn't never go for that sort of mummery. No, it's all on account of his mother's blood. I'd heard the rumors. Every man who served under Caim's father had at one point or another. They said she'd come from the Other Side."

"The Other Side?" The phrase pricked at something in her memory— something she hadn't thought about in a very long time, a tale she'd been told as a child on stormy nights when her nursemaid would bundle her up in blankets and tell her scary stories. "Do you mean the fey lands? Like elf mounds and unicorns?"

He shrugged his broad shoulders. "It's a northern legend. Way up beyond the marches and the wastes is said to be another world, a place of eternal twilight. The Other Side we called it. Most folk pass it off as drivel, but you've seen Caim. His father was a young knight when he returned from beyond the marches with a new bride, and their child. The woman was a rare beauty, with skin like mormorion crystal polished to a high luster, and the deepest, darkest eyes you've ever seen. It didn't take long for the stories to start around, but rumors are like mice. Try to stomp them out, but there's always a few scurrying under the floorboards."

"What about you? Did you believe the stories?"

"I believed Caim's father was a decent man and an honest lord, which is as rare a thing as an honest wage these days, and a good friend. As for the rest, it wasn't none of my concern."

"Does Caim know?"

"Hard to say. He was too young to understand such things when his parents were alive. Later on, I tried to spare him as much pain as I could, little as it was."

As she listened, Josey felt something stir in her chest. Emotions swirled beneath her calm surface, and she realized she had been holding Caim at a distance all this time. He had risked his life for her, and never deceived her or tried to take advantage. Take away the fact of his profession and he was the finest man she'd ever known.

She took a sip of wine.

"Another snoot?" Kas held up the wine bottle.

Josey was extending her cup when a noise creaked outside, like bony fingers scraping against the side of the cabin. She jumped in her seat. The crickets had fallen silent.

Kas clucked. "Don't fret. It's just the trees blowing. Nothing to worry—"

The door shivered in its frame as a heavy thud crashed against the oaken panels. Kas leapt out of his chair. Another blow flexed the stout planks. A splintered chunk of wood fell from the door. Josey clutched the table as a scream climbed up her throat.

Through the hole, Markus grinned at her.

CHAPTER
TWENTY-THREE

A chill slid up Caim's backbone and lodged in the base of his skull. How could Ral know? They must have been followed. He had to get back to the cabin. But first he'd finish his business here.

He approached Ral with measured steps, balanced on the balls of his feet. His knives came up like steel extensions of his hands, ready to carve out the life of this man who had turned his existence inside out. Ral stood calmly, hand resting on the sideboard. Caim didn't care. The bastard had to die.

As Caim gathered himself for a rush, a tingle ran across his body. Ral didn't move a muscle, but the room grew darker. For a moment, Caim thought his powers had emerged, unbidden again, but something was different. He didn't feel the pressure behind his breastbone. And yet, a prickling tingle danced along his skin like a march of ten thousand ants. The lamp wick flickered.

Caim half turned, keeping Ral in view, as a cloaked figure stepped out of the shadows of the other room and stopped under the archway. Sweat broke out under Caim's arms. He hadn't heard a sound. Shadows played across the man's ruined, colorless features. The eyes staring back at him, cold and black, catapulted Caim into a maelstrom of dark memories.

He had seen those eyes in his dreams, night after night, but never thought to see them again in the flesh. He was sure of it, as sure as he knew his own name. Once again he stood behind the fence on his father's estate. Bodies littered the bloodied courtyard. His father knelt before a man in black robes. White hands held his father's sword as if examining its balance. Then, the blade struck with stunning swiftness and Caim's father crumbled. A tiny voice screamed in the night, but Caim pushed past the cacophony to focus on the mysterious figure. The cowl was pulled back to reveal pale, ruined features like melted tallow, features without remorse or pity. And those eyes, sunken within their hollow sockets. Just as he saw them now.

Caim shifted to face his father's killer.

The stranger didn't move. Wrapped in his voluminous cloak, he watched Caim in the manner of someone observing the movements of an insect. Caim eyeballed the span between them. Six paces. A long lunge, but he could cover that distance in a heartbeat. He ignored his jangling nerves as his fingers tightened around the hilts of his knives.

Pasty hands emerged from the cloaked man's sleeves. Each held a short dagger, no longer than an eating knife, but their blades were as black as the stranger's cloak. Black as his father's sword. A greasy finger slid down Caim's spine, but he shook it off. He wouldn't be put off by odd weaponry or eerie stares. He was beginning his leap when a flash to his right triggered long-honed instincts. He stopped and ducked as Ral's stiletto traced a path over his head.

A spasm pulsed in Caim's chest, sudden and painful, as if his heart were trying to escape from his rib cage. He clamped down on the feeling and pushed it back down into the depths. He couldn't lose control. *Not now.*

Sword in hand, Ral advanced beside the cloaked man. Caim edged away. He could take Ral, but the stranger was a wild card. He didn't look like a fighter, but his movements were sure and quick. Caim didn't know if he could beat them both at once.

"I'll give you one last chance." Ral sounded genuine despite the patronizing sneer plastered across his too-perfect face. "Join us and reap the benefits. You can be my lieutenant, elevated above the slime of this city. You'll have power, money, women—everything you've ever wanted."

Caim didn't bother answering. Because of him Josey was going to die. She might be dead already, but he could still perform one last act as penance for his failure. He eyed Ral's guard, sword held off-center, ready to strike at any angle, but it left a lot of territory unprotected. Caim bent his knees. The pressure in his chest expanded, making it hard to breathe.

"Your words are wasted on this one," the cloaked figure hissed. "Kill him and be done."

"Yes," Ral replied with a sigh. "Perhaps you're right, Levictus."

Levictus. Caim allowed his rage to filter through his body, down through his arms and legs, and banish the tingles from his flesh. His vengeance had a name.

Caim feinted at Ral, but shifted in midstride. His *suete* knives stabbed, and aimed for the chest and gut of his father's killer, but they found only air as the cloaked man drifted away like smoke on the breeze, then flowed back with astounding speed. The black blades wove at Caim in a complicated pattern. It was a fighting style he had never encountered before. The man flitted like a hummingbird, first coming from the left, and then the right, faster than anything Caim had ever seen.

At the same time, something wriggled in his peripheral vision. He spared a glance and was almost spitted on the cloaked man's knives before he extricated himself with a fast parry-and-backpedal. Tiny blobs of darkness detached from the room's shadows. They ran down the walls like monstrous black tears. For a moment, he panicked, thinking he had lost control of his powers again. But he still felt the pressure, bursting to be free. The inky things resembled the shadows he had summoned before, but they were different in some ineffable way. Meaner, perhaps. He thought he could hear them hissing like a nest of asps as they crawled across the floor. He deflected a thrust from Ral's sword. When he looked down, the darknesses were all around him.

But where had they come from? A sibilant hiss made him focus his attention forward as the cloaked man launched a concerted series of attacks. Caim dodged and wove. He spun his blades in circles to disengage, and then stomped forward to press an attack, anything to evade the cloaked man's sinister weapons. It was him. Somehow, the stranger had called the shadows, and that meant . . .

Caim swallowed hard. He had never met anyone like him, someone who could also interact with shadows. If the cloaked man shared his abilities, what else might they have in common?

Caim hissed as a host of teeth, like tiny needles of ice, pierced his boots. He stomped on the floor to dislodge the tiny beasts, and received a nick across his left forearm as a black knife slipped past his guard. He jumped back before the next flurry of attacks could strike home.

Caim couldn't afford to examine the wound, but it burned like fire. He flexed his forearm as the sensation crept up into his shoulder. His side was beginning to throb from the exertion. Step by step Ral and Levictus backed him into a corner, away from the window. Something cold and revolting crawled up his calf. An image of his father's face, racked with pain, emerged from the depths of his mind. His mother was screaming. Caim dipped under a swipe and lunged, and his side erupted in agony, but he blocked out the pain and extended to his fullest range. Levictus knocked the thrust aside, but Caim's left-hand knife followed behind with a high slash. The cloaked man jerked back just in time to save his eyes. Instead, the knife's tip cut a gash across his face from mouth to temple.

He recovered faster than Caim anticipated and came at him fiercer than before. Dark red blood coursed down his cheek. Caim hopped away from the teeming darknesses and maneuvered closer to the bed. Caim glanced across the coverlets. Ral had circled around the other side. The killer had one foot on the mattress, sword poised to strike. A lamp of blown glass hung over their heads.

As his enemies closed in, Caim leapt up onto the bed. He batted aside a cut from Ral and swung his other knife in a high arc as he dove from the bed to the tinkle of shattering glass. He landed behind his opponents, hit the carpet in a soft roll with a grunt, and spun around as he came to his feet. Burning oil rained from the ceiling. The bed's fine covers went up like tissue paper. In seconds the fire spread to a drapery on the wall and up the ceiling.

The cloaked man wheeled like an angry serpent as his shadowy minions flew across the room. Caim dove through the open window. He caught hold of a shutter as his legs cleared the sill. He hung there for a moment. Then, the silvery blur of a throwing knife sped past his face.

He let go and the pavement rushed up to meet him.

"Get down!"

Josey slid under the table as Kas tore the spear down from its mounts. Its steely head shone with an oily glint. He rushed to the door just as the latch broke and a mob of Sacred Brothers poured inside.

Kas skewered the first Brother through the door. As the soldier fell, Kas whipped the spearhead around and stabbed another through the arm.

Bright spurts of blood splashed on the floor. For a moment Josey saw a glimmer of hope. Maybe the old man could fend them off. But as Kas yanked his weapon free for another strike, the press of bodies shoved him back. His spear seemed a pitiful weapon against so many swords.

Josey screamed as something crashed through the window. A heavily built soldier with thick arms and a scraggly yellow beard crawled over the sill. She reached up onto the table for something to use as a weapon. Her fingers found a smooth, cool surface. She grabbed the half-empty bottle and hurled it at the invader. It struck him on the arm and broke, drenching his uniform in wine. The Brother yelped and clutched his elbow. Heartened, Josey reached for more ammunition. She threw plates and cutlery, but he batted the missiles aside and leapt at her. He caught her by the ankle. She kicked and screamed as he reeled her in like a fish on a line.

Kas staggered in the middle of the room. Blood streamed down his clothes from a host of wounds. He plied the spear with failing strength until a blade smote him across the brow. He stumbled to the floor with a gasp.

Josey shivered in the embrace of her captor. Wine from his soaked arm wetted her dress. His horrid breath whistled in her ear. He chuckled and took liberties in the placement of his hands as he hauled her to her feet. She squirmed and tried to bite him, and was rewarded with a sharp slap across the face.

"Now, none of that, Josephine," a voice spoke from the cabin's entrance.

A shudder seized hold of Josey as Markus stepped into the cabin. Bandages peeked from underneath a striking new uniform: a white jacket and pants with golden insignia along the sleeves and stiff collar. It was the uniform of the grand master of the Sacred Brotherhood. *Why is he . . . ?*

Josey's questions fled at the hideous sight of his face. The flesh of his sunken cheeks was rippled and crusted black. Drool leaked from the wet sores where his lips had been; they pulled back in a terrible grimace as he stood over Kas. The big man's eyes were open, but glassy and unfocused. Blood seeped between the fingers clutching his ample belly.

"Another valiant defender," Markus said. "You seem to collect them like pets."

"Leave him alone! Take me, but let him be."

Markus held up a gloved finger as the Brothers surrounded Kas. "Don't waste your breath. There's no rescue coming for you this time."

While their brethren stomped the old man with their hobnailed boots, two soldiers drew long daggers and approached Josey. A scream hovered in Josey's breast as the sharp instruments came toward her, but she refused to release it. She was a princess, heir to the throne of Nimea. She wouldn't debase herself with pleading or crying. She would show them how a lady of imperial blood could die.

Markus straightened his cuffs. "Do you like my new look?"

Josey hurled her most defiant glare at him over the shoulders of the soldiers. "How much gold did it take to convince you to betray your oath?"

"Times are changing, Princess," he said. "You would be wise to change with them."

"Go to hell."

He chuckled as the knives sliced off her clothing. "I was too kind before on the waterfront. This time, I'm going to take my time and enjoy it."

Josey gasped as she was lifted onto the table, the rough wood abrading her naked skin. Calloused hands pried apart her legs and exposed her intimate parts for all to see. She kicked and connected with something squishy. A gloved fist smashed into her mouth. Blood dripped from her lips, but she smiled through the pain. Let them do their worst. She wouldn't go quietly.

But a cold worm twisted in Josey's belly as Markus appeared over her. The scars on his face oozed clear pus.

"Don't worry, girl. I was told to return you alive and unharmed. We're not going to hurt you."

He unbuckled his trousers. "Just a little tickle."

Josey screamed as a lance of red-hot pain penetrated between her thighs. Golden starbursts filled the black space behind her clenched eyelids. So lovely, they carried her away from the horrors of the waking world.

CHAPTER
TWENTY-FOUR

Ral spewed profanity with a vengeance as a troupe of table dealers from the gaming room downstairs battled the flames burning his suite. The blaze was under control, but it had reduced his rooms to a burnt shambles. Everything reeked of fire and ashes. Damn Caim! He had the Horned One's own luck. The sorcerer was gone as well. Good riddance to both as far as he was concerned. They could kill each other for all he cared.

As Ral paced across charred carpet, he considered Vassili's papers, tucked inside his jacket. He hadn't been able to make out everything on those yellowed pages, but what he understood spelled out dire implications, not only for the Church, but for the entire country. The archpriest had been involved in dirty dealings, even by his standards. Trucking with sorcery, deviltry, regicide . . . Vassili hadn't just wanted to rule Nimea; he had wanted to spread the Church's influence throughout the entire world. What boldness! In the end, the archpriest's sin had not been a lack of ambition, but trust in the wrong persons. Ral wouldn't make that mistake. He didn't trust anyone, especially his new ally. But knowing what to expect from the sorcerer—secrets, lies, and eventual betrayal—was better than trust. It was a certainty upon which to base his decisions. To rule an empire. It could be done, if he was bold enough.

Ral stopped beside the sideboard table. The wooden boxes had survived the fire with a few singes, a minor miracle for which he was almost prepared to bend knee and offer a prayer of thanks. He had seen for himself the kind of power a symbol could hold over common folk. Give them a hero, especially one raised from their own ranks, and they would follow him to the gates of Hell. Everything was almost in place. When Markus returned with the prize, they could proceed to the final phase of the plan. The last throw of the dice. Ral could barely contain his excitement.

A centurion of the Sacred Brotherhood, a grizzled veteran with more gray in his hair than blond and deep lines crisscrossing his face, appeared at the door and saluted with a fist pressed to his heart.

"The surrounding streets are clear, sir. But I sent a squad after the culprit."

Ral turned over his left hand. The tower-shaped blot gleamed on his palm like a patch of wet ink. He had tried washing it with lye, brine, vinegar, and bourbon, but so far the stain proved indelible. More to boot, in the fight with Caim he could have sworn it had started to tingle, barely noticeable in the heat of the melee, but a strange sensation nonetheless.

"Recall them. Are we prepared for Master Arriston's return?"

"Yes, sir. I have Brothers posted at the Market Gate to receive him and the package."

"Good. Have them brought to Celestial Hill as soon as they arrive. We're going to the palace."

"As you command."

At the centurion's command, thirteen Sacred Brothers entered the suite. Each left carrying a wooden box. A jaunty tune played in Ral's head as he glanced down at his hand. The mark rippled with the supple contractions of his tendons. A noble mark. Perhaps he would use it in his new family crest, a black tower on a field of white. It had a touch of elegance to it.

He looked around the room for the last time. The mural of Dantos was singed beyond recognition. The hero now appeared to be disappearing into a black void, his love forever beyond his reach. Ral didn't intend to return here ever again. In fact, he would try to forget his time spent here. Rising stars had no need for memories of the earth below.

He hummed as he walked out of the suite.

There once was a man who danced with Death . . .

Levictus stepped from the shadow of a sagging oak tree and onto a carpet of soft loam. Night seeped between the boles of the ancient grove. The sweet promise of its power beckoned to him like a lover's perfume.

His cheek burned through lines of blood congealed along his jaw. He had attempted to pursue the one who injured him through the city, but finally lost the man somewhere in the labyrinthine alleyways.

With a curse, he seized one of the shadows crawling under his robe and tore it open. Its minuscule death shriek rattled the dying leaves on nearby trees as he stuffed its gelatinous body into his wound. Murmured spells halted the bleeding and set the flesh to mending. This man, Caim, was a devious foe, but only a man after all. He would be dealt with before long.

Levictus strode across the uneven ground. Moldy stones and fallen pillars of an old sacellum studded the earth under the canopy of interwoven branches. Built as a temple in Nimea's pagan past, the site also marked a fault point, a weakness in the fabric between realms. It was here, less than a league from the city walls, he had discovered his budding powers as a young man, here he taught himself how to access those abilities with sacrifices of small forest creatures and, eventually, larger victims. Later, Vassili, ever the supportive mentor when he wanted something, had supplied him with proscribed texts to further his education in the black arts. Now the archpriest was dead and he, a man remade in the torture cells of the Holy Inquest, manipulated the strings of an empire.

He went to the stone altar at the temple's center, the very spot where he had made his fateful pact so many years ago. The memory of that night was seared into his brain. He had sought to avenge his family, but what he summoned in his ignorance went beyond anything he had ever imagined. He had seen things that night he couldn't forget, no matter how he tried. By the following dawn, he'd been a changed man.

He ran his hands across the weathered stone and drank in the power permeating the temple, let it fill him to completeness. He hadn't been back to this place in years, but now he needed to make contact again. It was time to unleash the full measure of his powers upon those who had tormented him.

Raising his voice to the night, he began to chant. Shadows screamed as they were consumed in the sorcery. The wound ceased to bother him. In its place arose a wave of ecstasy far beyond any earthly pleasure. It raced through his body like lightning as his paean to the forces Beyond soared into the sky.

Above the altar, a window of nothingness opened.

He braced himself as a frigid wind erupted from the rift and stood firm, resolute in the powers at his command, even as a figure appeared in the aperture. Harsh words resounded from the void. They grated on his ears like gnashing mountains, like the grinding of the world's bones.

"Levictus. Long has it been since your last communication. Is this the manner in which you pay homage to the Lords of Unrelenting Dark?"

Levictus knelt on the broken ground. "I have summoned you to—"

His voice broke into a hoarse scream as a jet of black flames lashed out from the portal. Levictus dropped to the ground, wrapped in their searing embrace. When the flames departed, he was curled into a tight ball.

The figure leaned closer to the rift. A dark gown clung to voluptuous curves. Cascades of midnight hair framed eyes that glowed like the pits of hell.

"Such as you do not summon us," she intoned. "You are a servant, a slave of the Shadow, to be used in whatever manner we require."

Levictus pulled himself back onto his knees. The pain was subsiding. He held his hands up to the moonlight, expecting to see a mass of charred flesh. Instead, there was only smooth, healthy skin.

He genuflected before the altar. "Forgive me, mistress."

"Tell us why you have reached across the Void this night."

"I require . . . I *ask* for another infusion."

"You dare? You, to whom the Lords of Shadow have granted more power than any mortal in a thousand years, to whom the secrets of the Dark were laid bare? You dare to demand more?"

Levictus dared to lift his gaze. The words, so long withheld, poured out of him in a rush. "I do not demand. I merely beg for the strength to serve your will. Othir, the jewel of the empire, lies under the sun like a great, bloated whore, spreading her cancer to every land. I would tear down her scabrous walls and scatter her people to the four winds. I would bring the Shadow to this place and extinguish the light of Nimea forever."

The emissary's head tilted so that her hair fell across her face, hiding her dusky features. "What you desire is possible, but there is a danger."

Levictus lowered his forehead to the cool earth. "I accept the risks."

"And there is another price to be paid as well."

Levictus had feared as much when he hatched this plan. Sixteen years ago, he had been given a task to cement his original pact with the Other

Side. He didn't mind at the time; it gave him a chance to experiment with his newfound powers. Now, after freeing himself from Vassili's yoke, the idea of continued service enraged him, but he would have his final revenge on Othir and the man who had wounded him. Though his heart resisted, he bowed his head in assent.

He listened to the emissary's message, whispered across the Void, and all the while his chest grew heavy with dread as the Shadow's plans were divulged to him. And yet, what choice did he have? He had bound his fate to this path long ago. It was too late to break free.

When she finished, Levictus exhaled a long sigh, and then nodded once more. "I will do as you bid. When do I receive my boon?"

The figure faded from view as the window shriveled up like a dead leaf. "It comes."

The grove darkened, and black clouds gathered above to block out the moonlight. Branches scratched together as a breeze from the Other Side crept through the trees. The ground quivered under his feet. Levictus clenched his fists as the tides of magic coalesced around him, but he could not have prepared himself for the tsunami that crashed down upon his head. He gasped and shivered, helpless in the throes of power. It scoured the marrow from his bones. It pounded through his veins and swelled in his chest until he thought his heart would explode. Overhead, storm clouds crackled and spat.

Then, like the calm in the eye of a hurricane, the surge evaporated.

Levictus picked himself up from the patch of dry ground where the convulsions had thrown him. He was himself again, and yet he was changed. Things looked different. The darkness churned around him like a living, breathing thing. Glowing eyes watched him from the shadows.

The shadows.

They had changed, too. Looking upon them, he understood what had been given to him, and he accepted.

With a smile, Levictus wrapped his cloak around him. As the deep, cool blackness fell around him, his body lightened and he flew on the night winds, back to Othir to sow the seeds of destruction.

CHAPTER
TWENTY-FIVE

A cold wind flogged Caim as he crouched behind the neck of his stolen steed. He pushed the animal all the way from the city, cutting cross-country between villages to save precious minutes. The moon, full and red, tracked his progress over the plains. A blood moon, the sailors called it. Night of ill omens.

The wound he'd received from the sorcerer's knife, scrawled like a streak of bloody charcoal down his forearm, burned like the blazes, but the pain was nothing next to the rage boiling in his chest. He knew where he had seen a wound like the earl's and like Mat's.

He stood in the center of the corpse-strewn courtyard. A large man slumped at his feet. Strings of red-black blood ran from the wound in his chest. A tremor ran through Caim as the corpse opened its eyes, black spheres without irises or whites. A whisper issued from blue-tinged lips.

He had been presented with an opportunity he never thought to have in a hundred lifetimes, to avenge his father's death, and he had let it slip through his fingers like wet sand. Damn Ral. It was clear the man had made some kind of deal with that creature, Levictus. But what drew them together? What plan had they hatched, and how did it involve Josey? Caim knew Ral. The man's dreams were grandiose, but teamed up with one who could conjure the shadows, how far could he go? The questions haunted Caim all during the harrowing ride.

When his first horse foundered, he sidetracked to a wayside roadhouse and stole another. The second horse proved hardier, if not so fast as the first, but after an hour of cantering the beast labored for breath. Caim felt sorry for the animal, but he didn't let up as evening approached in deepening strands of purple and blue. Nothing mattered except reaching Josey.

He reached the first stand of trees. The path was an inky band that snaked through the woods. He slowed the horse to a walk as they passed under the roof of branches. Ral had sent people after Josey. Even now they could be at the cabin. For the hundredth time he cursed himself for not killing Ral when he had the chance. The man was a fiend, not fit to live among humanity.

The same could be said for me.

True enough, but he would gladly go to the gallows as long as Ral went before him. If anything happened to Josey, he'd never forgive himself. He should have gotten her farther away, hidden her in another city where she'd be safe. The recriminations battered at him as he peered through the forest's gloom. The cabin was not far off the path. If Kas had left a fire burning, he should see its light soon.

Caim almost passed by the cabin before he picked out its white lines of wattle in the darkness. He yanked his mount to a halt and was running as soon as his feet hit the ground, knives drawn. The front door hung open on loose hinges. Beyond it, darkness swathed the interior. Not a sound disturbed the stillness of the forest.

Caim leaned across the entrance. His gaze darted to the corners of the front room. The place had an empty feel, devoid of life. The hearth had been allowed to go out; the dying embers were sunken beneath a bed of ashes. The few pieces of furniture were scattered about in shambles. Pieces of clay dishes littered the floor amid half-dried pools of dark scarlet. A sharp odor hung in the air. As he stepped over the threshold, Caim spotted the still mound of a body.

Kas.

Three strides took Caim across the room. A pike with a shortened shaft lay beside the old man's limp hand. Caim looked down at the man who had raised him and didn't know how to react. Titanic weights pulled at his insides; conflicting emotions congested in his vital organs. The walls of the cabin closed around him, cutting him away from the night. The wind's whisper vanished like ghosts of years past as the stink of blood and burnt leather filled his head. For a moment Caim allowed himself to feel remorse for the way he had left things between them. He had loved this man, and yet hated him for not being his true father. With an effort that showed in the whites of his knuckles, he shut those feelings away and turned his mind to more immediate matters. Blood stained the weapon's point. So the old man hadn't gone down without a fight. *Good for you.*

Caim knelt beside the body. The blood was sticky, not yet fully dried. The rest of the room was empty. No sign of Josey. It looked like the bulk of Ral's men had entered through the front door, and one by a broken window. What he thought was blood spattered across the sill turned out to be wine.

The door to the back room was half closed. He nudged it open. Scant moonbeams fumbled across the crude floorboards. A garment was laid over the disarrayed covers of a crude cot. An icy fist closed around Caim's heart at the sight of Josey's borrowed gown. It had been slashed to bloody strips. He flinched as identical wounds made by imaginary swords and daggers pierced his flesh.

He searched the entire cabin for the body, but found nothing. He went back outside to make a sweep of the yard. There were marks in the dirt where one or more bodies had been dragged amid a crowd of hoofprints. Caim was no tracker, but he could see they had come from the direction of Othir and returned the same way. He must have just missed them. Of course, they would stay to the main roads, secure in their numbers.

Caim's breath burned in his throat. Rage filled his thoughts, at Ral, at himself, at the gods if they existed. The Brotherhood had Josey. A thought flashed through his head. If they were riding with wounded, he might still be able to catch them.

He started toward his steed, but stopped after a few paces. The horse shuddered like it had an ague. Strings of milk white foam drooled from its mouth. The damned thing was blown. Useless. It wouldn't run again tonight, if ever.

Caim gave the animal what mercy remained in him. He stripped off its bridle and saddle, and dropped them on the ground. A wasted effort. It would probably drop over dead before morning. He had failed them. Josey, Kas, Mathias, his parents—they were all gone now. He was alone. Grief sliced up his insides like a river of broken glass. He wanted to scream to the heavens, but the cry lodged in his throat. He had nothing left. Then, a whisper-light touch settled on his shoulder.

"I'm so sorry, Caim."

The words tickled his ear as Kit alighted beside him. Her inner radiance surrounded him like the light of a thousand fireflies. He wanted her comfort, wanted it more keenly than he had ever wanted anything in his life since the day his father died, but he couldn't accept it. The rage had rendered all his tender feelings down to a lump of useless, hardened tissue.

"Where have you been?" He made no effort to temper his tone. "Out in some meadow, picking flowers and dancing with starlings?"

She floated around to face him. Tears trickled down her face like falling stars. "I was here, Caim."

"Yet you did nothing."

"I couldn't!" she cried. "I saw them kill Kas and drag the girl away, but there wasn't anything I could do."

"You could have come to find me. I could have stopped it."

"Would you have listened?"

"Of course I would—"

"No." She retreated a few steps from him. "You stopped listening to me a long time ago, and it only got worse when you met that girl."

"Her name was Josey."

"If you want to know where they took her—"

"Say her name!" he screamed.

Kit wiped at her face with the back of her hands. "Josey, okay? Her name is Josey, but she's not dead."

"I saw the dress, Kit."

"Listen, you idiot!" A deep crimson blush stained her cheeks as she propped her tiny fists on her hips. "She's still alive. They took her and rode off like a pack of demons. They left the dress so you would get all hellfire mad and go riding after them without a thought in that wooden head of yours."

He strode through her as if she weren't there, walked up to the door of the cabin, and stood on the threshold. The emptiness within yawned before him like a great mouth.

"I never wanted this for you." She came up beside him. "Neither did your mother."

"Don't, Kit."

Her ethereal fingers brushed his face. "I was happy in my world, Caim, but I had to come when I heard your mother's call. She understood it would be hard for you in this place, born of two peoples, belonging to neither. And I knew the first time I saw you that I would love you forever. That's the curse of my people. We never forget and we never die. We love forever, even after the ones we love die and pass into the great dark."

"Kit . . ." Troubled feelings rumbled in the depths of his soul. They chipped away at his resolve and made him feel weak and pathetic.

"Don't you think I mourned for your loss, Caim? Don't you think I cried myself sick after what happened to your parents? But you were a stone. You never cried."

"What good would it have done them?" But tears, hot and bitter, sprang to his eyes now as her words dredged up his past.

Kit rested her head on his arm. "We don't cry for them, Caim. We cry for ourselves. Kas understood that."

"And now he's dead, too."

"He died doing what he knew was right."

Caim thought of the bloody spear. Kas had died a hero. Would the same be said of him when his time came? The gloom inside the cabin beckoned to him.

"It's funny," he said. "For years after they were gone, I thought losing my parents had made me a stronger person. Tougher. Now I wonder if I didn't lose the best part of myself that night. The man with the black blades. He's like me, isn't he? A monster."

An electric tingle ran along his jaw as she touched his chin. "You are *not* a monster."

"There's darkness inside me, Kit. I've always known it was there, just below the surface, and you've seen what happens when I lose control."

She turned away.

"He sent that shadow-snake after me, didn't he? Now he's working with Ral, and Josey is gone. So who the fuck is he, Kit?"

For a moment, he thought she wouldn't answer. Then, "He serves the Lords of the Shadow."

Caim swallowed past the knot in his throat. The taste of tears lingered in the back of his mouth. A thousand questions jostled in his throat, but only one was important.

"How do I kill him?"

"He is flesh and blood, just like you. Cut him and he will bleed."

"I tried that." The admission was torn from his throat in an angry growl. "I tried, Kit. He has powers I don't understand, magic I can't match."

Her slender finger touched the space over his heart. "The blood calls to its own, Caim. You are your mother's son. You already possess everything you need."

He laughed, a cruel sound even to his own ears. "Then I'm damned and so is Josey."

"They took her alive, so she must have some value to them. They won't kill her out of hand. There's still time to help her."

"Now you want to help her? You couldn't stand the sight of her before."

Kit folded her arms across her slender chest. "I'm glad you have a mud-woman in your life. I know I can't love you the way I've always dreamed, the way I wanted to."

"Kit, I—"

She smiled and shook away another bout of tears. "But I'll always be here for you, as your friend."

"You're my best friend, Kit. You always have been. That won't ever change."

She punched at his arm. "It better not!" Then, in a more somber tone, "We'll find her, Caim."

He watched the light play upon the shards of broken glass on the cabin floor.

"I already know where she is," he said. "Ral told me himself once. He said we were the most feared men in the empire, that we should be lording it up in the palace."

"You mean the *palace* palace? Like the big muckety-muck's digs?"

Caim walked into the cabin. A storm lantern hung from a hook on the wall. He took it down and lit the wick from the hearth embers. Light filled the cabin as the lantern sprang to life. He hurled it into the back room. Flames shot to the ceiling as he strode out the door. The growing fire threw harsh shadows across the grass and against the trunks of the surrounding trees as he went around to the back of the cabin. Thoughts of Josey swirled around in his head. He would go after her, and the gods help anyone or anything that got in his way.

Across the yard, the boulder hunched in the earth like the egg of a giant bird. While Kit floated over him, he squatted down beside it. He fit his hands underneath the stone and heaved. The boulder was sunk deep in its loamy home, but he would not be denied. He pulled for the memories of his father and mother, for Kas who'd become the father he wanted and needed even if he hadn't realized it until too late, for Josey who needed him now. He pulled until his tendons strained and his legs shook. The wound in his side ached, but he didn't let up until, inch by inch, the stone came free of its bed. With a groan he heaved it away.

Pale worms wriggled in the damp earth where the stone had lain. Kit crouched beside him as he pulled a moldy leather sack from the soil. He cracked it open to pull out the items inside, and set them on the ground with reverence. The first was a square of sturdy broadcloth. It unfolded into a dirty gray tabard. A great sablewood tree was stitched onto the breast in black thread, the sign of his father's house. The second item was wrapped in oilcloth. Caim pulled away the covering to reveal a portrait in a plain wooden frame. Caim's father was tall and imposing in the picture. His mother looked tiny beside her husband, like a dark-leafed sapling growing in the shade of a mighty rowan. Her hair was long and lustrous black, her eyes mysterious pools of obsidian.

While Kit mooned over the picture, Caim took out the third item. The sword's leather scabbard was in bad repair. He wiped away years of grit from the whorls carved into the pommel. This had been his father's blade. Though the hilt was cool to the touch, holding it produced a burning heat in the pit of his stomach. He had pulled this weapon from his father's corpse. Now, he would use it to sever the chains of death that had bound up his life for so long, or he would die. In either case, the matter would finally be resolved.

Caim set the sword aside and pushed the other items back into the hollow. Getting behind the boulder, he heaved it back into place.

Kit watched him with an intent expression. "You can't keep running from your past. It's part of who you are."

He snatched up the sword. "I'm not denying it. I'm finally accepting my true inheritance and everything that goes along with it."

He started back toward the trail. "You coming?"

She fell in beside him, but said nothing. He was glad for the silence. He had planning to do. The trees swayed over their heads as they followed the rutted path back to Othir. The tang of wet copper stung the back of his throat. A storm was coming. *Good. Let the heavens pour out their tears. I'll give them a slaughter worthy of their misery.*

Over the plain, flickers of lightning danced through the shroud of purple-black clouds and echoed with the growls of thunder.

CHAPTER TWENTY-SIX

J osey's hands, clenched in the folds of her skirt, trembled as she stood before the painting. A regal man astride a fierce charger gazed down at her. His wavy black hair was cut at shoulder length in the masculine style of the previous generation. Thick brows met over a prominent, aquiline nose. And the eyes—she knew them with intimate familiarity. They were her own.

Is this really my father?

A brass plaque below the portrait read:

Leonel II of the House Corrinada
Emperor of Nimea

She whispered the name, adding her own. Josephine Corrinada. The jumble of thoughts warmed her body like a hot bath. Then she thought of Earl Frenig's kindly face and the languor evaporated in a cool shiver. So many secrets, so many lies, all to preserve her identity. *How am I supposed to feel?* She didn't know, and that was the scary part. And on top of that, what had happened to her at the cabin . . .

She bit back tears as a wave of images crashed over her. The rough grasp of strange hands. Markus's face in the dim firelight, sweat dripping from his nose as he took her. Josey folded her hands over her stomach. She wanted to curl up into a ball and die.

No.

She pulled her hands away and stood up straight. With a sniff, she drew back the tears. To hell with them all. She wouldn't succumb to the terror. Father hadn't yielded when they took his post away. He was an old man, far past his prime, but he'd continued to fight unto his last breath, and so would she.

Angry voices interrupted her thoughts. Josey turned toward the center of the chamber. The Grand Hall of the Luccian Palace, named after the famous architect and composer Luccio Fernari, who had spent the last years of his remarkable life involved in its construction, was a masterpiece of traditional Mitric architecture. Once, vibrant frescos depicting significant events and persons of the empire's history had covered the domed ceiling, but they had been replaced by scenes of inferior quality showcasing the Church's rise to power. She recognized them from her catechism: the Hanging and Decapitation of Phebus, Conquest of the Nimites, and, finally, Revolution Day. Each picture was bordered in ornate molding of curling vines and leaves chased with gold. Enormous, hand-woven tapestries hung on the walls, separated by brass lanterns with frosted glass panes that bathed the chamber in stark, ghostly light.

On the floor, a dais of marble steps dominated the eastern wall. A semicircle of massive thrones, fashioned of deep-stained redwood and upholstered in purple silk, crowded the highest tier. The seats of the prelate and Elector Council, they represented the highest powers in both the spiritual and temporal worlds. On the wall above the dais, a giant sunburst was emblazoned in a mosaic of tiny white-and-gold tiles. Once, that august symbol of the Church's authority would have instilled a sense of awe within her. Now, knowing what she did about the Council and their murderous deeds, she felt only a touch of melancholy, as if for a treasured thing lost beyond recovery.

Thirteen wooden boxes rested on the bottom step of the dais. She had no idea what they were meant for, but it could be for nothing good. She harbored no illusions about why she was here. The Sacred Brotherhood had taken control of the palace, apparently under the command of the man who stood at the foot of the dais, and she was his captive as surely as if she wasted away in some dark dungeon cell. She shook her head at the uncomfortable image. There would be rats and lice, all manner of crawling things . . .

Caim will come for me.

That hope huddled close to her heart, and yet reminders of her dire predicament were all around. She had cried as they dragged her, naked as a babe, from Kas's cabin and tied her over a saddle. Then, she began to hate. Jarred and battered, she fantasized about Caim killing the men who

228

had abused her, cutting them into pieces for the carrion birds to devour. Hatred sustained her on the long ride back to Othir. By the time they reached the city she was a teary, sodden mess, bruised from thigh to collarbone. More soldiers met them at the gates and provided an escort to Celestial Hill. She had been appalled to see the state of her beloved city. People rioted in the streets, destroying property, burning and looting. Bodies lay in the gutters, both commoners and soldiers alike. She wished she could put a stop to it somehow, but trussed over her steed like a sack of parsnips, all she could do was watch the carnage.

Up the Processional they rode, each clop of the horse's hooves on the hard cobblestones driving the saddle horn deeper into her ribs, until they reached the palace. There she was taken down from her humiliating position and hustled through a number of gates to a small chamber where an old silent woman in a black shawl washed her with stubborn disregard for her comfort and shoved her into new clothes.

Josey looked down at the garment she had been forced to wear. Layers of white silk brocade trailed on the floor. Rows of tiny seed pearls were sewn to the low-cut bodice and down the puffy sleeves that encased her arms, but left the shoulders bare. She felt scandalous in the gown. It reminded her of a wedding dress for a virgin bride, something she would never be. That part of her had been stripped away. Just thinking about it made her feel sick.

The only other people in the hall were Markus and Ral, who was also an assassin, according to Caim. A dangerous man, supposedly, but he hardly looked the part. He wore a fine suit of black with starched white cuffs and collar. A slender blade with a silver guard hung at his side. Josey couldn't imagine Caim wearing such an extravagant weapon. Then, she spotted the assortment of blades hidden about the man's person, tucked into the tops of his boots and under his sleeves, and reconsidered her opinion of him. Maybe he wasn't such a dandy.

"I don't care." Ral's words rang across the hall. "Drive them away. Kill them, if need be. Just get them away from the gates."

Markus saluted and stalked out of the hall. When Ral looked over, Josey met his gaze without backing down.

"A vast improvement." He treated her to a slick smile as his gaze wandered up and down. "Now you look the part of a princess."

"I'd throw this dress in your face if I had anything else to wear."

"Tsk, tsk. No need for hostility, Josephine. We need each other."

"I don't need anything from you. You're the one who killed my father. Don't try to deny it. I know everything now."

"Everything? Do you know that without the Council to control the people, the city is tearing itself apart?" He stepped closer, until the scent of his oiled hair clogged her nose. "Do you know that you're completely alone, a young girl in a perilous place surrounded by perilous people?"

"Caim will—"

He cut her off with a laugh. "Caim is dead in some gutter, or soon will be. Look around you, Princess. I hold the palace, and with it, the city. Perhaps someday the entire country will bow to me. Forget Caim and whatever romantic notions have been bouncing around inside that little skull of yours. Think of the big picture. An alliance with me would benefit us both. You would enjoy my protection, and I would gain a measure of legitimacy."

Josey could have been slapped across the face for all the shock she felt.

"You mean marriage. Us? You're insane. I would never—"

"It's not so far-fetched, my dear." Ral sauntered toward the dais. "Worse unions have been forged for the sake of politics. Our marriage will cement my hold on the throne. You will be an empress with all the wealth and splendor a woman could ever want."

Josey resisted the impulse to lift a hand to her temple, where the beginnings of a frightful headache throbbed. Her bodice was too tight, making every breath more difficult to inhale.

"You might hold the palace for now," she said. "But the Church won't sit idle. Once the riots are quelled, they'll put you . . ."

Her words died away as Ral opened the wooden boxes on the dais, one by one lowering the front sides to reveal their gruesome contents. Thirteen pairs of glassy eyes stared at her in various states of shock. She recognized their pale features. From their wooden prisons, the heads of the prelate and the Elector Council confronted her.

"As you can see, the Church is no longer a concern. With the Brotherhood firmly under my command, thanks to the largess of my benefactor, none remain in the city who can challenge me." He laid a hand on the box holding the prelate's head. "Call it a wedding gift from your betrothed. After all, these are the men who killed your real father."

Josey shook her head. Tears wet her lashes and gathered in the corners of her eyes. She wouldn't give in to this fiend, wouldn't allow him to twist her thoughts. She drew herself up straight. "The people of Othir will never stand for it."

"The people will do whatever their lord governor demands of them."

"And what of the mob gathered outside your gate?"

A grimace broke the hard planes of Ral's face for a moment. She had scored a hit, but then the calm returned as if nothing had happened. "Those who refuse to obey will be dealt with harshly and permanently."

She scoffed. "There aren't enough Sacred Dogs in Othir to subdue the entire city. Even recalling the nearest garrison—"

"I have," he said with a mocking grin, and waved a hand, "other resources at my disposal, my dear."

Josey started as a shadow detached itself from the darkness draping the wall behind the throne. The shadow resolved into the shape of a man, tall and lean, garbed in a monk's robe of purest black. There was something eerie about his movements; the intensity of his gaze was unnerving. Everything about him suggested barely restrained violence, a dangerous animal coiled to spring at the least provocation. An image flashed through Josey's mind, of the ebon serpent uncoiling from the ceiling in Caim's apartment, and she knew what this creature was at once.

Sorcerer. Trafficker of the black arts. Agent of the Dark Ones.

"What have you leagued yourself with?" she whispered.

"A power from beyond this world." Ral nodded to the newcomer. "Enough to rule a nation and rebuild an empire. You should thank me, Princess. I intend to restore your birthright."

Whatever Ral intended to say next was interrupted by a commotion at the entrance. Sacred Brothers ushered a throng of men and women into the hall. She recognized one face in the group: Anastasia's father, Lord Farthington. She started to lift her hand to catch his attention, but hesitated when she got a better look at him. Lord Farthington looked drawn and haggard, his face more deeply lined than she remembered. His mouth quivered as he was herded inside with the others. *He's terrified.* A tiny shudder fluttered her belly. If such a powerful lord was afraid, what chance did she have?

"My lords and esteemed ladies." Ral lifted his voice. "Forgive this disturbance of your persons at such a late hour, but there are matters of great importance at hand which require your attention."

Josey chewed on her bottom lip. The words sounded rehearsed. Ral was playing some sort of game, and she wanted nothing to do with it. She cast her gaze about the chamber. The robed man had vanished when the aristocrats arrived, as silently as a phantom, but she got the feeling he was nearby. She sidled over to a side wall, pretending to admire the tapestries while she checked the exits. She didn't know the layout of the palace very well, but if she could get away from the hall she might be able to find a way out. Getting away was all she could think about.

Behind her, Ral climbed the dais as he addressed the nobles. He kicked over one of the wooden boxes on his way up the steps, sending its contents tumbling to the floor. Gasps rose from the crowd.

"Good people, don't be alarmed," he said. "This is a glorious moment. This is the day you shall long remember as the beginning of a new era of prosperity and majesty."

As Ral sat in the center throne, an old nobleman staggered forward as if to admonish him, but a hulking soldier shoved him back into the crowd.

"Nobles of Othir," Ral said. A pair of golden ravens rested atop the throne's tall back, as if perched upon his shoulders. "I proclaim myself your sovereign. As a merciful man, I am granting you the opportunity to be the first to bow to me and swear your allegiance."

He gestured to the wooden boxes. "Or be declared traitors and face immediate execution."

While the gentry sputtered and clamored in indignation, Josey picked up her skirt and tiptoed to a narrow archway tucked between two arrays. She was almost there when a large frame filled the opening. Her silk slippers slid to a halt as Markus loomed before her. His scarred cheeks twitched into a mockery of a smile as he stared at her with cruel intensity.

Ral's voice called from behind her. "Ah, it is time for your most excellent personages to meet my betrothed. Allow me to present Princess Josephine of the House Corrinada. My bride-to-be."

Tears formed in Josey's eyes as she turned to the crowd. They watched her with various degrees of astonishment.

Ral extended a hand from the throne. "Come, my dear. Stand beside me so we can address our subjects together."

As Markus took her arm in a painful grip, Josey moved her feet to keep from being dragged across the tiles. With every step the turmoil of dread grew within her bosom. She cast her gaze about the hall, hands bunched into the folds of her skirt.

Caim, where are you?

Nightfall greeted Caim on his return to Othir. He didn't need to use the Ereptos tomb tunnel; the soldiers had abandoned the gates, and for good reason. The city was destroying itself in a tumult of blood and fire.

He slipped in through the Black Gate and stalked down streets scarred by fighting and mayhem. A smoky miasma hung over the city. The Processional was in shambles, with sodden furniture, broken street-lamps, and heaps of trash, some draped with dead bodies. A team of slaughtered draft horses lay in Dawnbringer Square, still in their traces. Makeshift barriers showed where the city's forces had tried to contain the violence and failed. Above the carnage, Celestial Hill loomed over the rooftops, its pristine walls gleaming like ivory in the moonlight.

"This place is a mess," Kit said as she floated over his head. "Are you sure you're going to be able to find him?"

Caim turned down a narrow lane. "I'm going to try."

A light rain filled the cracks in the street and collected in shallow pools. With knives drawn, Caim watched the dark nooks and doorways on either side of his path. His father's sword hung between his shoulder blades with strange familiarity. He wasn't sure why he had taken it. His knives had served him well enough these many years, but he was running on instinct now, and taking it had felt like the right thing to do. From time to time he found himself reaching up to touch the shagreen-wrapped hilt, and a shiver would run through his arm. After this night was over, he'd be happy to bury the thing again.

As he entered the Gutters, Caim almost ran into the backs of a gang of citizens. They marched down the center of the street, truncheons in hand. With soot and bloodstains on their clothing, they looked like they had already seen some fighting. He waited until they passed. As he crossed the street, his gaze was drawn to the hulking specter of the workhouse, resolute against the city skyline, walls glistening in the rain, affecting everything in its vicinity like a bloated spider in the center of a tattered web. Caim's fingers tightened around his knives as he went on his way.

He dipped into a crooked side street. It was so dark he had to navigate mostly by feel, following its meandering length for two blocks to the mouth of a constricted intersection. Water dripped down onto him from the eaves above as he stood in the safety of the alley's shadows. By its looks, Ale Street had escaped the worst of the rioting so far. A man's body in the uniform of the night watch was sprawled in the gutter outside the Blue Vine beside an overturned cart. Blood clotted in the reddish hair where half his head had been caved in.

"I'll check around back." Kit darted away.

Caim stared across the street. Slivers of light leaked from gaps around the wineshop's shuttered windows. A soft clack on cobblestones drifted through the rain. A horse, its chestnut coat rain-soaked and soiled with grime, nosed through piles of garbage. The ends of leather reins trailed in the puddles.

Caim opened and closed his fists. What was he waiting for? Josey needed him, and yet he hesitated. He had fought for her, killed for her, sacrificed everything. Was he prepared to die for her, too? He could run. Start over. Kit would be ecstatic. All he had to do was leave Josey to her fate. Just walk away.

Caim caressed the ice-cold amulet that hung from his wrist. He couldn't do it. He couldn't leave her to Ral's tender mercies. And though he was loath to admit it, he had become fond of this tired old tramp of a city. If he ever left, it would be on his terms.

Having decided, he crossed the swampy street and nudged open the door. Faces looked up as he stepped into the common room. Half a dozen men and one woman sat around the hearth. Several hands stole inside clothing to reach for hidden surprises, but one look from him was enough to stop them cold. Mother stood behind the bar. A heavy mallet rested on the counter beside her, the kind used for breaking open cask bungs. *Or caving in the skulls of young soldiers.*

Caim scanned the room for a specific face, but didn't find it. "I'm looking for Hubert."

"He ain't here," Mistress Henninger replied in a terser tone than her usual. "Haven't seen him."

"Since when?"

She shrugged, one sleeve of her heavy blouse slipping off the shoulder. She reached up to put it back. "Earlier. Before sunset."

"Any idea where he is now?"

A bearded man stood up clutching a stick of firewood in his fist. "You'll get out of here if you know what's good, young buck."

Caim stared at the speaker. After half a dozen heartbeats, the bearded man settled back in his seat.

Mother came around the bar. "Don't mind him, Caim. You're a welcome sight. Hubert came by a few hours ago when the fighting took a turn for bad, and he grabbed up all the men to go with him." She shot a scornful look at the group huddled around the hearth. "At least, all the real men. Anyways, no telling when he'll be back."

"I'll wait." His voice, though hardly above a whisper, carried across the room. No one objected.

"Drink?" Mother asked.

With a nod, Caim took a seat. He tucked his knives away, but kept them loose in their sheaths. Kit floated down from the ceiling and alighted beside him.

"Nothing out there," she reported. "There's some skirmishing over in the next block, but it seems to be moving away from this part of town. The worst is down by the docks. I think someone set fire to the city granaries."

"That should keep the tinmen busy," he murmured under his breath.

"I don't know. The harbor is out of control. I didn't see any soldiers. Not any live ones, at least."

Mother brought over his drink and set it on the table. "Don't know if you'll want to be finding Hubert just now, Caim. He wasn't in his right mind when he left, if you take my meaning."

"No, I don't. What happened?"

She rubbed a hand over her prominent bosom. "Well, 'tisn't for me to say, but you got a right to know what you're walking into."

The front door banged open. All conversation ceased as three men entered. Caim almost didn't recognize the young man in their midst. Bloodstains marred Hubert's once-fine clothes, and his hat was missing.

By the gore slimed on its hilt, the rapier strapped to his hip had seen some use this night. The young nobleman's gaze had a strange cast as it swept through the taproom. When it settled on Caim, a vicious smile twisted Hubert's bruised lips.

"Mother," he said, "we have a hero among us. Set this man up with another drink on me."

Hubert's words were slurred, but there was an unmistakable air of menace behind them as he came over to Caim's table, followed by a pair of thick-shouldered goons.

"I'm not here to drink, Hubert. I came looking for your help."

Hubert plopped down in a chair. His bodyguards, or whatever they were, watched the room.

"My help? I'm a little busy right now, Caim. Tonight is the moment of our grand coup. We've got the Reds on the run, but you already know that, don't you? You paved the way, so to speak."

"What are you talking about, Hubert?"

Hubert laughed, a dry sound devoid of humor. "Playing the innocent, Caim? There's no need, I assure you. You can take full credit for my father. He was, after all, a tyrant at heart."

Caim had a sinking suspicion he knew the answer, but asked anyway. "What about him?"

"He's dead, Caim. Someone entered his rooms at the palace last night and killed him. Then they took his head. A bit macabre of you, but it was a nice touch."

Caim remembered Mathias lying in his bed with his heart cut out. What had Ral said at the Golden Wheel? Something about taking matters into his own hands. Vassili must have been Ral's secret patron. It made sense. With the backing of a Council member, Ral would have felt untouchable. But at some point, he'd decided he didn't need the archpriest. So he'd devised his own plans, which somehow involved Josey. It might already be too late. She could be dead. The thought ricocheted inside Caim's head, dashing all his thoughts to pieces. He took a deep breath. He had to remain in control. That was the only way to save her.

"And you think I had something to with it?"

Hubert leaned forward until their faces were inches apart. The reek of whiskey hit Caim like a punch to the jaw.

"You're Caim the Knife, slayer of the corrupt and powerful. But my father wasn't some goddamned monster. He did this city a lot of good."

"So good his own son was out to unseat him?"

"You don't know anything about it!" Hubert slammed his fists on the tabletop.

The other patrons huddled closer around the hearth while Hubert's bodyguards inched forward.

Kit materialized behind the bravos. "You better do something, Caim. These guys are carrying a lot of hardware."

Caim slouched back in his seat. He had never seen Hubert like this. The young man seemed on the verge of a maniacal rage.

"Listen to me, Hubert. I didn't kill your father, or any of the other Elector Councilors. That was Ral. He's working with someone, a foreigner. They're plotting to take over the government. *They* killed the archpriest."

Hubert sneered across the table. "A pretty tale, but there's no need to deny it. You've done us all a great service."

"I was out of the city taking Josey somewhere safe, or that I thought was safe."

"Ah, yes. The conspirator's daughter and her faithful knight in shining armor."

Hubert reached for the cup on the table, and Caim caught the young man's wrist in a hard grip. "That's enough."

Hubert's reddened eyes stabbed at Caim. Then his features crumbled into a ruin of misery. "Why did they have to butcher him like that? I know he could be a hard man, even cruel sometimes, but they had no right . . ."

Caim released Hubert. He sympathized, but his insides were ice. "The people responsible are the same ones I'm after. They took Josey and now they're holed up in the palace with a battalion of tinmen."

Hubert wiped his face with a coat sleeve. "What are you going to do?"

"Storm the palace and get her back."

"Really?" Kit blurted. "That's your plan?"

Caim clamped his jaws together to keep from yelling for her to keep quiet. "What about you?" he asked Hubert.

"I've been rousing the people. We already control most of Low Town.

We could use your help, but it sounds like you've got enough on your plate."

"We could work together."

Hubert looked more like his old self now. He sat up straighter in the chair and even managed a backhanded brush down each of his coat sleeves.

"How?"

"You might control Low Town, but the Brotherhood still holds everything above the Processional. You'll never take High Town with a rabble of shopkeeps and stevedores, so don't even try. Go straight to Celestial Hill."

"What will that accomplish?"

"We'll cut off the head of the beast. With Ral and his lieutenants out of the way, there'll be no one to coordinate their soldiers. Once we control the palace, the city will fall to us by default."

"That's a big risk. My father died taking a chance like that."

Caim drew his knives and set them on the table. The bodyguards shifted, but kept their distance.

"You're not your father, Hubert. Prove it tonight. Help me save Josey and put down this menace for good. She's the heir to the old emperor. We found the documents to prove it. She's royalty."

"Royalty, eh? Well, she certainly acted the part. But why should my people risk their lives just to trade one tyrant for another?"

"Because she's not her father either. She's what this country needs to knit itself back together. You always talk about a return to the old ways. This is your chance to prove it. This could either be Nimea's last night as a unified realm, or the beginning of a better life for us all."

Hubert eyed the blades, and then nodded. "I'm in. What do you want me to do?"

Caim smiled across the table. "I've got a plan."

CHAPTER
TWENTY-SEVEN

Rain pelted Caim as he crouched in the half-finished bell tower of the new cathedral. The wind howled in his ears. Rain pounded on the stone roof. No stars shined this night, and no moon, only a screen of tumultuous storm clouds stretched across the city.

A good night for killing.

High Town spread below him in a carpet of gray and black. Celestial Hill rose against the sky like a great wave. Lightning flashed, and the bleached shoals of white rooftops appeared before the night washed back over the city. Flames flickered along the Celestial's broad avenues, where a thousand plebeians struggled against the city militias. True to his word, young Vassili had assembled an army: milliners and bakers, porters and servants armed with all manner of weapons, from torches and lengths of raw timber to pikes stolen from slain tinmen.

Their goal was the Luccian Palace, sprawled atop Celestial like a crowning jewel, surrounded by concentric walls with watchtowers and massive barbicans. Hubert's spies reported Ral had withdrawn all of his pet soldiers inside in anticipation of a siege. Exactly what Caim wanted him to do.

"They're almost in position," Kit said. "Hubert says he doesn't expect much resistance."

The rain was freezing cold, but Caim paid it no mind. "They'll fight back. They don't have any choice."

"It's really burning out of control."

Caim turned his head. Billows of ugly black smoke shrouded the boroughs of Low Town. Fire had claimed entire blocks, devouring homes, storefronts, and public buildings in its wrath. The rain was the only thing keeping the blazes contained, but many would die before morning. More would die if his plan didn't succeed.

Hubert's people had finally reached the palace gates. The young nobleman was a tiny figure striding at their head, his sword flashing in the torchlight. His assault got a reaction. Like a kicked anthill, masses of soldiers rushed to defend the walls. Arrows filled the air and men spilled their lives into the overflowing gutters.

Caim descended from the tower. He had seen enough. Hubert was buying him the window of opportunity he needed. Kit floated beside him as he dropped to the cathedral's marshy grounds and started up the winding boulevards to Celestial Hill. Within minutes they reached the outer wall of the palace at a spot well away from the fighting. Caim had already scouted his entry point. The stone of this section of wall was riddled with cracks and creeping vegetation that created convenient handholds. He took his time and made sure each hold was firm before trusting his weight to it. At the top, he crawled over the smooth apex and dropped down the other side.

Caim paused at the foot of the wall. A manicured lawn extended toward his next obstacle, the forty-foot interior wall of the palace. Beautiful gardens filled the space between, adorned with delicate flower trees and swollen streams. The sweet fragrances of lilac and oleander lingered in the damp air. Caim passed through the luxurious grounds without a second glance.

Kit spotted the first sentry under the branches of a redbud tree. Caim squatted behind a hedge of flowery bushes and watched. The soldier was looking toward the palace gatehouse, possibly waiting for his relief. Every few moments he blew into his hands and rubbed them together, his spear propped against the tree trunk.

While he watched, Caim thought about Kas, lying dead in his cabin, blood seeping from gouges in his torso. The old man hadn't asked for trouble, but it had come to his door nonetheless, garbed in the Church's flimsy excuse for the law. Caim imagined Josey as she was stripped naked and dragged away, cursing him for leaving her alone. An image of a corpse-strewn courtyard formed in his mind.

Moments dripped by like the falling rain, and all the while Caim's anger burned hotter, a smoldering coal in the pit of his stomach fueled by recrimination. He had been fooling himself. He'd only ever been good at one thing his entire life. It was time he went back to it and forgot about being the hero.

With images of Josey gnawing at his mind, he got up and started toward the tree. He kept low and worked his way around behind the sentry. He could pass by, unseen, but tonight wasn't a time for taking chances.

As he moved into position, Caim found not a knife in his hands, but the leather cord from Josey's necklace, wrapped around his palms with a foot of length stretched between. He clenched the key amulet in his fist as he stole up behind the sentry. His heart beat harder. He had never strangled anyone before; some stray dogs, years ago when he had been living on the streets and it had been kill or starve to death, but never a man. He supposed it was all the same.

Then, the moment was upon him. Caim slipped the cord around the guard's neck and pulled tight. His arms were nearly wrenched from their sockets as the man lurched forward. The guard kicked and grunted like a wild animal. Caim slammed a knee into his back and hung on. If not for the key, which Caim gripped like a garrote handle, the cord would have been ripped from him. As it was, the loops of leather sawed into his left hand until he started to fear he might lose the fingers.

The sentry stumbled to the wet grass and Caim kept up his hold, and it was a lucky thing because his victim fought for a good long time. Minutes passed before the guard was still. Caim stood up, a little shaky. His hands and wrists ached like he'd been wrestling a bear. As he unwound the cord from his stiff fingers, a flicker of lightning lit up the gardens and he got a glimpse of his victim's face. It was a sight he could have done without. The man's features had turned an ugly shade of purple. His tongue lolled from his mouth like a swollen red worm, his eyes open wide. Worse, he was a kid, maybe seventeen at most.

Caim's gaze fell to the crimson surcoat covering the youth's armor. Not a kid. A soldier. An enemy. *Older than I was when I chose my path.* He wrapped the cord around his wrist again.

After hiding the body in a clump of tall fronds, Caim continued onward. Another fifty paces brought him to the foot of the inner wall. No sign of additional sentries. He ran a hand across the granite facing, too smooth to climb and too hard for pitons. From around his waist he uncoiled ten fathoms of braided silk cord, a gift from one of Hubert's contacts.

"Are you sure you can manage this?" Kit asked.

"I'll meet you on the other side. You remember the plan?"

She gave him a withering look. "I'll be there. Just don't take too long." Then she was gone.

He attached his grapnel to the line and measured out seven times his own height. Fortune favored him. The sharp prongs caught on the first try. Caim pulled the line taut and listened for signs of movement above. After sixty heartbeats of silence, he began his ascent. Foot by foot he climbed. It was difficult to find purchase on the slick stone. Several times his feet slipped and nearly wrenched the cord from his grip, but he held on. At the top he grabbed hold and hoisted himself onto the curved capstone.

He lay there, heart pounding against the stone as he peeked over the side. Several large buildings crowded the inner bailey, which was floored with rectangular blocks of pale gray stone. The old imperial residence, where the Elector Council now held its sessions, dominated the center. Flying buttresses radiated out from the main structure like the legs of a colossal insect. Lofty towers surrounded the great central dome, painted in gold leaf.

Lesser buildings abutted along the inside of the wall: a barracks and stables for the Palace Guard on the bailey's east end; on the west side, the Thurim House. The Thurim had been the body of state elders responsible for advising the emperors of old. Of course, as one of its first acts after gaining power the Church abolished the assembly. For many Nimeans, it remained the singular most heinous misuse of power and was the spark for rebellious elements like the Azure Hawks. A few cloaked sentries patrolled the courtyard in pairs, but the majority, it seemed, had taken Hubert's bait and rushed to the outer walls. Caim prayed they would remain there. He didn't fancy the idea of running into a patrol of angry soldiers as he wandered the citadel.

Kit appeared on the wall beside him, her legs dangling over the side. Not a drop of rain touched her. "Is this as far as you've gotten? You need to get moving or we'll be here till midsummer."

He stifled an acrid reply. "I count eight down below."

"And four in a guard shack."

"No one up top?"

She shook her head, sending her silver tresses swinging. "I guess they're afraid of a little rain."

"That's good for us."

Caim unhooked the grapnel and let the line fall to the ground. Pulling with his arms and pushing with his toes, he slithered along the top of the wall while the rain beat a tattoo on his back, until he reached the near corner of the Thurim House.

Caim got to his feet. While Kit levitated beside him, he tried to dry his hands on his sodden tunic. The Thurim House was an older style of building, with tall lancet windows, deep ledges, and elaborate fluting; ideal for climbing, but the edifice rose more than a hundred feet above the bailey. One slip would mean a quick end to his career.

"Get on with it, will you?" Kit said. "Before daybreak."

Caim shot her a nasty glare as he found his first handholds and started up. He put his mind on other matters while he climbed. His next problem was how to find Josey within the confines of the palace. He was counting on the belief that Ral wouldn't harm her until the last of the riots were put down and he had firm control of the city. A cold shiver of dread that had nothing to do with the rain passed through Caim's body as he considered the idea she might be dead already. In that case, Ral would pay.

Chilled by his thoughts, Caim didn't realize he had climbed so far until he reached the ornamental cornice jutting from the edge of the roof. Teetering on a narrow shelf, he leaned out to grasp the overhang. Then, with a deep breath and a prayer, he let go with his feet. The palace grounds spun beneath Caim as he swung out over empty space. The guards' torches were tiny sparks far below. His side burned like a hot coal shoved under his skin. With a grunt, he pulled himself over the lip.

He rested on the rooftop to catch his breath. The rain felt good on his skin.

"Come on, Caim," Kit called.

He groaned and rolled to his feet. With the wind whipping past his head, Caim crossed the slippery roof. Scaling down the building's eastern façade was easier. Halfway down the wall, he stopped and inched along a narrow ledge. A tapered buttress arched out like a slender bridge from a corbel set in the side of the building to support the towering walls of the imperial residence. Caim didn't stop to think. He just stepped onto the slick stone blocks and walked, arms held out to either side like a tightrope acrobat. He only tottered once. Halfway across a gust of wind swirled from below to disrupt his balance. He froze as his feet began to slip out from under him, but he clenched his toes and forced himself to stand rigid until the gust died down. With a racing pulse, he continued on and reached the other side without further delay.

As he touched down on the roof of the residence, Caim took a moment to gain his bearings. Battlements studded the top of the building like rows of teeth. Minarets rose at each of the four corners. Once, fires had burned atop each slender tower, a symbol of imperial rule, but those braziers had lain cold these past seventeen years.

Caim leaned over an embrasure between two stone merlons. The soldiers below marched in the same pattern as before. No one had seen him. Satisfied, he jogged over to where Kit hovered above a massive chimney stack. He jumped to catch the top and pulled himself up. Balanced over the black abyss of the flue, he unlimbered the bundles from his back and tied them to his belt.

"I hate this part."

Kit twirled a piece of her hair. "I'm sure it won't be so bad. Just think happy thoughts."

With a sigh he lowered himself into the chimney. The space was not as tight as he'd feared. With his back braced against one side, he could use his knees and hands to control his descent. Fifteen feet down he came to the first branch shaft. The top floor. He levered himself inside the chute and crawled down its dark, narrow passage, dragging the bundles behind him. He encountered a low-hanging projection with his head and, after rubbing his bruised brow with a sooty hand, he dropped to his belly to wriggle underneath. A wave of claustrophobia hit him midway through the process. The walls suddenly seemed to press in on him, crushing him from all directions. He paused for a moment to catch his breath. Then, he pulled himself through the aperture.

As Caim continued down the chute, he came to a junction of four shafts. He hesitated a moment, comparing his position to his mental layout of the palace. Straight ahead should take him to the central hall. So decided, he continued. A current of warm air buffeted him as he crawled around a slight bend. He stopped at the edge of a pit.

Specks of burning cinders floated up from the opening, which glowed with the light of a roaring fire below. He peered over the edge and had to squint against the scorching heat. The crackle of blazing pinewood logs echoed off the chimney walls a dozen paces below. The shaft continued on the other side. Five paces. On his feet, he could have made the jump without a second thought, but it was a long way to leap on his hands and knees.

Kit chose that moment to appear from the ceiling. "You're almost there. Just a few more paces and a short dip."

"Dip?"

"Just hurry, will you?"

Caim fought the urge to say something she would make him regret later. Instead, he gathered his legs under him as best he could and braced his hands against the walls. He took a deep breath of the heated air, let it fill his lungs, and he leapt. The fire's heat bathed his torso as he sailed across the distance. Caim stretched his body to its fullest extension. For one long instant, time slowed to a trickle. Then, his fingertips caught the ledge. Muscles rigid, he held himself aloft. The two bundles dangled beneath him. Smoke stung his eyes. For several seconds he dangled over the chasm like a hog on a spit. When his heart stilled its maddening pace, Caim kicked with both legs. His hands grasped at the smooth stone of the shaft, and he pulled himself the rest of the way up in scrambling wriggles. Once he was across, he flipped onto his back and took several long breaths.

Kit poked her head through the ceiling. "You all right?"

"You might have mentioned the fireplace."

"And deprive you of a little fun? You know, you're getting boring in your old age. I might have to go looking for a younger guy, someone with a sense of adventure."

"I could be so lucky." Caim rolled over onto his stomach and resumed his crawl.

"What?"

"Nothing, dear."

The shaft extended a dozen paces farther before it sloped downward at a sharp angle. Faint light filtered through a gap at the bottom of the drop-off. Caim took a few moments to figure out how to best tackle this obstacle. He tried to twist around to put his feet forward, but the shaft was too narrow. He finally decided to drop headfirst. With luck, he wouldn't come down too hard.

As he was bracing himself for the descent, Caim was surrounded by a sudden chill in the air. It cut through his thin clothing and bit deeper, down into his bones. For a moment, he felt as if his heart were going to stop. Then, it was gone.

With a shiver, he said, "I don't like this, Kit. Keep an eye out, eh?"

She didn't reply.

"Kit?"

He looked around as much as the shaft allowed, but there was no sign of her. She could be scouting ahead without being told, although that sounded too good to be true. *Wonderful goddamn time to wander off.* But he didn't have time to ponder her sudden absence. He had to keep moving. Josey needed him.

Caim wedged his hands against opposite walls and let go.

CHAPTER
TWENTY-EIGHT

Caim bit down on his tongue as the bottom of the chute rushed up faster than he anticipated. He shoved both hands hard against the walls. The blackened stone gouged his palms, but he kept up the pressure until he hit the bottom. Somehow he managed to land without bashing his skull open. He started to relax when clanks from above announced the falling bundles. They landed beside him with a loud crash.

Caim cursed and disengaged himself from the tether. He touched the tip of his tongue to his lips and winced. *At least it's still attached.*

He was in the fireplace of a large chamber. The slight illumination he had detected before came from an open doorway on the other side leading to a corridor that glowed with soft candlelight. The plain coverlets draped over the plush, oversized bed, along with the lack of personal effects, led him to believe this was a guest room, presently unused. But why was the door open? It was rather late for a dusting by the chambermaid.

Suspicious, Caim gathered up the bundles and padded across the pale sea green rug. Outside in the hallway, colorful arrays lined the walls in both directions. Candles flickered in brass holders, the wax dripping into reservoirs.

His soft-soled boots made no sound as he stalked down the corridor. He chose the right-hand branch, followed it to a T-section, and turned left until he came to another intersection. Caim was considering his next choice when a faint sound reached his ears. Voices. Judging by the reverberation, the speakers were in a large room. Like the Grand Hall.

Caim stole toward the noise. Every time he passed a candle, he reached up to snuff its wick. The passage behind him filled with darkness.

The corridor opened into a wide gallery. A carved marble balustrade overlooked the massive chamber below. Sacred Brothers were stationed at regular intervals around the balcony, four in all.

Caim left the bundles in the dark of the hallway and drew his knives. Two Brothers died without realizing their lives were in danger. He allowed the third to utter a muffled croak, which drew the last sentry into the shadows. Only when the gallery was clear did Caim take a moment to peer over the railing. His throat constricted as he spotted Josey, still alive—thank the gods—standing at the foot of a broad dais in a white gown. She didn't appear to have suffered any harm. In fact, she looked better than when he had left her at the cabin. A weight he hadn't fully realized he was carrying lifted from his chest. He hadn't failed her yet.

A large crowd filled the chamber below, surrounded by a platoon of Sacred Brothers. Despite their bedraggled appearance, the captives seemed to be aristocrats, many of them in their senior years. Expressions of fear and indignation played across their pinched faces.

Josey wasn't the only one Caim recognized. Ral, in a fancy black suit, sat in a gaudy throne atop the dais. One at a time, the captives were brought before him and made to kneel.

While Caim watched, the Brothers escorted an elderly lord in a night jacket to the steps of the dais. When they released him, the nobleman stood up as tall as his stooped back allowed.

"I will bow to no usurper!" he shouted in a powerful voice that belied his age. "I would rather die."

Ral made a shooing gesture with one hand. "And I shall gladly grant your wish, my lord."

The old lord sputtered and coughed as the Brothers dragged him from the hall.

Mystified, Caim went to retrieve the bundles. When he grasped the sword's worn hilt, a voice whispered in his head. He knew it well. He'd heard it in his dreams a thousand times. The voice of his father's ghost.

"Justice . . ."

Caim's hand shook. He wanted to throw away the blade, but a powerful force held him back. He shook his head, as much to deny the unease churning inside him as to clear it, and slung the sword onto his back. He carried the second bundle to the balcony, cut the strings binding its oilskin covering, and unlimbered his other gift from Hubert: the curved bronzewood shaft of a bow to replace the one he'd lost in the fire.

Caim strung the weapon with quick, sure motions. As he stood up, he placed an arrow across the rest and drew the string to full tension. The confusing maelstrom of emotions roiling in his chest—for Josey, for his father, for Kit's disappearance—they all vanished as he sighted on the throne. He was back in his element. This was business, pure and uncomplicated.

Caim took in a deep breath, and let it out slow and steady. In the space between one breath and the next, he fired.

The bowstring thrummed against his forearm as the arrow flew. He followed its path across the hall. A perfect shot. In his mind's eye, Ral slumped dead on the throne, his eyes turned misty with the fog of death. The image was so real he almost believed it had already happened, until the torchlight surrounding the dais flickered and the arrow dipped to the side, not much, just a hand's breadth, but enough to miss its mark. Instead of taking Ral through the throat, it sliced a furrow across the sleeve of his jacket.

The hairs on the back of Caim's neck tingled as he remembered another night, in Ostergoth's castle, and another perfect shot ruined at the last moment. Sorcery. His hands tightened around the stave of the bow.

Levictus.

Everyone in the hall looked up. Josey's eyes blossomed wide. The lordlings lurched to their feet and retreated from the dais. Their mutterings swirled up to Caim. Some of the Brothers drew weapons, but none moved to protect their liege. As for Ral, he hardly moved except to grimace and press his left hand against his chest.

Caim snatched another arrow from the bundle at his feet. Sweat drenched his shirt. Tremors chased each other through his stomach like a pack of angry dogs. But his hands were steady.

"Let her go, Ral!" he shouted. "Or the next one goes through your heart."

The assassin's dry chuckle ascended to the gallery. "We've been expecting you, Caim, but you're a bit late. Release my betrothed? No, I don't believe I will. The city is mine, and these good nobles were just swearing their loyalty to me. It would go better if you laid down your weapons and surrendered. Perhaps I'll grant you an imperial pardon."

"I don't think so. There are five thousand angry citizens outside the gates. Your pet soldiers won't be able to hold them off forever."

Ral stood with his hands at his sides, seemingly at rest, but Caim knew how fast the man could move. He kept the arrow centered on Ral's chest.

"Not forever. Just until reinforcements arrive from the outer garrisons. Then your little rebellion will be crushed in time for my coronation and subsequent wedding to this fine lady."

Caim's gaze flickered to Josey, and fingers of dread closed around his heart. In concentrating on Ral, he hadn't noticed Markus's arrival. Bandages peeked over the collar of the man's uniform, which was now white instead of red. Waxy scars dimpled his face as he stood behind Josey, one arm around her waist and the other holding a dirk to her slender throat.

"You should have joined me," Ral said. "You could have been my viceroy, a man of wealth and power, but you have proved too untrustworthy. I'm afraid you'll have to die."

He nodded to Markus. "Or perhaps you'd prefer to watch her bleed to death before your eyes first?"

Caim pulled the bowstring back another inch, making the bronzewood creak. "You won't kill her. You need her too much."

"Are you certain about that?"

Ral lifted a finger. Josey gasped as a line of blood trickled down her neck. Markus's burn-scarred lips curved upward in a grin.

Caim cursed under his breath. His plan was falling apart. Rather than rescuing Josey, he had placed her in even greater danger. Retreat wasn't an option. Come morning, Ral's hold over the city might be impregnable. He could shoot, but Markus might kill Josey out of hand. They were at an impasse, and he was out of options. The string strained against his fingers.

The clack of boots on the marble flagstones stole everyone's attention. All heads turned as a soldier in militia livery dashed into the audience hall. An angry clamor followed in his wake. Ral took the opportunity to descend a couple of steps. Caim's aim didn't waver.

"The outer gates have fallen!" the militiaman shouted.

Ral swore a vile oath. "What of the bailey?"

"We hold it yet, but it may not stand for long."

Caim smiled. "Looks like your plot is unraveling around you, Ral. Maybe you should give up now and save everyone the trouble."

As Ral opened his mouth to speak, a metallic twang pricked at Caim's ears. He threw himself aside as the baluster before him shattered in a shower of marble shrapnel. Caim reaimed and let fly. The arrow sped like a diving falcon, but Ral ducked behind a powdered dowager. The missile passed over their shoulders to thud into the leg of the vacated throne.

Caim reached for another arrow, but Ral was already darting across the crowded hall. He threw down the bow and vaulted over the broken balustrade. His knives cleared their sheaths before he hit the floor. Heels stinging from the impact, he raced after his adversary.

"Caim!" Josey screamed as Ral and Markus hustled her through a side exit and slammed the door behind them. Three Brothers took up positions in front of the exit with weapons bared.

Caim smiled as a familiar feeling spread through him, a tingling that started in the tips of his fingers and vibrated up his arms until it coursed through his entire being. Sparks of light glimmered on weapon points and flashed from rings of mail, igniting his blood. An insistent pressure throbbed behind his breastbone as his powers awakened, but this time he welcomed it like a long-lost brother. It was time to put aside the veneer of civilization and revel in pure barbarity.

With a snarl, he launched himself at the soldiers.

CHAPTER
TWENTY-NINE

Josey's breath rushed from her lungs in a gasp as she thrust out her hands to cushion the impact with the wall.

Ral didn't give her time to recuperate before he dragged her along the candlelit hallway, raving as he devoured the passage in long strides. "This doesn't change anything! One madman can't change the course of history."

Josey was too jubilant to care what Ral said. Ever since her assault at the cabin, she had been terrified to discover what Ral and Markus would do next. But when she'd seen Caim in the Grand Hall, her heart had jumped. He had come for her! She looked around for some means to get away from her captors, but there wasn't much hope of that. Ral was much stronger than he looked, and Markus followed them with a squad of Sacred Brothers.

She was racking her brain for a plan when the corridor opened into a wide anteroom. Display stands and trophy cases crowded the floor. A menagerie of stuffed animal heads on the walls seemed to watch as Ral hustled her through.

"We'll go north," he said. "Assurances have been given. Whatever else they take, I'm to have the capital. I've done my part. Then, after the city's been tamed, I will return to begin my reign. He'll see who's the better man!"

"You sound frightened." Josey couldn't help herself from taunting him, trying to hurt him as she had been hurt. She didn't know whom he meant by "they," but she hardly cared anymore. She was tired of being yanked back and forth between hands like some tawdry carnival prize. "You should be. Caim's not going to show you any mercy."

"He had his chance two nights ago and fled like the coward he is."

Despite his bluster, Josey didn't believe a word of it. Caim was like a force of nature, as unstoppable as the tide. However, if Ral could get outside the city, he might be able to take her beyond Caim's reach.

Ral stopped on the other side of the trophy room and pointed to one of the sergeants. "You come with me. The rest of you wait here." Then to Markus, "Do whatever it takes, but stop him. When I return, you'll have everything I promised, lands and title."

Markus glanced at Josey, his scarred face rigid with tight lines. Clearly, he wanted to object, but he merely nodded. "He won't get past us. Phebus speed your journey and hasten your return. My liege."

With the barest nod, Ral dragged Josey along. He thrust her down another corridor. She looked around for something, anything, to slow their progress. She dragged her heels, only to have Ral tighten his grip to a painful, viselike clamp and pull her all the faster. She scratched his hand and received a slap across the face.

When they passed a steep flight of stairs, Josey bit down hard on Ral's knuckles. Blood filled her mouth as the skin split beneath her teeth. An unholy screech erupted from Ral. He shoved her away. Josey kicked off her slippers and dashed up the steps. The hard stamp of boots pounded close behind.

The staircase turned back on itself twice before letting out in a narrow passageway of bare stone. Josey hiked up her skirt and ran. She passed a bas-relief carving on the wall depicting a regal griffon in the same style as the design on the cellar floor at the earl's manor. The floor was caked with thick dust. Cobwebs drooped from the ceiling. She needed someplace to hide. She turned a corner and ran past several closed doors. She grabbed at their handles, but they were all locked. Her breath burned in the back of her throat as she came to another flight of steps. Josey rushed up them without a pause.

The stairs rose on and on above her in a dizzying tunnel of steps and railings. As she rounded a heavy stone newel post, a sinewy hand grasped her ankle and wrenched her to a standstill. She kicked and clawed. They had molested and abused her, killed her foster father and oppressed her people. She would not give in! But the grip wouldn't let go. Ral pulled himself up her body, crawling over her in a disturbing imitation of a lover's ardor. She didn't see his other hand until it smashed into her cheek. The buffet knocked her against a wall and scattered her senses. She slumped, hardly aware as he draped her over his shoulder.

Josey struggled to keep her eyes open even as a gray blankness threatened to overtake her. She was swung around several times, then carried down some stairs and through a winding passageway. Ral's shoulder ground against her stomach, making her want to throw up. It was over. She had lost. Now Caim would never find them.

Then, a gust of freezing wind blew up her dress. Raindrops splattered on her back. Josey shivered despite her fogginess. When she lifted her head, she saw not the pavers of the outer courtyard she expected, but sloping gray tiles. They were on the roof, of a side wing by the look of it. The bailey wall loomed in the darkness like the spiked back of a slumbering monster. Torch fires blazed beyond the rampart, where a great mass of people swarmed. Flashes of steel and iron. No sounds reached her between gusts of wind, but she imagined the cries of pain and death.

Ral came to the end of the roof and stood at the edge of the abyss. There was nowhere to go. Cursing, he turned back, but something gave him pause. He set her down and drew his sword, pressing the tip against her back.

"Don't move a hair on that pretty head, Princess," he breathed into her ear. "I wouldn't want you to fall to your death."

Josey swayed in his grip. The tiles were ice cold under her feet. The rain saturated her sodden gown to penetrate her undergarments. At a nod from Ral, the sergeant took a position behind the door back into the palace and lifted a black-headed mace with wicked flanges. *They're waiting for someone to come through the doorway.*

Talons of fear constricted around her throat. *Caim!*

Josey tried to wriggle free, but Ral tightened his grip and jabbed her with the sword point. Blinking back raindrops, she watched the open door with growing trepidation.

Blood dripped from Caim's knives as he stole through the palace corridors. The shadows flew before him, a malevolent whirlwind of darkness and death snuffing out the candles along the walls with their passage. Caim saw just fine. The ache in his side was gone. He felt rejuvenated.

The Sacred Brothers in the throne room had fallen to him in a handful of heartbeats. Driven by anger, it took him almost as long to kick open the locked door. The screams of the nobles as they fled reminded him of another slaughter. His parents' faces hovered before him. Their mouths moved, but no sounds emerged, only the pained expressions they'd worn the last time he saw them, a lifetime ago. An image of Josey imprinted over the carnage of his father's estate, her body sprawled on the cold palace tiles, Ral's sword protruding from her chest. Her eyes stared up at him in horror. He slashed the air and the figment vanished, but his fury redoubled, so hot he felt he might explode at the slightest touch.

He rounded a corner and skidded to a halt at the entrance to a spacious room. Rows of glass cases covered the floor beneath the stiff heads of a dozen hunting trophies. Five men awaited him.

Markus stood sideways, his sword leveled at Caim. "It's over. You're done interfering with our plans."

The other Brothers flanked Caim with careful steps. One sported a crop of gray hairs sprinkled through his short beard and a row of stripes on his sleeve. He had probably seen all sorts of action from tavern brawls to brutal murders.

But he hasn't seen anything like me.

"Nice suit," Caim said to Markus. "Did it come with a leash?"

Markus sneered through the mass of burns encrusting his face. "I'm grand master now, and soon I'll be a lord."

Caim let his hands rest at his sides as the soldiers moved in. The veteran Brother lifted his hand as a prelude to attack.

Then, the darkness exploded.

Shouts resounded off the high walls as the Brothers were under assault by hundreds of tiny mouths. Caim watched without malice or mercy as the soldiers fell, one by one, and were consumed. All except for Markus, who stood in a shrunken circle of light, untouched. He slashed at the darkness around him as his men cried out for help, but he did not budge from the circle.

When the shadows finished their feast, they parted before Caim as if they knew his mind. Perhaps they did. He didn't know and he didn't care. The remains of the soldiers lay in huddled masses, their flesh gnawed away down to the bone.

The color fled from Markus's marred features as he stared at Caim. "What kind of devil are you?"

Caim slunk forward, his knives held low.

Markus turned and revealed a round shield strapped to his other arm. A little larger than a buckler, it looked like a relic from another century. Caim lunged with a double cut, low and high. The links of a mail shirt stopped his left-hand *suete*. The other was knocked aside by the edge of the targe. Caim spun away as Markus's sword whistled past his ear.

From behind the protection of his shield, Markus harried Caim around the room with an onslaught of vicious stabs. Caim stepped around a glass trophy case. Markus shattered it with a side-armed blow.

"You should have stayed away." He centered his sword point on Caim's chest. "You should have let us take the girl. Now you're going to die."

Caim launched a feint and counterthrust, but Markus batted it aside with the shield.

"You're already dead," Caim said. "You're just not smart enough to realize it yet."

Markus growled as he charged. Caim twisted away from the sword, but the shield's boss caught him in the chest and drove him back into the wall. His left arm was trapped between the shield and the room's partition. The broadsword fell, and he caught it with a desperate parry. Markus's stale breath blew in Caim's face as they strained against each other, chest to chest. The air was filled with their grunting and huffing.

Around the periphery of the room, the shadows quivered with agitation. Caim heard them hissing in the back of his head, eager to attack.

Back! he shouted at them. *This is my fight.*

But he couldn't push free. Markus was bigger, stronger, and he had the leverage. Moment by moment, he crushed the breath from Caim's lungs. Inch by inch, the sword's edge dipped closer to his head.

"Not so dangerous now, are you?" Markus smiled over the edge of his shield. Sweat dripped from the tip of his nose. "Caim the Knife, the most feared man in Low Town, chopped up and gutted like a market hog."

Caim's chest burned. His right arm was shaking, and he'd lost feeling in his left. The sword fell a few more inches. He could see his reflection in the surface of the blade.

"I wonder," Markus said. "Will you scream like your lady-love did when I stuck her with my prick?"

Caim spat full in his face.

Markus drew back his sword as he blinked away the sputum. The motion made some space for Caim, enough to catch a breath of air.

Markus's eyes narrowed to bloodshot slits as he swung. Caim's knife flicked out. A heartbeat later, the sword clattered to the floor and Markus staggered backward, one hand pressed to the side of his neck. Ruby red arterial blood streamed down the front of his fine uniform. Disbelief and annoyance vied in his gaze as he slipped to the flagstones.

The blood roared in Caim's ears like a rushing flood. His hands shook from the exertion. He took a deep breath. The shadows had quieted at the edge of his vision. He could feel their impatience as he let out the breath. Flicking the blood from his blades, he resumed his hunt.

Caim jogged through a groined archway into another wing of the palace. As he passed a flight of stairs, distant sounds caught his ear: the slam of a door followed by a wailing roar. The storm.

Caim shook the excess gore from his knives as he turned onto the steps.

The shadows coursed before him.

CHAPTER THIRTY

"Our chariot awaits, Princess," Ral crooned into Josey's ear.
She tried to bite him, but he kept his arm well away from her mouth.
The sharp point of his sword pressed into her back.

A carriage awaited in the bailey courtyard below, surrounded by fluttering torches held aloft by rain-drenched soldiers. Ral shouted to catch
their attention, but his words were lost in the storm. Josey almost laughed
at his predicament. Besides the door there was no other way off the roof
except for a fifty-foot drop to unforgiving stone.

"Your lover," he said, "is dead by now, darling. A pity I didn't get the
chance to cut his throat myself. Shall we go see the corpse?"

Before he could take a step, however, a shape appeared in the doorway.
Josey didn't have to see the face to know who it was. A gasp broke from
her lips, and relief, so long withheld, suffused her body and drove away
the bitter chill as Caim stepped out onto the roof. He moved with his cus-
tomary grace, but Josey could see his side was paining him by the way he
walked. His long knives glittered in his hands, their blades stained
scarlet. And he wore something new. The hilt of a sword jutted over his
right shoulder.

While Josey took in the sight of her savior, a hulking figure moved
from behind the door. She opened her mouth to warn Caim, but Ral
mashed his forearm hard against her lips. The Brother swung. Josey's
muscles went rigid as she witnessed what happened next, for she had seen
it before in the cellar beneath her father's house.

The night came *alive*.

One moment the mace was sailing toward Caim's head, and then he
was gone, wrapped in impenetrable shadows. Red stains blossomed on the

Brother's uniform, at his side, his arm, his chest. Slack-jawed, the soldier collapsed and did not move again.

Josey sighed as Caim emerged from the darkness.

"Bloody Phebus." Ral yanked Josey sideways. "Not another step! The princess and I are leaving. You'll stand aside if you don't want to see her insides splattered all over the yard."

Caim stopped a dozen paces away. "I don't think so, Ral. Without Josey you're just an upstart with dreams of grandeur."

"I've got important friends, people who want to see me on the throne. Princess or no princess, I will rule Othir."

"Then prove it." Caim took another step. "Kill her."

Josey shuddered as she looked into his eyes. He wasn't bluffing.

"Stay back!" Ral shouted.

But Caim took yet another step, closing the distance between them.

Ral shifted his grip, and Josey felt herself slipping. Her bare feet scrabbled on the slick tiles. Caim leapt for her. He had dropped his knives. *Pick them up!* she cried inside her head even as she reached for him.

They slid down the slope, both of them straining to reach the other, but all she could think about was Ral, lurking above them, ready to pounce at any moment. A scream lodged in Josey's throat as the roof ended and empty space yawned beneath her feet.

Their fingers missed by inches.

Then, she was falling. Josey closed her eyes, the cry forgotten, and resigned herself to a swift death.

Something seized her arm and jerked her plummet to a halt. She looked up through the pouring rain, thinking Caim had somehow managed to catch her, but what she saw instead brought the scream rushing up her throat. Black as coal, so dark she couldn't make out its outline at first, it perched on a stone rainspout like a gargoyle. It looked like an overgrown wolfhound or a great jungle cat, with deep black holes for eyes and huge fangs like sooty icicles. Though the thing looked monstrous, it held her arm gingerly in its massive jaws.

Josey shook with body-jarring sobs as she hung from the mouth of the beast. Choking on tears of joy and fear, she contemplated the stones of the courtyard below. With firm resignation, she reached up around the creature's neck with her other arm. Rough bristles scraped against her wet skin.

With a rumbling growl, the creature shook its head and let go. Josey's piercing wail sliced through the storm as she fell, but her scream was cut short when her heels landed on firm footing. Shivering, she clutched at the wall. Her fingers found purchase on an entablature of ornamental scrollwork below the building's cornice.

Josey looked up. The beast was gone, vanished like a phantom, but the silhouette of a head peered over the edge of the roof above. She cried for help, but the wind snatched the words from her mouth. Lightning split the sky, followed by an epic crash of thunder that shook the palace walls, and the head disappeared.

Eyes squeezed shut, Josey tightened her grip and prayed.

Thunder rattled the roof tiles as Caim attacked.

He had recovered one of his *suetes*—a small miracle—but his thoughts were on Josey, dangling below. He didn't know what she had managed to grab onto; he couldn't see five strides in front of him through the storm's gloom. Whatever it was, he didn't think her grip would hold for long. He had to finish this fast. He feinted and cut low.

Ral beat the strikes aside and countered with a jab of his slender blade, but Caim was already moving. He slashed for the head, but the bastard jumped out of range. Something else was bothering him as well. When Josey had fallen over the side of the roof, he panicked. She was going to die and it was his fault. He deserved to die with her, but when he reached the edge, time had slowed to a crawl. In that instant, the shadows had scattered and he'd felt the presence again—the same presence he had felt in the Vine and again in Josey's cellar. The sensation had jangled his nerves like a splash of ice water. He'd stopped himself as his feet started over the side, but the feeling was gone.

Caim wiped his face with his free hand. The bizarre presence might have left, but his situation had deteriorated. The shadows were gone, back to wherever they came from, and his side ached worse than ever.

Ral adopted a casual fencing stance, sword arm halfway extended, feet apart. The gleaming point of his weapon wove small circles between them as he glanced to Caim's shoulder.

"Pick up a new toy, Caim? Watch out. You might pick up a little style and ruin your reputation."

Knees bent, knife held low, Caim slunk toward his prey. "Worry about how you're going to get away."

"Get away?" Ral laughed. "This is exactly where I want to be. You and me, the winner takes all."

Caim couldn't believe the man's hubris. Ral was no slouch with the sword and as cold-blooded as any killer on the street, but even he couldn't hope to defeat Caim in a fair fight. "Do you really think you can—?"

A sudden motion cut off his words. Caim dropped flat to the rooftop as a steel sliver sailed from Ral's off-hand. The throwing blade spun over Caim's head to strike the wall behind with a metallic clink. Caim ground his teeth together, pissed at himself for forgetting Ral's penchant for dirty tricks. Ral didn't give him time to browbeat himself, but rushed in behind the throw.

Caim pushed off the wet tiles. He blocked the first thrust and spun away from the follow-up. In turning, however, his foot slipped on a loose tile. Pitched off balance, he parried a swift slash, but the impact knocked him on his back. He grunted as a tearing sensation ripped through his side. A trickle of warmth oozed down his ribs. He rolled back to his feet on the unsteady surface and scuttled sideways. All the while, Ral hounded him with cuts and jabs. Somehow during the exchange they had traded places. Now Ral backed him toward the precipice above the bailey. Caim kept low and made himself as small a target as possible. He reacted a split second too late to an attack and paid the price with a slice down his right biceps, not too deep, but it bled with a vengeance. Caim switched the knife to his left hand and responded with a riposte to create some space between them.

"How does it feel?" Ral advanced on light steps. His sword cut lazy figure eights in the air. "Knowing you're about to die at my hands? It has to hurt. I know you've always considered yourself the better man."

Caim's breath came in shallow puffs as he gazed into the eyes of his enemy. Behind the arrogant twist of Ral's feature dwelt a frightened man, a man who had lived in Caim's shadow for so long he couldn't imagine a future without him. Caim tilted his head to let the cool rain patter on his face. He and Ral were two edges of the same blade, more alike than he had ever realized. With a momentous effort, Caim let the anger pour out of him, and he smiled.

Ral's lips twisted into an ugly frown.

When Ral glided forward behind a long thrust, Caim didn't retreat or dodge the attack. Instead, he leapt to meet it straight-on. Ral dug in his heels, but he couldn't curtail his lunge before Caim's blade caught the outthrust sword and twisted it away. A stiletto came up in Ral's other hand for a swift stop-thrust, but Caim grabbed the wrist. They grappled, chest to chest, both heaving for advantage. Caim drove with his hips, and the *suete* knife punched into Ral's navel like a blade returning to its sheath.

Ral convulsed against Caim's shoulder. His breath wheezed in Caim's ear. "You aren't . . . better . . . than . . ."

Caim pushed.

Ral sprawled on the tiles, one hand pressed to his abdomen, the other stretched over his head as if reaching for something that wasn't there. A livid welt pulsed on his open palm.

Caim left the man to gasp out his final breaths alone. He went over to the roof's edge. The storm had intensified. He couldn't see anything. He called out to Josey. If there was any response, he couldn't hear it over the wind.

He was searching the face of the building for a way down when a shiver that had nothing to do with the cold skittered up his spine. The *queticoux* flashed through his mind, and the voracious shadows he had faced in Ral's suite.

Caim's fingers tightened around the hilt of his knife as he moved.

CHAPTER THIRTY-ONE

Caim toppled toward the roof's edge as a line of fire sliced across his lower back. His hands slipped on the wet tiles; his right leg was dead weight beneath him. With a frantic heave, he lurched sideways and saved himself.

A black-robed shape perched on the roof's peak. Amid flashes of lightning, the sorcerer's stoic features emerged, glistening like alabaster under his gaping cowl.

Caim took stock as he watched his enemy through the haze of rain and mist. He was hurt. How bad, he couldn't tell, but every movement sent rippling talons of agony clawing through his body. The twinge in his chest returned, pulsing under his heart, whispering its seductive call into his ears. Just surrender, it said, and the pain will be gone. Part of him wanted to give in. It would be easy to let the power take over.

With a deep breath, Caim pushed himself to his feet.

Sensation returned to his leg as he staggered away from the edge of the roof. His aches faded into the background when a small, almost innocuous knife appeared in the sorcerer's hand. Where did its matte black metal come from? The same metal as his father's sword. The answer was staring him in the face, so simple, and yet the implications reverberated to the core of his being.

"You killed the earl." Caim climbed the roof's sloped pitch. "You killed my friend Mathias. And sixteen years ago, you killed my father. I want to know why."

Levictus rose to his full height like an uncoiling serpent. His voice echoed in the darkness, as cold and forlorn as a tomb. "Before, we were an instrument; we went where bidden, unseen, unheard. To take those who were marked for death. Baron Du'Vartha was one of many."

Baron? His father was nobility? *And I never knew.* Red-hot anger flooded his thoughts as he brooded over all the things he'd never gotten the chance to know about his parents, but he tamped it down. He had to stay in control.

"Why? Of what value was my father's death to you?"

"Our masters commanded it. We obeyed without knowing the reason, but now we know many things that were mysteries before. About secret dealings. About the heir of House Tenebrae, born of a mortal father and a daughter of Shadow."

"What are—?" Caim swallowed the question before it passed his lips. His mind turned in a dozen different directions. "Daughter of Shadow. You mean my mother?"

The sorcerer took a step toward him, not threatening in itself, but Caim had seen the man move and felt the measure of his strength. Although thin of frame, this foe was more lethal than a dozen thugs like Ral. Something moved in Caim's peripheral vision. Dark shapes gathered in the gloom surrounding the rooftop.

"We considered allowing you to live." The sorcerer produced a second knife from the folds of his robe. "But the Lords of Shadow have demanded your extermination, and we must obey in order to be free."

Caim braced himself, but nothing could have prepared him as a thousand points of darkness swarmed from every direction. The shadows crawled up his boots, latched onto his cloak, and stung him with tiny needle-sharp fangs. He lashed out with his knife, but they came too fast, flowing like quicksilver around his attacks. Pain burst anew from his back, accompanied by the sickening sensation of things trying to wriggle into his wound.

Levictus glided through the mass of his pets, his knives glittering like black jewels in the night. Caim thrust to halt the advance, but the sorcerer shifted without moving and the *suete*'s point met empty air. Caim jerked back just in time as the black knife traced a searing incision down his cheek. Two inches lower and it would have severed his throat. He spun and attacked from a different angle, but his enemy was gone. The shadows vanished as well, but Caim could feel their presence in the dark, stalking him.

He turned in place, all senses tuned for the slightest sign of the sorcerer. His face burned like he had been tagged with a hot iron. The knife dragged in his hand, almost too heavy to lift. He longed to close his eyes, just for a moment, but the sorcerer lurked somewhere in the darkness, watching him, waiting for an opening.

His ears caught a sound, a near-silent whisper of a foot dragging across wet slate, as black metal gleamed out of the corner of his eye. He closed his stance a moment too late. Two lightning-quick cuts left him disarmed and bleeding from fresh wounds across his injured side. Bile filled his mouth as his knife hit the tiles and clattered over the side. Again, Levictus vanished.

Tears of frustration burned in Caim's eyes as he limped in a slow circle. "What did you do with my mother?!" he screamed. "Did you kill her, too?"

A mocking voice floated in the wind. "You know the truth, but you cannot face it. Cannot embrace it, as I have."

"Stop talking in riddles and tell me where she is!"

The wind died down for a moment, making the sorcerer's next words resound like thunder crashing over Caim's head. "She dwells in the peerless realm of her ancestors, beyond the Veil in the Land of Shadow."

The words echoed inside Caim. In his memory he was looking up at his mother, standing on the widow's walk of their family home, her features framed in black tresses like the waters of a tempestuous sea. Her dusky skin glowed in the light of the setting sun as she faced the wild Northlands and the great dark forest beyond his father's demesne. Caim tried to swallow in a mouth gone dry. He hadn't been able to believe it before, but now, like a blind man feeling the surf on his toes for the first time, he couldn't deny it any longer. His mother really was one of the Shadowfolk. His father, a mortal man, had brought her home as his new bride, never guessing the Shadow would come to reclaim its own. He was a half-breed, a freak caught between two worlds, and now he was going to die without the chance to discover what he had lost.

His chest contracted in a painful spasm.

Caim hissed as the breath left his body. Then he caught sight of a dark mass looming in the sky over the palace. He looked up, dreading some new attack, but a familiar voice called to him from the storm-shrouded sky.

"Caim!"

Kit! Her voice sounded distant, as though she were shouting from the other side of the city.

"Kit, where are you? I need you."

"I'm trapped. He's blocking me."

"What?" Caim glanced up and around. The rounded dome of the palace was topped by a narrow steeple, but the dark cloud hovered above even that.

"Caim . . . Help!"

She sounded weaker. A gust tickled the nape of his neck and Caim spun around, only to be confronted with a wall of dense shadows. He could feel his death approaching on silent footsteps. "What can I do, Kit?"

But she was gone. Caim ground his teeth together. Just when he needed Kit most, she was beyond his reach. But something she said nipped at his brain. *He's blocking me.* What did that mean? Was she talking about Levictus? How could he . . . ?

Shadow magic. The sorcerer must have detected Kit's presence and taken steps to separate them. But how could he help her?

Kit's words at the cabin came back to him. *The blood calls to its own, Caim. You already possess everything you need.*

The blood calls to its own.

The sorcerer appeared out of nowhere. Caim backpedaled across the slippery tiles as the black blades sought his flesh. He evaded their touch with a roll and came up on his feet perilously near to the edge. He was trapped. The rage returned, fiercer than before, burning away his fear. If he was going to die, he would do it as he had lived, on his feet and facing his enemies. As Levictus approached with firm, steady strides, Caim reached up over his shoulder.

An electric shiver ran through him as his fingers closed around the smooth hilt of his father's sword. A vision appeared before his eyes: his father's estate as it had been sixteen years ago. The villa in flames. Glowing embers fluttering into the night sky like a cloud of angry fireflies. Levictus standing over his father. Above the wrappings of long black robes, the sorcerer's pallid features shone in the moonlight. The blade pierced his father's chest and Caim cried out, pain bursting from his insides as if the weapon had pierced his flesh instead.

Caim blinked.

He ran through a field of wildflowers in every hue and variety. His parents chased after him, their laughter ringing in the summer air. He glanced over his shoulder, but they had fallen far behind. He could barely see them. Yet their eyes latched onto him from across the distance, watching him, waiting for . . .

Caim blinked.

He was back on the palace rooftop. The sword shimmered like a shard of black ice in his hand. Water danced along the temper of its razor-keen edges. It felt odd, holding it, and at the same time familiar, like coming home. His father's voice reached across the years.

Justice.

Levictus had stopped half a dozen paces away. The sorcerer stood there with raindrops streaming down the hard planes of his face. Watching. Waiting.

With a grim smile, Caim stepped toward his enemy, and the ache in his chest exploded. Kit appeared as a sensation of weightlessness enveloped him. Joy radiated from her smile like the dawn of the first morning. He had never seen her like this before. Gone was the girlish ingénue. In her place was a woman in full bloom, the woman Caim had always imagined she could be.

She bent down to him, and the darkness flowed along her body like a second skin, but it wasn't entirely black. Murky patterns twisted within the dark. As he reached up, they played along the flesh of his hand and arm like tiny vibrations, and then penetrated his skin, through the muscles and sinews down into his bones. Colors beyond description spun around him, striations of light and shadow cast into physical form.

"Trust yourself," she whispered.

Caim took a deep breath. He knew what had to be done, but could he do it? Could he release the bands of self-control that had held him together for so long? If he let go, would he lose himself? He took another glance over the side. The darkness parted around him like a veil of sheerest gossamer and he saw Josey, clinging to a stone projection. How she fought for life! She wouldn't give up, not as long as a single breath remained within her. Yes. He could do it, for her.

Caim released the breath, and with it all his reservations. The sorcerer stood like a statue of some forgotten demigod of the night. But Kit had said he could bleed. If he could bleed, he could die.

Caim saluted with the sword. *His* sword now. Levictus nodded as if they had come to some agreement, and then advanced across the rain-splattered tiles. Again the shadows darted at Caim. He could see them better now, not as amorphous blobs, but as small, sleek creatures with sharp teeth and glittering black eyes. But before they could reach him, a black shape erupted from the darkness. The tiny shadows scurried out of the beast's path. It was huge. Striding on four big paws, it resembled a great sable mastiff.

Caim leveled his sword at the creature. But instead of attacking him, the thing turned to pursue the shadows, scooping them up in its massive jaws and tearing them to bits. Then he realized this was the same shadow creature he had seen before, at the Vine and in the cellar under Josey's manor. It had never threatened him, only his enemies, and by the vibration thrumming in his head as the beast tore through the sorcerer's pets, this thing was somehow bound to him.

A violent hiss was the only warning Caim got. He lifted the sword in time to deflect a black knife aimed at his throat. Phosphoric sparks flew as the weapons connected, recoiled, and clashed again. The shadows had fled into the darkness, and the beast with them. Caim almost felt like his old self. On the next pass, he beat the sorcerer's counterattack by a fraction of a heartbeat. He feinted high and slashed. The sword tore through black fabric and found flesh underneath.

Levictus vanished, leaving behind a few spots of blood. But this time, Caim witnessed something he hadn't before. As the sorcerer disappeared, he stepped into a hole in the air, like a window into nothingness. It slammed shut behind him, but tendrils of dark luminescence remained. Caim turned, following them with his eyes. He was ready when Levictus reappeared on the other side of the roof. He struck. The sorcerer nearly fell on his back evading the lunge. His knives deflected the sword's path enough to avoid being spitted. Then, like a cat he righted himself and kept coming.

Around and around they circled while Kit danced above their heads. Her laughter rivaled the thunder. Caim took a scratch on his left hand, a shallow wound, but Levictus followed up with a series of stabs that put him on the defensive. Yet the sorcerer was slowing with every step, while Caim felt his stamina improving. The sword twitched in his hand like a living thing. He pressed with a riposte, but Levictus parried and leapt at him. Caim tried to reverse his momentum as the tip of a black knife raced toward his unprotected chest. He didn't have time to think as he twisted to avoid the deadly strike. The edge of the roof reared up toward him. Off balance, he would have fallen, *should* have fallen, except that the darkness billowed around him, cradling him in its grasp. His feet left the tiles, and came down a moment later behind the sorcerer. Somehow, he had been transported a dozen feet through thin air. Levictus turned, his knives moving. Even as his brain boggled at what had just happened, Caim lunged.

Levictus made no sound, but the tendons of his neck stood out like taut cables. His eyes stabbed at Caim with the hatred of the damned for one interminable moment. Then, he slumped to his knees.

Caim shoved the blade deeper and stepped back. The sword's hilt quivered in the sorcerer's chest like the masthead of a floundering ship. In his mind, Caim saw his father, kneeling in the blood-drenched yard of their family estate.

Justice. At last.

Sibilant whispers echoed in the darkness. Caim balled his hands into fists as the shadows returned, but they ignored him. Skittering like tiny spiders, they adhered themselves to the sorcerer's body until they encased it in a black cocoon. The corpse dissolved before Caim's eyes, melted away with the rain and ran down the cracks between the roof tiles. A minute later, nothing was left but his father's sword and an empty, sodden cloak.

Caim watched the black garment flap in the wind. The presence was gone, the beast and the little shadows with it, and something else as well. His fear. A weight had been lifted from his mind. He was different—he accepted that—but he wasn't a monster.

A faint wail rode the storm's howl. *Josey!*

He limped toward the roof's edge, but froze as a barrage of lightning strokes illuminated the night. Ral blocked his path, face streaked with pink lines of blood, sword drawn back. Caim recoiled, but there was nowhere to go. Even an old woman couldn't miss from so close. Ral grinned through his gory mask as the sword shot forth like a bolt from an arbalest. Caim grabbed at the blade with his naked hands, but it slid between his fingers and plunged into his stomach. Warm blood bubbled over Caim's hands as he braced himself for the disemboweling twist, but the sword dropped from the killer's hand to clatter on the tiles. Ral gaped with a stunned expression as he collapsed at Caim's feet for the second time.

Caim lifted his gaze to the slight figure in drenched rags standing behind the dead assassin, one of his *suetes* clutched in her shaking, blood-stained hands.

"Jo—" Caim tried to say, but the roof jumped up to smash his face.

Then, he was on his back. Josey and Kit knelt on either side of him. Their hands tugged his jacket in different directions, each trying to pull him upright, but the darkness held him in its embrace. His thoughts were slow to come. Water coursed down Josey's face. Overhead, the heavens roiled in their wrath, but an expanding sense of peace filled the hollow spaces of his soul. She was safe.

"It's all right," he whispered with a smile that took all of his dwindling strength.

"Don't leave!" Josey and Kit shouted in his ears. "Stay with me!"

He wanted to stay, but he had to disappoint them both as the night pulled him down into its unfathomable depths.

CHAPTER
THIRTY-TWO

Morning brought a fresh glow to the city. Breezes laden with the sea's cleansing tang blew across the cemetery grounds and banished the lingering stenches of smoke and death. Low strains from a six-piece orchestra filled the grassy strips between long rows of tombs while people gathered around the freshly dug plot.

An imposing marble gravestone stood in the midst of the assembly, the beveled edges of the words engraved upon it glinting in the pale sunlight.

Caim Du'Vartha
1218–1242
Dear Friend and Loyal Subject.
It is Not the Night We Fear,
But the Gathering Shadows Beyond Our Ken.

From his vantage in a thicket of aged brushwood Caim read those words, their letters seared into his brain like harbingers from the next world. Although the faux funeral had been his idea, Josey had come up with the epitaph. He wasn't keen on the "loyal subject" part.

It was an odd thing to observe his own funeral. He supposed this was how ghosts, recently evicted from their corporeal bodies, must feel as they watched their friends and loved ones gather to pay final tribute. In all, he found it rather dreary.

Then again, the world had taken on a different shade since the events on the palace roof. The trees, the grass underfoot, even the people attending his memorial—none of them seemed completely real. A new presence flitted in and out of his awareness, always on the periphery. Every so often he would catch a glimpse of a shadow—low to the ground, moving swiftly—and then it would be gone. It was as if he had stepped through a doorway into another world, one deeper and more profound than the one he had known all his life, and there was no going back.

Kit hadn't changed, of course. Or rather, she had returned to the same waif she had always been, ever youthful and bubbling with effervescence. Whatever transformation happened to her that night, it had reversed back by the time he regained consciousness. She refused to discuss the beastly presence, refused even to admit she'd seen it, which shouldn't have surprised him. Same old Kit.

But everything else was different, much of it oddly so. For a known assassin to enter the palace was unnerving enough. To awaken in the imperial bedchamber, attended by dozens of physicians and nurses and servants, had almost been too much for him. But then Josey had appeared and everything seemed right again. Even now the sight of her, dolled up in full regalia as she officiated over the ceremony, made his pulse race. She looked every bit an empress. Her hair had been dyed back to something close to its natural color. A gown of crushed velvet in somber purple lined with snow leopard fur accented her complexion and set off the jewels dripping from her neck, ears, and wrists. She was every man's fantasy: young, beautiful, kind-hearted, yet tough enough to stand on her own. *And as far beyond your reach as the moon and stars.*

A graceful young woman stood beside Josey. Anastasia, a friend from some important family. Fetching enough for a blonde, but she was outshone by the empress. A stooped, elderly man in a plain gray suit perched at Josey's elbow. Earl Frenig's manservant had been squirreled away in the palace dungeons after his master's murder. Besides being a bit undernourished, the old codger was little worse for wear.

Hubert stood in the front row amid several palace ministers. Head bowed, his left arm in a sling, the new Duke Vassili was a hero. In Low Town they were calling him "Lord of the Gutters." Not the most charming title, but he had taken to it like a kitten to cream. Just days after taking over his father's affairs, Hubert had spearheaded an effort to revive the Thurim. Their first item of business was a salvo of bold reforms aimed at relieving the plight of Othir's poorest citizens, including a plan to rebuild the parts of the city destroyed in the fire. Together, Hubert and Josey were going to accomplish magnificent things.

Another initiative coming out of the palace was the disbanding of the Sacred Brotherhood and the stripping of lands from wealthy priests. In the aftermath of the People's Revolt, as it was being called, the remaining hierarchs of the True Church had convened to elect a new prelate, one favorably disposed toward the restored imperium. Fresh proclamations of friendship and mutual assistance flowed from Castle DiVecci daily. To all appearances, it was the beginning of a new era in Nimea. For the first time in a long time, the future on the horizon looked brighter than the fading glories of the past.

Kit leaned on Caim's shoulder while he watched the proceedings.

"Isn't this all a bit much?" she asked. "I mean, it's not like most of these people actually gave two figs about you when you were alive."

"Yes. Well, people have to have their pretenses." Caim snapped off a twig from a tree branch and dropped it to the ground. A leather pack sat at his feet, beside a pair of wrapped bundles the length of his arm. Some victuals and a couple bottles liberated from the palace wine cellars, his bow, and his father's sword. Along with the clothes on his back and his knives, they were everything he owned in the world. The thought was oddly liberating.

"You think anyone will fall for this?" Kit asked.

"Why not? After the murders and the riots, everyone just wants to get back to some semblance of normalcy. If the burial of one poor thug is enough to satisfy them, isn't that a small price to pay?"

As the last notes of the dirge died away, the guests began to file away from the gravesite. Hubert offered his good arm to Josey, but she declined with a shake of her head. Caim couldn't suppress a chuckle, appreciating this new side to the girl he had risked his life to protect. Her performance was flawless as well-wishers offered their condolences. By now the story was known throughout the city, how a lowborn man had saved the long-lost princess from traitors in the True Church and made the ultimate sacrifice in her service. If whispers arose of how attached the young empress had become to her rescuer during their escapades, none could reproach her. Indeed, they served to make her more accessible to her new subjects. After all, weren't such romantic notions the stuff of bard's songs?

With a gesture for her attendants to remain behind, Josey wandered among the headstones, head bent in quiet contemplation. As if by chance, she entered the grove and stopped a few paces away from him.

He took her in and attempted to penetrate the layers of pomp and regalia to find the young woman he had come to know. It wasn't easy. She had already become the symbol of her office, the mother of a nation.

Then, her mouth contorted into a frown. The Josey he knew was back.

"You shouldn't be out of bed so soon. The doctors said it would be weeks before you'd be well enough to move about."

Caim pressed a hand against his stomach. A dull ache pulled at his muscles there, but something stronger pulled at his spirit. "I'm just here to say good-bye."

Her bottom lip disappeared into her mouth. "You don't have to leave. Hubert has an idea to change your identity. We could put you into some better clothes, change your hair, and not even your grandmother would recognize you."

"That would be curious, as I've never met either of my grandmothers."

Josey twisted her fingers, heedless of the fortune in sapphires festooning them. Her gaze had dropped to his chest, as if she couldn't bring herself to look him in the eye anymore.

"I would be dead, if not for you."

"As I remember it, you were the one who saved me."

She shook her head. "When I was hanging in the dark, I couldn't see anything. My hands were numb. My heart was numb. I started to give up. Then I remembered the way you fought, how you never gave up—no matter the odds. That gave me the strength to pull myself up."

She looked up with a new light shining in her eyes, a glorious flame of pride. "Whatever comes now, I know I can face it. You did more than save my life, Caim. What I'm saying is you could have a family here. You and I . . . we could be . . ."

He shook his head. She started to reach out, and he caught her hand in a gentle grasp. Her nails had been cleaned of gutter filth and polished with a bright indigo lacquer. Her perfume filled his head, weakening his resistance.

"I can't stay. I've made a lot of enemies in this town. Anyway, it wouldn't be proper for an empress to be seen in the company of assassins, even if they're wearing silks and pomades."

He took her chin in his other hand. She moved closer until the hem of her wide skirt brushed his boots. Their lips came together in a kiss. The sweetness of her taste lingered in his mouth for a long time after he pulled away.

"I could come with you." Her eyes were cloudy with emotion. "Wherever you're going. I don't care."

Pulling away from her was the hardest thing he'd ever done. Only the knowledge of what he was sparing her kept him from toppling back into her arms.

"You have a lot of work to do here, Josey. Othir needs her empress. Our paths lead in different directions. For now."

Her hands started to rise, but then dropped back to her sides. Moisture glistened in her eyes. He smiled with care, afraid even the smallest gesture would crack the armor he had erected around his heart. He wanted her badly, wanted to stay and protect her, serve her, whatever she desired just for the chance to be with her. But they were as different as the sun and moon. Forever bound together, forever apart.

"Where will you go?" she asked.

He turned his gaze northward. Somewhere beyond the trees of the grove and the city walls lay the land of his birth. He didn't know what he would find once he got there, but the need to know about his past throbbed in him like a second heartbeat.

"I have questions that need answering and a long road to travel before I reach my destination."

"What if the answers you want aren't there?"

"Then I'll keep searching."

Josey reached into a fur muff dangling from her sleeve and pulled out a bundle of papers wrapped in black cord. "Take this. There's a writ of safe passage inside, although I don't know how far that will extend. There's been no news out of the northern provinces for weeks. I intend to send a military detachment up there as soon as I can find the resources."

"You're starting to sound like an empress already." He accepted the package. Nestled among the documents was a thin book, like a diary. He started to pull it out. "And this?"

She put her hands over his. "Read it later, after you've left the city environs. There might be information in there you can use. And, Caim, if you don't find what you're looking for, promise me you'll come back."

Caim pressed his lips to her fingers. "I promise, my lady."

Then he turned and left before the trembling in his legs could betray him. A breeze swirled through the trees and ruffled his hair as he trod across the carpet of fallen leaves. The sky was deepening to purple twilight. Kit danced before him in the failing light, her hair flowing free like a silver banner. He touched the golden talisman hung by a simple leather cord around his neck. He wanted to look back and catch one last glimpse of the woman he loved, of Othir's gleaming towers, of the life he was leaving behind.

But he kept walking, through the gates and into the gathering shadows beyond.

ABOUT THE AUTHOR

JON SPRUNK lives in central Pennsylvania with his wife and son. Between his day job as a juvenile detention specialist and time spent with his family, he is hard at work on the sequel to *Shadow's Son*. For more on his life and works, visit www.jonsprunk.com.

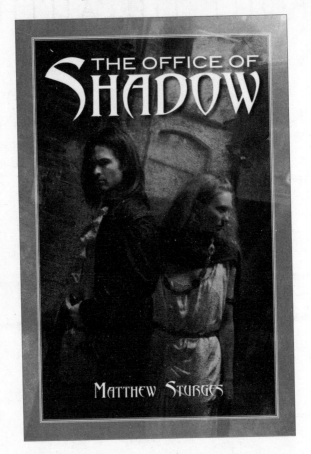